IMPYRIUM

D0372456

SACRED ISLE

OLD TOM

HOUND'S TRENCH

Île de Réves

0   0.5   1 MI

10

Han
Sylva   Castile

Jain
Yamato   Palantine

Eluvan

Hyde
Menlo   Klauss

Chen
7

Khan

New
College   6

Rowan   3   4   1   8
5
2   9

Old College

TUR AN GHRIAN   IMPYRIAL PALACE

1. IMPYRIAL PALACE   6. DIREWOOD
2. TUR AN GHRIAN   7. HOUND'S TRENCH
3. MANSE   8. KIRIN POINT
4. OLD TOM   9. LIRLANDER EMBASSY
5. MAGGIE   10. ÎLE DE RÊVES

HENRY H. NEFF

IMPYRIUM

IMPYRIUM

HARPER
An Imprint of HarperCollinsPublishers

Impyrium

Copyright © 2016 by Henry H. Neff
All rights reserved. Printed in the United States of America.
No part of this book may be used or reproduced in any manner whatsoever without
written permission except in the case of brief quotations embodied in critical articles
and reviews. For information address HarperCollins Children's Books, a division of
HarperCollins Publishers, 195 Broadway, New York, NY 10007.
www.harpercollinschildrens.com

Library of Congress Control Number: 2016013337
ISBN 978-0-06-239206-0

17 18 19 20 21   OPM/BVG   10 9 8 7 6 5 4 3 2 1
❖
First paperback edition, 2017

For my mother, Terry Ann Zimmerman

IMPY

GRISLANDS

SACRED ISLE

MUIRLANDS

Azaelian
Sea

Grislands

Muirlands

Rowana

Bregan
Sea

RIUM

Baalaskir
Sea

Prusian
Sea

7

9

8

Afrique

Hadesian
Deeps

LIRLANDS

WORKSHOP

PROLOGUE

At three o'clock in the morning, a monster entered Founders Hall. The vye might have been wearing scholarly robes and spectacles, but it still counted as a monster. What else did one call an eight-foot wolf that walked on two legs?

Despite this disquieting sight, Private Marcus Finch remained at attention: chin up, shoulders back, his carabine resting against his epaulette. Impyrial guardsmen did not stare, slouch, or fidget. Not even when a monster approached.

But Marcus was not a machine. When he recognized the figure walking beside the vye, his heart beat even faster. Lord Basil Faeregine was the Divine Empress's only living son. He was arguably the most important man in Impyrium.

Fortunately for Marcus, Founders Hall spanned three hundred feet from its pillared entry to the great vault. He had time to appreciate the occasion and rejoice inwardly. The new year was just a few hours old and he'd just seen his first vye and a member of the royal family. It was going to be a very good year. As the pair drew nearer, Marcus tried to decide which sight was more thrilling: the Faeregine or the monster?

The boy in him leaned toward the monster. Vyes had served the Faeregines since Mina I, but the creatures were rarely seen in other parts of Impyrium. Back in his village, parents invoked them as bogeymen to frighten disobedient children: *Get to bed or a vye will carry you off to the Grislands!* As Marcus watched it approach, he wished it would snarl or lope or exhibit some other savage quality. Instead, the vye advanced with a stately grace.

Such civilized behavior was disappointing but not a surprise. Dr. Razael was a famous scholar, a Rowan valedictorian who had been advising Basil Faeregine since his lordship was a boy. Marcus was pleased with himself for recalling these facts. He'd only been on the Sacred Isle a week, but he'd spent his free time studying profiles in his handbook. Dr. Razael looked just like her photograph.

Basil Faeregine did not. Marcus had imagined Faeregines would be resplendent figures whose magic and heritage would be apparent at first glance. His handbook had shown a tanned gentleman with silver hair, an impeccably tailored suit, and the complacent smile of one whose family ruled the world. This present version was still handsome, but older and thicker than expected. He was also slightly disheveled, with a sheen of sweat upon his florid face.

Still, Marcus tried not to judge. Here on the Sacred Isle, New Year's was not merely a holiday but a major state function. Throughout the week, visitors from all over Impyrium had been arriving to conduct important business with the Bank of Rowan. As the bank's chairman and managing director, His Excellency was undoubtedly spent.

When he reached the vault, Lord Faeregine muttered a distracted "Happy New Year" and reached for something in his suit pocket. He did not bother looking at the guardsmen, but Marcus was not offended. Members of the royal family were surrounded by servants from birth. They might bond with nannies and tutors, but the rest were background elements: nameless, faceless, and interchangeable. To a man like Basil Faeregine, Impyrial guardsmen might have been tall red vases that happened to flank palace doorways.

And that was how it should be, thought Marcus. *The family had an empire to run.*

But as Lord Faeregine removed something from his pocket, he paused to peer at the other guardsman, a sergeant standing fifteen feet to Marcus's right.

"Why, it's Beecher isn't it?"

From the corner of his eye, Marcus saw the sergeant bow. "I'm flattered you remember me, sir." The man's gravelly burr contrasted sharply with his lordship's patrician tenor.

"Not at all," said Lord Faeregine genially. "You were with me when those miserable Caterwauls blocked the road to Port Royal. Knocked several flat as I recall. Good man."

"Your lordship's very kind."

Lord Faeregine turned in Marcus's direction. "And who's this poor lad? He looks like he's going to topple over."

Do not slouch. Marcus focused on a distant portrait.

"Private Finch is new," replied the sergeant. "This is his first night on palace duty."

"My word, they get younger every year," Lord Faeregine muttered. "May I ask your age, Private Finch?"

Marcus cleared his throat. "Eighteen, your lordship."

"Well," said Lord Faeregine, "all I can say is that I envy your youth, your height, and your good fortune to serve with the sergeant. Welcome aboard, soldier."

Marcus shook the proffered hand, unable to suppress a grin. A Faeregine was speaking to him! His reply was barely coherent, but his sincerity appeared to please Lord Faeregine, who chuckled and introduced him to Dr. Razael.

The vye had towered silently over the humans throughout the pleasantries. Now she fixed Marcus with a pair of tawny, unblinking eyes. Marcus's smile faded. Never before had he looked into a face that was so intelligent and yet so feral. The combination was so unsettling that Marcus quickly averted his eyes. Dr. Razael exuded no overt hostility but also no warmth. Her gaze wandered over Private Finch, found little of interest, and returned to the vault door.

Lord Faeregine held up what he'd taken from his pocket. The object looked like a palm-sized nautilus crafted of a coppery metal. "If you two will give us a moment, we'll pop inside and confirm everything's in order. Tonight's auction set a new record."

Sergeant Beecher bowed. "Congratulations, your lordship. "

Shouldering his carabine, the sergeant walked forward ten paces and stood with his back to the vault. Marcus followed his lead. A moment later, there was a mechanical clicking, followed by the sounds of his lordship murmuring strange words in a lyrical undertone. A shiver ran down Marcus's spine.

Lingua Mystica. Lord Faeregine was speaking the language of sorcery! The Lirlander Seals were undoubtedly protected by all kinds of spells and enchantments, but this was the first time Marcus had ever heard it spoken aloud. He almost giggled at his good fortune. He'd only been posted here a few hours ago, when a guardsman had taken ill, and already he was brushing shoulders with Faeregines. Not to mention that palace duty was infinitely warmer and dryer than patrolling the harbor and eyeing those boatmen in their black skiffs. Marcus did not care for the boatmen.

A tremor shook the floor as the vault's heavy door began to roll aside. As it did, light spilled from within, so dazzling and bright it chased the shadows from the vast hall. The vault might have contained a fallen star. Marcus broke into another grin.

When Lord Faeregine and Dr. Razael entered, they sealed the vault behind them. The glorious light retreated, ebbing like a swift sunset. Sergeant Beecher sighed.

"Well, Private Finch. I'll guess you won't be forgetting this night anytime soon."

Marcus remained at attention. "No, sir."

A pause. "You don't 'sir' me, lad. I'm a sergeant."

"Sorry," said Marcus quickly. "I guess I'm just a little . . ."

"The word is *nervous*. A tot will take off the edge. It is New Year's after all."

The sergeant slipped a flask out from beneath his sash. Marcus stared. Members of the Impyrial Guard were not permitted to drink, to swear, to smoke tobacco, or generally do *anything* that might besmirch their impeccable image. They were the elite, and expected to behave as such. What was the sergeant playing at?

Now that he was getting a good look, Marcus saw that Beecher was rather ancient for a guardsman—forty at least—and barely met the regiment's height requirements. And there were other shortcomings:

sloping shoulders, a slight paunch, and a trace of stubble. His face was genial but homely, with bushy black eyebrows and a slight cast in one eye. The man resembled a dairy farmer more than a crack soldier. Small wonder he'd never risen past sergeant.

"No, thank you," said Marcus. He spun back to face the distant portraits.

The sergeant unscrewed the cap and took a sip. "I see we have a stickler."

Chin up, shoulders back. "Not a stickler, Sergeant. A professional."

This brought a dry chuckle. "Ah, you take me back. I'll wager you've been studying your handbook and dreaming about the day you get to go home and strut about in that uniform. Every girl for miles is sure to sally out in her best homespun for a look at Private Finch, the pride of Backwater Village. Am I close?"

Marcus flushed scarlet.

The sergeant took another sip. "You're going to burn out, Finch. Save the spit and polish for when it matters."

"And guarding the Lirlander Seals doesn't qualify?" Marcus retorted. "They're the crown jewels of the empire."

"Sounds like you're an expert," said Beecher. "Ever seen one up close?"

Marcus had only been on one ship in his life, a leaking tub that brought him down from New Halifax. It did not have a Seal, and thus had no choice but to hug the rocky coastline. Ships without Seals did not venture beyond sight of the land. If they did, they risked entering the Lirlands, territory controlled by demons that inhabited undersea kingdoms. An ancient treaty confined the Lirlanders within their borders, but they did not tolerate trespassers. Ships that entered their waters suffered a terrible fate unless they bore an enchanted relic upon their prow. These were known as Lirlander Seals, and they were among the most valuable objects in Impyrium.

"No," said Marcus sheepishly. "I haven't."

"Come have a look," said Beecher. Turning, he walked back to the vault door.

Marcus remained rooted to the spot. He spoke in a pleading whisper. "What are you doing? Lord Faeregine's inside!"

"Oh, he'll be in there for a while yet," said the sergeant. "And don't worry about him hearing us. The door's three feet thick."

"But what about . . . ?" Marcus glanced anxiously about the hall. Legend held that unseen servants—*fiendish* servants—tallied every whisper within the palace.

The sergeant appeared to read his mind. "Nothing's listening from the shadows, lad. I've been on the Sacred Isle for twenty-two years. The ghost stories are bunk. Come have a look. You might never get another chance to touch a dragon."

A dragon? There were only a handful in the entire world, and none in Founders Hall. But the sergeant had aroused Marcus's interest. He came to stand by the man and craned his neck at the famous Lirlander Vault. Marcus had seen it when he came in, but he had not taken a close look. It was his duty to guard, not to gawk, and he'd swiftly turned his back upon taking up his new post.

But now, he indulged his curiosity. His first impression was one of ancient strength. The vault's door was simply massive: a circular slab of bronze some fifteen feet across, green with age and etched with runes about its periphery. Its center had been sculpted with marvelous artistry into a relief showing a Hadesian galleon braving wild seas with a bright, mother-of-pearl inlay on its prow. A kraken and several other monsters could be seen among the waves, but nothing that resembled a dragon.

"Where is it?" said Marcus, searching in vain.

Beecher stood on tiptoe and tapped the pearl at the galleon's prow.

"That's not a dragon," said a disappointed Marcus. "It's a pearl."

Beecher took another sip and wiped his mouth on his sleeve. "No, lad. That there is a scale—just a fragment, mind—from Ember the Golden. The big ones are on the other side of that door. You're looking at the world's tiniest Lirlander Seal."

Marcus gave a laugh of pure boyish delight. The Seals were made from dragon scales! And not just any dragon but the greatest to ever walk the earth. He stood on tiptoe and rubbed the wondrous thing for luck. The surface was slick and smooth, like oiled horn.

"Do they really cost a million solars?" he asked, gazing up in awe.

"Heard they were fetching two at tonight's auction," the sergeant replied. "Two million in bullion, no paper. And that's just to rent one for twelve months. Once the year's up, you've got to come back, kiss some Faeregine behinds, and ante up again."

Private Finch raised his eyebrows. House Faeregine had ruled Impyrium for over three thousand years. Faeregine magic was the strongest, their coffers the deepest. Only Faeregine women could rule, but even the men were reputed to be sorcerers of rare ability. It was dangerous for anyone, much less a member of the guard, to speak of them so flippantly.

"We should return to our posts," Marcus muttered. He marched back to his spot and rested his carabine against his shoulder. *Chin up, shoulders back.*

Beecher followed suit. "I told you no one's listening."

"*I'm* listening, Sergeant. And I don't want to hear any blasphemy."

A grunt. "You can't blaspheme your fellow man, Finch. The Faeregines aren't gods. They're flesh and blood, same as us."

Marcus stared at a distant portrait of Mina II. The man had to be drunk.

"That's bordering on treason."

The sergeant scoffed. "If truth is treason, I've lived long enough."

Do not slouch. "My father says my uncle used to talk like that," said Marcus stiffly. "They hanged him during the last rebellion."

The sergeant took another sip. "Let's hope I didn't hold the rope. Strung up plenty for the Faeregines in those days. Bad business."

Marcus turned and glared at the sergeant. "If you think so little of the Faeregines, why serve in the Impyrial Guard?"

Beecher looked genuinely amused. "Who said I think little of 'em? They've convinced the world they're masters of heaven and hell and everything in between. I tip my bloody cap."

It was Marcus's turn to scoff. "So it's all just smoke and mirrors?"

The sergeant's expression became surprisingly thoughtful. "Not all," he murmured. "I'd guess there's still some magic in the family. Maybe in those triplets. But it ain't what it was. Mina the First might have been a goddess, but it's Mina the Forty-second that sits the throne now. Ever see our 'Divine Empress' in person?"

Marcus pursed his lips. Lord Faeregine was the only family member he'd ever seen and his lordship had not quite lived up to Marcus's expectations. Maybe the Divine Empress wasn't the ageless, scintillating figure whose image adorned coins and banknotes.

He must have looked crestfallen for the sergeant softened his tone.

"Don't mistake me. I honor the Faeregines. But I honor 'em as men and women, as folk born to rule like I was born to soldier. Sooner you ditch the fairy tales, the better off you'll be."

Marcus almost asked for the flask. "You know," he said pensively, "I'm not quite sure if this has been the best night of my life or the worst."

This made Beecher chuckle. "It's not over yet."

As though in answer to the sergeant's quip, rapid footsteps echoed from the corridor outside the hall. A hooded figure appeared in the distant archway and ran toward them. The sergeant's grin vanished. He held up a hand.

"Halt and show yourself."

Marcus shifted anxiously as Sergeant Beecher repeated the order.

When the figure ignored a second command, the sergeant brought up his carabine. The figure skittered to a stop some twenty yards away. Beecher's voice was iron.

"Not another step. Let's see your face."

The figure gasped for breath. "Stand aside, Sergeant."

"Three seconds," Beecher replied coolly. "Lose the hood or lose that head."

Marcus's weapon shook in his trembling hands. His marksmanship scores had always been excellent, but the firing range was nothing like a live situation. Thank the gods he'd underestimated the sergeant. Beecher might be old and cynical, but he was also experienced. Nothing about him wavered—not his voice, his weapon, or his apparent resolve to use it. The visitor yanked back his hood and glared at the sergeant. Marcus gasped when he saw the man's face.

The visitor was Lord Faeregine.

Sergeant Beecher's carabine remained leveled. "Good. Now tell me who you really are."

The man stared at the guardsman with a look of puzzled outrage. "I'm Basil Faeregine, you buffoon. Lower that weapon and stand aside or I'll have you tossed down Hound's Trench!"

Beecher smirked. "Sorry, friend. You can't be Lord Faeregine."

"Is that so?" the man said with a sneer. "And pray tell me, why not?"

"Because Lord Faeregine's in the vault."

Blood drained from the man's face. He looked at the two soldiers as if they were insane. "B-but that's not possible!" he sputtered. "It must be an imposter! *I'm* Lord Faeregine!"

The grim sergeant shook his head. "I think Dr. Razael would know the difference."

"But Razael's dead." The man announced this with a soft croak, his eyes filling with tears. "Her body was found near the orchards. Murdered."

The sergeant frowned. "What's tonight's password?"

"Ambergris," replied the newcomer. "What? Did the imposter know it?"

Sergeant Beecher cursed softly and lowered his weapon.

The visitor looked appalled. "Sergeant, did you neglect to ask for the password?"

Beecher flushed. "The gentleman had the nautilus. He knew the spells—"

Marcus went numb as a low rumbling sounded behind them. Once again, bright light streamed into the hall as the vault began to open. Raising his weapon, Sergeant Beecher turned about to face the sliding door. His voice was eerily calm and professional.

"Private Finch, imposters have infiltrated the Lirlander Vault. Escort Lord Faeregine to safety and raise the alarm."

Marcus hesitated.

"Now, Finch!"

Beecher's shout propelled Marcus into action. Dashing forward, he seized Lord Faeregine by the wrist and made for the distant exit. Their footsteps rang on the marble as the room brightened. Lord Faeregine stumbled along as though in a state of shock.

Crack!

A bullet's sharp report echoed in the hall. Two more came in quick succession, followed by a scream.

Lord Faeregine gave a cry and tangled his feet. Marcus nearly tumbled with him but kept his balance and pulled his lordship up. The pair staggered on.

Marcus heard sounds of pursuit. He glimpsed a shadow on the wall: a wolfish shape bounding on all fours and closing rapidly. Escape was out of the question. Thrusting Lord Faeregine ahead, Marcus whirled about to confront their pursuers.

He saw nothing but the vault's blinding light. An instant later, something slammed into his chest, huge and snarling, heavy as a sledge. The impact sent Marcus flying. As he fell, a thought flashed in his mind, a thought so absurd that he almost laughed.

Do not slouch.

When his skull struck the floor the world went black.

CHAPTER 1
HAZEL

Everyone sees what you appear to be,
few really know what you are.

—Niccolò Machiavelli, Pre-Cataclysm philosopher
(544–486 P.C.)

O n New Year's Day, some people spring out of bed determined to
be kinder, thinner, more industrious, more outgoing. No matter
the resolution, they all share something in common: they believe
this year will be better than the last.

Hazel Faeregine was not one of those people.

Despite the hour, she lay abed with two magical tomes, an ancient
fairy tale, a stuffed giraffe, and a sense of impending invasion. Below,
bells were clanging in Rowan's Old College. Evidently it was not enough

to chime nine o'clock—the ringer needed to add whimsical flourishes lest anyone fail to realize it was New Year's Day. Hazel sighed. Those bells were as ancient as the empire. They should be played with dignity, not enthusiasm.

An invader arrived. As usual, it was Isabel. Picking the lock, she burst into the room, assessed the situation, and advanced. Hazel flung a bolster, which her sister ducked.

"You're not squirming out of this," said Isabel. "If I have to go, then so do you."

When Isabel reached the footboard, Hazel launched her last pillow with a cry. She tried to sound ferocious, like some beast from the Grislands. What came out was a squawk.

Isabel merely caught the cushion and used it to bat Hazel about the head.

Left, right. Left, right . . .

"Why do you make me do this?" Isabel moaned, actually sounding bored as Hazel retreated beneath the covers. Thumping her one last time, Isabel dropped the pillow and sat carefully on the bed. Her bustle crinkled. A maid gasped in the doorway.

"The dress, Your Highness! The embroidery—"

"Is lovely," said Isabel brightly. "Olo, pick out some different shoes while I gab with Hazel. These ones pinch."

"But the Red Branch is here to escort you," Olo whispered. "One's waiting in the vestibule!"

"I don't care if the Spider's in the vestibule," said Isabel. Hazel admired her sister's cheek, but knew she'd never say such things if their grandmother were really lurking about.

Olo made a face but withdrew. Isabel set her lockpick—a bejeweled hairpin—artfully among her black braids before fixing Hazel with a pair of dark, doe-like eyes. They were set unusually far apart and gave Isabel what was commonly known as the "Faeregine look." Similar pairs graced family portraits dating back to Mina I. Indeed, with her olive skin, aquiline nose, and dancer's carriage, Isabel was a shining example of the breed.

"Do we need to have the Talk?" she asked.

Hazel hugged her knees. "Which talk? The horrid one about our changing bodies? Or the one where you remind me who I am and why I can't do as I like?"

"The second," said Isabel, adjusting her corset. "You know we have to go."

"Not me," said Hazel. "I'm the youngest."

This made Isabel laugh—a fine, fetching laugh that boys tended to notice. "By seventeen minutes. No, you're going even if I have to drag you. I'm surprised Rascha hasn't already. Where is she?"

"I don't know," said Hazel. She'd been pleased that her tutor, Dàme Rascha, was uncharacteristically late. But now her absence was puzzling—almost as puzzling as the presence of a Red Branch in the triplets' sitting room. The Red Branch did many things but babysitting was not among them. Where was the regular guard?

Again, the door opened.

Violet and Isabel Faeregine were identical, but people never confused the two. Violet never rushed or raised her voice. Her posture was always perfect and her expression seldom stirred from one of serene composure. If Isabel was fire, Violet was ice. Even her dress was pale blue. She surveyed the room with detached disapproval.

"Are we ready?" she inquired.

"Do we look ready?" said Isabel.

Violet gave a prim smile. "No. We don't."

"Say 'we' one more time and I'm going to throttle you," said Isabel. Hazel crossed her fingers.

Violet tutted. "Are *we* forgetting I'm the eldest?"

Technically, this was true. Violet had been born nine minutes before Isabel, a fact she often cited. She never bothered telling anyone that she was twenty-six minutes older than Hazel. That gulf was self-evident.

Isabel snorted. "As though nine minutes matter."

Violet's eyes twinkled. "You'll find that they matter very much. See you down there."

She left in a soft rustle of silk. Isabel turned to Hazel.

"You don't think the Spider's going to *announce* anything, do you?"

"About her successor?" said Hazel. "No idea."

Scooting off the bed, Isabel smoothed her dress—crimson silk embroidered with rubies. Hazel's was green silk dotted with emeralds. It lay on the velvet chaise, still wrapped in muslin.

"Hurry up and get ready," Isabel muttered. "I'm going to catch up with Violet."

Before Hazel could reply, Dàme Rascha swept through the door.

"My apologies, Your Highness. This morning has been—"

The vye paused. Wolfish blue eyes swept over the mess before settling on her charge—a charge still abed in her nightclothes and whose fine white hair was sticking up like dandelion wisps. Isabel seized the chance to escape. Ducking past Hazel's tutor, she scampered out to the common room and shut the door behind her. Dàme Rascha glanced down at a bolster. Her voice was hoarse, its accent tinged from years living in the Witchpeaks.

"What is the meaning of this?"

"I was . . . redecorating?" said Hazel. "Bad idea. I'll fix it."

With a flick of her wrist, Hazel sent the scattered pillows flying to their places. They obeyed marvelously, landing with soft, simultaneous thuds. Hazel could not quite suppress a grin; she was getting good at these little cantrips. She offered a hopeful glance at her tutor.

As vyes went, Dàme Rascha was not particularly imposing. The mystic stood no more than seven feet and her fur, once an inky black, had faded to muted gray. Her teeth were worn, and her clawed hands trembled when she took her afternoon tea. But that glare was dark as thunder. She did not speak so much as growl.

"Casual magic is vulgar. Get up."

The command cracked like a whip. Hazel slid sheepishly out from under her covers and fidgeted with her nightgown. Dàme Rascha marched her to a full-length mirror.

"Raise your arms," she ordered.

When Hazel did so, Dàme Rascha whisked off her nightgown as though changing a toddler. Hazel swallowed her indignation. There was no arguing with Rascha when she was in a mood. While the vye fetched hot water, Hazel stared at her reflection.

You do not have the "Faeregine look."

Isabel and Violet were tall. Hazel stood a foot shorter. Her sisters were developing curves. Cubes had more curves than she did. Every summer, Isabel and Violet ripened into bronze, but Hazel's skin was the color of bleached ivory, so pale she stayed indoors on sunny days. When she did go outside, Rascha swaddled her in so much linen she resembled a skittish beekeeper. Even her eyes stood out, and not in the distinctive Faeregine way. They were tapering and reddish, more suited to a rabbit than a girl.

Hazel's appearance was a popular topic in Impyrium. Folklore held that twins were unlucky and triplets even more so. That Elana Faeregine had died birthing three girls on All Hallows' Eve was fine fuel for gossip, particularly as Hazel was albino. The average commoner, and even many among the nobility, believed Hazel's mother must have practiced necromancy or consorted with nefarious spirits. What else could explain this white-faced changeling?

Dàme Rascha returned with a basin of warm water, a cake of creamsoap, and a rough sea sponge. Kneeling, the vye began scrubbing Hazel as she had a thousand times before. Unlike Isabel's and Violet's tutors, Rascha did far more than simply teach her charge the magical arts. Ever since Hazel could remember, the vye had been her primary caretaker and companion. Whether this was because Hazel required closer supervision (she had been a sickly child) or the vye assumed the role from maternal instinct, Dàme Rascha took her duties seriously. Being raised by an overprotective vye had its advantages—no one teased Hazel if Rascha was near—but it came at a price. Hazel winced as her shins were scoured raw.

"A bath would be more comfortable," she observed.

Dàme Rascha was unmoved. "Turn."

Hazel complied, happy to look away from the mirror. Squeezing out the sponge, Rascha resumed her work, grunting now and again lest her ungrateful pupil forget she had rheumatism.

"Ouch!" said Hazel. "You might have said 'Happy New Year' before flaying me."

"Happy New Year."

"You're only saying that because I brought it up."

The vye shrugged.

"Well, it's very inconsiderate," said Hazel, flicking a bubble. "You might think of others."

Rascha scoffed. "Says the girl who lounges in bed."

"I wasn't lounging," said Hazel. "In fact, I think I'm coming down with a cold." She gave an unconvincing cough. "Anyway, what does my lying about matter when *you* showed up late?"

Water streamed down her back as Rascha rinsed away the soap. She draped a towel over Hazel's shoulders.

"I do apologize," she muttered. "The morning has been . . . difficult."

To Hazel's dismay, there were tears in her tutor's eyes. Hazel had never seen such a thing, had not even known that vyes *could* shed tears.

"Oh, Rascha!" she cried. "I was only teasing."

The vye gave an affectionate growl and lifted her from the basin. "No, child. It's not that. Something has happened."

"What's wrong?" said Hazel softly. "What has happened?"

The vye handed her a chemise. "It is not for me to say."

Hazel studied her tutor before beginning the tedious process of dressing. So many layers before one even put on the gown: small-clothes, a chemise, stockings. She could call Olo in to help, but that would be the end of the conversation; Rascha would never talk freely in front of a maid.

Fetching Hazel's corset from the wardrobe, her tutor fastened it about her waist. Hazel never understood why her twiggy form required a corset but she obliged and sucked in her tummy.

"Does it have anything to do with the Red Branch?" she asked.

Silence as the vye tightened the corset. Once it was torturously snug, Rascha tied the laces. Hazel exhaled slowly.

"Olo said one was in the vestibule," she continued. "Did you see him?"

"The Red Branch took your sisters down to the throne room. She will return for us."

Hazel's ears pricked up. *She will return for us.* The agent was a woman! There was only one person that could be, and Hazel longed to meet her. Still, it was strange that the Red Branch should handle such mundane duties.

"Why isn't the regular guard escorting us? What's wrong?"

The vye did not answer as she unwrapped the dress. Smoothing the silk, she lowered it carefully over Hazel and began arranging the bustle.

"Please tell me, Rascha," said Hazel. "I'm not a baby."

A pause. "There may be enemies in the palace. Last night, criminals broke into the Lirlander Vault."

Hazel turned. The Lirlander Seals were her family's prized assets. The Sacred Isle had been teeming with visitors from all over the world who came for the sole purpose of acquiring one. The auction had been last night, but Hazel had gone to bed before it started.

"You're joking," she said.

The vye gathered Hazel's fine white hair in a barrette. "No. And that is not the worst of it. There were two murders."

Hazel's arms turned to gooseflesh.

"Who?" she whispered.

The vye cleared her throat. "Sergeant Beecher of the Impyrial Guard and . . . Dr. Razael."

Hazel stared. "Uncle Basil's old tutor?"

Dàme Rascha nodded and dabbed a bit of rouge on Hazel's pallid cheeks. "Dr. Razael was my cousin. That is why I was late."

Hazel did not know what to say. She studied the vye's grieving face. More tears would be shed, but later and in private. "I'm so sorry,"

Hazel said quietly. Her thoughts turned to her uncle, who was rarely seen without the company of his beloved tutor. "What about—?"

The vye patted her cheek. "Lord Faeregine was also attacked, child. No—let me finish—your uncle is fine. His injuries were minor, thank the gods. And nothing was taken from the vault. The imposters were discovered before they could complete their crime."

"So, they were caught," said Hazel.

The vye shook her head grimly. "No. Which is why we wait for the Red Branch. You will be safer in their care."

"But they're assassins."

"The best," said Dàme Rascha. "Who better to protect you from killers?"

Hazel hugged her giraffe. "Why would I be in danger? I don't have any enemies."

The vye bared her teeth in a sudden grimace. "You are Hazel Faeregine, granddaughter of the Divine Empress. You've had enemies before you were born!"

Hazel backed up a step. "Rascha, you're frightening me."

"Good," Rascha snapped. "I've kept you too sheltered. You are the most talented mystic I've ever taught, yet you waste your gifts making pillows fly. It's time you woke up!"

Snatching the stuffed giraffe from Hazel, Dàme Rascha flung it on the bed. Hazel flushed an angry pink, but could not help lingering on what her tutor had said.

"You really think I'm talented?" she said hesitantly. Rascha was notoriously spare with praise.

The vye sighed and cupped Hazel's chin. "Your Highness, you have more magic than both your sisters put together. I can see it. Why can't you?"

Before Hazel could reply, there was a knock at the door.

"Who is it?" said Dàme Rascha.

The answer was curt. "Sigga."

Hazel felt a rush of nervous excitement. She had never seen Sigga Fenn in the flesh, but the agent was already famous. Even her origins were interesting. The newspapers said she was a native Grislander. Few humans dared set foot in the Grislands, much less grew up in those barren wastes.

And this Grislander was not only the youngest member of the Red Branch but the order's only female. In ancient times, the Red Branch had been revered as mystic-knights, champions of the realm. But that was long ago. Nowadays, the order did not inspire reverence so much as a respectful dread. They were the Spider's prized soldiers, lethal shadows she deployed like chess pieces throughout her empire.

Hazel tried not to gape as Dàme Rascha opened the door.

Her first impression was that Sigga Fenn looked nothing like the Impyrial Guardsmen. The Red Branch did not stand at attention or dress in a starched uniform. She wore no gloves and her black boots were scuffed beyond polishing. Guardsmen carried pistols and carabines, but they were just regular humans, *muir* in the old tongue. Magical humans, or *mehrùn*, did not use firearms. Indeed, such weapons were considered so far beneath their station one would have been ridiculed, or even shunned, for doing so. Mehrùn were expected to possess more sophisticated means of defense. Blades were another matter, however, for there was honor in them. Sigga Fenn carried two black daggers, one sheathed at each hip.

Sigga was very lean and tall—six feet at least—with brown hair shorn very close to a narrow skull. She wore no makeup or jewelry but her aspect was not masculine. The Grislander looked *functional*, as though she had no use for anything decorative or extraneous. Her only distinguishing mark was a tattoo of a crimson, upraised hand on her inner right wrist: the symbol of the Red Branch. Only twelve people bore that tattoo, and they were the deadliest killers in the world.

Sigga Fenn glanced at Dàme Rascha with eyes so green and catlike Hazel wondered if there were demons in her ancestry. Such things were not unknown.

"You're Rascha," she said, not asking.

The vye bristled. "*Dàme* Rascha."

Sigga merely nodded and glanced down at Hazel. "Hello."

"You will address the princess as *Your Highness*," said Dàme Rascha sharply. "And you are to bow."

A faint smile played about Sigga's lips. "Forgive me, Your Highness. I spend little time among royalty."

She bent deeply at the waist. Hazel acknowledged her with a minuscule nod. Faeregines bowed rarely, and never to servants. When Dàme Rascha slipped emerald slippers on her tiny feet, Hazel selected a pair of spectacles with round green lenses and hurried out after the famous fighter.

The triplets' chambers were atop one of the palace's southwest towers and gazed down upon Old College, an ancient quad at the heart of Rowan, the world's greatest school of magic. A lovely view, but also a long walk to the throne room.

Normally, Hazel found the journey tedious and wished the empress was less of a traditionalist. An elevator would be just the thing in such an enormous palace, but the Spider detested "clockwork" and the Workshop, whose members sought to preserve technology in a world dominated by magic. Given the choice, the Spider would have done away with the engineers and razed their subterranean cities, but an ancient treaty protected their little guild. So long as the Workshop obeyed the rules and abstained from unauthorized innovations, the empress had no choice but to endure it. But you would find no electric lights or moving walkways in her home. In any case, the long trek gave Hazel an opportunity to study Sigga Fenn as the agent walked ahead of them.

Hazel registered every detail of the woman's stride, noting how servants scurried to get out of her path. Even the Impyrial Guard seemed to fidget and look away at the assassin's approach. Hazel felt like she had a Cheshirewulf padding before her—a Cheshirewulf that had traveled the world and braved countless perils. It was impossible not to admire and envy her. Hazel had never even visited the mainland. There were many questions she would have liked to ask the Grislander, but protocol did not allow casual conversation. Instead, Hazel turned her mind to last night's murders.

She was still shocked that such terrible things had happened, and in the very palace. Isabel was the history buff, but Hazel was certain nothing like a murder had occurred in many years. There had been hundreds of dueling deaths, of course, but those weren't remotely the same thing. The most recent murder she could think of happened fifty years ago, when some distant aunt or cousin had pushed her husband out of Gloaming Tower.

But that had been a lover's quarrel, whereas last night's murders sounded like part of an orchestrated crime. After all, Dàme Rascha said the perpetrators had been imposters. Who had they been pretending to be and how had they fooled the Impyrial Guard?

Hazel glanced suspiciously at the soldiers they passed. They were practically interchangeable. What was the name of the one who'd been killed? Beecher. The name sounded familiar. Hazel vaguely recalled a man who had accompanied the triplets to a concert last year. Homely for the guard, but he'd had a kind face. Isabel had joked that he looked like a mastiff. Hazel frowned. Was that the man who'd died?

Descending a final stairway, they reached the hallway leading to the throne room. Its scale always made Hazel feel like an insect. The ceilings were eighty feet high with massive caryatids depicting the dynasty's early empresses. Each column was carved with a craftsmanship and skill that no longer existed. Hazel glanced up at her ancestors as she passed: Mina I, an angelic goddess; Mina II, the ruthless visionary; Mina III, the hopeful peacemaker; Mina IV, the faceless tyrant.

As the dynasty's forty-second empress, Hazel's grandmother would not get a caryatid in the entry hall. Her legacy would most likely consist of a tasteful portrait in a palace gallery along with a grander memorial somewhere on the mainland. Space on the Sacred Isle had grown too scarce for the sprawling tombs and temples of yesteryear.

Some joked that the Spider would never need a tomb. The empress was one hundred and eleven years old, but clung to life with grim tenacity. As they reached the final caryatids, Hazel could make out a small, hunched figure sitting on a golden throne high atop a dais. Even at a distance, Hazel found her grandmother intimidating. She hoped her late arrival would go unnoticed.

She hoped in vain.

Antoine Bole, the palace's omnipresent chamberlain, was stationed near the doors, dressed in a rose-colored suit that matched his small horns. Fauns were famously exact and Antoine was no exception. Giving Hazel a reproachful look, he led her to the midst of the Impyrial court.

Dàme Rascha did not accompany them into this inner circle. Neither did Sigga Fenn. There were rules governing who could stand where during official gatherings. Since the vye and Grislander were servants, they were confined to the periphery, beyond the ring of wealthy muir, senior officials, and Workshop emissaries. Lesser nobles and mehrùn from Houses Minor formed the middle ring. The innermost circle was restricted to members of the twelve Great Houses.

These individuals were arranged like small battalions around the empress's dais. They were the most prominent magical families in the world and could trace their roots to fabled heroes and sorcerers of ages past. While the Faeregines controlled the throne, Lirlander Seals, and Otherland Gates, the Great Houses each had their own spheres of influence. Rivalries were intense and feuds could last generations, but the families banded together when threatened by outsiders or upstarts. For every mehrùn, there were a thousand muir who tended to revolt every century or two. Without cooperation among one another, the nobles would have been overrun long ago.

Hazel saw Isabel and Violet ahead, standing amid the ladies-in-waiting, girls from Great Houses who were deemed acceptable companions for the triplets. Her sisters looked bored and aloof, while their uncle Basil stood at a distant podium droning on about the Lirlander Seals. One eye was bandaged and his arm was in a sling, but he seemed to be his chipper self as he detailed how auction proceeds would be used to build roads and schools throughout the Muirlands.

Antoine nudged Hazel forward. She obliged him, weaving her way through the ladies-in-waiting to stand near her sisters as their uncle introduced Lord Kraavh, the new ambassador from the demonic Lirlands.

Excited whispers rippled across the assembly as the ambassador emerged from an antechamber. A frustrated Hazel could see nothing but elaborate hair and dresses. All of the girls were taller than she was, except for Isis Palantine, who was only eight and practically drowning in cream chiffon.

"Can you see anything?" Isis whispered.

Hazel shook her head.

Someone murmured in her ear. "Should we get you a footstool? You're just so itty-bitty."

Hazel glared at the speaker but said nothing. Imogene was fourteen, even taller than the twins, and she had famously pinchy fingers. She was also a Hyde, an obscenely wealthy family and the Faeregines' oldest rival.

"Shut your face, Imogene," whispered a voice.

Isabel had turned about to fix Imogene with a steely look. Hazel's sister really was a tigress, particularly where the Hydes were concerned. Imogene's lip curled. She opened her mouth to retort, but stopped when the ambassador began speaking.

When Hazel heard that voice, a shiver ran through her. Lord Kraavh sounded nothing like the last emissary. This wasn't some squeaky imp; this was a daemon true. She stood on tiptoe.

"What is he?" she whispered, still unable to see.

A wide-eyed Isabel mouthed the word "rakshasa."

Hazel gripped her arm. Rakshasas were exceedingly powerful demons that had undergone *koukerros*—daemonic metamorphosis— many times to reach their state of being. Most were many centuries old. The Lirlanders normally appointed an imp to the Faeregine court out of surly obligation. They never named anyone important to be ambassador, much less a rakshasa.

Hazel fidgeted impatiently. She desperately wanted to see the demon, not merely hear that purring baritone as Lord Kraavh began reciting the Lirlanders' oath of fealty.

"Three thousand years ago," he began, "your ancestors conquered my people. In exchange for our freedom, we agreed to forsake the lands of men and live beneath the seas. Thus the deepwater daemonia—the Lirlanders—came to be . . ."

Someone squeezed next to Hazel and thrust a glowing rectangle under her nose.

"Birthday present from my father," whispered Mei-Mei Han. "What do you think?"

The tiny screen showed a towering, tiger-headed figure with curling ram's horns. Hazel stared at the demon, practically spellbound.

She did not bother mentioning that the device was undoubtedly illegal. Mei-Mei would not care. The Hans played a role in Workshop relations and Mei-Mei prided herself on having the latest gadgets. It was an open secret that many Great Houses employed expensive— even illicit—technologies. So long as transgressions were minor and discreet, the empress chose to overlook them.

"Where's the camera?" Hazel whispered, dimly aware that something must be transmitting the images.

Mei-Mei nodded at Esmerelda, middle daughter of the Castiles. Despite her fifteen years, Esmerelda had always been pleasantly clueless. Even now, she was oblivious to the small device perched atop her nest of auburn hair.

"Have you ever seen a rakshasa before?" Hazel whispered.

Mei-Mei shook her head, her eyes glued to the screen.

"Why do you think he's wearing armor?" said Hazel. Granted, it was splendid—a suit of pearly, nacreous plate—but it seemed peculiar dress for an ambassador.

Mei-Mei shrugged as Isabel shot them a look to be quiet. Lord Kraavh continued his address.

"And finally, we will continue to honor our ancient pledge. The Lirlanders shall attack no ship that crosses our borders, provided it bears a sacred Seal from the *true* Faeregine."

Hazel looked up. *The true Faeregine?* What did he mean by that?

A hush filled the audience chamber. Hazel glanced at her grandmother upon her elevated throne. Many others did likewise. The Spider sat motionless with her customary scowl. Those Faeregine eyes—dark and impenetrable—were fixed, unblinking, on Lord Kraavh.

"Three millennia is a long time," said the ambassador coldly. "Even for daemonia. And so I have come to inform Her Radiance that this is the final year we will honor the Red Winter Treaty. The Lirlanders look forward to negotiating a new agreement with the Faeregines—and others—who wish safe passage across our seas."

Hazel was dumbstruck. The ambassador was not requesting a change to the treaty's terms; he was declaring the treaty finished, and in highly public fashion. It was unspeakably insulting.

"My, my," whispered Imogene Hyde.

Hazel looked to her sisters. Violet and Isabel appeared grave and composed. They, like everyone else, were waiting to see how the Divine Empress would respond.

The Spider did not disappoint.

The empress did not rise or stir but stared impassively at the rakshasa. When she finally spoke, she used a dialect of Old Impyrian that went back to the Cataclysm, whose devastation not only ushered in a new age for mankind but literally reshaped the world. Few people could speak that tongue, and most of them were in this room.

The Spider was sending an unmistakable message: *My roots are deep.*

"We honor Lord Kraavh for renewing the ancient vows and ensuring peace between our peoples. Three thousand years is indeed a long time. But perhaps Lord Kraavh has forgotten that the treaty required his people to honor the Seals in *perpetuity.* Perhaps he has also forgotten that the treaty also benefits his people by prohibiting the binding of daemonia . . ."

The rakshasa's three emerald eyes narrowed.

"If the Lirlanders should abandon this agreement," the Spider continued, "I cannot punish those who engage in forced summonings. Even Lord Kraavh may find himself subject to the whims of those who possess the means to call upon him. Such knowledge is old but not forgotten." The Spider raised a bony finger. "There may even be some who recall the eleven letters of your truename . . ."

The threat hung in the air, plain as a drawn blade. If the Divine Empress really knew Lord Kraavh's truename, she could summon the demon against his will or even destroy him outright. Such practices were forbidden since the Red Winter Treaty brought an end to the Cataclysm and the wars between humans and demonkind.

A nimbus of pale fire flickered about the ambassador. "That would be an end to the peace."

The Spider nodded. "Which is why the ambassador will wish to reconsider his proposal—and his etiquette—before addressing this court again. He now has my permission to leave."

Lord Kraavh grimaced as he bent stiffly at the waist, bowing his great head. Turning upon his cloven hoof, he withdrew silently from the hall. Hazel nearly grinned. *Score one for the Spider.*

Mei-Mei gave a low whistle. "That was a spanking."

The throne room was now abuzz with excited chatter. Even Imogene Hyde's smirk had vanished. Hazel's uncle, looking somewhat flustered, made some rambling remarks that garnered little attention.

Poor Uncle Basil, thought Hazel. *Attacked last night and now upstaged by his mother. What else could go wrong?*

A sharp rapping answered her question.

The sound came from the empress's dais, where the Archmage Elias Menlo was striking his staff upon the marble. The archmage came from a long line of famous witches and sorcerers. He was not a handsome man but rangy and rawboned with a plaited gray beard and a crimson skullcap that marked his high office. Hazel felt no affinity when she looked at him, which always struck her as a little sad. After all, the man was most likely her father.

Paternity counted for a great deal among other houses, but not the Faeregines. Direct descendants of the empress rarely married or even learned their father's identity. This ensured their loyalty remained solely to the Faeregines. Ancient birth records revealed that Impyrium's archmages fathered many of the early empresses; the rest were sired by patriarchs or sorcerers from the Great Houses. Whether that was still the practice, Hazel could not say.

The archmage ceased his rapping as the chamber fell silent. His voice was warm and rich as a cello's. "Her Radiance the Divine Empress, ruler of all Impyrium, has chosen this day—this New Year's Day—to make an edict regarding the succession."

Hazel froze as eyes turned toward her and her sisters. In a few seconds, one of them (Hazel hoped it would be Isabel) would be designated *Your Impyrial Highness*. Violet was technically the oldest, but she and her sisters had been born on the same day, which allowed the Spider to choose her successor from the three. The instant the empress died or abdicated, the heir would discard her birth name and become Mina XLIII.

The other two sisters would remain *Your Highness* until the new empress produced a daughter. Once that occurred, they would be reduced to *your grace*, which was how one addressed a duke or duchess. Impyrium had lots of dukes and duchesses. They would be given titles and estates and have certain responsibilities—perhaps even some that mattered. But they would never sit the throne.

Hazel's heart beat like a kettledrum. There were so many people in the audience chamber, people gawking and standing too close. Imogene mouthed something. What was she saying?

It won't be you.

Hazel was tempted to cackle "Good!" but remained silent. She had no desire to be Divine Empress, had dreaded the possibility since she was five. "Hazel" was a perfectly good name, earthy and unassuming. She had no wish to change it to Mina XLIII. And she'd much rather study magic than rule, particularly now given Rascha's faith in her potential. As far as titles were concerned, she could eventually be "Duchess of the Dawn" or the "Duchess of Spring" or any one of the ridiculous names they conferred upon irrelevant royals. Whatever happened, the course of her life was about to change, to crystallize into something different. Wetting her lips, Hazel stared defiantly at her grandmother.

Out with it!

The Divine Empress cleared her throat.

"I hereby designate my granddaughter Violet Gabriela Faeregine as heir to the throne of Impyrium. In the event she cannot serve and remains daughterless, Her Highness Isabel Athena Faeregine will succeed her. Further contingencies will be handled in accordance with our laws. All hail Her Impyrial Highness!"

It took Hazel a moment to process everything. She registered commotion, a tide of silk and chiffon as girls surged past to congratulate their future ruler. Violet lifted her perfect chin in graceful acknowledgment of what she had always regarded as her birthright. The rulers of the Great Houses bowed as she made her way to the dais.

Hazel glanced anxiously at Isabel. She knew her sister must be crushed. It was no secret Isabel regarded herself as the most capable, but she betrayed no hint of envy or disappointment. Indeed, there was nothing but pride in Isabel's eyes as she watched her sister ascend the steps.

For her part, Hazel was glad she had worn tinted lenses. Dàme Rascha said that mouths could lie but eyes could not. At the moment, Hazel's were brimming with joy. Relief spread through her body, making her toes and fingertips tingle. She would not be Divine Empress! She had not even been mentioned! Twelve years of numbing anxiety had vanished. She could have floated out a skylight.

A pair of fingers pinched her arm like steel pliers. Imogene Hyde leaned close.

"Congratulations. You're not only the last Faeregine, you're officially the least. How does that feel?"

Hazel exhaled. "Wonderful."

It was late afternoon when Sigga Fenn escorted Hazel and her sisters back to their tower. There were more receptions that evening, but Hazel begged Dàme Rascha to let her skip them.

To Hazel's surprise, her tutor relented. She imagined this had more to do with the vye's need to mourn her cousin than coddling her pupil.

Indeed, Hazel's presence had barely caused a ripple that afternoon. The palace was humming with talk of the Lirlander Vault, the Spider's rebuke of Lord Kraavh, and the new Impyrial Highness. But no one bothered discussing these events with her. For Hazel, the afternoon had consisted of tiny cakes and even tinier conversation.

As the triplets reached their common room, the tutors took their leave while Sigga remained in the vestibule. Olo remained to undress her sisters, who were already bickering as Hazel walked through the door.

"I'm serious, Violet," said Isabel. Her irritation was interrupted by a sigh of relief as Olo unlaced her corset. "I refuse to be some 'Duchess of Begonias.' I want a real title with real responsibilities. If I don't get one, I'll move to the Grislands and organize a revolt."

Stepping out of her dress, Violet somehow managed to sniff her armpit with style. "I think it's noble you want to serve my empire, Isabel, but you mustn't talk that way. It's treason."

Hazel snuck away and let her sisters bicker.

Slipping into her bedroom, she closed the door, and turned its useless lock. She and Rascha had not yet covered warding spells. When they did, she would make her room impregnable.

Kicking off her shoes, Hazel set about escaping from her embroidered prison. Shimmying out of her dress, she unfastened her corset. In three minutes, she'd molted from a colorful bird into something pale and spindly.

Blissfully free, Hazel slipped into a nightgown that had been left on a bed whose soft sheets were scented with lavender. A fire was burning in the hearth, its light dancing on frost-laced windows. Hazel did not want to think about succession or murder or palace imposters. All she wanted was to cocoon in her bed with her giraffe and an ancient tale of a mermaid who longed to become a human. If she got hungry, a maid could bring her soup and crackers. Any Faeregine—even a demoted princess—could call for soup and crackers. And that was a comfort.

Less comforting was the paper that fell from the book when she opened it. Hazel stared at it a moment. She did not use bookmarks and had never seen it before. Setting down her giraffe, she flipped the paper over.

Spiders weave and Spiders lie
in wait for easy prey,
but we can spin a web ourselves
and catch you any day.

With love,
the Butcher, the Baker, the Candlestick Maker

Hazel read it again, utterly perplexed. What did the note mean and who could have written it? Was it some kind of threat? And how had someone gotten into her room to slip the paper in her book? The tower was off-limits to visitors and heavily guarded. Rascha's warning suddenly rang in Hazel's ears: *There may be enemies in the palace.*

Taking the note, she leaped out of bed and raced into the common room, where Violet and Isabel were still arguing. Dashing past them,

Hazel flung open the door to the vestibule where Sigga Fenn was reading *The Impyrial Chronicle*. Hazel thrust the note at her.

"This was in my book!"

Holding the paper by its corners, Sigga scanned its contents. She promptly stood and checked that the outer door was locked. Her affect was eerily calm.

"Remain here, Your Highness."

Slipping a black dagger from its sheath, the Grislander ordered Isabel and Violet to the vestibule while she made for Hazel's room. Hazel's blood turned to ice. It had not occurred to her that the intruder might still be in their chambers.

While Sigga searched the bedrooms, the sisters watched in tense, terrified silence. Clutching Isabel's hand, Hazel wished they could be somewhere quiet and safe, where no one knew their names or cared about their family. A little village in the Muirlands would do, someplace far removed from the Sacred Isle. Life would be so much simpler.

But she knew no such place existed. At least not for her.

She was Hazel Faeregine. And the world would not let her forget it.

CHAPTER 2
HOB

A likely young lad sought his fortune.
He set out one day in July
with shoes newly soled and a rucksack too old,
he strode past fields of barley and rye.

His ma had not wished him to leave.
She offered two bits of advice:
If you're looking for gold,
best be lucky I'm told.
And if not,
Learn to reef, knot, and splice.

—From "One Day in July," a Muirlander folk song

Smoke lay thick about Mother Howell's, veiling the rafters and masking the smell of its patrons. These arrived in a steady flow, miners and timbermen who clomped in from the cold to cluster three deep about the bar while Mother Howell's daughters rushed to and fro, drawing beer from taps or dipping ladles into buckets of pungent spirits.

The faces around the bar were hard but not unfriendly. Conversations were genial, as were the nods at newcomers who stomped snow from their boots and warmed their hands by the potbellied stove. The place was always busy throughout the long winter, but on movie nights half of Dusk shouldered in.

To accommodate them, Mother Howell had conscripted the young people into setting up extra chairs and benches in the open spaces between tables, barrels, and grain sacks. This extended to the balcony, where a boy in a threadbare army jacket was placing seats on either side of a projector.

The boy was tall for his age and stocky with jet-black hair that fell in tangles over his ears. His skin was nut brown; his eyes an incongruent green, the color of sea glass. They were sharp eyes, quick and alert beneath a pair of straight, heavy brows. He possessed the broad face and square jaw common among the many tribes that inhabited the Northwest, but his nose was narrow and had been broken once upon a time. Now and again, he peered over the railing to scowl at another boy loitering by a post.

"Come on!" he mouthed.

His accomplice surveyed the crowded bar, blinked anxiously, and shook his head. With a groan, the boy on the balcony swore loud enough for the projectionist behind him to hear.

"Kiss your mother with that mouth, Hobson?"

The boy turned to see Porridge Nansük hunched over a table and squinting as he spliced film together. The projectionist was in his early twenties, wiry with a long ponytail and a visible share of tribal blood.

"Twice on Sundays," the boy replied. "And it's *Hob*."

Porridge grunted and applied a drop of adhesive using a teaspoon's handle. "What's the matter, then?"

"Mole won't swipe a whiskey."

"Swipe one yourself."

"Mother Howell said she'd beat me the next time I tried. Her hands are like tombstones."

Porridge laughed. "She spent twenty years working the Sentries. You'd best behave. Besides, you're too young to be dabbling in hard stuff. Stick to cider."

Hob squared a chair. "I'm thirteen."

"Exactly. You should be in school."

Hob reached for the tobacco pouch on a nearby stool. "School doesn't pay."

Porridge snatched the pouch away. "What fool said that?"

"A fool who's behind on his rent."

Porridge returned to his splicing. When Hob asked what they'd be seeing, the man merely chuckled and promised the film was sure to get everyone's attention. It was on odd statement, one that caused Hob to scan the crowd for a flash of Impyrial crimson, any prospect of *official* trouble. But he found none. There hadn't been any soldiers quartered in Dusk for months. At first frost, the soldiers and scientists locked up their archaeological site and drove their sledges south to catch the trains at Cey-Atül. The closest thing to crimson in Mother Howell's was Hob's jacket, but its color had faded. These days, it was little more than a patched, rusty rag that reached to Hob's knees, but he couldn't bring himself to part with it. His mother had made him a new coat last winter, but it hung on its hook, pristine and unworn. Hob tried not to feel too guilty. His adopted sister, Anja, could wear it someday.

Mother Howell's anvil of a face appeared atop the balcony's narrow staircase. Hob would have sworn she was half ogre.

"Hey-o," she called. "You ready yet?"

Porridge remained hunched over his work. "Five minutes."

The woman's beady eyes fell on Hob. "Don't stand there gawking."

Hob gestured indignantly at the chairs. "I set these up."

Mother Howell hooked her thumb at the stairs. "Get down there and herd the nippers forward."

"Yes, ma'am," said Hob, squeezing past her. A meaty fist seized him by the collar.

"That wouldn't be you that's got Mole trying to weasel drinks, would it?" she growled.

"No, ma'am. I'm hurt you'd even think it."

She cuffed him before turning her abuse on Porridge. Hob hurried down the steps, shooed a mutt aside, and cornered his sheepish partner.

"She was watching me!" said Mole, blinking in the manner that earned him his nickname. His real name was Barnabus, but who wanted a friend named Barnabus?

"Forget it," said Hob, plucking Izu Maycroft up from an armchair and carrying the toddler to a bench near the screen. Other children scooted over to make room, clutching mugs of eider tea and staring expectantly at a canvas screen on the stage. Depositing Izu on the bench, Hob and Mole then transplanted some seven-year-olds who had commandeered one of the better couches.

"We could ask Bluestripe to get it," Mole suggested.

Hob shook his head. Bluestripe was Dusk's resident goblin, a creature so pitiful that no one had the heart to drive him off when he'd turned up years ago. The little fellow had been banished by his clan and nearly froze to death as he wandered down from the Sentries. When the miller found him huddled by the village well, his curving nose had turned permanently blue.

"Why not?" Mole persisted. "He's right over there."

Hob spied a beaver hat bobbing about the fringes of the bar crowd, pestering people to buy him a drink. The goblin's tipsy capering brought a frown to Hob's face.

"I don't want it that bad."

"But what about the girls?" Mole whined. "We said—"

"I know what we said," Hob muttered. "I'm the idiot who said it. Anyway, we've been outflanked."

He nodded to a corner where three girls their own age were giggling in conversation with a group of older boys. A husky fifteen-year-old named Angus Dane greeted a passing adult while slipping Bree Roule—a girl with flaxen braids and a tendency to appear in Hob's better dreams—a flask. Glancing at her girlfriends, she took a sip that promptly curdled her pretty face. The older boys howled with laughter, but Angus looped an encouraging arm about her shoulders. Hob's heart gave a funny twinge.

Above, Porridge cranked a kerosene generator to life. Cheers erupted as the ancient projector's light pierced the smoke to shine a jittery white rectangle on the screen. Mother Howell bellowed for one and all to find seats or stand in back. Even the mayor quaffed his drink and scurried for an armchair.

"Where should we sit?" asked Mole, scanning about. Bree and the other girls had joined Angus and his friends at one of the central tables. To Hob's dismay, the only remaining spots were on a neighboring bench where several toddlers were clutching blankets and staring at the screen with unblinking anticipation. Hob sighed. They either had to sit with the kiddies or on the floor among the sawdust and spittle.

He opted for the kiddies, sliding next to minuscule Jinny Hodge, who had stayed with his family when her mother got sick. She leaned against his shoulder and continued sucking her thumb.

"That's so cute!" cooed Bree from behind them.

Hob wished the world would end.

A boot nudged his back. "How long you two been together?" said Angus.

"Six months," replied Hob airily.

A grunt. "Been keeping it hush-hush, have ya?"

"We're trying to avoid a scandal."

The girls laughed. Mole shifted nervously in his seat. He was half Angus's size and had to go to school with him. But Hob could have cared less about Angus or his friends. Hob had spent three years mining up in the Sentries Mountains. Mining was hard and dangerous work—so hard and dangerous that Hob wasn't about to waste movie night worrying about Angus Dane. Fighting was common in the camps and Hob had scrapped with far rougher sorts than the landlord's son. Angus knew this perfectly well.

"What's on the program?" called a voice.

Leaving the balcony, Porridge bounded onstage and bowed in response to the cheerful boos.

"Ladies and gentlemen, we have a special treat tonight, culled from sources old and new, near and far, legal and . . . otherwise. It has been assembled with infinite care and a dash of genius."

He paused for the laughter and jeers to die down before raising his tankard. "I dedicate this film to our very own Hobson Smythe. May we never see his like again."

Hob reddened as the audience raised their glasses. Why on earth was this movie dedicated to him? And what did Porridge mean by that ridiculous toast? *May we never see his like again.* If it was a joke, why did he sound so earnest? Hob stared fixedly at the screen, ignoring the puzzled looks and rumblings.

All chatter died away the instant the film began, for the only sound came from the projector's tinny speakers. From them issued a warbling music as colorful images appeared on the screen.

"Ooh!" squealed Jinny. She pointed at a stern-looking sorcerer waving his arms over a smoke-spewing skull.

The smoke took form, winged and sinister. A child-sized mouse trudged up a flight of stone steps lugging two buckets of water. Mole elbowed Hob.

"Is that magic?"

"It's a movie."

"I *know* it's a movie," Mole whispered. "But can mehrùn really conjure stuff like that smoky thing? I never saw Salamandyr do anything like that."

Hob shot Mole an incredulous look. Salamandyr was a drifter who had passed through Dusk one spring claiming to be a sorcerer. His accent, voluminous robes, and spontaneous "trances" made a powerful impression on the locals until Mother Howell caught him stealing chickens. The only true gift he displayed was swiftness of foot when he fled the village. If Mole still believed Salamandyr was a sorcerer, he was beyond hope.

When Mole repeated his question, some adults shushed him. A grateful Hob watched the movie in peace. He loved it whenever Porridge got his hands on a Pre-Cataclysm film, particularly the cartoons with talking mice and ducks. Porridge maintained that people—regular people, not just mehrùn—once had boxes in their homes and watched such entertainments whenever they liked. In those days, said Porridge, mehrùn lived among plain folk and practiced their witchcraft in secret. He even insisted the Sacred Isle wasn't the center of the world, that it hadn't even always been an island. Porridge said lots of things.

And he was saying them now.

The mouse had dozed off and was dreaming of cosmic feats while an enchanted broom filled an overflowing cistern. The image suddenly vanished, replaced by a jarring chorus of trumpets. A headline from *The Impyrial Chronicle* appeared:

EMPIRE FLOWERS UNDER FAEREGINES
Divine Empress leads Impyrium into 31st century!

The headline dissolved into a grainy photograph of a wrinkled old woman slumped in a golden palanquin. She was wearing a crown of priceless lymra stamped with an *F* whose lower half was strung like a harp. Hob's mouth hung open.

Was that really the Divine Empress?

The picture was slightly blurred as though snapped in haste. The only images Hob had ever seen of the empress showed a much younger person enveloped by golden light. This woman looked no more divine than Bluestripe. Seeing it made Hob nervous.

ROYALS SACRIFICE DURING DROUGHT
"We're all in this together," says senior official.

Another photograph showed a garden party at a magnificent estate where mehrùn children were jumping into a swimming pool.

IMPYRIAL AUCTION RAISES MONEY FOR MUIRLANDS SCHOOLS
"Every child deserves a chance," declares Basil Faeregine.

The headline vanished, replaced by a crowded classroom in some desert province where boys and girls shared pages torn from old textbooks.

The crowd in Mother Howell's grew restless as more headlines appeared, each paired with a contrasting image.

EMPIRE SALUTES FAEREGINE TRIPLETS
Rumors of unprecedented powers

DIVINE EMPRESS NAMES NEXT GODDESS
Read on for an exclusive interview with Violet Faeregine

"What is this?" someone shouted.

"Bring back the mouse!" cried another.

Hob wholeheartedly agreed. The cartoon was just getting good and Porridge had to ruin it with this nonsense. Movie night was about having a laugh, not—

He froze. The next headline was not from *The Impyrial Chronicle* but *The Northwest Register*, a smaller paper that covered regional news.

DUSK BOY EARNS
TOP MARKS AT PROVINCES

Beneath the headline an Impyrial magistrate was presenting a nine-year-old Hob with a plaque. The boy in the picture was a virtual stranger, a beaming, round-faced cherub with a crew cut and his whole life ahead of him.

It vanished, replaced by rapidly alternating images of a colorful centennial poster and black-and-white photographs.

THE FUTURE IS HERE!

[A farmer repairing a wagon wheel.]

IT WILL BE BIGGER!

[Food lines in a ghetto.]

AND BRIGHTER!

[A recent shot of a filthy Hob shielding his eyes
as he emerged from a mine shaft.]

WITH OPPORTUNITIES
FOR ALL!

[Portraits of the Dusk Eleven:
a group of young men and women
who'd joined the revolts twenty years ago.
None had returned.]

Angry shouts erupted. Relatives of the Eleven were present and Hob imagined they did not appreciate being ambushed with such painful memories. Jinny flinched as a tankard struck the screen on which two words were flashing:

WAKE UP!
WAKE UP!
WAKE UP!

Mother Howell hurried onstage. "Shut it off!" she yelled. Righting the screen, she wheeled on the balcony. "Shut it off before I come up there and brain ya!"

The projector flicked off, its message fading on Mother Howell's broad apron. She eyed the packed house.

"Pipe down," she rumbled. "No one's throwing drinks in my place or starting some tomfool riot. There's squeakers here if ya haven't noticed." She wagged an angry finger up at Porridge. "You want to spout tripe, you do it in your *own* place with your *own* customers. Understand me, boy?"

Porridge's voice almost broke. "Yes, ma'am."

"All right," said Mother Howell, simmering down. "Here's what we're going to do. While Porridge sets up another movie, we're all gonna chitchat, spend lots of money, and have a grand old time."

The crowd laughed and someone started a cheer for Mother Howell. Patrons surged toward the bar. As Hob watched them, he considered just how foolish Porridge had been. That film was dangerous. If any official, if any outsider had seen it . . .

He did a double take.

An outsider *had* seen it.

A stranger was standing just beside the door, sipping from a tankard and looking quietly amused by all the activity. He was a tall man in late middle age, slighter than most Duskers, with graying brown hair and a well-trimmed beard. The beard marked him as an outsider right away. Locals didn't groom theirs.

A boot nudged his shoulder. Hob turned to see Angus finish a sip from his flask.

"You help Porridge put that trash together?"

"What?" said Hob, distracted. "No."

Angus smirked. "He dedicated it to you, Golden Boy. Why would he do that?"

"No idea."

"Fine plaque," Angus continued. "Can I see it sometime? Or did it fall down the mines?"

"It's at my house," replied Hob. "Come polish it anytime."

Angus grinned. "You mean it's at *my* house. Or did ya forget my family owns that little rattrap?"

Hob swallowed his reply.

Emboldened, Angus took another sip and pretended to search the crowd. "Where's your ma? I'd hate to think she's missing out 'cause she's home washing my clothes. Is that what she's doing, Golden Boy? Washing my skivvies?"

Hob shrugged. "Your skivvies take a long time to wash, Angus. I'd see the doc if I were you. Something's leaking."

Mole gave a hoot and the girls dissolved into fits of giggling. Angus was still fumbling for a retort when someone shouted for quiet. The new movie was starting.

Turning back to the screen, Hob suppressed a grin. These little jousts with Angus were always satisfying. He settled in to watch a movie about a mermaid who wanted to become a human. The film was scratched and barely audible. But at least it was long.

Jinny was fast asleep when the film ended and her mother came to collect her. Other parents claimed their young ones while the remaining adults settled in at the bar. Angus and his friends made a noisy departure, leaving a mess on their table for Hob and Mole to clean. This they did, along with rearranging benches and stacking the chairs. For their efforts, Mother Howell gave each a copper and smelled their breath. When she sniffed no whiskey, she gave them a second.

Porridge came down from the balcony, lugging his projector and film canisters. He glanced apologetically at Hob.

"Sorry about putting you on the spot."

Hob waved it off. "I don't care about that. But you should be more careful, Porridge. I'd burn that before the wrong person finds it."

The young man shook his head. "We can't just live and die pretending everything's okay. You know what happens if we all sit quiet and watch our cartoons?"

"What?"

"Nothing."

Hob smiled, but Porridge didn't. Bidding Hob good night, he made for the door, giving Mother Howell a wide berth. Hob turned to Mole.

"Want to play skid?"

It was rare that the games table was available. But a yawning Mole shook his head and shuffled off to get his coat. He had school tomorrow. Hob did not.

The two left Mother Howell's, bundled for the bitter cold. Hob breathed the piney air through his muffler. At least there was no wind. No snow either, not even atop the Sentries, whose peaks loomed over Dusk like sleeping giants.

The square was nearly empty and dark, as only half the streetlamps were left burning. The pair crunched across the snow, making for the dingy row houses where Mole lived with his parents. Hob's cottage was two blocks beyond, past the little Ninespire temple.

As they neared Mole's house, they heard laughter, followed by a slurry grumbling that could only be Bluestripe. Poking his head around the corner, Hob saw Angus's friends holding the goblin by each arm near the temple steps. The creature sagged between them, staring blearily at his hat, which had fallen in the snow. Angus waved his flask beneath Bluestripe's nose.

"You scared off the girls. Least you can do is have a drink with us. Come on then."

The goblin mumbled something incoherent and tried to wriggle free. Mole crept up beside Hob.

"Don't," he whispered. "He'll take it out on me."

"Go inside," said Hob. "There won't be any trouble."

"Are you sure?"

"Yeah."

Mole was visibly relieved. "Okay. See you later."

When Hob heard Mole's door shut, he rounded the corner and walked down the lane with his hands in his pockets.

"Leave 'im be," he said wearily. "He can barely stand."

Angus turned around, his face a red blotch. "Mind your business, son. You've got enough to worry about."

"What's that then?"

A gloating grin appeared on Angus's face. "I spoke with my da. If you don't cough up every copper by next week, I get to put you out."

"You'll have the money."

Angus laughed. "How you gonna do that, eh? I know what you earn and I know what your ma pulls in. Little Anja gonna be a miner too?"

"You'll have the money," Hob repeated. "Let Bluestripe go."

"Not 'til he has a drink with us. And you'd best get home and learn some magic like in that cartoon. That's the only way you'll be scraping together what you owe."

Hob shrugged. "I already know magic."

The group laughed. "Go on then," Angus jeered. "Show us some magic, Golden Boy."

Kneeling down, Hob proceeded to pack two snowballs. The night was cold and the snow did not clump easily, but he pressed and molded them until they were adequate. A puzzled Angus and his friends looked on. Even Bluestripe raised his lumpy head.

"Now," said Hob. "Watch closely or you'll miss the trick."

Taking one of the snowballs, he displayed it before lobbing it high in the air. His audience followed its trajectory, staring up as if they expected it to sprout wings. As they did, Hob hurled the second snowball. It smashed into Angus's face, exploding in a glittering cloud.

Angus stumbled and slipped, causing the other boys to release Bluestripe in a failed bid to catch their falling friend. The goblin dashed down a nearby stairwell to the temple's cellar, where he lived in a nook behind some old prayer books. The cellar door slammed shut and Hob heard a bolt slide into place. He glanced back to Angus, who was wiping a spot of blood from his nose.

"You're a dead man," Angus spat.

Hob affected concern. "You didn't like the trick?"

Angus climbed unsteadily to his feet. "I'm serious."

Hob laughed. "Too serious, Angus. It's just snow."

"Maybe," Angus huffed, "but I don't take guff from bastards."

As soon as he uttered the word, a deathly silence fell over the group. Verbal jabs were traded freely in Dusk, but often with affection or as conversational seasoning. But certain words were never used in a joking fashion. They were grave insults requiring either a public retraction or a duel. Angus had just used one. It didn't matter if it was true.

The other three boys withdrew several paces as Hob removed his coat. As for Angus, he looked confused, even appalled as though he'd just realized what he'd said. His companions couldn't help him now. This was now an honor matter.

Dropping his coat, Hob went straight at the older boy. Angus could keep his teeth or his pride, but not both. When he raised his fists, however, an unfamiliar voice spoke out.

"That'll do."

They all turned as a figure emerged from the little cemetery behind the Ninespire temple. It was the stranger, the man Hob had glimpsed in Mother Howell's.

"Who the hell are you?" Angus demanded.

"A visitor," said the man, slipping through the gate. "And I'd be careful throwing that word about. Where I come from, it leads to worse than fistfights."

The man came to stand by the lamp at the temple's steps. Hob could see he was no trapper or trader, or even from the Northwest. The stranger's clothes were brand new and of excellent quality. He looked how a city man might outfit himself for an expedition. A city man with money.

"Where are you from?" said Angus suspiciously.

"Someplace else," the stranger quipped. "It's lovely. In fact, I suggest you go there."

The man exuded such a confident, sophisticated air that it seemed natural to obey him. To do otherwise would be rude, uncouth. Hob sensed it might even be dangerous. Wealthy city men didn't venture this far north, not unless they were suicidal. The stranger either had companions nearby, or there was more to him than met the eye.

Apparently Angus agreed, for he muttered something to his companions and they shuffled off. Before they left, however, he scowled at Hob.

"One week, golden boy. One week to settle up or you're bunking with Bluestripe."

Hob said nothing. When the boys had gone, the stranger plucked Hob's coat from the ground and brushed off the snow.

"Put this back on. You'll catch your death."

"Thank you, sir," said Hob, slipping on the coat.

The man grunted. "You have some manners, I see. Well, that's a start. Come on then."

Hob blinked. "Excuse me?"

"I need a guide. And I gather you need money."

"Where are you going?" asked Hob.

"That archaeological site," said the stranger. "You know it?"

Hob nodded. He knew it well, for it was not far from the mines. "Sure, but it's Impyrial property. Off-limits."

"Fascinating." said the man. He spoke as though this was a bit of interesting trivia and not a capital crime. "Let's get started."

"You want to go now? It's almost midnight."

"Are we scared of vyes in the woods?"

"No," said Hob, who had never seen a vye but heard plenty of tales. "But it's rough country and the trails are snowed over. We could go in the morning."

"Tradesmen start work in the morning," remarked the stranger. "I am not a tradesman. And I have no more time to waste. Do we have a deal?"

"How much?" said Hob flatly.

The man patted a coat pocket. It gave a promising clink. "Enough to settle your debts."

"Let me see the money."

The stranger sighed. "I feel like I'm in a souk." From his pocket he plucked a thick gold coin over an inch in diameter. Hob squinted at it, amazed.

"Is that a solar?"

The stranger smiled. "Never seen one before?"

Hob shook his head. It was hard to find bullion of any kind in

Dusk, much less Impyrial solars. Local trade was conducted with copper coins, scrimshaw, or nuggets from the mines. When these were scarce, people bartered. The only gold Hob had seen was in an old trapper's grin. His family could live for six months on that glorious coin. And Angus could go jump in Bear Lake.

The stranger dropped the solar in Hob's palm. Its weight was intoxicating. "Do we have a deal?"

Hob considered. The dig site wasn't far and he knew the area well enough to find the trail by moonlight. The night was cold but clear, no hint of a brewing snowstorm. If all went smoothly, he'd be back well before dawn. Still, something was off.

"Why me?" he asked. "Anyone could take you there."

The stranger sounded bored. "You seem like a capable lad. But if you don't need the money . . ."

He reached for the coin, but Hob closed his hand. "Where's your sledge?"

The stranger pointed to a sleek shape beyond the temple's rowan grove. Hob told him to wait there while he fetched his gear from his locker at the mining depot. One didn't venture lightly into the Sentries, and Hob had no faith that an outsider would have the proper equipment.

Once at his locker, Hob buckled a heavy work belt over his coat and slipped a leather baldric over his shoulder. To the belt, he attached a rock hammer, a chisel, and a sturdy canister that looked like a large canteen but contained retractable steel cable, useful for climbing or as a winch to raise or lower heavy tools. To these he added a flashlight, a small lantern, and his father's infantry knife. He wouldn't need a pick, but he did bring a short-handled spade in case the sledge got stuck.

Once he'd tossed some food tins in his satchel, he reached for his rifle, a muzzle-loading Boekka he'd purchased secondhand. Hob never left Dusk without it, not even to fish local streams.

The stranger chuckled when Hob returned clinking with gear.

"I see I picked the right guide."

Hob examined the man's sledge. The vehicle was new and obviously of Workshop make with a powerful engine under its gunmetal casing. It looked nothing like the noisy, fume-belching hulks Hob's company leased from scrap pirates. The man must have had serious connections; only the rich and powerful had access to decent technology. Dusk didn't even have electricity. Taking his mining goggles, Hob smeared them with phosphoroil, a waxy substance that gathered ambient light to help one see in the darkness. Once the lenses glowed a faint yellow, he slipped them on.

"I'll drive."

Hob hunched low over the sledge, adjusting the throttle with one hand while working the runner pedals with his feet. The machine was a delight to operate—swift and smooth, perfectly balanced. Wind whipped past his fox-fur cap, but the engine was almost eerily quiet.

He had been driving for almost an hour, steering a path through the forested hills until they began climbing Auld Ettyn, a mountain whose twin peaks served as a border between the human-populated Muirlands and the haunted Grislands—the Gray Lands—that began on the mountain's far slope. As they rounded a bend, Hob felt a tap on his back.

"Stop a moment," said the stranger.

Hob shook his head. The man tapped again.

"I need to relieve myself," he clarified irritably.

Hob pointed to the dark woods on their right where a pack of timber wolves was keeping pace. When his passenger failed to spot them, Hob removed his goggles and handed them back. Phosphoroil not only magnified light, it was particularly useful for spying a predator's eyeshine. The stranger gave a startled exclamation.

"How long have they been after us?"

"Ten minutes," said Hob, taking the goggles back. "There's a bridge ahead. I'll stop once we've crossed. They won't follow."

"Why not?"

"Wolves have more sense than we do."

Twenty minutes later, they reached an ungainly span of rusted girders that traversed a gorge some four hundred feet across. In warmer months, the bridge trembled from the roar of great waterfalls formed by the mountain's snowmelt. But winter had silenced them, leaving jagged sheets of ice to drape the chasm walls. Hob held his breath until they'd reached the other side. Looking back, he saw dozens of glittering eyes staring after them. Bringing the sledge to a skidding halt, Hob kept the engine idling while his passenger emptied his bladder and craned his neck at the bright crescent above. To Hob's surprise, the man addressed it in a theatrical tenor.

> *The moving Moon went up the sky,*
> *And nowhere did abide:*
> *Softly she was going up,*
> *And a star or two beside—*

With a laugh, he zipped his trousers and strolled back to the sledge. He was either a poet or a lunatic. Perhaps both.

"Did you write that?" asked Hob, shifting his rifle. The man did not answer right away but blew a ring of frosted air into the night.

"No," he said. "The credit goes to Samuel Taylor Coleridge."

"Never heard of him."

The stranger smiled. "Of course you haven't. He died three thousand years ago." He pointed up at the moon. "Would you believe that we ordinary humans—lowly little muir—once walked upon that?"

"Whatever you say," muttered Hob, rubbing his hands together. The man sounded like Porridge when he was in his cups.

His passenger chuckled. "You don't believe me?"

Hob shrugged. "If that's true, why aren't we there now?"

The man gave him a shrewd look. "That is an exceedingly intelligent question, Hobson Smythe."

Hob glanced up. "How do you know my name?"

"That film was dedicated to you," the stranger replied. "You're the boy in that photograph, the one receiving a plaque. Placed first in Provinces, did you?"

"Yes, sir."

"Why didn't you go off to an Impyrial college? The Faeregines would have paid your way. You might have become an administrator, a city magistrate even. What happened?"

A pause. "Life, sir."

The stranger grunted. "That projectionist was right, you know. A lad with your talents is wasted out here."

Hob said nothing. He'd had this conversation with himself countless times. The stranger let the matter drop.

"How much farther to that dig site?" he asked.

Hob pointed. "It's just past that ridge."

"Carry on, but stop a few hundred yards from the entrance. We'll cover the last stretch on foot."

"Why?"

The man gave him the same look that Hob often gave Mole. "Because the site will certainly be guarded."

"All the soldiers left," said Hob. "They won't be back until the thaw."

From his coat, the stranger produced a heavy revolver crafted of an oily black metal etched with strange markings. Hob had seen similar markings on the cairns near Whitebarrow. Opening the revolver's cylinder, the stranger loaded it with large silvery bullets.

"Who said the guardian would be human?"

CHAPTER 3
THE TRANSCONTINENTAL

A little rebellion now and then is a good thing,
and as necessary in the political world as storms in the physical.

—Thomas Jefferson, Pre-Cataclysm polymath (270–187 P.C.)

Hob kept his eyes on the stranger's gun, his mind on the Boekka slung across his back.

"I said I'd take you here. That's it."

The man's smirk suggested disappointment. "In my day, lads didn't flinch at a bit of adventure."

Hob had heard rumors about dig sites. "I'm not going in."

The stranger spun the revolver's cylinder shut. "I'm not asking you to. But I need a lookout and an extra pair of hands. I trust you can haul on a rope?"

Hob nodded.

"Splendid. There's another solar for you if you see this through. Two solars for driving a sledge and lowering a rope. Not bad for a night's work."

Hob couldn't argue. He'd have to exchange the coins for more practical currency in Wulfast, but he could manage that. He could even buy his mother something pretty just because. Lowering his goggles, he steered the sledge for the ridge.

Minutes later Hob pulled over and shut off the engine. The site was two hundred yards ahead, past a snow-spattered barricade warning visitors to keep out. A soaring white pine stood nearby, its trunk branded with the Faereginc's harp-shaped *F*. No villager could cut down that tree; the Divine Empress claimed it for a ship mast.

"Even out here they own us," said the stranger.

He dismounted to rummage through the sledge's storage compartment. A moment later, he'd produced rope, a set of pulleys, a powerful flashlight, and a dull metal camera that must have been acquired on the black market. Like many technologies, cameras were heavily regulated by the authorities. To Hob's puzzlement, the man also removed a newspaper—that week's edition of the *Northwest Register*. Handing the rope and flashlight to Hob, the stranger slipped the camera around his neck and marched ahead. He promptly sank into the moonlit snow.

Muttering an oath, he reached for Hob's hand. "You'd better go first."

Hob did so. He was lighter and had a knack for sensing where the snow would hold. It was good to focus on something, to distract himself from the fact he was breaking Impyrial law. His creeping shadow looked vaguely sinister, but really it was wariness. The wolves would not cross the bridge, but even wilder things prowled the Sentries at night.

Straight ahead, a derrick stood like a grave marker, ringed by piled boulders and debris. Heavy equipment and fuel drums were positioned nearby, covered by canvas tarps. A line of fallen trees ran up the mountain like a scar, a relic of the spring earthquake whose fault revealed caverns within. Two days later, Impyrial archaeologists arrived and declared the area off-limits.

When they reached the ring of slag and stones, Hob scanned their surroundings. The stranger breezed past him. Why wasn't the man anxious?

"Shouldn't we be looking for the guardian?" Hob whispered.

"The guardian will be inside," came the hushed reply.

"Then why did we have to walk?"

"If it's a golem—and they're always golems—it will be sensitive to vibrations. The sledge would alert it."

"What's a go-lem?" asked Hob.

"An animated construct," replied the stranger. "A statue that's been brought to life by an enchanted parchment placed in its mouth. The most famous golem was in Prague, but the magic goes much further back."

"And Prague is . . . ?"

The man shined his light on the derrick. "Pre-Cataclysm city. European."

None of this made any sense to Hob. Instead, he focused on topics most relevant to his health. "So, this golem. Can it climb out of the dig site?"

"Doubtful. Depends on its size, the cavern's depth, the powers of the mystic that created it. Lots of factors."

"How big can they be?" asked Hob nervously.

"I've seen a twenty footer, but ten's more likely."

Hob frowned. Ten feet was plenty big. "So what do you need me to do?"

"Lower your voice for one."

They reached the derrick, whose iron frame straddled a black chasm some fifteen feet across. The stranger swiftly assembled an apparatus using his rope and pulleys.

"Listen carefully," he whispered. "You're going to lower me down so I can take photographs. Don't worry about my weight; the pulleys will offset it. If all goes well, I'll be ten minutes."

"And if it doesn't?" Hob whispered.

The stranger clipped the rope to a belt beneath his coat. "If I tug once, wait until I tug again. If I tug twice, pull me up. Three times, haul for your life. Understand?"

Hob nodded at the cable canister on his belt. "This has a gear winch. It'll work faster than pulling you by hand."

"How long's the cable?"

"Two hundred feet."

The stranger shone his light into the chasm. "No good. I need to go deeper."

"What are you taking photos of?"

The man winked. "Truth."

Before Hob could ask another question, his companion stepped off the ledge. Hob was grateful for the pulleys. The stranger was lean, but he was also tall and wearing heavy clothes and equipment.

Sitting down, Hob braced his feet against the derrick and fed the rope through.

Foot by foot, the rope passed through Hob's gloves. After eighty feet or so, he felt a sharp tug and waited until a second signaled he should resume. Another hundred feet, another tug. Holding the rope fast, Hob listened for any nearby sounds. He felt horribly vulnerable with his back to the Sentries. If something happened upon them here, with Hob holding the man by a rope . . . He thanked Kayüta, the fox spirit, that the night was quiet with little breeze to carry their scent into the woods.

Another pull and Hob resumed his work. Almost half the coil remained. The rope must have been three hundred feet, and was woven of very strong and supple material. Another thirty feet, then forty. Hob's mind drifted to what the stranger had said. What did he mean he was photographing truth? *Something* must be down there, but Hob assumed it was precious metals or gemstones. The empress claimed their land's best trees, why wouldn't she claim its other riches?

His forearms griped as he continued lowering. Precious little slack remained when there was another tug. Hob tugged back to let the man know he was running out of rope.

Minutes passed. Hob felt an easing of tension as though the stranger had unhooked himself. He pulled slightly; no resistance. Hob frowned, but seized the chance to shake out his hands. What was this idiot doing?

Chill seeped through his army coat. Hob wore it for sentimental reasons, not because it was as warm as the fur-lined oilskins favored by Duskers. It was not made for sitting motionless on a slab of icy rock in the dead of night. The stranger said ten minutes. They were well past that.

A shiver ran through the earth like the pucker on a horse's flank. Hob sat up, peering intently at the black chasm. Was that a flicker of light or were his eyes playing tricks? Another tremor, stronger. The rope jerked forward in Hob's hands. Three sharp tugs.

Haul for your life.

Hob did so, pulling swiftly and steadily, hand over hand. The pulleys clinked and groaned as the rope piled up beside him. A shout echoed from within the earth.

Hob's pulse quickened. More flickers; a flashlight momentarily pierced the night. Tremors rumbled like millstones. Hob's arms and shoulders burned as coils of rope lay tangled about him. How much farther? A hundred feet? Two hundred? Hob blocked out the agony in his lungs, his hands, his back. One more heave, then another. Swift but steady. One more heave . . .

"Hurry!"

The stranger's hoarse cry was panicked. The rope swayed as though he was trying to climb it like an ungainly spider. Hob pursed his lips; he would snag it on something and—

The line went slack.

Tying the rope about the derrick, Hob hurried to the chasm's edge. Particles of dust and snow glittered in his flashlight's beam as his gaze followed the rope past forty feet of rock to an open space. The stranger's flashlight was below, its light illuminating the man who lay sprawled on what? A *building*?

"Can you hear me?" Hob called. The stranger rolled dazedly onto his back. The rumbling grew louder.

"Wake up!" Hob shouted. "Are you all right?"

The stranger gestured at his leg. "I think something's broken. The golem . . . it's coming."

"Where's your gun?"

The man pointed to something beyond Hob's field of vision. He must have dropped it.

"Can you splice two ropes together?" Hob called hopefully. There were many serviceable knots, but he doubted a city man would know them. The stranger confirmed his misgivings.

A ponderous footstep sounded. Gazing off into the darkness, the stranger gave a horrified gasp and crawled feebly in the direction of his revolver. He barely moved.

Hob wasted no time. In three seconds, he had clipped his cable to a beam and lowered himself down into the chasm. Below, the stranger had given up on his gun and lay clutching his leg. Beyond Hob's view, there was a sound like groaning metal. Hob squeezed his flashlight into a clip on his rifle.

"Stay there," he ordered.

The stranger was almost directly beneath him. As he descended, Hob saw that he was in a dim, impossibly vast cavern housing huge, rectangular buildings made of metal and glass. Many had collapsed, but some were intact and so tall they nearly scraped the rocky carapace that entombed them.

"Where's the golem?" Hob yelled, pointing his rifle this way and that. The cavern's acoustics made it difficult to pinpoint the rumbling. The stranger pointed to his right. Kicking his legs, Hob twisted about.

The flashlight's beam wavered on a face a stone's throw away. The golem was some twelve feet tall with long, simian arms that helped it support its ponderous weight. Its chiseled face was a crude approximation of a man's, but its onyx eyes did not blink and its mouth was frozen in a grimace. It lumbered toward them, dragging its granite feet over the roof.

Crack-crack-crack-crack-crack!

Hob's rifle shots echoed in the cavern. The bullets struck the golem's chest, sending up tiny flecks of stone, but the creature did not break stride.

"My gun," gasped the stranger.

Hob saw the revolver lying some fifteen feet away. The golem was closing quickly. If he went for the gun, he'd lose his window to escape. If he activated the winch, he'd be leaving a helpless man to die.

Pushing the cable release, Hob dropped swiftly to the roof. Ditching his rifle, he scrambled on all fours for the heavy revolver. The golem was mere steps from the stranger, who had curled into a ball. Seizing the gun, Hob aimed it at the golem's head and fired.

The revolver's roar was enormous. Its shocking recoil jolted Hob's arm, sending the shot wide. Bending slowly, the golem reached for the stranger as though it meant to tear him in two. Gripping the revolver with both hands, Hob took aim again.

This time, he did not miss.

Seven rounds slammed into the golem's head. It staggered back at each impact, its hands clutching at its cracked and splintered skull. An angry orange glow began to radiate from the bullet holes.

"Cover your eyes!" the stranger shouted.

The golem's head exploded in a spray of granite shards. They pelted Hob's arms and jacket, stinging whatever exposed flesh they could find. A concussive jolt shook the building's roof, followed by a shower of breaking glass.

Opening his eyes, Hob saw the headless golem in a smoking heap, grasping blindly at anything within reach. Seizing Hob's rifle, its hands twisted his beloved Boekka and flashlight into scrap. Was the creature dying? *Could* such a thing die? Hob had no idea, but the stranger was far too close to it.

Scrambling to his feet, Hob dragged his companion away from those searching fingers. The stranger clutched his knee and grunted with pain as Hob deposited him a safe distance away. Giving the golem a wide berth, Hob retrieved the stranger's flashlight to assess their situation.

There was good news and bad.

They were fortunate Hob's cable was not pinned beneath many tons of sentient stone. But it still dangled close to the golem. They would have to venture within reach of those searching hands before Hob could activate the cable's winch. To complicate matters, he doubted the device would bear their combined weight.

"How's your leg?" said Hob.

The man exhaled slowly. "I don't think anything's broken. Just twisted my knee badly."

Hob removed his belt attached to the cable canister.

"I don't think the winch can pull us both up together. I'm going to send you up first while I distract it. Once you reach the top, press this lever and send the belt back down. Understand?"

The man coughed into his fist. "I think so."

Hob frowned. Snatching the camera, he snapped the man's picture. "Unless I get out of here, officials are going to find my body when they come back. And they're going to find this camera with your photograph. Do you understand that?"

The man met Hob's eyes. "Message received, Mr. Smythe. I didn't intend to be cavalier. I'm well aware you saved my life. Please demonstrate how to operate the winch."

Hob did so twice before buckling the sturdy belt around the man's midsection. When all was ready, Hob dragged him as close as possible to where the cable was dangling. Ten feet away, the golem now lay motionless.

"On my signal," he whispered. He padded quietly around the golem so that he was on its other side. "Ready . . . now!"

Hob kicked a large metal box bolted to the roof. A stony hand shot toward the vibrations, grasping wildly. The stranger activated the winch, rising into the air as the cable went taut. Hob caught his breath. The man's boots were going to graze the golem. With a gasp, the stranger tucked up his legs, clearing the monster by inches as he ascended toward the derrick.

Gazing out at the cavern, Hob tried to remain calm. It was not just the golem that had his heart racing. He shone the stranger's flashlight on a building and gazed at its rusted skeleton. What was this place? Who had lived here? Hob recalled the man's claim that muir had walked on the moon thousands of years ago. It was impossible—nonsensical—but so was an ancient city buried beneath the mountains.

A voice called out from above. Hobs belt and cable canister were descending. Once again, he kicked the metal box whose vibrations occupied the golem. Edging around it, he caught the belt, buckled it securely round his waist, and activated the winch.

A beautiful clicking sounded from within the canister as the mechanism began spooling. Hob was lifted smoothly off his feet. He held the camera out at arm's length and snapped a photograph of the scene. There was a pulse of light and the camera hummed briefly. Hob was impressed it had survived the fall. He ran his fingers over the casing. Maybe the workshop had made it too. Had they made the stranger's gun? The revolver sat in his coat pocket, warm as a bed brick.

Hob had never been so happy to see the stars. Emerging from the chasm, he found the stranger sitting with his back against the derrick. Swinging to safety, Hob untied the cable's anchor and returned the man's camera and revolver.

"I must say you're a remarkable young man," remarked the stranger, laying the gun on his lap. "Few people could handle themselves like you just did." He fished a second gold coin from his coat. "You're owed this, I believe."

Hob took the solar, ashamed by the rush of greedy pleasure it gave him. He'd made a year's wages for a few hours work. Sure it had been dangerous, but so was mining. Pocketing the coin, he glanced up at a sky that was showing the first gray hints of dawn. "I'll get the sledge."

Hob's companion held up a hand. "I have a proposition."

"No thanks," said Hob, turning away.

"A wise man always listens to a proposition," said the stranger slowly. "Your father taught me that."

Hob turned back sharply. "You knew my father?"

The stranger was gazing at him thoughtfully. "I did. Ulrich and I were very close."

Hob felt a sting of disappointment. "My father's name was Anders Smythe. He was a soldier in the Impyrial Guard."

A sympathetic glint shone in the stranger's eyes. "No, Hob. Your father only took that name when we infiltrated the guard. His name was Ulrich Doyle, and he was a far greater man than any of those traitors that serve the Faeregines. Ulrich was a member of the Fellowship."

Hob had heard of the Fellowship. Porridge talked of joining them, said they were some kind of revolutionary group. Hob backed a step, sorry that he'd returned the stranger's revolver.

"You're lying," he said softly. "You didn't know my father. Who are you?"

The stranger slipped a photograph from his breast pocket and handed it to Hob. "My name is Edmund Burke."

Hob shone the flashlight on the photograph. The only picture of his father he'd ever seen was on his mother's bedside table. He'd studied it a thousand times, knew every detail. As Hob examined this new photograph, an icy prickling crept down his spine. It showed the same man.

His father was much younger in this photo—no older than twenty—with short black hair, light eyes, and a workman's shirt. He was sitting with a group of men in a tavern. Most of the others looked drunk, but not Hob's father. He gazed at the camera with the same inward, soulful expression Hob recognized from his mother's picture. The person next to him was older and appeared to be smiling with tolerant amusement at one of their rowdier companions. That man was Mr. Burke.

Hob studied the picture in silence, finding unmistakable traces of himself in his father's nose and dimpled chin. The clearest link, however, were the eyes. Hob's were shaped like his mother's, but they were green like this man's. They marked him as a bastard, the shame of some pale-skinned skänder. His mother's tribe had made Hob painfully well aware of this. Hob switched off the flashlight.

"So you knew my father," he muttered. "Am I supposed to care?"

The man gestured at Hob's coat. "You don't wear that for warmth."

Hob sniffed. "Why are you showing me this? What do you want?"

Mr. Burke looked intently at him. "I want you to come with me. The Fellowship needs people like you."

"I don't know anything about the Fellowship," said Hob. "Besides, I'm needed here."

"Why? To provide for your family? You'll earn more in a few months with me than twenty years breaking your back in the mines."

Mr. Burke produced a roll of solars wrapped in silver foil. Hob felt dizzy.

"How many are in that?" he asked hoarsely.

"Twenty. Come with me and they're yours. Your mother could give up washing and buy a proper house. Can she do that if you stay?"

Hob considered. "How do you know I won't just take the gold and ditch you?"

Burke shook his head. "Not your nature. Besides, I'm not just giving you money. I'm giving you a chance to join something far bigger than you can imagine."

Hob laughed. "What's that then?"

The man gestured at the chasm. "Open your eyes. Magic folk, the 'Great Houses' that run the empire—they've been spooning us lies, hobbling us so we can't break free of their control."

"You sound like Porridge."

"The filmmaker? He's heavy-handed, but he isn't wrong. Most muir sleepwalk through life. Few know anything of our true history and scientific achievements. The Workshop has warehouses teeming with technology salvaged from before the Cataclysm, but it's locked away, collecting dust because the Faeregines won't let them reintroduce it. We can't be trusted with such toys, you see—our benevolent empress know best. Most of us spend our entire lives as lost little sheep.

Muir will always be in the dark so long as mehrùn rule Impyrium. We're slaves in all but name."

Hob lifted his chin. "We're not slaves. I was invited to attend the Impyrial college."

Mr. Burke looked as though he couldn't believe Ulrich Doyle's son could be so blind. "My boy, what do you think the Province exams are for?"

The question made Hob uneasy. "To find the best and brightest," he answered. "The empire needs administrators."

Mr. Burke chuckled at this. "Aye, that they do. Identify the most gifted muir—those most likely to pose a threat—and indoctrinate them while they're young. Instead of fighting the system, they become a part of it while their positions maintain the illusion of opportunity. Rather ingenious, eh?"

Hob's cheeks burned. His performance on those exams was a point of pride, a ready rebuttal to those that turned up their nose. Hobson Smythe might be a lowly miner, but he was also the brightest thirteen-year-old in the entire Northwest province. A broken plaque said so.

"I guess you think I'm one of those sheep," he muttered.

Burke's eyes blazed. "You don't have to be! Come with me, Hob. Stay here and you'll spend a dismal life wondering what might have been."

Hob shook his head. "I can't just leave. I don't even know you."

"But I know you," said Mr. Burke gently. "I've visited Dusk four— no, five—times since you were born. Mostly as a trader, once as a magician."

Hob's mouth nearly fell open. *"Salamandyr?"*

Mr. Burke inclined his head. "In the flesh, although that disguise nearly proved my ruin. I'll never steal a chicken again."

Hob tried to smile. "My friend, Mole, still thinks you're the real thing."

But Mr. Burke did not appear to hear this. He leaned forward with an intense, serious expression. "Listen, Hob. I swore to your father that I'd check up on you if anything happened to him. I've kept that promise. He also wanted me to guarantee you a place in the Fellowship, but I couldn't do that. We all have to prove ourselves worthy. Tonight, you did so."

Rising to his feet, the man casually brushed snow from his pants. He betrayed no trace of any injury.

"I don't understand," said Hob. "This was all a test?"

"Not all," Mr. Burke allowed. "Verifying this city's existence is of immense importance. But my visit also gave me an opportunity to see what you're made of. You have your father's courage. Not many people would have risked their life to save a stranger."

Hob was appalled. "But what if I hadn't?" he exclaimed. "Or what if I'd missed? You were unarmed. The golem would have crushed you!"

From a hidden holster, Mr. Burke produced a second revolver. "I'm never unarmed. But I am out of time. The Cey-Atül Transcontinental is departing for the capital at noon and I need to be on that train. I'd like you to accompany me as my assistant." He cocked his head. "What do you say, Hob? Are you ready to take up your father's mantle?"

Hob stood silently in the frigid darkness, clutching the photograph and pondering this bizarre turn of events. He had so many questions for this man: questions about his father and the Fellowship, about the ancient city entombed beneath them. He almost laughed. How often had he raged against the injustice of his life and circumstances? He had never forgiven the Fates for giving him brains and then snatching away his opportunity to get out, to leave Dusk and make something of himself. But opportunity had returned to pluck at his sleeve. Hob glanced at the dark chasm. He did not have to mine ore; he could mine truth—truth about his father, the Faeregines, and the world they ruled. And he could support his mother and Anja in the bargain.

He blinked, realizing suddenly that it was snowing. How long had he been standing there? Mr. Burke looked inquisitively at him.

"Am I buying one train ticket or two?"

Hob exhaled. He knew what he wanted to say, but had no idea what was going to come out of his mouth. His reply was barely a whisper.

"Two."

A grin broke out on Mr. Burke's face. He gripped Hob's arm. "Good lad. Your father would be proud. Let's get moving. I've a motorcar waiting in Wulfast."

Hob felt almost giddy as he ran to the sledge. The evening's events and their ramifications swirled like flurries about his head. Minutes later, they were speeding down the mountain toward Dusk. No wolves were waiting at the bridge, which was fortunate for the wolves. In his present high spirits, Hob might have eaten them.

Forty minutes later, the realities of leaving had doused Hob's euphoria. He sat on the idling sledge, gazing forlornly at the cottage's dark windows.

"I'd only go in for a minute," he said, hoping for a different answer.

"I'm sorry," said Mr. Burke, not unkindly. "We're already running late and mothers don't give up their sons so easily. Leave the note and the money. I know it's hard, but you're doing them a kindness."

Steeling himself, Hob scrawled a hasty message that he was off to make his fortune. Wrapping the letter around the roll of solars, he slipped them in the sack of dirty linens by the front door. His ma would find it when she woke.

She would miss him, of course, and curse him for not kissing her good-bye, but Freyka Nansook had grown up the daughter of a Hauja shaman. Hers were a practical people, tough and stoic to a fault. She'd shed a tear or two in private before breaking the news to little Anja. Then she'd consult Mother Howell on how best to manage the gold.

Ten years without work or worry. That's worth a few tears.

Returning to the sledge, Hob eased it quietly down the alley behind the temple. He wanted to avoid the early risers.

Once they passed the mining depot, they had to descend a series of steep switchbacks until they reached paved roads. Edging round an overturned timber freight, Hob banked onto the pitted highway that led south toward Wulfast. He was barely conscious of his passenger, or the rosy dawn. His eyes were on the road, his heart back in Dusk.

True to Mr. Burke's word, a motorcar awaited them in Wulfast. It was parked at a scrap lot on the city's outskirts, a wedge of polished black steel. Nearby, a group of vagrants warmed themselves by a small fire burning in an oil drum. As Hob brought the sledge to a stop, a uniformed driver exited the car, greeted Mr. Burke in a foreign tongue, and began loading his gear into the trunk. The man took almost no notice of Hob until Mr. Burke indicated he would be coming along. The driver merely nodded, glanced at Hob with a pair of watery blue eyes, and opened the back door for Mr. Burke.

Hob could not decide if the driver was being rude or professionally discreet. While he pondered this, one of the vagrants—a brutish man who reeked of drink—approached and tried to take the sledge. When Hob refused to give it up, Mr. Burke rolled down his window.

"It's all right. He's disposing of it for us. Get in."

Leaving the sledge to its new owner, Hob hurried over to the door now being held open by the driver. He had never been in a motorcar before, had only seen one when the magistrate awarded him his plaque.

Hob climbed in, careful not to let his boots muddy the leather or lacquered wood. The air inside was warm and smelled faintly of cedar. Moments later, they were speeding south, leaving Wulfast's soot-blackened buildings and refineries in their wake. Mr. Burke pulled off his gloves and settled low in his seat.

"I intend to sleep. I suggest you do the same."

Hob tried to close his eyes, but sleep was utterly out of the question. Instead, he gazed out the window as the car's powerful engine gobbled up the miles between Wulfast and Cey-Atül. They passed a few villages and towns, but the view was largely tundra and the dwindling Sentries curving toward the horizon. Now and then, Hob would pinch his palm. He felt like he was entering a different world.

This was confirmed when he beheld Cey-Atül. Its skyline jutted against the sky, ringed by a halo of haze and smoke that poured from factories on its outskirts. He saw tall buildings that reminded him of those beneath the Impyrial dig site. Empty freight cars glinted on a labyrinth of train tracks outside the city walls. These walls were much higher than the ones surrounding Wulfast. Bands of raiders plagued the Northwest and some numbered in the hundreds. Cities took precautions, but villages like Hob's had limited resources. Dusk's only defense was a wooden palisade.

But Cey-Atül was civilized. In addition to high walls and motor-cars, it boasted a harbor teeming with ships, and an Impyrium flag that flew from the tallest tower, rippling above the Faeregine banner. Hob gaped at it, his breath fogging the window as the car approached a gated archway. Behind him, Mr. Burke stirred.

"Don't stare," he yawned. "You'll look like a rube."

Hob laughed. "I am a rube."

But Hob leaned back as Impyrial Guardsmen waved them through the archway and directed them to a special lane free of the common carts and wagons clogging the commercial avenues. The lane fun-neled them toward a massive building with great stone columns and a statue of Mina I in aged bronze. Impyrium's first empress was always depicted as a child—an angelic girl making a sign of benediction.

The first Faeregine. Nothing like that crone in Porridge's film.

A large crowd of shabbily dressed people were gathered about the statue's base and overflowed into the street, blocking their way. Many carried old suitcases or carpetbags. Some carried nothing at all. A guardsman was trying to herd them with little success. Mr. Burke told the driver to pull over.

"We'll get out here," he said. "Purchase fares for some of the poorer souls. Ten in steerage, three families in coach. Have my things sent aboard. Take care with that camera."

Hob tried not to turn about and stare as he followed Mr. Burke toward what Hob now realized was the train station. Broad flights of steps led to the entrance, but Hob caught sight of an official waving at them from a door at street level. Mr. Burke was evidently a known and respected figure, for the official bowed and promptly led them down a series of narrow corridors so they could bypass the crowds.

Ten minutes later they emerged from a private door onto a platform where one of the famous Transcontinentals was boarding.

Hob had never seen anything like it. The Transcontinental utterly dwarfed the freight trains littering the city's outskirts. Its steam-hissing engine must have been fifty feet in diameter with a ring of giant floodlights set in its copper plating. Behind it were scores of triple-decker cars with oval windows and elegant scrollwork. Their escort took them to a forward car where a man in a crisp suit stood by a ramp. Pleasantries were exchanged, sums passed hands, and the suited man—their escort called him a *concierge*—led them into a luxurious cabin twice the size of Hob's cottage.

Mr. Burke let the concierge take his coat. "Bring us brunch and the latest papers," he said. "And send for the barber. The lad needs a haircut."

Once the concierge withdrew, Mr. Burke sat on an elegant couch and began looking over some travel documents. Unsure what to do, Hob sat at a small dining table by the window. Throughout the station, swarms of hunched, spindly goblins were running about, shining lanterns beneath cars and making sure all was ready to depart. Many passengers were still boarding. Among the well-dressed crowd, Hob spied a hooded shape towering conspicuously above the rest. The figure turned, revealing a wolfish profile as it spoke to an elderly woman. Hob stood for a better view. Mr. Burke looked up from his papers.

"What are you gawking at?" he asked.

"A vye, I think."

Mr. Burke returned to his reading. "You'll still find them in the bigger cities. A hundred or so still live in the capital. Is it alone?"

"No," said Hob. "It's talking to a woman in black robes with orange cuffs."

"Amber cuffs," Mr. Burke corrected. "Sounds like a Promethean scholar. Unusual sight this far west. They rarely leave the Sacred Isle."

"What are they?" asked Hob.

"Mystics," said Mr. Burke. "They advise our beloved empress on all things magical."

Hob gaped so openly he might have had *rube* tattooed on his forehead. He didn't care. A vye and a mystic were standing right outside! The two were boarding the train now, locked in close conversation while an entourage of soldiers and officials followed them up the ramp. Hob sat back down and drummed his fingers.

"Another habit we shall have to break," muttered Mr. Burke.

"Sorry. I can't sit still. I've never been anywhere before."

Mr. Burke tutted. "Nonsense. You've just been someplace rare and wonderful. Not five people have stood where we stood last night. Not for thousands of years."

"I mean someplace with a name," said Hob.

"But it has a name. Before the Cataclysm, it was called Vancouver."

There was a knock at the cabin's interior door. When Hob opened it, an elderly gentleman wished them good day and rolled in a barber's chair along with a small cart. A minute later, Hob sat beneath a clean white cloth. Mr. Burke directed from his chair.

"Clean and neat. Side part."

The barber nodded and poured a kettle of steaming water into a basin to wash Hob's hair. The concierge returned, pushing another cart laden with covered dishes, a silver carafe, and several newspapers. The aroma of bacon filled the car.

The train sounded a long whistle, triggering a flurry of commotion outside. But Hob did not have to run or hurry. He sat in the comfortable barber's chair and glimpsed Mr. Burke's reflection in a gilded mirror.

Hob's new employer did not even blink when the doors closed and the massive train eased into motion. He was wholly engrossed with an article on the front page of *The Dryad*, a popular penny rag. A faint smile appeared as his eyes traveled down a column. When he turned the page, Hob glimpsed the main headline:

PALACE KILLERS STILL AT LARGE
No arrests in attempted theft of Lirlander Seals.
Royal family "terrified" says court insider.

Hob glimpsed other headlines: rising wheat prices, the disappearance of rare creatures from Workshop's biological exhibits, and the latest victory by Hellfyre, an undefeated racehorse making a bid for the Impyrial Stakes.

He wanted to read more, but the barber tilted his chair back to wet his hair. Instead of a newspaper, Hob found himself gazing at a chandelier, its crystals clinking as the train eased slowly out of the station. Hob tried to keep his breathing steady. On the other side of this vast continent, Impyria awaited them: a city of sorcery, the heart of the empire, and home to the dreaded Faeregines.

CHAPTER 4
SUPPER WITH THE SPIDER

*Excellence and contentment
are fundamentally incompatible.*

—David Menlo, archmage (17 P.C.–72 A.C.)

Master Montague was an unpleasant person: ill-tempered, half-deaf, and uncommonly flatulent. The combination was unfortunate for, unlike her more mature classmates, Hazel could not keep from giggling. Whenever he noticed her silent contortions, the master would glare and demand to know what was so funny. It was a question that could not be answered. Not without driving the man into retirement.

And so Hazel sat in the back, near the radiator whose soft hissing drowned out the master's lapses. It also drowned out his lectures, which often meant Hazel only had a foggy grasp of the day's topic. Master Montague's expertise was Muirlands history, geography, and political economy. Violet and Isabel might need to study such things, but Hazel found them torturous. She wasn't going to be Divine Empress or conduct affairs of state; she was going to focus on magic. Instead of memorizing useless facts, she could have been learning Anatovsky's Spectrum, or any one of the intriguing new spells Rascha promised to teach her this spring. Besides, how could she possibly concentrate on transportation networks after what happened last week?

Dr. Razael and Sergeant Beecher had been buried, Private Finch remained hospitalized, and Lord Faeregine had practically vanished. Hazel understood Uncle Basil's reclusiveness. Despite interrogating scores of suspects, investigators had yet to arrest anyone for the crimes committed on New Year's Day. While Hazel could not blame her uncle, she did miss him. Aside from Isabel, he was her favorite relative, and they often had Sunday brunch together. His secretary had canceled the last one, citing his lord's "present condition."

Her own condition was rather fragile. Since discovering that terrifying note in her book, Hazel's life had changed. Sigga Fenn escorted her and Isabel everywhere from their general classes in Old College to their private Mystics lessons. She could not go anywhere without that lithe figure trailing like a shadow. Hazel wondered if the Grislander ever slept.

She glanced back at Sigga, who sat in one of the chairs by the door. If anyone could put the Red Branch to sleep, it was Master Montague. To Hazel's horror, she found that her bodyguard was not only awake but had been joined by Dàme Rascha. At some point during the class, the vye must have slipped in to observe her pupil. Judging by her scowl, she was not impressed.

The master's voice boomed out.

"Your Highness, if you would be so kind as to answer the question."

Hazel turned to find the master staring at her expectantly. So were sixteen other girls, her sisters among them. Isabel looked hopeful, Violet detached. Hazel reddened. "Could you repeat it?"

"Of course," said the master sarcastically. "Why should someone of my knowledge and experience expect young royalty to pay attention? Surely, Her Highness has all the answers."

"I am sorry," said Hazel earnestly. "If you would please repeat the question."

The master resumed his customary pacing. "What are the Transcontinentals, where do their branches originate, and why were they founded?"

Hazel was mortified. She knew nothing about the Transcontinentals other than they were trains that presumably traveled long distances. Somehow, she did not think this would satisfy the master. Still, a bit of fluff could go a long way. She'd seen Uncle Basil talk for hours without saying anything.

"The Transcontinentals," she began, "are locomotive trains. Specific branch locations are a matter for debate, but they almost certainly originate far away. The trains were created to convey people from one place to another. We should all be very grateful for their existence."

The class laughed, but the master simmered. He cast a disparaging glance at Dàme Rascha as though she was to blame for Hazel's ignorance. "I'm an old man," he replied drily. "My remaining time is too precious to waste on such drivel. Who can provide a satisfactory answer?"

Isabel's hand shot in the air. The master ignored it and turned his attention to Imogene Hyde, who spoke with languid superiority.

"Transcontinentals are colossal locomotives capable of traveling at one hundred miles per hour. There are five branches that converge upon Crossroads Station in Impyria. Their points of origin are Cey-Atül, Santa Mina, Navaché in the Archipelago Tropique, Ferropolis, and Saltmarsh. They came into being after the Rising of 648 when farmers demanded a cheaper way of getting their crops to market. In response, Empress Mina the Seventh authorized the Workshop to lay tracks and revive steam engine technology that had been lost to muir during the Cataclysm. By the early 900s, regional freight networks allowed the Transcontinentals to be repurposed as passenger trains to convey mehrùn and wealthy muir throughout the western empire."

"And why are trains preferable to widespread highways and motor-cars?" pressed the master.

Imogene lifted her chin. "They're far easier to control. Mobility is limited to those who can afford tickets. As a result, few muir ever journey more than thirty miles from their birthplace. This reduces unrest."

The master bowed his bald, shining head. "Excellent, Lady Imogene. I am gratified to see someone apply herself. Others could learn from your example."

Hazel stared daggers at the master. This was Imogene's third year learning this muirish gobbledygook while the Faeregines had barely begun taking classes at Rowan. Until this past September, Hazel had studied solely with Rascha, who had spent her entire life with mystics and witches. The vye knew little more than she did about the Muirlands or Workshop contraptions. Besides, the master was a Montague, a house dependent on Hyde patronage. It was shameless how he favored Imogene. So what if she'd been right?

Straight above them, Old Tom's bells tolled five o'clock. A piebald homunculus, a man-shaped creature with bat-like wings, flew from its window perch and settled on the master's shoulder as he wrote their homework on the board in meticulous copperplate. That was another reason to dislike him, Hazel decided. People with perfect handwriting never had a sense of humor. Violet had flawless penmanship. Hazel's defied legibility.

"You're making us look bad," Isabel muttered as they filed behind their classmates toward the door. Violet had already left, gliding past Dàme Rascha and Sigga where Omani Kruger, another member of the Red Branch, was waiting in the hallway. As Heiress, Violet had her own bodyguard.

Hazel shifted the heavy book under her arm. "What do I care about trains? I've never been on one. Probably never will."

"It's not about trains," said Isabel. "And you know that perfectly well."

Before Hazel could reply, they had reached Dàme Rascha and Sigga. The vye handed the girls their coats and scarves from the nearby stand and managed a curt nod to the master as he swept past them to meet with his graduate students. It was common knowledge that the master viewed his time with the "court brats" as a distraction from his real work. But he had little choice in the matter. It was tradition that the young nobility should study under Rowan's top scholars.

The master would have to grin and bear it. Unfortunately, so would Hazel.

As this was the final class of the afternoon, Hazel, Isabel, Dàme Rascha, and Sigga walked down the portrait-lined hallway to the stairwell where older Rowan students conversed in little cliques. From their robes, Hazel could see they were fifth and sixth years. Most would hail from houses of lesser nobility; some would even be mehrùn born to muir parents in the outer provinces. All would be brilliant.

Only the very best students received invitations to study at Rowan. The rest attended other schools of magic scattered throughout the empire. The fact that children from the Great Houses received automatic admission triggered resentment from those who had to earn their places. It was evident in the stony looks as they passed. Even so, Hazel wished she could stay put. Rascha would not reprimand her in front of strangers, and Hazel knew a storm was brewing.

The storm broke once they descended Old Tom's steps.

". . . never been so humiliated," the vye seethed, as the four walked toward Tùr an Ghrian's gleaming white spire. "One would think you spend all day playing with dolls. What have you to say?"

"Nothing," said Hazel, who was not in the mood to be lectured. An icy wind was swirling about the quad, whipping her white hair about. Pulling up her hood, she began planning her evening. If she mastered Anatovsky's Spectrum on her own, that might appease Rascha. Afterward, she could send for cocoa and read a story while snowflakes melted on her window. If Uncle Basil were around, she might have borrowed one of his storybooks. Lord Faeregine collected Pre-Cataclysm texts and spent a small fortune to have them magically restored. Hazel cast a longing glance at Maggie, a sprawling gray building where he kept an office. To her surprise, a light shone in the window.

"Uncle Basil's in!" she cried, darting past several professors conversing beneath a witchfire lamp.

Isabel groaned. "Come back. We've got Mystics now."

"So?" said Hazel, hurrying toward the building.

"There's only one Sigga."

"Go with Violet," said Hazel, pointing ahead where their sister was talking with the Castile twins. On Mondays, Isabel and Violet studied Mystics with their tutors atop Tùr an Ghrian. They would be in different rooms, but the rooms were practically adjoining. Surely a Red Branch would watch two princesses for a few hours.

As Isabel caught up with Violet, Dàme Rascha and Sigga followed Hazel into Maggie and down the long hallway where a pair of Impyrial guards stood outside her uncle's office.

"I'm here to see Lord Faeregine," said Hazel.

One of the soldiers shook his head. "I'm sorry, Your Highness, his lordship is not to be disturbed—"

Her uncle's cheerful voice crackled from an intercom. "Is that my niece? Send her in. Princesses don't need appointments."

Bowing, the guardsman opened the door for Hazel, but balked at admitting Sigga. The Grislander brushed past him.

"I go where she goes."

Hazel always liked visiting Uncle Basil's office. It was richly decorated in a masculine sort of way with dark wood, old paintings, and fascinating objects lining the glass-fronted bookcases. His work with the Bank of Rowan took him all over the empire, and there was always something new and unusual to be found: carved femurs from the witch ossuaries, a length of enchanted rope, or some taboo figurine from the Lirlanders. At the moment, her uncle was not cooing over a recent acquisition but pouring over ledgers with two junior ministers. He beckoned Hazel over with his unbandaged arm. She offered her customary peck and asked how he was.

"Physically, emotionally, or spiritually?" he quipped. "The arm is mending, thank you. And I flatter myself that I'm becoming less grotesque by the day."

Hazel considered him. The whites of his eyes were no longer bloody and his nose had recovered its original shape. But despite his attempts at humor, his face betrayed the heavy toll recent events had taken.

"I think you look wonderful," said Hazel.

Her uncle sighed. "You've always been a terrible liar." He nodded to Hazel's companions. "Nice to see you again, Dàme Rascha. Agent Fenn, I believe this is our first meeting, but I'm well acquainted with your reputation."

Sigga bowed.

"Why aren't you working at the bank?" asked Hazel.

He gestured with his good arm at the mountain of ledgers. "Can't get anything done in the city. Reporters hounding me, crying questions from the street. 'Have any arrests been made? Are the Lirlander Seals safe?'" A squiggly vein throbbed at his temple. "One had the temerity to ask if I thought nepotism was to blame. Insufferable little twit."

Hazel peered at a sheet covered in cryptic names and numbers. "It all looks very complicated."

Lord Faeregine laughed. "If only it was that simple. These aren't accounts, my dear. It's the lineup for the Impyrial Stakes."

That ridiculous horse race, Hazel thought. She hoped he hadn't seen her roll her eyes.

"It should be splendid, particularly if Hellfyre and Mistral remain unbeaten."

Hazel knew nothing about racing other than it seemed fussy and anticlimactic. Such drama over an event that lasted a few minutes. This time her uncle read her disinterest.

"I take it you didn't stop by to discuss Thoroughbreds?"

"No," said Hazel. "I wanted to see you. And perhaps borrow a book?"

"Ah," said Lord Faeregine. "The truth comes out. Where's my *Little Mermaid*?"

"On my nightstand," said Hazel coyly. "I'll return it later."

Her uncle scoffed and turned to his ministers. "Forget those vault imposters. My niece is the cleverest thief in the empire. Slowly but surely, she's transferring my collection to her bookcase. Behold the evidence." He pointed to the top shelf of a glassed case where a row of priceless books had several vacancies.

"Your collection is safe, Lord Faeregine," said Dàme Rascha. "Her Highness will not be borrowing any more stories until she gets her studies in order."

Lord Faeregine raised an eyebrow at his niece. "Which class?"

Hazel scowled. "Master Montague. He's the worst."

Uncle Basil gave an understanding nod. "I had him too. Prickly fellow. Rather uncompromising."

"Exactly!" said Hazel, glancing triumphantly at Dàme Rascha. She wasn't the problem—Montague was a beast!

The vye folded her arms. "Repeat your definition of the Transcontinentals."

Hazel readily complied, knowing Uncle Basil was always one for a laugh. To her chagrin, he looked anything but amused.

"Dàme Rascha's right," he said sternly. "No more storybooks until you make a better showing. The Transcontinentals are critical, particularly with the Lirlanders threatening to challenge our agreement. If ocean travel is jeopardized, trains become more important than ever. You're a bright girl, Hazel. Surely you see that."

"She does *not* see that," said Dàme Rascha stiffly.

Hazel regretted coming. Rascha was going to use this opportunity to air her grievances.

"Her Highness's knowledge of everything but Mystics and fairy tales is negligible," the vye continued. "Isabel knew more about practical matters at eight than Hazel does at twelve."

"Come now," said Lord Faeregine. "Surely you exaggerate."

"I do not. Her Highness cannot even name the greater provinces of the western empire. Don't even bother asking her about those in the east or Zenuvia."

"I don't need to know these things," Hazel insisted. "Violet's going to be empress. And Isabel will be a diplomat or something important."

"And what do you intend to be?" asked Dàme Rascha quietly.

Hazel glanced about the office, at its sumptuous trappings and treasures. "A banker."

Her uncle sighed. "I know you're joking, but even bankers have to know geography, Hazel. Just the other—"

He broke off as a knock sounded at the door. A page entered the room wearing a chain displaying the Faeregine crest encircled by a serpentine dragon. The young man stood at attention.

"The Divine Empress requests your company for supper."

Lord Faeregine groaned at the formalities. "She's my mother for heaven's sake. Of course I'll dine with her."

The page bowed. "The invitation is for Her Highness."

Hazel stared. "For *me?*"

"Will you be joining Her Radiance?"

"I . . . of course," said Hazel. What other answer could she give? One did not refuse an invitation from the empress. Not that Hazel had much experience weighing invitations from her grandmother; this was the first she had ever received. The day was shaping up to be a disaster.

Uncle Basil looked equally shocked. "What does my mother want with her?" he asked.

"The empress does not confide in servants, my lord."

Uncle Basil frowned. "Will her sisters be attending?"

"I am required only to fetch Her Highness."

Hazel's legs felt rubbery. The Spider wanted to see her *alone?* Sitting across from those black, unblinking eyes would be terrifying. She pursed her lips.

"Well," said Uncle Basil, "I'm afraid you'd better go. Thank you for visiting. When you've righted your academic ship, you may steal another book."

To Hazel's surprise, Sigga Fenn spoke up.

"Where is your guard, my lord?"

Lord Faeregine looked puzzled. "Just outside the door."

"Not the toy soldiers," said the agent bluntly. "Your real guard. Surely Lord Faeregine has proper security after what happened at the vault. It would concern me if you did not."

A twinkle shone in Uncle Basil's eyes. "You're in good hands,

Hazel. Let's put Agent Fenn at ease, shall we, Harkün?"

A shadow materialized in the corner and solidified into a very tall, cadaverous man with ancient ogham runes carved into his black skin. He carried no weapons that Hazel could see, but she almost recoiled from him. He did not speak, but raised his hand upright. He also bore a Red Branch tattoo.

"Satisfied?" said Lord Faeregine.

Sigga nodded curtly. "Yes, my lord. Good night."

Laying a hand on Hazel's shoulder, Agent Fenn steered her out the door. She did not let go until they had reached the bottom of Maggie's steps.

"What was that about?" asked Hazel.

Sigga glanced back at the curtained window. "I don't like that he remained hidden. Harkün could have posed a danger to you."

"Why?" said Hazel. "You're both in the Red Branch."

Sigga shook her head. "If Harkün's assigned to Lord Faeregine, that's his only concern. He wouldn't hesitate to neutralize anyone he deemed a threat. Even you. I prefer to know when someone like that is nearby."

Hazel shook off a shudder. "He felt like death."

The Grislander eyed a group of passing students. "I'm not surprised. I've heard Harkün's fond of graveyards."

Dàme Rascha chuffed. "Nonsense. Necromancy's illegal."

This was true. The vye would not even touch upon anything to do with necromancy in their lessons, but Hazel knew that its practitioners sought mastery over death. The study reputedly involved all manner of grisly spellwork and experiments.

Sigga was less squeamish. "It's hard to hunt necromancers if you don't understand their practices. Everyone in the Red Branch has dabbled. Some more than others."

The page was ahead, waiting at a respectful distance on the shoveled walk. They followed him through the ancient gates that separated Rowan from the palace grounds. Straight ahead, a turreted sculpture of reddish stone loomed against the cloudless evening. Lights shone in countless windows, including those in a relatively inconspicuous tower overlooking a courtyard. Hazel eyed it with dread.

The page led them into a Faeregine wing that was off-limits to visitors. Up, up the marble steps they climbed, past sculptures and portraits, reflecting pools and fountains. Their footsteps could not drown out the thumping of Hazel's heart.

What did her grandmother want with her? She ruled out anything do with the master. The empress did not deal with trivialities. This had to be something bigger, something family related. Hazel reflected that the Spider had not even mentioned her in the succession announcement. Could she be sending Hazel away? Was she going to be disowned? Hazel had never felt or even looked like a Faeregine. Only Isabel and Uncle Basil had ever showed her kindness; the rest of the family—even distant cousins—seemed to endure her out of necessity. Now that succession was settled, what if she was expendable?

By the time they arrived at the Spider's tower, Hazel had convinced herself that a ship would be taking her to a jungle island teeming with cannibals. In Uncle Basil's books, jungle islands were always teeming with cannibals. She had often wondered how they got any sleep. How could you go to bed knowing your neighbor wanted to eat you?

The page stopped at a pair of golden doors. Two shedu flanked them, gargantuan winged bulls with bearded human heads. These specimens were so ancient that their skin had hardened. To a casual observer, they resembled onyx statues more than living creatures. But they did move. One dipped its head slightly to appraise them. Hazel felt a tingling in her gut, as though its gemstone eyes were boring through her. The Faeregine seal pulsed with an inner light and the page pushed the doors open.

Hazel, Sigga, and Dàme Rascha followed him past a dozen guardsmen into a vast atrium. A moist breeze was blowing, heavy with the scent of plants and flowers that rose up on either side. Birds twittered and called from lofted perches, swooping occasionally in colorful flashes of plumage. The atrium was far larger than the tower's external dimensions. Hazel's senses told her this was not some illusion or architectural trick. Old Magic saturated the dense air.

True to her epithet, the Spider was waiting at the room's center. Hazel was accustomed to seeing her grandmother wearing her crown and court regalia. But here, in her private quarters, she wore only a simple red robe and sat at a table for two. She glanced up as they approached, her gaze sharp as a scalpel. When they bowed, she pointed a bony talon at the opposite seat.

Hazel slid stiffly into the chair, conscious of her posture. The Spider's eyes never left her as she sent the others off with a dismissive wave. Rascha and Sigga followed the page down a path lined with rhododendrons.

The two sat in silence for several minutes while servants brought water, wine, and little dishes of greens, nuts, and fruit. Hazel fought the urge to fidget. She longed to break the silence, but etiquette dictated one should wait for the hostess. When the Spider finally spoke, her voice was a gravel croak.

"Are you really so frightened of me?"

Hazel met those wide-set Faeregine eyes, so alert and impenetrable. "I suppose I am."

The empress nodded. "I'm not fond of children," she remarked. "A century has passed since I was a child. I no longer understand them. But it is time I understood you."

Hazel glanced down at plate. "There's not so much to understand."

"That is not what I've been led to believe."

"I do not know what you've been told, Your Radiance."

"Do you not?"

Hazel winced slightly. "Does it have to do with the master?" She did not know why she brought this up other than it was exceedingly uncomfortable to sit before this woman and guess what she wanted to hear. Silence and authority were a powerful combination.

"Are your referring to your abominable progress with Masters Montague, Plath, and Strovsky?"

Gods, this woman was terrifying. "Yes."

"That is *a* concern but not *the* concern," said the empress. "I am referring to your abilities with magic. I have reason to believe they are considerable."

"Dàme Rascha flatters me."

A pause. "Do not patronize me. I want a demonstration."

Hazel wiped her clammy palms on her robes. "What would you like me to do?"

The empress gestured at the veritable jungle surrounding them. "A hibiscus has recently been planted in this atrium. Find it and make it grow."

Hazel pushed back from the table. This would be child's play.

The empress shook her balding head. "Remain seated."

Hazel's shoulders slumped. Sitting back down, she gazed round at the lush greenery. The plant would not be in plain sight. Sipping her water, she closed her eyes and cast her mind out into the room. The process was the opposite of squinting to bring something into focus. Instead, Hazel relaxed her eye muscles and let the sensation trickle back into her brain. Images became soft and blurred, buoyant and pliant. She did not try to steer this inner sense but let it drift like a balloon. The feat required instinct, not intellect.

The hibiscus was fifty feet above them, planted in a ceramic pot upon a balcony. Hazel's mind burrowed to find the seed suspended in rich black soil. She coaxed it gently, whispering words of waking and growth. From far off, she heard her grandmother's voice.

"That's it, child. Bring it here."

Hazel transported the hibiscus as surely as if she cradled it in her hands. Her back was to the balcony, but her mind's eye showed the pot floating down to them even as the plant twined through the soil and bloomed into a brilliant pink flower. Once it set down gently on the table, Hazel opened her eyes to see a hummingbird feeding at the blossoms, its wings a shimmery blur.

"Very good," said the Spider. "Now incinerate it."

Hazel blinked. Why would she burn something so beautiful? A second hummingbird arrived and the two began a darting, dancing contest for the right to feed. Hazel shook her head.

"No."

"Incinerate it."

Hazel felt a flash of defiance. "I won't. If you're so eager to see it burn, you do it."

Amusement shone in the Spider's cold eyes. "I can't."

"Of course you can. You're the Divine Empress."

"I am many things," the Spider mused. "A linguist, a strategist, a survivor. But I am no sorceress. Neither was my predecessor."

Hazel was confused. "I don't understand. You faced down that Lirlander. You knew his truename."

The empress shook her head. "No. I merely have spies. We've known for months that Lord Kraavh would be named ambassador and that he was hostile to the treaty. My spies agreed to share details concerning the demon's truename but not the name itself. This was sufficient to make the desired impression."

Hazel was staggered by the implications. "What if your spies were wrong? What if they had lied?"

The empress shrugged. "Ruling requires calculated risks."

"Well, it worked."

"For now," said the Spider. "But our seams are showing and our enemies have noticed. Magic is unpredictable, the Old Magic even more so. Over the centuries, it has dwindled in our bloodline. Our family's abilities no longer surpass those of our rivals. There may even be Houses Minor that equal us in this regard. In the past, we Faeregines dominated the world with magic. Today we must rely on propaganda and institutions we control. Even these are under threat."

"The Lirlander Seals," Hazel breathed.

The Spider nodded and mixed a little water with her wine. "The Seals make us masters of the seas. We control them and the Otherland Gates. Our family still has the bank and what remains of our mystique: they are all under siege. The world must see that the Faeregine fire has not gone out. Our family requires a weapon."

Her meaning was perfectly clear. "I don't want to be a weapon," said Hazel.

"It is your ambition to study magic, is it not?"

Hazel lifted her chin. "Yes. But I want to create things, not destroy them. If that's what's required to rule, perhaps our family has ruled long enough."

The Spider's thin lips pressed tightly together. Her eyes glittered with cold malevolence. "I envy your ignorance," she muttered. "You've no notion of what your ancestors have kept at bay these many centuries. But you will understand soon enough. The burdens our family bears far outweigh our privileges."

"I'm well acquainted with the burdens of being a Faeregine," said Hazel.

A terrible smile appeared on her grandmother's face. "Are you indeed? We shall talk again after Midsummer when you've made your first pilgrimage. Your views may change once you've stood before a dragon and peered beyond the Otherland Gates. Humans have short memories, my dear. People have forgotten why people begged Mina the First to become Divine Empress all those years ago. They clamor for technology, having forgotten that it would have destroyed them if Astaroth and his Cataclysm had not taken such dangerous toys away. That is the people's privilege. It is a Faeregine's burden to remember."

These words struck a profound chill. Hazel could no longer meet that terrible gaze, but she clung stubbornly to her position.

"Perhaps it is. But I'm not going to become a family weapon."

"You will do what is required," said the Spider simply. "Your powers will sow doubt among those who conspire to overtake us. When the Great Houses see that we remain formidable, they will fall in line. When the masses witness new Faeregine miracles, rebellions will cease. Much depends on you, child. Why do you think I left you out of the succession?"

Hazel glanced up. "I thought you'd forgotten about me."

The Spider sipped her wine. "I forget nothing. Your sisters meet the public's expectations of how a Faeregine should look and behave. You do not. While they occupy our rivals' attention and fulfill their royal duties, you will be free to develop your abilities. I have great plans for you, but you must be forged with a hotter fire. The vye's leniency has nearly ruined you. She's more of a nursemaid than a proper tutor."

"Dàme Rascha is the finest tutor in Impyrium," said Hazel, her voice rising. She would not let anyone—not even the empress—speak ill of Rascha.

The Spider did not reply, but studied Hazel in silence. At length, she rang a little bell and ordered a servant to fetch Dàme Rascha and Sigga Fenn. When the pair returned, the Divine Empress addressed the Grislander first.

"You are responsible for this one," she said, gesturing lazily at Hazel. "We will assign another Red Branch to Isabel. You will not divulge a single detail of my granddaughter's activities to anyone. Is that understood?"

Sigga bowed.

The empress turned to Rascha. "Do you believe the Old Magic still exists among us?"

The vye looked taken aback. "There have always been mortals who possess sparks of stronger, more primal magic than that of other mehrùn. But such beings were exceedingly rare, even among your ancestors. I do not know if any exist today."

"You lie," said the Spider. "You believe my granddaughter is one. Why else would you have asked the Promethean scholars how to verify its presence?"

Rascha's face fell. Her glance at Hazel was oddly apologetic, as though she knew and regretted where this was heading. "Nothing has been confirmed," she conceded. "But there are signs. In several areas, the princess's abilities surpass those of qualified mystics. With time—"

The empress cut her off. "She is to qualify as a Third Rank by her birthday."

Dàme Rascha opened her mouth and shut it. Hazel had never seen her look so unsettled.

"Your Radiance," said the vye delicately, "profoundly gifted individuals require years of study to achieve even First Rank. The volume of knowledge, the nuances—"

Again, the Spider interrupted. "Excuses do not interest me. My granddaughter will meet every requirement of a Third Rank by her thirteenth birthday. If she fails, you will be pilloried and exiled to the Grislands."

The vye bowed.

Hazel was stupefied. She stared at her grandmother, hating her with every fiber of her being. The woman was evil. The instant Hazel betrayed her love for Rascha, the Spider saw a weakness she could exploit. The ultimatum had not been issued with any anger or malice but a detachment that was infinitely more unsettling. The Spider did not make idle threats.

"One more thing," she added, looking sharply at Hazel. "This task does not excuse you from your other studies. You will pass each class—with honors—or I will have to reconsider my leniency with your tutor. Do I make myself clear?"

Hazel did not want to know what that might mean. All she could do was nod.

The empress returned to her supper. "Good. Dàme Rascha, you shall have access to anything that you feel my granddaughter requires. I expect weekly reports on her progress."

The vye bowed. "It will be as you wish. But I must voice my concerns. These demands will place profound, perhaps unbearable, strain upon your granddaughter. Old Magic is powerful, Your Radiance, and it must be nurtured carefully. There are disturbing precedents. Her Highness is but twelve years old. She is the last Faeregine."

At this, the empress actually laughed.

"She's not the last Faeregine, you fool. She's the first in a thousand years!"

CHAPTER 5
THE BIG LIE

Good men weep for justice.
Better men bleed for it.

—Pablo Antola, heretic. Executed 898 P.C.

Six days after boarding the Transcontinental, Hob finally beheld Impyria. Framed by the window of his sleeping compartment the city looked like a painting, a sprawling silhouette of domes and spires against the dawn. Even at this distance, the capital's scale was astounding. By comparison, Cey-Atül had been a fishing village.

He dressed quickly, washing his face and putting on the gray suit the train's tailor had made for him. By the time his employer emerged from his sleeper, Hob was immaculate. Yawning, Mr. Burke tucked a worn bronze pendant inside his dressing gown and selected one of the newspapers arranged neatly on the table.

"Eager to depart, I see."

"Yes, sir."

Mr. Burke glanced out the window. "We'll have inspection soon. Are you ready?"

Hob nodded as he poured their coffee.

"Good," said Mr. Burke. "Let me see your papers."

Four days earlier, a young woman had visited their car and taken Hob's photograph. She returned the next evening with an identification card, travel visa, and work permit. Now Hob promptly thrust the stack at Mr. Burke, who shook his head.

"Remember, submitting one's documents is a bore. The intrusion is a nuisance."

Hob tried again.

"Better," said Mr. Burke. "Inspectors are small men. Make them feel it, but not too much or they'll get officious. What's your name?"

Hob answered. He had memorized every detail, even serial numbers. The documents were fakes, of course, but the information was accurate whenever possible. The purpose was not to create an entirely new identity but legitimize Hob's presence. The authorities had cracked down since the last uprising; all visitors were screened and muir needed special permission to live or work in the capital. Mr. Burke peppered Hob with questions about his home province and their affiliation. Hob answered each in turn, weaving lies with truth. Satisfied, Mr. Burke returned to his compartment to dress.

Forty minutes later, the train idled at a security checkpoint. Two inspectors entered. The tall one ordered Mr. Burke to the far end of the compartment. The other followed him, noting something on a clipboard. Hob remained where he was and produced his papers. The inspector held them up to the chandelier as though searching for a watermark or some flaw in the paper.

"From the Northwest, I see. How long have you worked for this Mr. Burke?"

"Eight months."

"What does your Mr. Burke do?"

"He owns Impyrial Imports on South Market Street. Near Hangman's Square."

The inspector gazed about the luxurious cabin. "Must do a brisk business."

"Yes, sir."

"What were you doing in Cey-Atül?"

"Mr. Burke's thinking of opening a northwest branch."

"And what do you do for him?"

"Run errands, keep accounts. Whatever he needs."

The inspector suddenly seized him by the wrist. Turned Hob's hand over, he stared at the tough and callused skin.

"Rough hands for an errand boy."

Hob tried not to panic as he met that piercing gaze. "Woodworking. It's a hobby."

The inspector remained inscrutable. A moment later, he released Hob and returned the documents. "Fair enough," he muttered. "But soak 'em in bath salts, son, or the next fellow might think you're lying."

"Yes, sir."

The inspector whistled to his colleague. "We're done here."

After the two men departed, Mr. Burke laughed at Hob's account of the interview.

"Woodworking, eh? Quick thinking. We'll see to those hands."

Hob remained somewhat shaken. "Why did he let me go?"

Mr. Burke peered out the window where officials were rooting through suitcases. "Don't assume he did. The craftier ones will squeeze out a bribe and then have you followed anyway. We'll take precautions."

The two disembarked at Crossroads Station twenty minutes later. While a porter fetched their luggage, Hob gazed up at the sun, a watery white disk beyond the green glass roof. Hundreds of birds wheeled in colorful flights, their calls mingling with the din of droning loudspeakers and hissing steam engines.

Hob fell in step with Mr. Burke as the porter followed with their bags. He tried to mimic the brisk-but-bored affectation of a passersby, but he practically twitched with excitement. He was in Impyria, the very heart of the empire. The people he was passing were important— they made laws and wove magic and imposed order on the world. Dusk was cold and dull, a tiny outpost smothered in snow and pine needles. Here everything was light, an explosion of colors and sound, swift riptides of people and money.

Money. It was everywhere. Even muir servants dressed in tailored suits or clothes trimmed in ermine or sable. They trailed after silk-robed mystics, or hurried ahead to summon palanquins or carriages from the ranks of those waiting in front of a glowing glass mosaic.

Minutes later, Hob sat in back of a carriage clattering down a cobbled street teeming with people, rickshaws, and trolleys gliding on iron rails. Hob glanced up as they passed a streetlamp ablaze with scarlet flames.

"Is that witchfire?"

"Yes," said Mr. Burke. "There are no gas lamps in the capital. Our rulers like to remind us that magic reigns supreme. The lamps burn a different color in each district. Useful if you get lost. Red means we're in the Magistrate District. There's the Bank of Rowan."

He pointed across a crowded plaza where a copper-domed building flew a trio of whipping flags. Behind it was a towering white structure with nine needlelike spires that pierced the pale blue sky.

"The Grand Temple," said Hob to himself. He'd seen photographs, but they failed to convey its true scale.

His gaze traveled past it to the horizon where he spied a low, solitary cloud that hung motionless over the sea. He squinted. "Is that what I think it is?"

Mr. Burke chuckled. "The Sacred Isle itself. You're lucky it's a clear day or you wouldn't be able to see it from here."

"I can hardly see it now."

"That mist is always present, even during hurricanes. The Faeregines like their privacy."

The carriage rattled onward, parting crowds and stopping only when streetcars trundled past. Government buildings gave way to fancy shops and elegant stone residences with little balconies and gardens. The higher they climbed, the larger the houses until they reached a neighborhood where towering mansions loomed behind gated wall with posted guards.

"Who lives there?" asked Hob.

Mr. Burke peered out. "Nobles from Houses Minor and their little armies of maids, soldiers, and domanocti."

"Domanocti?"

"Night servants. Imps and other such spirits that make bargains with spellcasters."

Devils, thought Hob. He'd been so awed by Impyria's splendor he'd momentarily forgotten what it was. The ancient city must be riddled with dark sorcery. His eyes fell upon a well-dressed girl of eight or nine walking in a park with a tutor or governess. Was she a witch? A necromancer-in-training?

The carriage made a sharp turn. Mr. Burke glanced behind to see if they were being followed. "You'll learn more about domanocti during orientation."

Mr. Burke had mentioned orientation during their journey. Hob was not altogether happy about the idea.

"I could learn on the job," he said.

Mr. Burke sighed. "Everyone who joins the Fellowship undergoes training. How else would you learn to be of use? How else would we learn where to place you?"

"I thought I'd be working directly with you."

"Not until you've been trained properly," said Mr. Burke firmly. "You're bright, but you're also rough around the edges. You must learn how to behave in polite society and interact with mehrùn. Ms. Marlowe will teach you these things."

Hob looked out the window. They were now in a seedier section of the capital, one where alley shops advertised homunculi and poisonous herbs, magical trinkets and spellwork. His gaze fell upon a woman crouching in a doorway. She looked up as the carriage passed, revealing a gaunt face covered with blue sigils. Her eyes locked with his. Hob looked away.

"I guess I'm just homesick," he muttered.

"Perfectly natural," said Mr. Burke. "I know this is all new and bizarre, but you'll settle in soon enough. Your father did."

Hob turned. "So he went through orientation too?" He'd asked about his father several times aboard the Transcontinental, but Mr.

Burke's answers were frustratingly vague. When pressed, the man offered only a sad smile and promised Hob would learn everything when the time was right. But now he seemed more inclined to talk.

"Of course he went through orientation," replied Mr. Burke. "Ulrich was older than you, though. Sixteen, I think. Fresh off a boat with no education and an accent so thick we never thought he'd pass for anything but what he was—a runaway serf from Novaslo. But he proved us wrong. Not for the last time."

"He was good, then," said Hob.

Mr. Burke reflected a moment. "I don't think I've ever stumbled across a finer human being," he said thoughtfully. "I'm not talking about decency, though Ulrich had an admirable character. No, Ulrich was a fundamentally superior person—tougher and smarter than the rest. I used to joke he was some kind of Workshop experiment. Best recruit I ever had. You have some big shoes to fill, young man."

And I'll fill them, thought Hob, his pride kindling.

At last, the carriage stopped at a narrow brick building tucked between two warehouses on the waterfront. As Mr. Burke paid the driver, Hob climbed out, inhaling frigid gusts that smelled of brine, fish, and coal smoke. Some dockworkers came over to fetch their baggage.

Hob followed the men inside the brick building, where a girl in her late teens was filing paperwork. Her skin was darker than Hob's.

"Welcome back," she said to Mr. Burke. Hob had never heard such a languorous accent. Was she from the tropics? She smiled at Hob and offered to take his coat.

"I'm Sou-Sou. And you are?"

He tried desperately to sound older. "I'm Hob."

She draped his coat over her arm. "You need anything you let me know, okay? I remember my first days."

When she laughed, Hob felt lightheaded. Dusk didn't have girls who looked or sounded anything like this. Bree Roule now seemed plain as a peeled turnip. Sou-Sou handed several folders to Mr. Burke and led them to the door behind her desk.

"Ms. Marlowe's expecting you."

Hob was sorry to leave her company, but he followed Mr. Burke up a flight of stairs that led to a row of offices overlooking the warehouse floor. Below, dozens of workers were unloading crates stamped *Impyrial Imports*.

Ms. Marlowe awaited them in a tidy office with a small fire burning in its grate. She was a petite woman with a straight back and reserved demeanor whose silver hair was worn in a tight bun. She welcomed them without ceremony and directed them to a pair of cushioned chairs beneath a painting of fishermen. Hob watched in silence as she made three cups of tea, her movements brisk and precise.

"Ms. Marlowe," said Mr. Burke. "Allow me to present Mr. Hobson Smythe."

Setting the tea tray before them, she extended a fragile hand to Hob before appraising him like a collector. She spoke almost as if he was not in the room.

"So, this is Ulrich's son," she said. "A good face. Pleasing but not a distraction. Proud but trustworthy. Many possibilities, but we'll have to fix that nose. Is there a brain behind that face?"

"Indeed there is," said Mr. Burke. "He placed first in Provinces."

The woman grunted. "Did you have a placement in mind?"

"Military, I think. The lad's a natural."

Ms. Marlowe frowned, her eyes wandering over Hob. "We've soldiers aplenty. If he's as bright as you say, I'd rather use polish than a whetstone."

Mr. Burke cocked an eyebrow. "Servant?"

She nodded. "We may have an interesting opportunity."

"I don't want to be a servant," Hob blurted out. He had not left his family and traveled thousands of miles just to black someone's shoes.

Mr. Burke laughed. "It's a compliment, lad. Only top recruits train as servants. They're our best sources of intelligence. With any luck, you'll serve in a Great House."

"Perhaps the greatest," said Ms. Marlowe quietly. "But a good servant is obedient. Are you capable of obedience? I'm having doubts. Your father was headstrong."

Hob lifted his chin. "I can do anything you ask of me."

The lady blew on her tea. "Well, you don't lack for confidence. Let's get you settled."

Setting down her cup, Ms. Marlowe pressed a buzzer and Sou-Sou entered. "Escort Mr. Smythe to Brother Marcos's classroom. He'll join the blue cohort."

With a parting glance at Mr. Burke, Hob followed Sou-Sou out the door and down several flights of stairs. She chatted pleasantly throughout, asking about his homeland and journey.

"You rode a Transcontinental? I envy you." She laughed. "I came here on a smuggler's boat, half buried under cod."

She led him into a storage closet where she accessed a secret door behind some crates. Beyond was a small elevator. Sou-Sou unlatched its grate.

"Sorry for all the bother. We get raided now and again."

The elevator's cramped, rattling descent reminded Hob of his countless trips down into the mines. But miners rode in silence. Sou-Sou was talkative.

"Edmund must think highly of you. He's not ordinarily a recruiter."

"What is he?"

"A visionary," she replied. "And I'd do anything for Ms. Marlowe. I've only been here six years, but you wouldn't believe how much we've accomplished under their leadership. We're going to change the world, Hob."

"Is that why you came here?" he asked. "To change the world?"

She gazed solemnly at him. "It's why we all come."

The elevator came to a halt. Sou-Sou opened the grate to reveal an intersection of stone passageways, slick with moisture and exuding a pervasive odor.

"Impyria's original sewers," Sou-Sou explained. "Haven't been used in two thousand years but you'd never know it by the smell. Don't worry—we won't be down here long."

Hob pinched his nose and followed her along a curving ledge for several hundred yards until they reached a recessed doorway. When Sou-Sou pressed a buzzer, a red light flashed. She looked up, presumably so some hidden watcher could see her face. The door's bolt shot back.

Inside was another elevator. The ride up was even longer than their descent.

"Where are we?" asked Hob.

"Under the Market District," replied Sou-Sou. "The sewers let us travel between locations without being seen."

"How old is the Fellowship?"

"Depends on who you ask. Some would say our roots go back to Babylon."

"What's Babylon?"

A pitying smile. "You'll know soon enough."

The elevator opened onto a dim closet filled with mops and brooms. Hob followed her out of the closet and down a long hallway that smelled of floor wax and fresh paint. The doors they passed were closed and buzzed with muffled voices. Stopping at one, Sou-Sou knocked and poked her head in.

"We have a new addition."

Hob followed her inside, where a mixed group of teenagers sat around large wooden tables. They turned in near unison, offered looks of noncommittal curiosity that always greets newcomers. Hob's gaze drifted from them to the compact, thirtyish man standing before a blackboard.

"Brother Marcos, this is Hobson Smythe," said Sou-Sou. "He's only just arrived."

The teacher bowed, a gesture Hob found amusing. Muir didn't observe such formalities in Dusk. The only people Duskers ever bowed to were visiting officials, and only because it was the law. Even those bows came with wry looks. But Hob nodded and continued to look around the room. Some kind of model hung by wires from the ceiling, painted spheres arranged around a yellow orb.

As Sou-Sou took her leave, Brother Marcos gestured to an empty spot at the nearest table. "Have a seat, Mr. Smythe. Please tell us something about yourself."

Hob kept his descriptions brief, his manner guarded. He wasn't about to bare his soul to a roomful of strangers. Apparently, there was one other person from the Northwest, for a straw-haired boy said "Finally!" when Hob said he was from the Sentries. When a girl asked if he was skänder, Hob said he was half.

"What's the other half?" she asked bluntly.

"Something else."

Brother Marcos cut in. "Our skin, our hair, our homelands, our accents—these are just trappings. We're all brothers and sisters. Hob, we can best help you if you tell us something of your education?" His tone became delicate. "Can you read Impyrian?" Brother Marcos gave a you're-in-a-safe-place smile and made a middling gesture with his hand.

"Yes," Hob answered. "I can do calculus too."

His new classmates stared, some with interest, others with dubious sneers. Brother Marcos merely laughed.

"You must have done well at Provinces."

Hob shrugged. One advantage to being self-taught was that you didn't to go through silly classroom introductions. This was a waste of time. As Brother Marcos went to a cupboard and fetched a thick book along with paper and pens that he set on the table. Hob glanced at the book's black cover: *The Big Lie* by someone named Pablo Antola.

"Interesting you should mention calculus," said Brother Marcos. "Do you know who invented it?"

"No," said Hob. Several boys snickered.

Brother Marcos turned on them. "We do not mock ignorance here. We were all ignorant at one time. It is our duty to educate our fellow human beings. Mr. Gabriel, can you illuminate Mr. Smythe instead of making him feel unwelcome?"

A skinny black boy in his midteens glanced sheepishly at the floor before standing. "I might be wrong, but I think calculus was invented by a human named Isaac Newton."

Brother Marcos smiled. "Correct, Mr. Gabriel. Please create a timeline on the board and mark Isaac Newton's era. We'll use Mr. Smythe's arrival as an opportunity to review for next week's test."

The boy went to the blackboard and chalked a long horizontal line. He then made a prominent tick mark that he labeled *Cataclysm* before making a smaller tick several inches to its left. Apparently, this Isaac Newton's era occurred before the Cataclysm. But that's not what made Hob stare. According to the boy's timeline, the era following the Cataclysm was merely a fraction of man's recorded history.

Brother Marcos clapped. "Good. Please introduce yourself."

The boy wiped chalk from his hands. "I'm Badu Gabriel from Castelia, a city in Lebrim."

"And Lebrim's Pre-Cataclysm name?" said Brother Marcos.

Badu's grin flashed white against his blue-black skin. "Portugal."

"Excellent," said Brother Marcos. "Can you show Mr. Smythe where Portugal is on the Origins Map?"

Badu dragged over a large map propped on an easel by the door. Turning it to face Hob, he pointed to a coastal swath of land across the ocean. Hob studied the map intently, digesting it with a mixture of disbelief and excitement. He got up and came over for a closer look.

"What is this?" he said.

"You are looking at our world before the Cataclysm," said Brother Marcos. "No Faeregines, no Great Houses. No Impyrium. Nonmagical humans ruled everything you see."

If Hob had not beheld a lost city buried beneath the Sentries, he would have concluded Brother Marcos was insane. But he had—Hob had stood upon a building in what Mr. Burke said was Vancouver.

Hob found the city on the Origins Map. It looked to be hundreds of miles south of where Dusk was today. On this map, the mountains ran mostly north and south; there were no Sentries. But some coastlines and contours were recognizable. It looked like a giant hammer had shattered these continents and set their pieces adrift to form the world familiar to Hob. Apparently many lands were now below sea level.

He continued searching for landmarks. He tried to locate Impyria and the Sacred Isle. Normally, they were at the center of a map. But not in this world. There was no Impyria or Sacred Isle—just a tiny dot marked *Rowan* near the eastern boundary between two countries called the United States and Canada.

No one interrupted him. One girl even brought him a chair. Hob sat down, vaguely aware that his legs were trembling. He now noticed little stars penciled next to a number of cities. Perhaps their existence had been verified.

Brother Marcos spoke up behind him. "It's much to absorb," he said gently. "If you thought we were crazy, it would not surprise or offend anyone here. We've all been through it. But the story you're about to hear is true. I'll ask Miss Dauphine to get us started."

A tall, heavy-lidded girl rose from her seat and introduced herself as Eloise Dauphine. She was from Tarynia, which used to be part of a country called Brazil. Hob had to listen closely for she spoke with an accent he had never heard before.

"Civilization goes back well over ten thousand years," she said. "Before the Cataclysm, nonmagical humans ruled the world. They built great cities, crafted sky ships, and split matter into its smallest components. They did not did not need magic, only their intelligence and will. Magical humans lived among them, but hid their natures and studied witchcraft in secret."

Hob was confused. "Are 'nonmagical humans' the same as muir?"

"We try not to use words like *mehrùn* and *muir* in this class," Brother Marcos explained. "They are insulting and inaccurate. Did you know their very origins are daemonic?"

Hob shook his head.

"It's true," said Brother Marcos. "They were simply words that daemonia used to distinguish between humans that could summon them and those that could not. Over the centuries, their meaning has been corrupted. Today, the law classifies muir as lesser beings, as a subhuman species distinct from mehrùn. But this is not so. We are all humans."

"I don't understand," said Hob. "What changed?"

Brother Marcos invited a young man from Ferropolis to continue.

"Three thousand years ago, a spirit named Astaroth rose to power. He recovered a powerful book and used its magic to cause mankind's cities and technologies—even our memories—to fade. This sorcery had less effect upon magical humans. They remembered who they were and salvaged knowledge lost to others. They rose up against the demonic kingdoms that had replaced the nations you see on that map. Three champions defeated Astaroth, but not before he brought about terrible earthquakes that shook the world to its foundations."

Hob knew that last part. "Our priest tells that story on Imbolc. How Mina, David Menlo, and the Hound slew Astaroth atop the Witchpeaks. Trumpets and glory and all that."

"Trumpets and glory." The teacher sighed. "Alas, those three might have been heroes. When they destroyed Astaroth, they acquired the very book that might have restored mankind's memories, even the cities and craft that Astaroth had stolen."

Brother Marcos's face darkened. His voice trembled with anger. "But these 'heroes' failed us. They let us languish in ignorance. Their successors pretended our past did not exist and suppressed all evidence to the contrary. They even pretend to be a different race. Nonsense! If that were true, how can mehrùn be born to muir parents? Why would the authorities test every human child to see if they can perform magic?"

Hob had undergone these tests two years ago during the last census. Every child between nine and thirteen had been required to appear in the village square. When it was his turn, Hob entered a tent where a bored-looking mystic assessed his capacity to conjure lights, shape smoke, and extinguish a fire. She had not found his theatrical failures amusing.

Brother Marcos held up the book he'd given to Hob. "Miss Crenshaw, can you explain the theory behind the Big Lie?"

A young woman of eighteen or nineteen stood. "It's a propaganda technique used by a Pre-Cataclysm dictator named Adolf Hitler. It holds that people are less likely to question a big lie than a small one. The bigger the lie, the more people assume it must be true. The alternative is too outrageous."

"Excellent," said Brother Marcos. He brandished the heavy book. "This isn't made of paper, it's made of blood—the blood of those who had the courage to question the big lies and seek the truth. They paid a high price. Many lost their freedom, their families, even their lives. These heroes didn't sacrifice because they thought they'd ever see a free Impyrium. They did it so you might."

As Hob listened, his heart thundered in his chest. Was his father's blood in those pages? Mr. Burke would only say that Ulrich Doyle died a hero and that he'd explain more fully when Hob had a deeper understanding of the Fellowship. It was maddening. His mother still kept that photograph by her bed, but she never spoke of him. Hob could not really blame her; Anders Smythe had cost her everything. He wondered if she even knew his real name.

Brother Marcos's words stirred Hob's spirit, but they also troubled his conscience. He'd always realized that human civilization existed before the Cataclysm. After all, he'd watched Porridge's films and laughed at the silly, fantastical world they depicted. But he never thought too deeply about the implications. The films were just entertainment, a fun (and illegal) distraction. Daily life was so demanding, what was the point in questioning the ancient past? Hob stared at the book in Brother Marcos's hand. The Big Lie, indeed. He felt like a fool.

History with Brother Marcos lasted until early afternoon. Their next classes were designed to help them pass as servants in noble households. The first was held in a dining room where a Sister Wallenberg and several assistants demonstrated how to serve lunch in a formal setting. Hob had an uncommonly good memory, but even he was overwhelmed by the minutiae concerning what went where, which utensils to use with which dishes, and how to be invisible yet ever-present. At least they got to eat the food.

Once they had cleared the lunch service, the boys and girls went separate ways. Hob followed Badu to a richly decorated bedroom where Brother Caswell showed them how to prepare a gentleman's chambers. Hob stifled a yawn as they aired the room, sifted fireplace ashes, laid out his imaginary master's clothes, brushed a jacket, and polished riding boots. They stayed until each boy could repeat the routine while demonstrating perfect posture.

"Do we do this every day?" Hob whispered to Badu when they were in the hallway.

"Pretty much. It's got to be second nature if you're going to get placed with a house. Don't worry. Our next class is a lot more interesting."

The class was located in a dim, stuffy room whose shelves were lined with glass containers of various shapes and sizes. Each was inscribed with glowing runes and housed a different type of creature. Some were asleep; others glared out with as many as eight hideous eyes. He read the labels on the nearest shelf: *Common Imp, Stygian Crow, Summer Darkling, Brandybeak, Domovoi, Dewdrop Faerie, Vampyric Homunculus, Cacospider, Nile Croaker.* The latter puffed its milky dewlap when Hob peered through the glass.

"Mr. Smythe."

Hob turned to see Ms. Marlowe standing before a blackboard covered with detailed taxonomies. She indicated a seat in front and handed him a red leather book titled *Mystics, Magic, and Domanocti: A Guide to the World of Mehrùn.* "The first rule of infiltration is to know thy enemy. I expect a boy who aced Provinces to digest this within the week."

When she rang a small bell, Hob's classmates instantly took their seats. It was clear they held Ms. Marlowe in greater awe than Sister Wallenberg or Brother Caswell. Their teacher did not waste time. Clasping her hands, she began pacing.

"Miss Platt, what differentiates a mystic from a sorcerer?"

A young woman with curly black hair and glasses answered. "Mystics perform magic using proven spells. True sorcerers are rarer. They don't have to rely on formulae—they can improvise."

"Good. Mr. Klein, define Menlo's law of entropy."

A gangly boy drummed his fingers and furrowed his brow. "I'm sorry, but I don't know."

Ms. Marlowe shrugged. "Don't be sorry. Get out. Go polish shoes with Brother Caswell. Miss Mahmood?"

As a dejected Mr. Klein left the room, a soft-spoken girl wearing a colorful head scarf answered. "Magic has a price. Overuse can permanently drain magical energy or shorten one's life span. Powerful spells have been known to kill the caster."

"What do we call this?" said Ms. Marlowe.

"Our lucky day?" Badu quipped. Several students laughed.

Ms. Marlowe tapped her foot. "Do we know the answer, or are we just being cheeky?"

Badu flashed a cocky grin. "Mortemagia. It's a major risk for sorcerers since they tend to work stronger, more experimental magic."

"Very good, Mr. Gabriel," said Ms. Marlowe. She ceased pacing and returned to her lectern. "Now, if you will turn to page forty-six, we will begin today's discussion concerning domanocti. Those who serve mehrùn must know how to care for such creatures and be comfortable in their presence. Mr. Smythe, please bring me that runecage containing the vampyric homunculus . . ."

Classes did not end until eight o'clock, when Hob and his cohort joined other Fellowship members at a dining hall's long wooden tables and benches. Hob said little throughout dinner, preferring to listen and observe.

When they'd finished, Hob followed Badu and the other boys to a dormitory room furnished with bunk beds. He found his suitcase had been unpacked, his clothes neatly folded in a footlocker. While some of the boys undressed, Hob looked out a narrow window at Impyria.

They were seven or eight stories up: high enough to survey a sea of buildings, low enough to hear the bells and shouts from the street. The city was incandescent with shop lights and streetlamps, energy and sound. Carriages and rickshaws flowed like lava through the Market District, coursing through crowds of humans and nonhumans alike. Two specks of light flashed in the night. Hob spied a pair of domanocti clutching tiny lanterns and rolls of parchment, their wings a blur as they skimmed over tiled roofs and disappeared.

"Homesick?"

Hob turned to see Badu sitting on his bunk shining a pair of dress boots.

"Not yet," said Hob. "I want to go out and explore."

"You will," said Badu. "They send us out to get familiar with the city. Employers expect us to know it."

"And this is all so I can get hired by a Great House?"

Badu chuckled. "No, it's so *I* can get hired by a Great House. You'll end up with a fishmonger."

Hob only smiled and began to undress. When he removed his dress shirt, Badu put down his cloth and stared.

"Where are you from again?"

"Dusk."

Badu gestured at the tribal markings covering Hob's upper chest and shoulders. "Does everyone in Dusk have those?"

"Just me," said Hob, pulling on his sleeping shirt. He was by no means ashamed of his tattoos, but he didn't feel like answering questions about them. Badu cocked his shaven head.

"Were you a soldier?"

"No."

Badu sighed and returned to his polishing. "I can't gain a pound. What's the secret?"

"Swing a pick for three years." Taking a candle stub from the windowsill, Hob lit it and carried it up to his bunk. While the others talked and played cards, he cracked open *The Big Lie*.

Seven weeks later, Sou-Sou pulled Hob and four others out of history class and took them down to a large auditorium he had never seen before. Twenty other teenagers were already there, members of different cohorts. Most were eyeing a broad stage that had been partitioned into three sets: a dining room, bedroom, and parlor. All whispering stopped as Ms. Marlowe swept into the auditorium trailed by Sister Wallenberg and Brother Caswell. She wasted no time as she consulted her clipboard.

"Platt, Smythe, Cruz, Reynara, Vaslo, and Gabriel. Onstage, please."

What followed were a series of tests requiring the students to demonstrate every skill and bit of knowledge they'd acquired concerning a servant's duties. Those who made mistakes were dismissed. Those who hesitated or betrayed uncertainty were also excused. One boy was removed for slouching while he waited for his turn.

After three hours of painstaking exercises, Sou-Sou led Hob and the nine remaining students from the auditorium to a small, plain room. She lined them up against a wall, bid them good luck, and closed the door behind her. No teachers were present, no instructions had been given. Hob felt like he was in a firing line. Nevertheless, he stood tall and stared at their reflections in the mirror across the way. He was happy to see Badu had made it.

Questions began crackling from a hidden speaker:

"Which empress issued the Ninespire Edicts?"

"Why do phantasmals prefer brandybeaks as familiars?"

"What is the proper way to address a duke?"

"When did you last steal?"

Some questions were addressed to specific individuals; others required each of them to respond. Whenever it was his turn, Hob answered in the clearest, simplest terms possible. The questions were not difficult, the attempts to fluster them irritating but transparent. Hob never lost focus, not even when strangers randomly entered and left the room.

"Mr. Smythe," said the loudspeaker, "describe each of the six people who interrupted this interview."

Hob shook his head. "There were only five entrances by four people." He described each in detail, including the woman who had come in twice, once disguised as a man.

A full minute passed before the voice returned.

"The rest of you may leave."

The others filed past him. Some looked disappointed, others relieved. Badu closed the door, but not before making an obscene gesture from the doorway. Hob tried not to grin.

Mr. Burke and Ms. Marlowe entered the room. Hob had not seen

Mr. Burke since orientation started, but there was no formality. He gazed proudly at Hob before shooting a triumphant glance at his colleague.

"Didn't I tell you, Ms. Marlowe? Just like his daddy."

The old woman frowned. "He'll need to be better."

CHAPTER 6
A TEDIOUS AFFAIR

There's daggers in men's smiles.

—William Shakespeare, Pre-Cataclysm playwright
(449–397 P.C.)

Hazel used to love Tùr an Ghrian. The tower's topmost chamber
was ringed with summoning stones, huge monoliths anchored
in rune-scribed malachite. Some of the world's most powerful
magic had been worked in this room, and Hazel often wondered what
secrets those ancient stones could tell. But of late, it was just a place, a
crucible of trials and failure. Dàme Rascha's stern voice sounded across
the chamber.

"You're drifting, child. Go back to progressions."

Again? thought Hazel. Progressions were basic exercises to develop control, similar to a violinist practicing scales. She blew the damp hair from her eyes and glanced out the nearest window. No view tonight, just pale mist clinging to the glass. Rascha's staff rapped the floor.

"Focus."

Hazel stared at the brazier thirty feet away. Raising her arm, she pointed a finger.

"*Isu*," she whispered.

Flames kindled in the iron bowl, their light dancing on the summoning stones. Closing her eyes, Hazel prepared to shape the flames into whatever Rascha requested.

Tree. Rune. Sparrow. Girl.

The vye called them out, one after another. Hazel sensed the flames bending to her will, their contours buckling and shifting to assume the proper forms.

"Circle," called Rascha.

Hazel scribbled the shape in her mind and waited patiently for the next command. If nothing else, progessions were good for a breather.

"Circle," said Rascha again.

Hazel furrowed her brow. "You want two?"

"One will do."

Confused, Hazel opened her eyes. A ring of bright fire hovered above the brazier. "But it's right in front of you," she said.

The vye folded her arms. "I do not see a circle."

Hazel glanced at Sigga, who watched in silence by one of the monoliths. "Do you see it?"

Sigga did not reply; she never interfered with Dàme Rascha's lessons. Hazel turned back to the brazier. She'd been getting very little sleep. Perhaps her mind was playing tricks.

Dàme Rascha spoke with ominous calm. "Define a circle."

"A round shape," said Hazel.

"Define it mathematically."

"A round plane." *Where was Rascha going with this?*

"And what do its points have in common?"

Hazel considered a moment. "I suppose they're all the same distance from its center."

Calm Rascha vanished. "You *suppose*?" she snarled. "I ask again. Is *that* a circle?"

Hazel gazed reluctantly at the flames . . . the wobbling, visibly oval flames. She hated when Rascha was right. "No," she conceded. "It isn't a circle."

"But a circle is what I asked for," Rascha huffed. "You know what it is, but fail to give me one. Why?"

"Anyone but you would say that's a circle," Hazel groaned. "It's good enough!"

Dàme Rascha extinguished the flames with an impatient sweep of her arm. Smoke curled from the brazier as the vye stalked toward her. "It is *not* good enough," she growled. "It is lazy. It is imprecise. I give you a simple task and you cannot be bothered to do it properly."

Hazel threw up her hands. "What difference does it make?"

At this, Dàme Rascha marched Hazel to a storage cabinet where she kept extra supplies for their lessons. The vye unlocked it and dragged out a wooden chest wedged beneath shelves stocked with spell books, astronomy charts, and reagents. Muttering a command, she tapped the chest with her staff and opened it. Hazel watched in puzzled silence as her tutor crouched and emptied the chest of old junk: tattered spell books; crusted alchemical equipment; and a stuffed, beaky creature with orange fur and bulging, accusatory eyes. Tossing it aside, Dàme Rascha reached within the chest and turned something. Hazel heard a soft click. A moment later, the vye lifted out a wooden panel.

"A secret compartment?" said Hazel. "Very sneaky, Rascha. What are you hiding?"

The vye did not answer but carefully removed a bundle enfolded in black velvet. When Rascha unwrapped it, Hazel saw that it was a painting set in a gilded frame.

Her tutor held it up. "Look closely."

The painting's varnish had yellowed and some of the paint had flaked away, but the work appeared to be a portrait of a girl not much older than Hazel. The subject was slight and very pale with long auburn hair and a golden songbird perched on her finger. Her pose and modest smile were typical, but there was something subtle in her expression: a sad, even haunted quality. Who was she? Hazel spied the Impyrial signet ring on her finger—the very ring that now adorned Violet's hand. Hazel was amazed. How could this girl be a Faeregine? Her hair and skin were too light. And those eyes weren't large and wide-set like those synonymous with the "Facregine look." The girl's eyes were smaller and almond shaped, a translucent blue instead of inky black. . . .

Hazel clapped a hand over her mouth. "She looks like me!"

The instant she said it, the similarities appeared all the more obvious. They shared the same delicate nose, the same elfin bone structure. If Hazel hadn't been albino, they might have been twins. A confusing tide of emotions welled up within her.

Hazel had never felt like a Faeregine. When the triplets were old enough to attend court, Violet and Isabel were greeted with deep bows and solicitous inquiries. Hazel was usually met with frigid indifference. Even worse, the culprits were often her own relatives, particularly those who occupied less notable branches of the family tree. It rankled these "minor" Faeregines that someone they deemed unworthy of their name stood to inherit more power and wealth than they did.

Hazel still had tried to win them over. For years, she mimicked her sisters' gestures and mannerisms, even the imperious way Violet held her head. It did not have the intended effect. By the time she was seven, she understood that her presence was merely tolerated, not welcomed. Gradually, Hazel withdrew from court life. Now, she appeared only when required.

Naturally, there were times when Hazel wondered if there was something to the rumors. Perhaps she didn't truly belong; perhaps there had been some kind of mistake. In all her life, she had never come across a single Faeregine who looked anything like her.

Until now.

She touched the frame's edge. "Who is she, Rascha? Why haven't I seen her before?"

"The first question answers the second," said the vye. "You have never seen her because it is against the law to display her image. Even her monuments are faceless."

Elation turned to horror. Hazel recoiled from the canvas. "You're playing a trick on me. This . . . this can't possibly be her!"

Rascha remained solemn. "No tricks, child. We are looking at Mina the Fourth."

It took a moment for Hazel to digest this. Disturbing as the revelation was, it also made her intensely curious. She inched forward. "It's uncanny," she murmured. "How can I look so much like her? She died ages ago."

The vye placed the portrait in Hazel's uncertain hands. "Nature can be unpredictable. Sometimes a child does not take after either parent but a distant relation. Even a long-dead ancestor."

"Like reincarnation," Hazel breathed.

The vye grunted. "Nothing so extraordinary. It is merely atavism."

Hazel's gaze wandered over the fine brushstrokes. "Where did you find it, Rascha? I thought every picture of her was destroyed."

"I did too. Three years ago, I found it in the archives, misplaced among portraits of past scholars. Her likeness to you startled me, but I did not realize who she might be until I noticed the signet ring. When I checked the date, I hid the painting so that no one else would find it. Enough rumors surround you."

Hazel was profoundly grateful. The last thing she needed was anyone making connections between her and the monster in this picture. A terrible thought suddenly occurred to Hazel. "Does my grandmother know?"

The vye shook her head. "I told no one. Even if another portrait survived, it would have to be an early one for anyone to notice similarities between you. Mina the Fourth's experiments radically altered her appearance. The adult looked nothing like this child."

The adult looked nothing like a human, thought Hazel, recalling the dreadful tales she'd heard.

"Why do you keep calling her Mina the Fourth?" said Hazel. "Everyone else calls her the Reaper."

"That is why I am showing this to you," said Dàme Rascha. The vye tapped the gilded frame. "This child is *not* the Reaper. Not yet. This was painted two years before Arianna Faeregine's coronation, when her talents were just beginning to emerge. This girl had limitless potential. But her teachers failed her."

Hazel wrinkled her brow. "They must have taught her something. She's the greatest sorceress in history."

Rascha shook her head. "Merely the most powerful. She never learned control, and for that, I blame her teachers. In their eagerness to stoke a fire, they did not notice its flames spreading beyond the hearth. Those flames nearly consumed the world."

Hazel took a deep breath. "So . . . I suppose this is your way of asking for perfect circles."

The vye laid a hand on her shoulder. "Little things make big differences, Your Highness. In magic and in life."

Hazel gazed down at the girl in the canvas. Instead of horror, she felt sympathy, even a sense of kinship. "Could I have this? I'll keep it secret, I promise."

"Let me think on it," said Rascha. She turned to face Sigga Fenn, who remained a silent, watchful presence in the shadows. Hazel had forgotten the agent was even there. "You are not to speak of this. Not even to Her Radiance."

The Grislander rose. "The Red Branch answers only to the empress, Dàme Rascha. Not her devoted servants."

"Please don't tell her," said Hazel. "I'm begging you."

The agent gave her a considering look. "I will not volunteer anything, Your Highness. But if the empress asks, I must answer."

Sigga displayed the tattoo on her wrist as though it were a handcuff and not merely a symbol. Hazel understood. The Red Branch did not merely swear allegiance to the empress; its members were bound by magical oaths that could not be ignored. Such measures were required to ensure the empress's safety in the presence of such dangerous persons. Sigga was free to despise the Spider's orders, but she could not disobey them. None of them could.

Far below, Old Tom chimed six o'clock. Hazel looked uncertainly at her tutor. "Maybe I shouldn't go. We didn't cover half of what you wanted to."

Dàme Rascha blinked, as though whisked from deeper thoughts. Almost two months had passed since their fateful interview with the Spider. The empress's mandate had taken a heavy toll on Hazel, but it was taking an even greater one on the aged vye. Up close, Rascha looked drawn and grizzled, almost faded.

If you fail, she's the one who pays, thought Hazel. She tried not to fixate on the Spider's ultimatum, but the idea of Rascha suffering for her own shortcomings was paralyzing. Hazel could not bear to think of her tutor's head thrust through a stockade and exposed to the jeers and stones of a hired mob. Pillory was bad enough for human criminals; it would be even worse for a vye. Hazel would have to dig deeper.

"I'm staying," she insisted. "We'll sup here and keep at it until I make a perfect circle."

"No," said the vye wearily. "You must attend. Besides, a break will do you good."

"A dinner party's not a break," Hazel groused. "All that smiling and worrying about whether you're using the correct spoon. Why do there have to be so many?"

The vye grunted. "Such engagements can be tedious, but you must go. These things are expected of a Faeregine." Taking the portrait, she placed it back in the chest. "Go get ready. The coach leaves at seven and you must not keep your sister waiting."

Hazel did not have to ask which sister Dàme Rascha was referring to. Since the Spider's proclamation, a small army trailed perpetually in

Violet's wake. Guards, servants, and lesser nobles all eager to protect, pamper, or flatter the future empress.

An hour later, Hazel arrived at the turnabout near the winter gardens to find them buzzing about Her Impyrial Highness like midges. Apparently, the triplets would be traveling in style this evening, for the scream of the empress's prized stallianas pierced the night air. The instant the cavalry escort's mounts heard these terrible cries, they flattened their ears and turned anxiously about. Hazel understood why. Stallianas were to horses what tigers were to house cats.

A moment later, the stallianas came into view. They rounded a coach house at a trot, eight gargantuan, rust-red horses with braided black manes and bared, jagged teeth. Sparks flew from their hooves as they pulled the empress's luminous golden coach. With every lash of the driver's iron whip, the animals screamed in a chilling chorus. They came to a panting halt before the Faeregines, tossing their great heads and appraising the cavalry horses with wild, predatory eyes. Tongues of blue flame danced and flickered about the creatures' forelegs, for stallianas were creatures of both fire and flesh, bred by Mina XXV some thousand years ago.

Isabel was almost giddy at the sight. She loved horses—even ones that could eat her. "Gorgeous," she cooed, standing on tiptoe to pat the nearest's shoulder.

The driver leaped down to open the coach's door and help the triplets into its sumptuous interior. Violet offered a prim nod and sank into the cushion opposite her sisters. Her thick black hair was braided, a tiara winking in the soft lamplight.

"Ladies," she purred, plucking at her gloves. Isabel opened her bag and removed her math book. Dinner or not, they had classes tomorrow. "Hello, Violet."

Violet pursed her lips. "You're forgetting your etiquette."

"Sorry, Vi," murmured Isabel. "I'm not saying 'Your Impyrial Highness' when it's just the three of us. I'll do my duty in public, but I'm not kissing your behind in here. Incidentally, how'd you convince the Spider to let us use the stallianas? They're the only things she loves."

"I have every right to use the Impyrial coach." Violet sniffed. "I'm your future empress. You might show some respect."

Isabella turned the page. "I share a bathroom with my future empress. It dispels the awe."

"You're impossible," Violet muttered. Outside, there was a stamp and clash as the cavalry took up formation around the coach. An honor guard would escort the Faeregine triplets to supper, and that did not include the Red Branch. Hazel peeked through a velvet curtain.

"Don't do that," said Violet. "We'll look like kids."

"We *are* kids," said Hazel excitedly. "Don't get twisty. I just wanted to see where Sigga was."

"Like it matters," said Violet.

Outside, the driver gave a whistle and lashed the stallianas. The carriage gave a jerk as it lurched into motion. For several seconds the girls were jostled about, but then their progress became wonderfully smooth. Looking out, Hazel saw that they were now airborne. Their escort meant they could not leave the ground entirely, but the carriage seemed to skim just above the cobbled drive as the stallianas pulled the carriage in their fiery wake. The cavalry was nearing a gallop just to keep up with their easy, powerful gait. It was a marvelous sight. Too bad Violet had to ruin it. Letting the curtain fall back across the window, Hazel turned to face her sister.

"What's that supposed to mean?" she said quietly.

"Nothing," said Violet, sounding bored. "No need to get 'twisty.'"

Isabel closed her book. "You meant *something* by it."

Her Impyrial Highness took a deep breath; apparently one needed patience to deal with lesser beings. "All I meant is that Hazel needn't fret over protection. No one's coming after her. Why would they bother?"

"Because she's a Faeregine," said Isabel pointedly.

"Really?" said Violet. "Could have fooled me."

Hazel's mouth fell open. She could not decide which was more painful, her sister's words or the sneer that accompanied them. Violet had always been distant but never cruel.

Isabel leaned forward. "Take that back or I'll black your eye, dinner or no!"

"I won't," said Violet. "I'm tired of making excuses for Hazel. She doesn't belong in our classes; she refuses to fit in our circle. Did you know she actually failed Montague's last exam? She barely passed Strovsky's."

Isabel looked aghast. "Is that true, Hazel?"

Hazel did not answer. What was she supposed to say? That she had a secret mandate from their grandmother to become a Third Rank by her birthday and was barely sleeping? That she was so desperate to keep Rascha safe she could scarcely breathe, much less concentrate when she'd taken that test? It didn't help that the Muirlands bored her to tears. She was doing the best she could.

"Of course it's true," said Violet. "Imogene overheard the masters discussing whether Hazel should be held back. Can you imagine? Grandmother would never allow it, but that doesn't mean Imogene won't blab—she's a Hyde. The situation is humiliating."

Isabel ignored her. "Hazel, you should have talked to me. I've barely even seen you outside of class lately. What's going on?"

Hazel could not look at her. She wanted to confide in Isabel. And pride howled to inform Violet that the Spider was counting on *her*, not Her Impyrial Highness, to resurrect the family mystique. But she swallowed the temptation. Violet could think whatever she wanted.

"Hello?" pressed Isabel.

"Nothing's going on," said Hazel. "I'm sorry I'm such an embarrassment, Violet. It must be very trying for you."

Violet rolled her eyes. "Don't be a martyr, Hazel. It's hardly attractive. Just do us a favor and stay quiet when talk turns to politics."

"Fine. I'll gossip quietly with Uncle Basil."

"Uncle Basil won't be there," said Isabel.

Hazel was about to ask why, when she recalled where they were going. The Sylvas were barely a Great House. Uncle Basil would never cross the island to dine with the likes of them. This raised a question Hazel neglected to ask when the social secretary told her of the engagement.

"Wait," she said wearily. "If it's just the Sylvas, then why are we going?"

Isabel sighed. "They cashed in a Debt, the crafty buggers."

Even Hazel, despite an almost willful ignorance of such things, knew the difference between debts and *Debts*. The latter were contracts between noble families, obligations that had to be met whenever and however the holder chose. Families like the Faeregines and Hydes collected House Debts like chess pieces, hoarding them for years, even centuries, until they were needed. Hazel was amazed a family like the

Sylvas possessed one from the Faeregines.

"How did they get it?" she asked.

Isabel shrugged. "Some ancestor of ours probably got drunk and lost a fortune to some ancestor of theirs. It's got to be old. Mina the Twenty-first forbade Faeregine House Debts ages ago."

"Then it must be very valuable," Hazel mused. "Why would they waste it on a dinner party?"

"They want to honor me," said Violet. "Besides, the visit brings their house glory. After all, their future ruler is coming to call in the royal coach. They requested the stallianas specifically."

Hazel snorted. "But that's absurd."

Violet stiffened. "It is *not* absurd. Unlike some, the Sylvas realize a new empress means new opportunities. I'm impressed such a commercial family—they're practically merchants—would use a House Debt to pay their respects. It's gracious."

"It's grasping," Isabel countered. "Don't fool yourself. They want something. And what changes are you talking about?"

Violet gazed about the compartment. "This is all very nice, but it's ridiculous that we're using the same antiques as our ancestors. Grandmother's old-fashioned to a fault. She's far too strict with the Workshop, but she's ruled so long she won't listen to reason."

Isabel clucked her tongue. "Maybe she's ruled so long *because* she's been strict with the Workshop. You've heard stories about life before the Cataclysm. People had all kinds of advanced technologies—explosives and computation machines—and they nearly ended everything. There's a reason they were outlawed. Ever consider that?"

Violet removed her stole. The carriage was growing stuffy. "You argue for sport."

Isabel grinned. "It's fun."

"It's common." Violet sniffed. "Where are we, anyway?"

Hazel peeked out the window to see dead, petrified trees lining a jagged chasm. "Hound's Trench."

Violet sighed and rearranged her bracelets.

Hazel continued staring out the window. "Do you believe the stories?"

"Do I believe a hero made it with a spear?" said Isabel. "Um . . . no."

Hazel followed an owl as it soared over the chasm. "Nothing grows there. People say it's haunted. Olo told me—"

Isabel cackled. "Stop right there. I love Olo, but she's an idiot. Last year, I told her I was becoming a vampire. I'd swear she still believes it. Muir are pitifully gullible creatures."

"Hmmm," said Hazel. Isabel had no patience for things she couldn't see or touch, no use for myths or fairy tales unless they had practical application.

The Sacred Isle was not large, but the Sylva estate was still several miles away, perched on a spit of wind-lashed rock. Hazel gazed quietly out the window. Across the channel, Impyria's lights twinkled on distant headlands. So many lights, so many people doing as they wished. Hazel felt a stab of envy.

The stallianas gave a scream as they passed between two enormous maples flanking a wrought-iron gate. A horn sounded ahead. Others joined in, their notes mingling into one. Violet sat up, her face a mask of regal composure.

"Be sure to smile for the cameras," said Isabel, tossing her book aside and batting her eyelashes.

Hazel grimaced. It had not occurred to her that there would be photographers at a private dinner party. She hated having her picture taken, particularly with her sisters. Cameras adored them, but they did cruel and unusual things to Hazel. In private, she could—given proper light and squinting—detect a certain charm to her features. But cameras did not squint. Pictures never showed the cute little pixie in Hazel's bedroom mirror. Instead they captured a minuscule ghost trailing a pair of goddesses.

Hazel slipped on her tinted glasses from the purse on her lap. Violet didn't notice until the carriage wheels touched gently down and they came to a halt.

"Take those off. It's dark out."

But Hazel would not. Her glasses were a pacifier, a shield between her and the world. Immature? Maybe. Necessary? Absolutely. She practically leaped out the instant a groom opened the coach's door. The sooner she was out, the sooner this phase would be over.

She stood in the cold, pinching her clutch, head submerged in furs while flashbulbs rippled like broadsides. They were not for her, of course, but for Violet, who stepped lightly down from the coach and posed by the stallianas.

The three sisters walked between an escort of soldiers toward a weathered manor of rough stone twined with pale ivy. Countless windows blazed with light, illuminating an ornamental moat where black swans turned lazy circles. Swans were the Sylvas' sigil. A sculpted pair graced the entry, their features blurred by time and the elements. The same could not be said for Lord and Lady Sylva.

For the patriarch of a Great House, Eduardo Sylva was very young, having inherited the mantle when his father died during a voyage to Zenuvia. He was perhaps thirty with a trim red mustache and beard. A slew of medals were pinned to his suit: Order of Orion, the Vanguard, Gryffon Society. On soldiers, they represented real achievements. For men like Lord Sylva, they were virtual birthrights, awarded on any pretense of valor or merit. Almost all the patriarchs trotted them out on special occasions. Hazel thought they looked ridiculous, like overgrown boys in costume.

Lady Sylva was far more interesting. She was a Yamato by birth, but had the misfortune of being the youngest daughter. Her older sisters married Hydes, Jains, and Castiles, she had to make do with a Sylva, an undeniable step down until the Fates saw fit to sink her father-in-law's ship. Now, at the tender age of twenty-five, Akiko Yamato Sylva was already matriarch of a Great House. None of her sisters stood to rule theirs for many years, which may have explained why she looked so content. She stood beside her husband, fair and petite, black hair arranged in an artful mess. That she was reputed to be a Second Rank mystic only enhanced her aura.

Spreading her arms, Lady Sylva bowed so deeply she was nearly prostrate. Her words rang out like an incantation. "Daughters of Heaven, your presence honors us beyond measure. From Magic, truth; from Blood, honor; from Unity, strength. Suns unconquerable."

It was a traditional greeting. The sisters' response was automatic.

"Sol Invictus."

The formalities observed, Lord and Lady Sylva welcomed them inside. More flashbulbs as they entered a foyer packed with guests who promptly bowed. Hazel spied Dàme Rascha by the double staircase. Violet and Isabel's bodyguards were present, but there was no sign of the Grislander. Where was she? An image flashed in her mind: Sigga unveiling Rascha's painting to an attentive Spider.

This troubling image persisted as Lord Sylva gave his guests a painfully thorough tour of his ancestral home. Hazel's stomach was growling when they finally arrived at a dining room whose curving windows provided a spectacular view of Impyria. Hazel hoped her seat would face them; she needed the distraction.

She hoped in vain. Violet was seated on Lord Sylva's right hand, Isabel at Lady Sylva's left. To Hazel's dismay, her place was between Dàme Rascha and their host's fossilized aunt. As Hazel sat, the lady whirled about.

"Who are you?" she demanded.

"Hazel Faeregine."

"You astonish me."

Hazel was equally astonished. "I beg your pardon?"

Her neighbor did not reply, but proceeded to inspect Hazel with great intensity and suspicion. A footman appeared and murmured to Hazel that Lady Bethunia was a "spirited" ninety-seven and that no offense was intended.

The inspection continued.

Since teleportation was beyond Hazel's skill, she merely placed her napkin upon her lap and glanced sidelong at Dàme Rascha. "Have you seen Sigga?"

"No," said the vye, plainly irritated. "But your sister's bodyguards are here. I've already spoken with them. You will be safe."

Again, Hazel thought of the painting. "Do you think Sigga went to . . . *her*?"

The vye declined wine from a servant and shot Hazel a look to let the matter drop. Hazel eyed the dish set before her, a glistening cube of lobster held together by grains and seaweed. She poked it with a tiny fork before raising a glass as their hostess toasted Violet and pledged eternal friendship from House Sylva.

Conversation soon flowed around Hazel in a steady stream. The topics were trade and politics, shortages of this, prices of that. Hazel ate in silence, managing a facade of polite interest until talk turned to the Lirlanders. When the ocean dwellers were mentioned, Hazel set down her fork and turned her head toward the speaker.

"Trouble's brewing in the deeps," rumbled Baron Palantine, his face the color of his wine. "It's no coincidence the Lirlanders appointed Lord Kraavh. He's a warlord, not a diplomat."

"Warlord?" exclaimed his wife. "The demons have never made war on us. Not since the treaty. How can the ambassador be a warlord?"

"They make war on one another, my dear. It's said Kraavh's done monstrous things to his rivals. Tales that would freeze your blood. And Prusias—!"

"But as you say," interjected Lord Sylva, "the Lirlanders war with one another. Their squabbles don't affect us."

The baron was clearly relishing a fight. He thumped the table with his fist. "The very night Kraavh arrived, the Lirlander Vault was breached. Only a blind man would think that's a coincidence. He openly declared that the demons have tired of the treaty. Naturally, they'd want to steal the Seals. No Seals, no treaty!"

Lord Sylva dismissed the theory with a chuckle. "The demons aren't fools. Why would Kraavh do such a thing when he knows perfectly well he'd be the obvious suspect?"

The baron scowled and began attacking his quiche. "Don't ask me to fathom a demon's mind. They're twisted creatures, evil. You'll find no domanocti under my roof."

Hazel sat up. The evening was finally getting interesting. The Sylvas employed many domanocti. She'd spied no less than seven toddler-sized imps wearing velvet dinner jackets during their tour.

The baron was insulting his hosts!

Lord Sylva set down his wine. "Nineteen domanocti have served House Sylva for generations. Legions serve the Faeregines. I trust you didn't intend to offend our guests."

"What?" said the baron. "No. I was merely stating my policy on the creatures. If others employ them, that is their affair."

"Of course," said Lord Sylva. "Still, a retraction would be most gracious."

The baron flushed an angry purple. Hazel's eyes flitted from one man to the other. Was this going to turn into a duel? They weren't uncommon, but she'd never seen one. She tried not to betray her disappointment when the baron extracted his bulk from his chair and bowed. "I apologize if my comments were misconstrued. No personal reflection was intended."

Lord Sylva raised his glass. Tensions dissipated further as servants brought yet another course—a quivering mound that Hazel prayed was rice pudding and not a soft cheese.

A cheese it was. Her neighbor inhaled deeply.

"Most astonishing."

No duel. Stinky cheese. And now some other man was holding court. Men were always pontificating. Who was it this time?

Hazel did not recognize the speaker, a spare man in a gray suit wearing rimless glasses. His voice was mild, his brown face intelligent. No medals adorned his chest.

"It's a shame we must speculate about what happened at the Lirlander Vault. If Her Radiance permitted more technology on this island, the culprits could be readily identified."

"The criminals were disguised," said Isabel.

The man gave a complacent smile. "We have surveillance capable of piercing most disguises, even many types of illusion."

Isabel frowned. "I assume these have been authorized."

"Of course, Your Highness. The Workshop does nothing without the permission of the Divine Empress and her compliance officers. If it's of interest, I'd be happy to arrange a tour of our laboratories. We have some just outside Impyria."

"I would like that," said Violet. "Could we take a motorcar? I long to ride in one."

The Workshop man bowed. "One will be waiting."

"Make sure it's a Phantom," put in Lady Sylva, winking at Violet. "It's even faster than a stalliana and it won't bite off your arm. I drove one from Impyria all the way to Southhaven. Deliciously fun."

Violet's awe was readily apparent. "You drove one?"

"Of course," said Lady Sylva. "We keep several at our mainland estates. It's all very nice to ride in back, but the real excitement is behind the wheel."

"You don't think it's too . . . *muirish*?" said Violet. "Driving, I mean."

Lady Sylva laughed. "It would be muirish to worry what others think."

Violet nodded, clearly entranced by their hostess. Across the table, a viscount wiped a glob of cheese from his freckled chin. "You take great risks, Lady Sylva, motoring about the mainland. It's only a matter of time before the rabble revolts again. Very dangerous, indeed."

The viscount held forth on a recent piece of legislation he'd proposed. Evidently it aimed to expand the rights of the Houses Minor and had not been well received.

"My fear," he said to Violet, "is that unless we bolster the lesser nobles, there will be naught between us and the mob. If Her Impyrial Highness voiced her support, I'm confident—"

"Ernst," chided Lady Sylva, "don't be dreary. Our guests don't want to be harangued on matters best left to council. You're boring that young lady to tears."

To Hazel's horror, she realized Lady Sylva was looking at her. She stopped probing her cheese and sat up. "You're kind to think of me, but I find the Muirlands perfectly riveting."

"Indeed?" said Lady Sylva. "Well then, what do you think we should do? Do you agree with Ernst's proposal, or do your views align with the Hyde camp?"

Hazel was at a complete and utter loss. Her only hope was to affect a knowing, superior look while saying something pleasantly noncommittal. She'd seen it work for Uncle Basil. Lifting her water glass, she began to swirl it like wine. Ice cubes spilled over the rim.

"I think they both make valid points."

Lady Sylva smiled like a cat who'd stumbled upon a crippled canary. "Diplomatic. But which do you find most compelling? Have you done much traveling throughout the Muirlands?"

Cursing silently, Hazel feigned deep thoughts as she stalled for time. She gazed past her hostess at the servants lining the wall. The one directly behind Lady Sylva was a stocky black-haired boy with straight brows and a broad, earnest face. For an instant their eyes met and Hazel caught a glint of something. What was it? Amusement? Sympathy?

"It would be premature to comment," said Violet tightly. "The proposal's ink is barely dry. Besides, my sister's passion is magic, not affairs of state."

Lady Sylva bowed to both Violet and Hazel. "Forgive me. We

can certainly discuss magic. I'm particular to aeromancy. Has Her Highness studied it?"

Before Hazel could answer, Dàme Rascha spoke up. "Her Highness's studies are a private matter."

"Ah," said Lady Sylva. "I'd forgotten the secrecy surrounding Faeregine sorcery. I am confident she must be making great progress under your expert tutelage."

The vye said nothing. An unmistakable pall settled over the table. To Hazel's relief, a servant whisked away the cheese and replaced it with an iced sherbet. Sweets at last! A liver-spotted hand reached across and buried a spoon in Hazel's dessert.

"Most astonishing," said Lady Bethunia, helping herself to a second bite. Hazel felt like elbowing her. Why couldn't the old bat have stolen the cheese?

"Well," said Lady Sylva. "Let's lighten the mood, shall we? It's a tradition at House Sylva to play a game at the end of meals. Childish, I know, but merry on winter nights." She turned to Violet. "Do you like riddles?"

Violet nodded. "Very much so."

Hazel and Isabel exchanged incredulous glances. Their sister had never been interested in games of any kind.

"Wonderful," cooed their hostess. "Let's begin. A muir ferryman has to transport a goblin, a wolf, and a basket of toadstools across a river. However, his rowboat is so small he can only take one at a time. Herein lies the problem: if the ferryman leaves the wolf alone with the goblin, the wolf will kill it. If he leaves the goblin with the toadstools, it will gobble every last one. So what's our poor ferryman to do?"

Silence ensued as the guests tried to work out a solution. Brows furrowed. Some looked pensive, others gassy. Hazel felt a slight tap.

She glanced over to see Rascha give an almost imperceptible shake of her head. The meaning was plain.

Do not answer.

Hazel became indignant. Why shouldn't she take a guess? She could figure it out.

"It's a muirish riddle," said the vye in an undertone. "You know nothing about muir."

"Now, now," laughed Lady Sylva. "No cooperation. Has anyone worked it out?"

"It's obvious," said the viscount. "The ferryman must take the wolf across first. Then he can come back and get the toadstools . . ."

"The goblin will eat the toadstools," observed his companion.

The man considered. "Can he bribe the goblin?"

Laughter was followed by several other half-formed guesses. Hazel sat in silence, stewing over Rascha's blunt remark. It might have been true, but Hazel was feeling defensive after fumbling Lady Sylva's question. Besides, it's not like Rascha was some sort of Muirlands expert. The vye has spent her entire life among mystics, witches, and royalty.

More guesses were made, but no one managed to keep the goblin alive or unfed. When one lord threatened to flay "that damnable pest," Lady Sylva invited the servants to answer.

Lord Sylva chuckled. "They haven't the education, my dear."

Ignoring her husband, Lady Sylva perused the many servants spaced about the room. "You there," she said to a petrified maid. "What should our poor ferryman do?"

The maid looked like she might faint. "I—I beg your pardon, milady, but I don't know."

Undaunted, their hostess addressed an aged butler. "What about you, Barnes? Surely you've got a bit of country wisdom in you."

The gentleman gave a dignified bow. "Alas, my knowledge is confined to avoiding goblins, not preserving them."

A visibly relieved Barnes was excused.

"Really, Akiko," said Lord Sylva, "it's not kind to tease the servants like this."

"Don't be silly," said his wife. "I'd wager anything one of them has figured it out. What about you? Lady Harwell boasted that you placed at Provinces. I bought you just to shut her up."

The guests snickered at Lady Harwell's misfortune. Poaching servants from other houses was a popular pastime among nobles, a form of social warfare.

The person Lady Sylva addressed was the very boy Hazel had noticed earlier. For an instant, his face lost that habitually blank expression so common to servants.

He knows the answer, thought Hazel excitedly.

The boy bowed. "I couldn't say, my lady."

Evidently Lady Sylva had spied the same glimmer as Hazel. "You 'couldn't say' or you don't know? Which is it?"

"I . . . might have an idea how to work it out."

"Then let's hear it," said Lady Sylva.

Baron Palantine tossed a heavy purse on the table. "Fifty solars say he hasn't a clue."

"Done," said Lady Sylva. She turned back to the servant. "That's twice what I paid for you. Don't disappoint me."

Looking down, the boy gave an almost helpless smile. He was trapped. If he solved the riddle, he would upstage a roomful of nobles, including his future empress. The alternative would cost his employer a large sum of money. It was a lose-lose proposition.

Exhaling slowly, he closed his eyes.

"The ferryman should take the goblin across and leave the wolf with the toadstools. Next, he should bring the wolf across but take the goblin back with him so the wolf doesn't kill it. Once he's returned the goblin to the original bank, he can bring the toadstools across before making a final trip back to fetch the goblin."

Hazel almost smacked her forehead. *Of course!* Like most riddles, the answer was absurdly obvious in hindsight. She'd assumed the ferryman couldn't bring something back across the river, but Lady Sylva never set that as a condition. Clever muir.

"Bravo!" cried Lady Sylva, clapping.

Her guests followed her lead, but Hazel glimpsed displeasure on several faces, including Violet's. Isabel clapped heartily, however. So did Lady Bethunia, who declared the feat "most astonishing" and consumed the last of Hazel's dessert.

Baron Palantine glared at the boy. His jaw muscles twitched. "What is your name?"

The servant bowed. "Hobson Smythe, my lord."

"And where do you come from, boy?"

"I believe he just told you his name," said Lady Sylva.

"I'll call him whatever I like. I just paid fifty solars for the privilege."

"The Northwest, your lordship. A village called Dusk."

The baron sniffed. "Savages live in the Northwest," he observed. "Little muir savages that squat in huts, gobble seals, and worship rocks instead of their empress. I hear they mate with vyes."

Everyone glanced at Dàme Rascha, who sat perfectly rigid, her eyes fixed on the baron.

He returned her glare with a smirk. "Present company excluded."

Lady Sylva rose. "Ladies," she said pointedly, "I invite you to join me in the parlor. We'll leave the gentlemen to discuss whatever it is gentlemen discuss when we're not present." She turned to the servant boy. "Mr. Smythe, please come along as my guest and educate me about your homeland. I refuse to believe such a witty creature gobbles huts or squats on seals or whatever it was the baron said. For shame, Vardon."

Most of the guests laughed, but Baron Palantine merely stood with the other lords as the women prepared to leave. His eyes never left the muir boy.

A dozen ladies followed Lady Sylva to the parlor. While the hostess chatted with Violet, Hazel and Dàme Rascha were forced to walk behind Lady Bethunia, who halted periodically to inspect them. Hazel gazed up at her tutor. The baron had been unspeakably insulting.

"Are you all right?" Hazel asked.

"Yes," replied Dàme Rascha.

"That boy isn't," said Hazel. "Did you see the way the baron was looking at him? I think he's in danger."

"I should say he is."

"We have to help him."

The vye glanced down at her. "It's not our affair."

But this did not satisfy Hazel, who felt a nagging concern for the servant boy's welfare. Why did she even care? Isabel would tease that it was because he was handsome, but that wasn't the reason. No, they had shared something earlier, something strangely intimate and comically depressing. In a single glance, this muir boy—a total stranger—had shown her more empathy and kindness than Violet had in a lifetime.

"Make it our affair," said Hazel.

"And how should I do that, Your Highness?"

"Poach him."

The vye raised her bristly eyebrows. "You wish me to poach our hostess's servant?"

"Yes, I do," said Hazel. Just ahead, Lady Bethunia veered urgently into a powder room. Apparently, there was justice in the universe.

"On what pretense?" said the vye.

Hazel felt a rush of excitement. *Would Rascha actually do it?* "I don't know. Make something up."

The pair entered the parlor, a tacky, old-fashioned chamber their hostess assured them would be redecorated now that she was in charge. A trio of imps brought drinks, and the ladies settled into superficial conversation on the many settees. Lady Sylva monopolized Violet, discussing art and politics, the time she'd snuck aboard a galleon bound for Zenuvia. Her father sent every ship in his fleet after her! Violet doted on every word, flushing a giddy pink when her hostess made a confidential aside. They were like two girls at a slumber party.

Lady Sylva had forgotten about the muir boy. Hazel was not surprised, nor could she blame her. The young matriarch had invested the Sylva's House Debt to make inroads with the next empress. She wasn't going to waste the evening on a servant's tales about blubber and tundra. It was enough she'd whisked him away from a semi-murderous baron.

Still, the boy made a pitiful spectacle. He stood off by a palm, looking obscurely troubled and painfully out of place. An imp had brought him a drink—he was here by Lady Sylva's invitation after all—but he dared not take a sip. Eventually, he set the glass down and reverted from awkward guest back to servant. Perhaps it was a relief; he no longer had to be clever.

Isabel appeared at Hazel's side after having spent twenty minutes nodding at whatever the viscount's wife had to say. She massaged her neck. "I see Violet's smitten," she muttered. "How much longer do you think we have to stay?"

Hazel shrugged. It was past midnight, but that meant nothing. They would leave when Violet was ready and not before.

"Where's Sigga?" asked Isabel, gazing about the room. Her own bodyguard and Violet's were standing by the doorway.

"No idea," said Hazel. She watched a refreshed Lady Bethunia enter the parlor and harangue her footman, whom she blamed for letting her nap right through dinner. The servant knew better than to argue. Weathering the abuse, he led the confused duchess to a chaise while a maid fetched another sherbet.

"Have Sigga fired," said Isabel testily. "What kind of bodyguard doesn't show up? She's got to be the worst agent in Impyrium."

Hazel nodded absently. She couldn't pretend she wasn't disappointed—Sigga Fenn had been one of her heroes. She wondered if Rascha would seek to have her replaced.

She turned to ask, but discovered her tutor had slipped away to speak with the servant boy. The vye loomed above him, dark and feral, a grizzled wolf in crimson robes. It was clear the boy had spent little time with vyes, but he appeared to be holding his own. As the leading expert on Rascha's body language, Hazel could tell her tutor was not displeased.

Isabel yawned again. "Enough. I'm dragging our dear sister away. I have fencing at six."

Ever fearless, Isabel knifed through the ladies and laid an arm on Violet's shoulder. Quiet words were exchanged, accompanied by tight, unblinking smiles. Their hostess discreetly excused herself, leaving the sisters to continue their chat behind an ornamental screen.

Dàme Rascha pounced. Abandoning the boy midsentence, she intercepted their hostess before she could join another group. Lady Sylva looked somewhat surprised, but smiled pleasantly until she realized Dàme Rascha's intentions. Then the smile faded. Still, there was nothing she could do. Dàme Rascha spoke on behalf of the royal family. If a Faeregine expressed interest in one her servants, Lady Sylva was obliged to surrender him. The only issue to negotiate was compensation.

The practice wasn't very nice, but Hazel consoled herself that Lady Sylva had herself poached the boy out of spite, while she was doing it for a noble cause. Vile as the baron was, he would never harm a Faeregine servant. The muir would be safe in the palace, peeling potatoes or doing whatever the butlers found for him to do. It was better than being dead.

Isabel emerged from behind the screen and told a servant to fetch their things. Coats were fetched, along with a photographer who took a final picture of Lady Sylva and Her Impyrial Highness. Twenty minutes later, the girls were bundled into their coach while the stallianas stamped their fiery hoofs on the gravel.

Kicking off her shoes, Violet glared at Isabel. "Don't ever embarrass me like that again."

Isabel's lids were already closing. "Come off it, Vi. It's late."

There was a knock on the window. Hazel pulled back the curtain and was shocked to see Sigga Fenn holding Hazel's clutch.

"You left this in the dining room," said the agent.

Opening the door, Hazel snatched her purse. "Where have you been?" she hissed. "You're supposed to be my bodyguard. I didn't see you all evening!"

"That may be, but you haven't left my sight. For the record, I do not find sherbet 'astonishing.'"

Hazel's jaw dropped. *"Lady Bethunia?"*

The Grislander bowed. "Good night, Your Highness."

Shutting the coach door, Sigga Fenn ordered the driver to depart. As the stallianas raced up the drive, Isabel yawned and settled deeper in her furs.

"That woman's the best agent in Impyrium."

CHAPTER 7
IN THE HOUSE OF GOD

Promptness and an intelligent mind are essential to a page.
If a lad also has a good address, a pleasing figure, and a correct
manner of speaking, he is destined to rise in his calling.

—manual on servant etiquette

Late the next morning, Hob sat across from Mr. Burke and Ms.
Marlowe in the latter's office.

"Well," said Mr. Burke, "last night certainly exceeded my
expectations. Masterful planning, Ms. Marlowe."

She inclined her head. "The boy deserves praise. Our sources were
most complimentary."

"Thank you," said Hob, trying not to yawn as he declined one
of the petite cakes on Ms. Marlowe's tray. He'd returned to Impyria

shortly after dawn on the pretense of retrieving some belongings.

"Tell us about your conversation with Dàme Rascha," said Ms. Marlowe.

Hob recalled his interview with the vye, his apprehension at her size and intensity. "She wanted to know about my background and education. Asked if I could read, if I knew much geography. She she wants someone to teach Hazel Faeregine about the Muirlands. Apparently, she doesn't know much about them."

"Why do you think the vye picked you?" said Mr. Burke.

"Maybe she thinks Her Highness would prefer learning about the Muirlands from someone who's lived there or from someone her own age. Maybe the vye just wanted to get me away from Baron Palantine. He'd insulted her too."

"I hear he played his part well," said Mr. Burke. "Public men with private debts are most useful."

"I'll remember that," said Hob.

The baron might have acted on cue, but Hob did not doubt the man's loathing for vyes and Muirlanders. One couldn't fake the hatred in those bloodshot eyes. Perhaps that's why they chose him.

Hob was still amazed by the planning that had gone into last night's affair. The riddle, the baron's wager, his drunken insults had all been a carefully orchestrated performance. Nothing was by chance: not Lady Sylva addressing Hazel Faeregine, her casual reference to servant poaching, or even Hob's placement just past the hostess's shoulder, precisely where the princess might chance to look at him. Countless little details and manipulations, all designed to bait a subtle hook.

And it had worked.

"We're in uncharted waters," Mr. Burke reflected. "We've never assigned a new recruit to such a plum. You've barely learned how to be a proper servant, much less a proper spy. Are you up to this, Hob? Be honest."

"It depends on what my duties are."

"You will do whatever it is Dàme Rascha wishes," said Ms. Marlowe simply. "Did she elaborate?"

"I'm to spend a few hours a week talking about my life in the Northwest," said Hob. "The palace underbutlers will assign the rest of my duties. She did say that my lessons with Her Highness are to be kept secret."

"Good," said Mr. Burke. "The more private your interactions, the greater the chance to win her trust."

"So, you want me to become Her Highness's friend," said Hob.

"No," said Ms. Marlowe firmly. "Mehrùn, much less Faeregines, do not socialize with servants. If you are familiar or—gods forbid—flirtatious, you will be removed. Patience and professionalism will earn you greater access. We are particularly interested in the princess's magical abilities."

"Really?" said Hob. "What about her sisters? They seem far more—"

Mr. Burke cut him off. "Your focus is Hazel Faeregine. We know little about her. We do not think it's by accident."

"Very well," said Hob. "How should I send my reports?"

"We've considered that," said Ms. Marlowe. "You haven't been here long enough to learn sufficient encryption, so we have to entrust you with this."

She held up an Impyrial handbook that contained a sterilized history of the empire, the Great Houses, and biographies of their more famous members, past and present.

"Every servant on the Sacred Isle possesses one of these," she continued. "This copy contains an embedded sheet of spypaper, which you will use to communicate with us. It works . . ."

Using her fingernail, Ms. Marlowe traced a message on the inside of the book's back cover. As she did so, Mr. Burke held up a separate sheet of yellowed parchment. Two words appeared on its surface as though penned by invisible hands:

Like this.

Hob grinned. "That's amazing."

"Indeed," said Ms. Marlowe. "Spypaper is exceedingly rare and unspeakably valuable. You will *not* lose this book."

Hob listened closely as they discussed further details regarding communication protocol.

"This brings us to our last point," said Ms. Marlowe. "Safety. Yours and ours."

"Each of the Faeregine girls is protected by a member of the Red Branch," said Mr. Burke. "The one assigned to Hazel Faeregine is Sigga Fenn. She's the order's newest member, but she's also a native Grislander who's been killing since she was six. If she thinks—even for a moment—that you're a threat to Her Highness, she'll snuff you like a candle."

Hob studied the photograph Mr. Burke held up. It showed a tall, wiry woman with a shaved head and cold, feline eyes.

"I didn't see her at the dinner," said Hob.

Mr. Burke slipped the photo into a file. "That doesn't mean she wasn't there. Red Branch aren't soldiers, they're the empress's hand-picked assassins. Sigga Fenn has mastered arts so dark and insidious they'd turn your stomach. Never break character, not even when you think you're alone."

Hob looked from one to the other. "That's . . . a little terrifying."

Ms. Marlowe sipped her tea. "Sigga Fenn's not a monster; she's a professional assigned to protect the princess. Remember, you are *not* a threat; you are merely a servant that the Faeregines decided to poach from Lady Sylva. Do your job and you have nothing to fear."

Mr. Burke rose. "And to ensure the Fellowship has nothing to fear, allow us to introduce Brother Jakob."

The person who entered the office looked like some kind of monk or beggar. He was a bald, elderly man in a threadbare robe, and his mottled brown skin was covered in witchlike tattoos. One eye was missing, as were the tips of thumbs and several fingers. Despite his unsettling appearance, the smile he offered was kind and reassuring.

"I'm honored to make your acquaintance."

Hob nodded. "Yours too. Er, what is this about?"

"Brother Jakob is an expert on psychnosis," explained Mr. Burke. "It's an ancient technique to plant restraints in your mind. If you're discovered, you won't be able to give us away. Standard precaution."

Hob was wary. "I don't want to be some kind of zombie."

Brother Jakob chuckled and eased himself down on a couch. "A zombie would make a very poor spy. Psychnosis will not change you. It merely prevents you from divulging anything about the Fellowship. Surely you see the wisdom. Please sit beside me."

Hob did so. Brother Jakob smelled like tallow and incense. The man chuckled at Hob's anxiety. "It doesn't hurt. I'm just going to talk to you. Close your eyes and focus on your breathing. Deep and slow, like a sleepy elephant. That's it."

Brother Jakob began to hum in a low, lilting murmur. He

encouraged Hob to relax, to let his consciousness soften like a sponge. Doing so would protect his new brothers and sisters, wall them off from the wicked Faeregines and the unholy forces at their command. Brother Jakob could sense Hob had a noble heart, had always protected those he loved. He wanted Hob to picture those people, wade through his earliest memories . . .

Hob felt like a feather skimming on a breeze through time. Memories surfaced: snow blowing off Sentries peaks; the face of a dead miner he'd found in a tunnel; winds howling about the cottage while he and Anja slept, furs tucked under their chins. Sweet little Anja. Hob saw her on cottage floor, playing with a doll while their mother sorted laundry. His mother, kind but careworn, her black hair streaked with gray, hands boiled to leather in washing tubs.

But now she was younger, even beautiful. He gazed up at her from a box. No, a crib. She was cooing and holding out a pinkie for him to squeeze. Someone was beside her, a tall man in a red coat. Hob knew him from his photograph. He smiled down at Hob, not with his mouth but with his eyes. He turned suddenly. A figure had appeared in the doorway. Hob could not make out a face, but it was also wearing a red coat. Hob's father was called away . . .

"He's coming out of it."

Hob opened his eyes at Ms. Marlowe's voice. A damp cloth lay on his forehead and his legs had been propped on the coffee table. He was not entirely certain when he had moved to the couch. Mr. Burke and Ms. Marlowe sat in nearby chairs watching him attentively.

"How do you feel?" said Mr. Burke.

"Okay," said Hob. Dreamlike scenes were receding, settling like silt on a riverbed. What had just happened?

"You remember what we discussed?" said Ms. Marlowe.

Hob nodded. That was all clear as day, everything until the moment someone entered the room. *Had* someone entered the room?

Mr. Burke extended his hand. "Ready to do your duty?"

"I am," said Hob, taking the hand and rising. Despite a sleepless night, he felt refreshed and energized, eager for the task at hand. All his life, he'd wanted to matter, to make a difference in the world. Now he was going to get that chance.

Ms. Marlowe handed him an envelope. "Run along to the Dragon Pier. Don't be late."

Thirty minutes later, Hob emerged from an apartment in the Market District. He walked briskly, suitcase in hand and Lady Sylva's letter—a signed transfer of his services—tucked into the inner pocket of his greatcoat.

The Market District drew all sorts: merchants and mystics, servants and bodyguards, schoolchildren and pickpockets lurking in doorways looking for marks. Skirting a phalanx of magistrates, Hob stopped at a food stall and bought some dumplings plucked from the sizzling oil. He sank his teeth into one, wiped his chin, and tossed his change into a beggar's cup.

A bell sounded behind him. Turning, Hob saw the crowds parting for a streetcar. As it trundled past, he swung aboard. Two dumplings and a cheerful hello were enough to satisfy the driver, who made room for Hob's suitcase by the hand brake.

For twelve chilly blocks, Hob clutched a leather strap and gazed down at the harbor through gaps in the buildings. The day was overcast and the sky promised snow, but nothing was going to dampen his spirits.

He hopped off the streetcar at the Grand Temple. Hundreds of beggars dozed upon its steps, ignoring a dozen or so Caterwauls who were scourging their own flesh and wailing about corruption in the faith. Hob had little patience for them. It was hard enough to get along in this life, much less worry about the next.

Hefting his suitcase, he descended the Wyrm's Way, a steep avenue that zigzagged from the Grand Temple down to the harbor. Legend held that when Mina I was very old and in the midst of addressing her worshippers, her dragon, Ember the Golden, suddenly snatched her in his jaws and made for the sea. Thousands witnessed the event, which Mina II commemorated by having the dragon's trail designated a holy place. No new buildings had ever replaced those that were demolished; Ember's path was immortalized so that pilgrims could commune with the first Faeregine. According to official histories, the empress's demise had not been death by dragon but something glorious, a final testament to her godhood.

Hob found this fairly convenient. He imagined other ways one might reinterpret life's little challenges. Mismatched socks? Divine creativity. Untimely belch? The gods have spoken! Running late . . . ?

Bells rang across the ancient city. Cursing, Hob tossed away the rest of his dumplings and hurried down the steps. He was due at the Dragon Pier by noon. It was straight ahead, a golden dome flying the Faeregine flag. Hob wove swiftly between tourists and pilgrims, palanquins and soldiers.

When he reached the pier, a panting Hob handed a guard captain his letter and identification documents. The man turned them over to a small, bat-winged homunculus who inspected them while he consulted a list.

"Here you are. Hobson Smythe to enter service with the royal family. If you're carrying any weapons or contraband, I advise you to leave them here. Mystics search you on the other side. If they find anything amiss, your day won't end well."

Hob thought of the spypaper embedded in his handbook. Would a mystic detect it? The captain returned his documents.

"Skiff's at the end of the pier. Give this to the boatman." He handed Hob a copper coin.

"Boatman?" said Hob. "I thought I'd be going across in that." He pointed to a yacht moored nearby, the one he'd taken back from last night's dinner party.

The captain shook his head. "You're going to the Faeregine side of the isle. Can't enter without navigating the maze. Can't navigate the maze without a boatman. Get along now."

Hob proceeded past several soldiers to where a pair of stone dragons flanked a ramp down to the water. A lone black skiff was moored there, bobbing slowly on the blue-gray swell. Clutching the coin, Hob addressed the hunched and hooded figure at its prow.

"Hello. I'm going to the palace."

The figure held out a black-gloved hand. When Hob dropped the copper in its palm, it pointed at a little seat in the prow. Hob stepped uneasily aboard as the boatman untied the skiff and took up the oars.

Hob had discovered he did not care much for the sea. He'd grown up among mountains; open water was a stranger. Gradually, his unease turned to dread.

With each stroke, the boatman rowed them faster and farther from shore than Hob would have thought possible. Once they passed the seawall, whitecaps dotted the open channel, but no water sloshed into the boat or even sprayed his face. Hob gripped the sides tightly. Witchcraft was at work here, some devilry that smoothed the waves and sped them toward the Sacred Isle. Was it the skiff or the boatman? Hob glanced at the hooded figure pulling smoothly on his oars. Its face remained downcast, perpetually shadowed.

"How long will the trip take?" asked Hob.

No answer.

"We're going so fast," he remarked. "Are you a mystic?"

Silence.

The man certainly wasn't talkative. But as they rowed farther from land, Hob could not shake the suspicion that the boatman was not a man at all.

He glanced up at the sky. Clouds were scattering to reveal peeps of winter sun. Surely a fiend could not move about so in daylight. Evil spirits abhorred the sun and running water, would not cross a stream at sunset, much less brave an ocean channel in early afternoon. Every Dusk child knew that. Even Mole knew that!

Yet with every minute, Hob's misgivings intensified. He sat in the skiff, huddled in his greatcoat, eyes trained on the silvery mist that enveloped the island.

Where is this Faeregine devil taking you? To the palace or the underworld?

He wondered if there was a difference.

The boatman had been rowing for some time when Hob glimpsed the maze. Its true scale was not apparent until they slipped within the mist.

In his Fellowship classes, Hob had been taught that the Faeregines relied on propaganda to perpetuate their mystique. On Wyrm's Way, their legends seemed like amusing stories to dupe the gullible. But there was nothing amusing about the chalk-white cliffs towering hundreds of feet above them. The maze's walls looked like they were tilting forward, poised to topple and crush them like insects. Hob craned his neck, utterly speechless. No mortals—not even mehrùn—could have built such things. What if Mr. Burke and Ms. Marlowe were wrong? What if the Faeregines really were gods?

The skiff began spinning like a broken compass needle. The boatman pulled mightily on one oar, driving them toward a wall. Hob gave an involuntary cry, braced himself to be dashed to pieces, only to exhale as they shot through a narrow opening hidden by some trick of engineering. More walls, some straight others curving. They continued spinning. Hob could not keep his bearings as the boatman allowed the skiff to hurtle past wider passages only to row down others so narrow that Hob was certain they'd be crushed. The boatman never looked up, but seemed to steer by some unholy instinct. With a retch, Hob bid farewell to that morning's dumplings.

And then, all at once, the spinning stopped.

Relaxing his death grip, Hob cracked an eye to behold a placid harbor filled with ships of every size and description. Straight ahead, high upon its promontory, stood the Impyrial palace. Its architecture was almost organic and unlike anything Hob had ever seen. It looked like a crimson, many-spined sea creature sheltering patches of white barnacles clinging to the cliffs below. Except those weren't barnacles. They were mansions.

To its left, a gleaming white spire rose higher than anything else on the Sacred Isle. Hob knew it at once: Tùr an Ghrian, Tower of the Rising Sun. Beyond that monument of sorcery was Rowan itself, the ancient school of magic whose graduates dominated the world.

Hob's awe dwindled, replaced by a sense of purpose.

Someday, we'll tear all this down. Someday, it won't matter if a kid's born muir or mehrùn. They'll all go to schools where they can learn the truth instead of Faeregine lies.

Wiping his mouth with a handkerchief, Hob checked to make sure he hadn't gotten sick on his coat. Someone would be meeting him at the pier and he wanted to look his best. Squaring his suitcase, he sat up straight and tried not to gape at the ships docked or anchored about the harbor. One black and gold galleon must have been four hundred feet long. Tiny figures moved about decks high above the waterline. Hob wondered how the maze could accommodate such a gargantuan vessel, much less its escort of warships. Were there different paths through the maze?

A flash caught his eye. A beacon was burning on the galleon's prow, so bright it looked like a tiny star. It must have been a Lirlander Seal, one of those passkeys to cross demon waters. Hob had read about them aboard the Transcontinental.

When Hob had asked why someone would steal them, Mr. Burke explained that many parties wished to do away with the Lirlander Seals. They were one of the main props supporting the Divine Empress. Snatch them away and the royal family would no longer be gatekeepers to the sea. Any of the Great Houses could be responsible—all stood to benefit if the Faeregines lost control over trade. As for the Lirlanders, they'd hated the Seals ever since Mina I created them. Accounts of the crime had interested Hob greatly. Gazing back at that galleon, he wondered if the authorities would ever catch the culprits.

Just do your job, a little voice reminded him.

Lirlander Seals were not his concern. His priority was Hazel Faeregine. His first report was due later that week. Turning back to the palace, he scanned hundreds of windows among the spiraling towers. Which one belonged to Her Highness?

The boatman made for a smaller dock. Hob saw identical skiffs rising and falling on the swell, their occupants hunched against the February gales. Bells pealed from inland, chiming a faint melody before tolling one o'clock. Could that be right? Hob glanced at the cloaked figure across from him. Whatever it was, it had rowed him across fifteen miles of windswept chop in less than an hour. Sorcery indeed.

A robust, elderly man with thick gray hair and a dark suit was waiting at the pier. As the skiff bumped the dock, he extended a hand down to take Hob's suitcase.

"I'm Oliveiro, seventh underbutler. And you must be Mr. Smythe. Welcome to Rowan."

"Thank you," said Hob. He reached in his pocket. "Do I tip the boatman?"

The man laughed. "No. Just get out before it rows you back."

The earthy welcome comforted Hob, who took the man's hand and stepped up onto the pier. The warm feeling died when he glanced back at the departing skiff.

The boatman was looking up at them. Beneath its hood, Hob beheld an almost featureless face of gray, puckered skin. No nose or mouth, just two wide-set eyes whose lids were sewn shut with heavy black thread. The creature resembled an old doll left outside to rot.

You're a stranger in a strange land.

Oliveiro waved it away. "Begone you! Back with the others."

Lowering its head, the boatman slowly backed its oars.

"What are they?" asked Hob.

Oliveiro hefted his suitcase. "Never you mind. First rule of life on the Sacred Isle: don't ask too many questions. You'll see lots of things you've never come across in— Where are you from?"

"Dusk."

"I'm sorry to say I've never heard of it," he said genially. "Don't be too offended. I don't know much of the Muirlands. My family's served the Faeregines for twelve generations."

"Are you mehrùn?"

Oliveiro shook his head. "Muir as beer. Come on."

The man led Hob over a frozen beach to a guardhouse built into the cliff base. A pair of Impyrial Guardsman flanked a doorway whose braziers blazed with witchfire. Inside, a mystic in navy robes was playing arcadia with a domovoi. With a cackle, the gnomish creature jumped his wyvern two levels to capture a marble witch. The mystic groaned.

"Looks like we've arrived just in time," said Oliveiro.

The mystic sighed. "I'm down six lunes. Twelve if I don't reclaim my gate."

"Well," said Oliveiro, "forestall poverty a moment to scan our young friend. Dàme Rascha just poached him."

The woman looked up from the game to assess Hob. Like many mystics, her pupils were different colors: one an inhuman orange, the other a silvery splash of mercury. Holding his gaze, she rose from the table.

"You haven't spent much time consorting with mehrùn," she observed. "Repeat that for me."

"I . . . haven't spent much time with mehrùn."

"*Consorting* with mehrùn," she corrected.

Hob repeated the phrase exactly as she wished.

She nodded and turned her attention to the paperwork Oliveiro handed her. "So tell me, Mr. Smythe, do you intend harm to any member of the royal family?"

"No," said Hob. It was no lie; his duties were simply to observe Hazel Faeregine and report on her activities.

The mystic asked several more questions with a cool, detached air that belied their seriousness. Hob's answers tumbled forth as though plucked by nimble fingers.

"Are you in league with another noble house, the Atropos, the Fellowship, the Grislands Confederates, any Zenuvian interests, or Lirlanders?"

"No," said Hob.

To his surprise and relief, the mystic appeared satisfied. "Very well. Open your bag and step within that circle."

She gestured to a silver pentagram etched in the floor. Hob stared at it with deep mistrust. Mehrùn used such inscriptions to summon beings from spirit realms. If he stepped inside, would it banish him to another world? The mystic laughed.

"You're on the Sacred Isle. Gods help you if you balk at basic scrying circles."

Hob stepped carefully within the diagram, tensing as its inscriptions gleamed. Meanwhile, the mystic was sorting through his suitcase. She picked up his Impyrial handbook and flipped through several pages. Surely those strange eyes would detect the spypaper. But she merely set it aside and glanced at the pentagram whose sigils were pulsing green.

"You're free to go, muir."

I guess the Fellowship knows what it's doing, thought Hob gratefully. He followed Oliveiro through a tunnel leading into the cliffs.

"Please, sir. You don't have to carry my suitcase."

The underbutler laughed. "I carry everyone's bag their first day. Savor it, Mr. Smythe. You'll curse my name soon enough. While we make our way up, let me familiarize you with our rules. The Sylvas are a fine family, but you serve the Faeregines now. This is the House of God."

There was no irony in the man's tone, only a sincere, almost endearing reverence. Did Oliveiro really believe the Divine Empresses were deities? Maybe he did. His family had served the Faeregines for twelve generations.

Palace life might be all Oliveiro knew, but he certainly knew a lot and shared his knowledge with Hob as they ascended a series of tunnels and ramps. His first love seemed to be the dos and don'ts of service etiquette.

"An exemplary page anticipates needs. He is honest, forthright, and obeys his superiors at all times. Do not maintain eye contact with royal persons. Do not address mehrùn by their first names unless given permission. I take it you've memorized your handbook?"

"Yes, sir."

"How many siblings does the Divine Empress have?"

"Seven, although six are deceased."

"Who remains?"

"Lady Herra. The grand duchess resides in South Tracey."

Oliveiro grunted. "What's the sigil of House Hyde?"

"A red sword on a black field."

"Who commissioned the palace expansion of 1788?"

"Mina the Twenty-third."

"Hmph," said Oliveiro. "Wipe that smirk off your face. It's unbecoming."

"Yes, sir."

"Tell me, young man, who is our head butler?"

"Mr. Oswald Dunn. Mrs. Bhargava is the housekeeper."

"What about the sous-chef?"

Hob searched his mind. "I . . . have no idea. Was that in the handbook?"

Oliveiro looked pleased. "The handbook covers basic information, but over two thousand merry souls serve in the palace. And that doesn't include the Impyrial Guard or Rowan's faculty and staff. I expect you to know each in due time. But first we must get you sniffed."

Hob glanced at Oliveiro as they paused at a pair of swinging doors. Did the man just say *sniffed*? "I don't understand, sir. Are there dogs?"

Thrusting the doors inward, Oliveiro ushered Hob through a cloud of fragrant steam into an enormous, low-ceilinged kitchen.

"Not dogs, Mr. Smythe. Hags."

Hob found himself staring at dozens of squat, burly figures dicing vegetables and tenderizing meats. The nearest gave a sniff, and raised a vaguely female head to peer at Hob with a pair of piggish eyes. Dropping her cleaver, she hurried over to pinch and knead his arm.

"Nicely marbled," she muttered. "Good work, Olly. He'll go down smooth."

"Now, now," said the underbutler uneasily. "You know perfectly well he's a new employee and not a meal."

The hag ignored him and started flinging seasonings at Hob from nearby bowls. She scented the air as they settled upon him. "Sage," she decided. "Maybe some parsley . . ."

By now the other hags had noticed—or smelled—the new arrival. Abandoning their stations, they swarmed down the aisles, swatting aside the hanging hams and cheeses.

Oliveiro took a firm hold of Hob's wrist as the mob enveloped him. "Ladies! Ladies, control yourselves," he cried. "Where's Bombasta?"

"Present," grunted the brute who had Hob in a headlock.

Oliveiro gasped. "Madam, you have forgotten yourself. Perhaps Gorgo should run the kitchens."

The hag instantly released Hob and wheeled on the others. *"Line up!"*

Cursing and muttering, the hags shuffled off to arrange themselves by height before a row of gleaming ovens. Bombasta swaggered after them, cuffing those who dragged their clogs. A minute later, thirty-seven hags stood at surly, drooling attention.

Oliveiro brushed flour and crushed bay leaves from Hob's coat. "I'm terribly sorry. They can get a trifle enthusiastic."

Lights swam before Hob's eyes. He massaged his throat, trying to fathom why the Faeregines would even keep hags. They were infamous creatures: cunning, cruel, and ravenous. Dusk drove them off the instant any were seen prowling about the palisades. Hob couldn't possibly stay here; he'd be eaten within the week.

Oliveiro explained that kitchen hags were a Rowan tradition predating even Mina I. Beastly but gifted in the culinary line, and manageable if proper precautions were taken.

"They were *not* in the handbook," Hob croaked.

"Naturally," said Oliveiro. "But once you've been sniffed you needn't worry."

He led Hob to the head of the line where Bombasta was adjusting her wimple. It was hard to reconcile the flowery apron and frock with the glowering enormity that wore them. That face! The only explanation was some primordial romance between a crocodile and a pig.

"Whatchoo starin' at?" she growled.

"Nothing," Hob blurted. "I've never met a hag before."

"You ain't meeting a hag. You is meeting *the* hag. Bombasta Shrope at your service."

"*You ain't no Shrope!*" hissed her neighbor, a pasty horror with sparse, carroty hair.

Bombasta ignored her. "I'm head chef," she continued proudly. "You need anything down here, I'm the gal to see. Let's have a look at that arm, eh?"

At Oliveiro's prodding (and against all natural instinct) Hob removed his greatcoat and jacket and rolled up his sleeve. Seizing it without ceremony, Bombasta pressed her wet nostrils to his wrist. A guttural moan escaped her lips as she dragged her snout up to his elbow. If this was not horrifying enough (and it was fairly horrifying), the hag provided running commentary.

"Rustic flavors. Nice with horseradish. No . . . too bold. Stew 'im with sage. Done!"

With a shriek, the hag flung his arm away as though it suddenly repelled her. Her snarky neighbor snatched it and offered the toothiest, most petrifying grin Hob had ever encountered.

"I'm Gorgo, dearie. First sous and—unlike some I could mention—direct spawn of the Shropes."

Oliveiro groaned. "Now is not the time for feuds."

The hag scowled at him before pressing her nose to the slimy trail Bombasta had left behind. She gave a derisive snort.

"This boy ain't no stew! He's a pastry! Peasant pie with a side o' greens. You only said stew 'cause you bake like a ninny. Done!"

Once again Hob's arm was flung aside and snatched by the next hag. More sniffings ensued, some sufficiently vigorous that Oliveiro intervened. Hob endured the ordeal with as much stoicism as he could muster. By his count, nineteen hags proclaimed him a perfectly obvious stew, while seventeen insisted he was a pie. A saucier remained undecided.

When they finally left the kitchens, Hob needed a moment to recover. The underbutler had intended to show him the palace laundry and mail room but changed tack when he noticed that Hob had sweated through his suit.

"Boatmen and hags are enough for one afternoon," he said kindly. "Let's get you settled. I'll have your things laundered and you can start fresh tomorrow."

An infinitely grateful Hob followed him down a corridor and up a broad staircase past a bevy of busy maids and pages. Hob gave a start as a blip of golden light whooshed over his head and rounded a corner, nimble as a hummingbird.

"What was that?"

"Zephyss," said Oliveiro, holding a door. "Messenger orbs. Someone probably wants his shoes polished. Come along. Two more flights and we're almost home."

Hob followed, taking in aromas of tweed, wood polish, and old stone. The Sylva manor had been saturated with the smell of candles and perfume. They were still below ground, but Hob could already sense a profound difference. The Sylvas had money and ambition; the Faeregines had taste and tradition. One wanted power; the other had it.

That tradition was even more evident as they reached the servant quarters where portraits of past head butlers and housekeepers were hung in neat rows: ladies adorning the left-hand corridor, the men on the right. A pretty maid of about fourteen brushed past them carrying a silver tray. Glancing at Hob, she flashed a smile, which he was happy to return. Oliveiro promptly ushered Hob down the page's hallway and resumed his earlier lecture.

"An exemplary page is modest and discreet. He does not grin like a baboon or fraternize with the young ladies with whom he is privileged to work. Do I make myself clear?"

"Very clear, sir."

"Excellent," said Oliveiro, stopping at a door and producing a set of keys. "I've got a good feeling about you, Mr. Smythe. I'd hate to see you put a foot out of line."

Ducking another zephyss, the underbutler opened the door and gave a horrified gasp.

"What are you doing?" Oliveiro cried. "Where is your uniform?"

"Steaming in the showers," replied an unconcerned voice. "Bit wrinkled."

"That's no excuse to be naked!"

"Oh, come off it, Olly. I am not naked."

Oliveiro sighed and gestured for Hob to enter. "Hobson Smythe, it is my tragic duty to introduce you to your roommate, Mr. Viktor Grayson."

Hob entered to see a gawky teenager with wet blond hair sitting on a bed in a pair of skimpy briefs. The two glanced at each other with equal disinterest, and Viktor returned to polishing some boots. Oliveiro cleared his throat.

"Viktor, your new roommate is younger than the last and I expect you to set a good example. You can start by not lounging about in what can only be described as a loincloth."

Viktor shrugged. "They're comfortable."

"They're indecent," retorted Oliveiro. He set down Hob's suitcase. "Mr. Smythe, if you'll let me have your coat and jacket."

Once Oliveiro had the garments, he handed Hob an envelope containing his schedule and several maps. Bidding them good day, the seventh underbutler closed the door.

"What happened to your suit?" asked Viktor.

Hob replied "Hags" and braced for ridicule. He was used to the hazing that came with being newest or youngest. Life in a mining camp required a thick skin and a sharp tongue.

To Hob's surprise, his new roommate did not pounce. "Ah, well. Don't feel too bad. When I got sniffed, it wasn't my jacket Olly had laundered."

"You're joking."

"Wish I was," said Viktor, reaching for an undershirt. Hob glanced around the room. It was small but had the necessities: cot, dresser, and a narrow closet with three page's uniforms and a pair of dress boots in his size. Being underground they had no view, but the room did have a window that opened upon an airshaft.

While Hob unpacked, he and Viktor chatted as companionably as two strangers could. He soon learned that Viktor had grown up a farmer's son outside Avalia, had left home during the Great Drought, and served a House Minor until they gifted half their staff to the Faeregines to cover their taxes. That was six years ago. He'd been on the Sacred Isle ever since.

And now he had to run. Giving his boots a final buff, Viktor dashed out to finish dressing in the bathroom. The instant he was gone, Hob shut the door and collapsed onto his bed. Dimming the lamp, he reached for Oliveiro's envelope. He scanned tomorrow's schedule; standard-looking stuff until late afternoon when he had a conspicuously vague "private appointment" in some building called Old Tom. Consulting the map, he found it on the Rowan school grounds, just behind Tùr an Ghrian.

Closing his eyes, Hob let the staggering reality of his situation wash over him. Here he was, flopped upon a cot in the ancestral abode of the Faeregines. He had never felt so exhausted, terrified, and elated.

This is it. This is where you make your mark.

Rolling over, he reached for the Impyrial handbook on his nightstand. The photo of the royal family was several years old, but there was no mistaking the ghostly wisp standing off to the side, half-obscured by an archduke's deerhound. Hob studied the princess's shy, almost wary expression. It was a face that would hold many secrets or none. Was Hazel Faeregine a goddess or just a poor little rich girl? He'd find out soon enough.

Flipping to the inside back cover, Hob traced two words with his fingernail:

I'm in.

CHAPTER 8
THE TUTOR AND THE *TYPHON*

If you have to ask how much it costs,
you can't afford it.

—John Pierpont Morgan, Pre-Cataclysm financier
(176–100 P.C.)

The following day, Hazel sat in tense anticipation as Master Montague addressed the court brats on their latest essays.

"While some of you show progress, others are falling behind. I name no names, but I have doubts some of you are fit to continue this course. Serious work is not for everyone."

He gestured at yesterday's *Chronicle*, whose society page showed the Faeregine triplets posing with the Sylvas.

"Class dismissed. Your essays are on my desk."

The girls filed down the aisles, some eagerly, others with reluctant dread. Hazel trailed behind, noting that Violet and Isabel looked pleased when they flipped to the last page of their essay booklets. They did not wait for Hazel but left in a chattering herd with the rest of their classmates. Master Montague was already sitting behind his desk, brow furrowed, an unlit pipe dangling from his mouth as he turned to a stack of graduate papers. He did not bother looking up as Hazel picked up her essay booklet. She held her breath as she opened it.

Hazel stared at the red slash and the master's brief but harsh remarks in stunned silence. She bit her lip, determined to keep any tears in check. Then she got angry.

"This isn't fair," she said, clutching the booklet. "This is about me, not what I wrote."

The master set down his pen and spoke in a measured tone. "I do not assign grades based on personal feelings, Your Highness. I assign them according to a work's merits."

"My essay was good," Hazel insisted. It was true—she had never written more.

"No," said the master. "It was an overlong series of observations tangential to the topic. Eloquent and sporadically interesting, but outside the question's scope. In short, a failure."

Weeks of frustration tumbled forth. "You just said it was interesting!"

"And out of scope," the master repeated. Leaning back, he laced his fingers upon his belly. "You may not believe this given my decrepitude, but I was a fair runner in my day. Tell me, Your Highness, if I enter a race and set a blistering pace in the wrong direction, do I deserve a ribbon?"

Hazel did not answer at once. "I'm trying my best," she said, a hint of defeat in her voice.

"Are you?"

"Of course I am. And I'm tired of you singling me out in class. You pick on me more than anyone else."

The master did not reply at once but lit his pipe and blew a plume of heady smoke toward the rafters. "Do you know what's the very worst sort of teacher?"

Hazel was not going to play this game. She crossed her arms and waited for the answer.

Master Montague looked her in the eye. "An easy one. Good day, Your Highness."

Hazel walked mechanically out of the classroom and shut the door behind her. Dàme Rascha and Sigga were just outside, the former holding her coat. Hazel put it on while glaring at the master through the door's window. There he sat, reading contentedly away. Behind the master, his homunculus set a record playing on the phonograph and fixed him a drink.

I hate that man!

"What was that about?" asked Rascha.

Hazel thrust the essay at her. "I don't want to talk about it."

Dàme Rascha glanced at the grade and slipped the essay in her coat pocket. The vye's expression was somber, but she said nothing, which was far more painful. Almost two months had passed since the Spider's mandate and Hazel was still failing Montague's class. And she had yet to make a major breakthrough in her magical studies. They were running out of time.

"Let's go to the tower," said Hazel glumly.

"We're not going to Tùr an Ghrian," said Rascha.

Hazel turned. "What about Mystics?"

"After supper. You have another lesson first."

Puzzled, Hazel ran through her schedule. "No, I don't. This is Tuesday. Etiquette meets Wednesdays and Fridays."

"This is a new class," the vye clarified, "to aid your studies with Master Montague."

Hazel's heart fluttered. She glanced at Sigga to confirm that someone had heard this insanity. The Grislander remained impassive. A panicked Hazel waited for a third year to pass.

"Rascha," she pleaded, "this is the last thing I need. I—I barely have time to sleep or even breathe! I can't deal with yet another scholar."

"It's not a scholar," said the vye calmly.

Hazel opened her mouth and promptly shut it. "Really? Who's the teacher?"

"You'll see soon enough. He's waiting for us in Rattlerafters."

Hazel was officially curious. Why had Rascha chosen Rattlerafters? Technically, it was a library, but really it was little more than an attic frequented by those who wanted a place to nap or copy homework. Few students even knew it existed since it was tucked just beneath Old Tom's bell tower.

As they climbed the many steps to Rattlerafters, Hazel recalled the times she and her sisters used to play hide and seek there. Once they'd chanced upon some fifth years kissing in the stacks, a spectacle that left Violet scandalized and Isabel in silent hysterics. Hazel had watched with fascinated revulsion until Isabel flung an eraser and the triplets fled, hooting like gibbons. She missed those days. Back then, Violet had almost been human.

When Hazel reached Rattlerafters, she did not find a teacher but the boy Rascha had poached from Lady Sylva. He stood at attention next to an easel displaying a large map of Impyrium, dressed in a page's uniform. A confused Hazel turned on one heel to survey the tables and stacks. "Where's the teacher?"

Dàme Rascha gestured at the boy. "The young man is going to talk to you about the Muirlands and answer any questions you may have about his life in the Northwest Province."

Hazel was horrified. "You mean the *page?*" she whispered.

"Yes."

She glanced at the boy, embarrassed for both of them. She lowered her voice even more. "Rascha, I cannot possibly take lessons from a page. If my sisters—if *anyone*—heard of such a thing . . ." Hazel could not even imagine the fallout.

"You need to learn about the Muirlands," said her tutor simply. "Who better to acquaint you with them than a native?"

"Absolutely not."

The vye held up a finger. "One hour. If it isn't valuable, we will not do it again."

Hazel exhaled and glanced miserably at the map. The debacle would take even longer if she argued. "Very well," she whispered. "But this means I get the painting."

The vye agreed, and Hazel promptly sat at the nearest table, back straight, hands clasped, the embodiment of academic piety. Channeling her inner Violet, she offered the page a prim smile. "Good afternoon."

He bowed. "Good afternoon, Your Highness."

"May I ask is your name?"

"Hobson Smythe."

Hazel nodded. "I remember you from Lady Sylva's dinner party. I don't wish to be nosy but would you please share your teaching qualifications? Where were you educated?"

"Dusk Elementary, Your Highness. But I never graduated."

Hazel shot Rascha a disbelieving look.

"I had to take a mining job in the Sentries, Your Highness."

Hazel considered chiding him for speaking out of turn, but decided against it. There was no sense in being rude.

He explained while pointing to a stretch of mountains in the map's northwest corner. They were so far away they might have been on another planet.

"Well," said Hazel, "you were clever for solving Lady Sylva's riddle—you needn't bow—but I don't see the point of this. With all due respect, I'm not studying to be a miner."

The page inclined his head to acknowledge that no offense was taken. Something about him struck Hazel as odd. He lacked the meek deference endemic to servants. Quite the opposite, in fact. He projected a self-assurance that she found puzzling, even daunting. In some ways, he reminded her of Sigga.

"How old are you?" she asked.

"Thirteen, Your Highness."

Hazel was shocked. She'd have guessed sixteen, even seventeen. None of the boys at court had shoulders like those, much less anyone so young. A result of manual labor, no doubt.

"Well, at your age, I doubt you could be such an expert, but if you claim to know so much about the Muirlands, I'm sure you can name every archduchy in Afrique." Master Montague had posed the same question on her last exam. Hazel had managed only three, but she would be surprised if the boy could name any. Afrique was halfway across the world.

The boy did not even blink. "Tippoh, Tythos, Acheral, Azalia, Südsteppe, Laothe, Islan, and Muirplein. Cairn-Fomora is the capital, but technically isn't a duchy."

Dàme Rascha chuffed with approval. Hazel frowned. "How do you know that? More important, why do you know that?"

"I learned it when studying for Provinces."

Hazel knew of the exams. *You'd be laughed out of Provinces* was a common refrain whenever Master Montague was particularly disgusted with the court brats. The tests were infamously grueling and competitive.

"And how did you place?" she asked.

"First, Your Highness."

Hazel blinked. "Out of how many?"

The boy considered a moment. "I could not say exactly. Fifty thousand? Perhaps more."

"I don't understand," said Hazel. "Why didn't you attend an Impyrial college? My family would have paid your way."

"I needed to support my mother and sister," he said simply. "My father is dead, and my mother's tribe wouldn't help us on account my father was a skänder."

"What's a skänder?" said Hazel.

The boy looked past her at Sigga. "Your Highness's bodyguard is a skänder."

"No, she isn't," said Hazel. "She's a Grislander."

"Forgive me," said the page. "*Skänder* is a term in the Northwest for someone with white skin. My father was skänder, but my mother's full Hauja. The Hauja are a tribe that goes back almost to the Cataclysm."

Hazel felt sorry for him. "They cast her out because she married someone different?"

"My parents weren't married, Your Highness. For a Hauja woman to wed, the tribe's shaman must perform the ceremony. He refused."

"So, you're a bastard," Hazel observed.

His mouth twitched. "If you like, Your Highness."

Had she said something wrong? Technically, Hazel was a bastard but it had never bothered her. With Faeregines, the maternal line was all that mattered. Paternity was a footnote.

Still, Hazel sensed she had offended him, which had not been her intention. "I make no reflection," she said quickly. "Did your lineage affect your standing with the Hauja?"

"I have no standing with them," he replied. "The tribe only allowed me to sit séyu—their rite of passage—because they assumed I would fail."

"Did you?"

A faint smile. "No. I survived the eight days, killed a Cheshirewulf, and ate its heart."

The statement made the entire lesson worthwhile. "You *ate* a Cheshirewulf's heart?" Hazel exclaimed.

"Yes, Your Highness. Every Hauja boy has to track and hunt a Cheshirewulf to prove himself. The tribe holds them sacred."

Hazel had seen many pictures of Cheshirewulfs in books. Monstrous creatures. It was said that some still prowled the Direwood, but she imagined those were just stories.

"Are they really as big as a horse?" she asked.

The boy considered. "More like a good-sized pony. But they're stealthy—can disappear entirely when they hold their breaths. But I was more worried about the weather. The elders send you off without any food or furs."

Hazel raised her eyebrows. "And you lived eight days like that?"

"No," replied the page. "Not even natives can survive long under those conditions. On the second day I got lucky and shot a caribou with my Boekka. It gave me what I needed."

Hazel sat transfixed as the page went on to tell her how he'd tracked the Cheshirewulf, tricked it with a reflection, and ate its steaming heart by a frozen river. It was like reading one of Uncle Basil's storybooks, except the hero was right in front of her wearing a page's uniform. Something about that struck her as profoundly sad.

"Why didn't you stay with the Hauja and live on Bear Lake?" she asked. "It sounds so interesting."

"My mother was in Dusk," he explained. "And I didn't want to live with the Hauja; I just wanted to prove I was as good as they were. Anyway, surviving séyu didn't matter to them. When I came back, the shaman tossed the Cheshirewulf's pelt on the bonfire and called me a skänder trickster. Warriors drove me out of the camp. Almost killed me." The page tapped a scar near his hairline.

What could have made that? thought Hazel. *An ax?*

She found it profoundly unjust. "What about your mother's family? Why didn't they stand up to the shaman?"

For the first time, the boy looked like a typical page. He appeared touchingly shy, even embarrassed by her question. He seemed to realize this and stood up very straight.

"The shaman was my grandfather, Your Highness. The warriors, my uncles."

"Oh," said Hazel, unsure what else to say. Bad as her family was, they weren't trying to exile or kill her. Violet might someday, but she wasn't empress yet.

Old Tom announced his presence. The page practically sprang

out of his boots as the clock's chimes—almost deafening at this proximity—began tolling the hour. Hazel could not help but laugh. He recovered quickly, however, and promptly straightened the map he'd nearly knocked over. She was still giggling when the windows stopped vibrating. The page glanced up at the low ceiling.

"I suppose that's why they call it Rattlerafters," he said.

"Yes, indeed," said Hazel. She cleared her throat. "Well, Mr. Smythe, your stories are very entertaining, but our hour is up. Have you anything else to add?"

"Just remember that Tipsy Tigers Almost Always Sleep Late Into Morning."

Hazel wrinkled her brow. Perhaps he was still rattled from the chimes. "Why would I want to remember that?"

He gave a cheerful, decidedly nonservant grin that she rather liked. "Afrique, Your Highness. The first letter of each word represents an archduchy: left to right, north to south. I was pressed for time when studying for Provinces so I devised little tricks to remember things."

A simple device but rather useful. How many more did this page have?

Rising from her seat, Hazel buttoned her long coat. "I think we'll try this again. Next Tuesday then."

He bowed. "Next Tuesday, Your Highness."

Hazel left Rattlerafters, descending the stairs briskly lest she give Rascha an opening to gloat. The vye and Sigga followed, neither speaking until they were outside. Dàme Rascha took a moment to warm her hands by a witchfire lamp.

"That went well," she observed complacently.

"Tolerable," said Hazel. "But it was beastly to ambush me like that."

The old vye smoothed her pupil's scarf. "If you'd known what was in store, you would not have gone."

"Of course I would have. I yearn for knowledge! Now, about that painting . . ."

Even Sigga smiled at this. As the three crossed the darkening grounds, Hazel was practically buoyant. She had just taken a one-hour vacation from herself and it was liberating. Not once had she fretted over the Spider's mandate, Mystics, or even Master Montague. She had been hunting caribou and Cheshirewulfs, fleeing Hauja across frozen lakes while vultures wheeled above.

"He ate a Cheshirewulf's heart!" she exclaimed to herself. She glanced up at Sigga, who was walking beside her. "Where he's from almost sounds like the Grislands."

"Not quite, Your Highness. In the Grislands, humans are in the minority."

"But both places are cold," Hazel observed. "Not like this," she said, brushing some snowflakes with her mitten. "But *really* cold. Freeze-your-blood cold."

"That is true."

Hazel turned her mind back to the boy. "We did well to poach him," she said. "I didn't know muir could be so interesting. How do you think he ended up all the way out here?"

Sigga smirked. "That's what I've been wondering."

"He's been vetted," said Rascha defensively. "By the Sylvas and our people. Security approved him."

The agent grunted. "If security was any good, I wouldn't be here."

Hazel began to feel sick. "Please stop. Both of you. That was the first hour I've enjoyed in weeks and now you're making me worry that the page is an assassin."

Sigga nodded. "My apologies, Your Highness. It's not your job to worry about your safety. It's mine. Would you agree, Dàme Rascha?"

The vye bowed. "I did not mean to imply—"

"What's going on?" said Hazel, looking ahead as they rounded some trees.

A celebration was under way in the palace's rose gardens. Bright glowspheres hovered over several hundred guests clustered about braziers, laughing and clinking glasses. As they approached, Hazel spied a familiar face by a semiscandalous statue of Mina VII, whose beauty (and vanity) was legendary. Uncle Basil was awkwardly shifting a toddler from hip to hip. When she got closer, he caught sight of her and beckoned her over.

"Hazel! Come meet a cousin and say hello. You've been neglecting me terribly."

"Sorry, Uncle Basil. I've been catching up on my classes."

"Never let school get in the way of your education," he said amiably. "Some wise fool said that. Anyway, this is your distant relation, Amelia. Her family's visiting from Southaven."

Hazel hated meeting young children for the simple fact that her appearance often frightened them. Nevertheless, she mustered a smile for the girl, who promptly recoiled.

"She's so white, Cousin Basil!"

"And you're rather chubby," he replied, pinching her and setting her on the ground. The girl giggled and ran off to her mother. Lord Faeregine sighed. "Sorry about that—unpromising brat. Anyway, come in and raise a glass to *Typhon*."

"What's *Typhon*?"

"She's a ship, my dear. The most glorious galleon Fenton's ship-yards ever built. She just came through the maze. Come have a look."

"I'd love to, Uncle, but really I can't. I'm just ducking inside for a bite and then it's back to work."

He looped an arm about her. "Nonsense. There's plenty of food here, including those little artichokes I know you like. Make a plate, say hello to a few people, and then trudge back to your books. It's a sad soul that never rejoices."

There was no resisting him. Hazel followed him into the midst of humorless bankers, gossiping socialites, and a crowd of boisterous merchants ("important men in the city," according to Uncle Basil), who were relieving a phlegmatic faun of his appetizers.

Sigga and Dàme Rascha followed as Lord Faeregine introduced Hazel to various lords and ladies. It was a game Hazel had been play-ing since birth. She said hello, smiled at insincere compliments, and politely clawed a path toward a table with chafing dishes.

"You must be starving," said Lord Faeregine, chuckling as she piled artichokes and crab cakes on a tiny plate. "Let's have someone fetch you a platter."

"That's okay," said Hazel, wolfing down a crab cake. "I've only got a minute. Where's Harkün?" Her uncle's bodyguard frightened her so much that Hazel always made a point of looking for him.

Uncle Basil was distracted. "What? Oh, I don't know. Harkün's always wandering here or there. Red Branch are notoriously indepen-dent. Unless you're the empress, it's like trying to herd cats. Isn't that right, Agent Fenn?"

Sigga inclined her head.

Unable to contain himself any longer, Lord Faeregine led Hazel to the nearest railing and pointed down at a vessel of such monstrous size it had to anchor in the middle of the harbor.

"Nine masts," Uncle Basil crowed. "Two hundred cannon to fend off any pirates in the Bloodshallows or Hadesian Deeps. She's a floating battery, Hazel. Look at *Legionnaire*. Compared to *Typhon* she's practically a dinghy."

This was true. *Legionnaire* was a magnificent ship, almost five hundred feet with a Lirlander Seal on her prow. But *Typhon* was twice that size. In the moonlight, her paintwork was practically luminous.

"She's beautiful, Uncle Basil," said Hazel. "Truly."

He laughed with pleasure. "The bank's sunk a mint of money into her, but I daresay the investment will pay off handsomely." He lowered his voice. "And between you and me, a certain someone is going to clear a fortune on the silk she's carrying. You wouldn't believe how much that ship holds. Once she's back from her voyage, I'll buy you a racehorse."

"What would I do with a racehorse?"

He clinked his glass against her plate. "You race it, my dear. Incidentally, where is my *Little Mermaid*? I read it every Yule and your theft made me break tradition."

"I promise I'll return it."

A disbelieving look. "When?"

"When I get my racehorse."

He groaned. "Perfectly criminal. Ah, there's Harkün." He nodded at the hollow-eyed giant slipping smoothly through the crowd. Brushing past Sigga, Harkün whispered something in Lord

Faeregine's ear. Uncle Basil made a face.

"But she promised she'd make an appearance." He glanced anxiously at several photographers by a fountain. "Excuse me, Hazel. I have to have a word with the empress."

Hazel shrugged and attacked her artichokes. If Uncle Basil thought the Spider would venture outdoors to coo over some ship, he didn't know his mother.

"Shall we go?" said Dàme Rascha.

"Two minutes," said Hazel, reloading her plate. There was something undeniably pleasant about eating hot food on a cold, clear night. She was about to take another bite when Sigga suddenly pulled Hazel behind her.

"What are you—?"

Hazel's exclamation died away. Guests were parting as the demon Lord Kraavh made his way toward them. The Lirlands ambassador towered over the humans, both terrifying and magnificent in robes of midnight silk. He must have been ten feet tall from the top of his curling horns down to his goatlike hooves. Three round green eyes were set in that tigerish face. Each was fixed on Hazel.

"That's close enough," Sigga warned.

The rakshasa halted, his imps and servants standing behind him. Heat radiated off his person, mephitic vapors that billowed and hissed as they wafted away on the breeze. Hazel had never been so close to such a being. The demon's aura was so overpowering it was like a gravitational field. Hazel could barely move.

The ambassador appeared amused by Sigga's caution. "I wish to make Her Highness's acquaintance. I haven't had the privilege."

The rakshasa bowed low. Hazel managed to follow protocol:

a curt nod accompanied by a minuscule bend at the waist. "Hazel Faeregine," she said.

Lord Kraavh gazed over the overlook's railing. He was so tall he could view the harbor from where he stood. "What do you think of the fleet's latest addition?"

"Very impressive," said Hazel.

"Indeed. But not as impressive as you, Your Highness."

"I'm afraid I don't understand you."

The demon glanced up at the night sky. "There's a full moon tonight. There's magic in such moons. They shine a surprising amount of light. On some more than others. You shine rather brightly, Your Highness."

He gave a knowing leer before gazing about the grounds.

"Would you believe I stood on this very spot during the Siege of Rowan?" he remarked. "I saw the Hound turn a battlefield red. I heard Prusias's roar when the first Faeregine shattered his crowns. It's the blessing and curse of my kind. We live so long that both triumph and shame are inevitable. Dynasties are no different. I could tell you many stories of your ancestors, Your Highness. One in particular."

He knows. The rakshasa was so ancient he would have been centuries old when Mina IV was still a girl. He had probably seen Arianna Faeregine in person, perhaps even met her. Hazel had no doubt that Kraavh recognized the likeness between them. "Perhaps some other time," she said quickly. "Unfortunately, I have to go."

"Pity," said the ambassador. "The party is just begin—"

BOOM!

The explosion sent Hazel careening into Dàme Rascha. Clutching the vye's robes, she turned her head as a gargantuan fireball rose in a crowning plume from the harbor.

There were sounds like falling hailstones. Rascha pulled Hazel to the ground, shielding her as splinters of burning wood rained from the sky. Lying on her stomach, Hazel gazed dazedly down at the harbor trying to process what had happened.

Typhon had exploded.

Yellow flames blazed where the galleon had been, an inferno vomiting torrents of black smoke. Other ships had also caught fire, including *Legionnaire* whose sails were burning. Empty skiffs bobbed on the flickering swells like matchsticks. Flashes erupted on Hazel's right. Photographers lined the railing, snapping pictures as quickly as they could. One turned his camera on her. She hid her face in Rascha's robes.

A voice rose above all others, an anguished cry that Hazel barely recognized. Peeking out, she saw her uncle nearly crash into a rosebush. He staggered to the railing and stared down at the harbor with an expression of wild, almost frenzied disbelief.

"No," he gasped. "Dear gods, no! *No!*" Whirling about, he stabbed a finger at someone. "You did this!"

Peering around Rascha, Hazel saw Lord Kraavh standing motionless. Sigga stood between the demon and Hazel, a dagger in each hand.

"That is a very serious charge," the ambassador remarked coldly. "The kind that leads to wars. I suggest you confer with the empress before making such accusations. In the meantime, call off your little dogs before I decide to get angry."

The demon gazed coolly at the Red Branch agents positioned between him and the two Faeregines. Hazel saw that Harkün had also drawn a dagger with a wavy black blade.

Uncle Basil did not reply at once but turned back to the harbor as though this was all a nightmare from which he must wake. But *Typhon* did not rematerialize, and the brilliant fires kept burning. He dipped his head.

"Harkün, stand down. Sigga, get my niece inside. Lord Kraavh, return to your embassy and remain there until we determine what has happened. Someone is going to pay for this outrage."

The demon turned and walked away. "Someone certainly will."

CHAPTER 9
THE DIREWOOD

This is the forest primeval.
The murmuring pines and the hemlocks
Bearded with moss, and in garments green,
indistinct in the twilight . . .

—"Evangeline" by Henry Wadsworth Longfellow,
Pre-Cataclysm poet (206–131 P.C.)

Two weeks after the *Typhon* exploded in Rowan Harbor, Hob lay atop his cot, wondering if their room would be searched that morning. Guardsmen had swarmed the servant quarters three times, twice with dogs. They hadn't found anything incriminating, but Hob knew they'd keep trying. He had the impression that the authorities *wanted* a servant to be responsible for the catastrophe. Far easier to deal with commoners than the Lirlanders or a rival house.

Across the way, Viktor was donning makeshift armor: a sock-padded hat, an apron lined with stale bread, and shin guards made from bundled newspapers.

"Last chance," he said.

"Can't," said Hob. "I've got work."

Viktor scoffed. "Allow me to observe it's Saturday and I made a side bet on the assumption you'd be playing."

Ordinarily, Hob would have been Viktor's partner in the weekly match of hall thumper. The game involved two-man teams trying to plow through a gauntlet of defenders in the narrow hallway housing the linen closets. Each team got one chance to claim a tarnished ladle hung from a hook at the end of the hall. Matches were rowdy, violent, and incredibly fun. It was also a centuries-old tradition, which meant that the underbutlers (who despised the game) could do little about it.

"Come on," Viktor pleaded. "If you don't play, I'll have to pair up with Zeke. We'll come in last and then it's good-bye, Viktor. Are you that desperate for another roommate?"

Hob chuckled but Viktor's fears were not entirely unfounded. In hall thumper, the pair that claimed the ladle the quickest won a pie. The team in last place had to provide said pie by whisking one that night from the kitchens. The hags, who knew perfectly well that pages tried to steal a pie every Saturday, prepared their defenses accordingly. And thus, while every team wanted to win hall thumper, the more desperate objective was not to lose. Since Hob's arrival, Viktor had enjoyed two victory pies and steered clear of fists, teeth, and booby traps.

Having donned his gear, Viktor cursed Hob for dooming him to death by hags and stormed out. Hob waited a minute before retrieving his handbook from his nightstand. Sitting up, he opened the back cover and wrote a message using a broken comb tooth as a stylus.

All well. Meeting twice per week with HF. Have not seen magic, but she and DR stay late in tower every night. No one else admitted but SF. Palace tense after Typhon. Multiple searches. Some think explosion was accident (spark in gunpowder room), but most blame Lirlanders. Ambassador confined to embassy.

Overheard following while on page duty:
Finance ministry considering tax increase on provinces.
Empress doubling troops in Eastern Blys in case of food riots.
Hydes blocking measure to strengthen Houses Minor.
SF had me followed first week but not since. Remain cautious.

DR invited me to attend HF class trip to Direwood today. Triplets will be there along with others from Great Houses. Will report.
For truth, equality, and a free Impy—

The door flew open as Viktor rushed back in the room. Keeping his cool, Hob laid the handbook casually aside.

"That was fast."

"I'm going back out, was just . . ." Viktor's eyes fell on the handbook. "Why are you reading that?"

"Brushing up on my houses," said Hob. "I'm working an outing with the fine young gentleman and the court brats."

"Lucky you. Pop quiz: What's the mascot for House Menlo?"

"An ulu."

"And the Jains?"

Hob yawned. "An afrit. How's Zeke?"

There was a split-second hesitation. "He's fine."

Hob glanced sideways at his roommate, who was now rummaging for something in his topmost drawer. Viktor's response was odd. It almost seemed like he'd forgotten who Zeke was. The hairs on Hob's neck prickled. He stared at Viktor a little closer.

"How 'bout a tune?" he said, nodding at the fiddle, which was Viktor's dearest love.

"Maybe later."

"Come on," pressed Hob. "One verse of 'Muirlander in July.'"

Snatching up a pair of socks, Viktor stowed them under his hat for extra padding. "Gotta run. Catch you later."

"Take these too," said Hob. He tossed another pair of socks well behind Viktor. Reaching back, his roommate snatched them without a glance.

When the door closed, Hob exhaled slowly. Viktor was all thumbs at everything but his fiddle. Whoever just came into the room, it was not Viktor Grayson.

Sigga Fenn has mastered arts so dark and insidious they'd turn your stomach. Never break character, not even when you think you're alone . . .

The recollection of Mr. Burke's warning made Hob queasy. His pulse pattered like a rabbit's. Had Sigga been lurking outside, waiting for Viktor to leave so she could mimic his appearance and pretend to barge back in? And if she had, was this the first time?

Hob felt foolish for thinking he'd won over the Grislander. It wasn't her nature to trust anyone, much less a newcomer to Her Highness's circle. He had to convince her he was an ordinary page. If her suspicions continued, she'd eventually uncover something. Despite Mr. Burke's assurances that he would pass any background checks, Hob still felt like he was hiding in plain sight. Closing his eyes, he massaged his temples.

Win Sigga over. Do that and you're golden. What would earn a bodyguard's trust?

Musing on this, he snatched his towel and headed off to the showers. He was due in Old College by eleven. As Oliveiro often quipped, not even death excused unpunctuality.

Hob was not late, but he had not dressed warmly enough. The March morning was raw, with wild gusts that shook the leafless trees. He stood with twenty other servants by a fountain in front of the Manse, an ancient manor that was Rowan's oldest building. None of the servants were dressed for the weather, having sacrificed warmth for smartness: gray topcoats, polished boots, and lambskin gloves. They stamped their feet, clutching various supplies for their outing. When one maid griped aloud, Oliveiro maintained that love of duty was enough to keep one warm. This earned a collective groan.

A page shivered next to Hob. "What are they waiting for?"

None of the court brats or the fine young gentlemen (otherwise known as FYGs) had poked their nose outside. Instead, they clustered within the Manse's comfortable foyer and parlors. Many of the FYGs and court brats lived there during the academic year. Hob envied them. He'd heard Manse bedrooms magically configured themselves to suit their occupants. One might bunk in a desert caravan, alchemical laboratory, or even a glass-domed observatory and gaze out upon the stars. Hob wondered what he'd get. Probably a shack in the Sentries.

"Why freeze your fanny off if you can wait inside?" said a maid from the Skeiner Isles. "The Faeregines aren't even here yet. Her Impyrial Highness must be powdering her nose."

Oliveiro cast a carping eye. "That's enough, Maeve."

Hob shifted his grip on the picnic baskets he was holding. "What is the Direwood? There's hardly anything on it in the handbook."

"That's because it's haunted," said a valet. "We're crazy to go in there."

"It is not haunted," said Oliveiro firmly.

"Then why's the gate locked and guarded?" asked the valet.

"Because wild animals live inside," Oliveiro explained. "Once, it served as a refuge for mystic creatures. During the Great War it was even a sanctuary for those who would found Impyria. But that was ages ago. The Direwood is no longer in active use."

"Then why don't they get rid of it?" said another page. "That's prime real estate."

Oliveiro rewrapped his muffler. "The Direwood is a living museum. You'll understand once we're inside. Consider yourselves fortunate. Precious few among the staff ever get a glimpse."

"Lucky us," said the page, stamping his feet.

"Ah," said Oliveiro. "Here they are."

Hob gazed across the quad to see the Faeregine triplets approaching, accompanied by their tutors and bodyguards. Violet and Isabel were in front, wearing robes of Impyrial crimson trimmed in black mink. Hazel walked behind, wearing a long quilted coat. Less glamorous, but more sensible.

As the Faeregines arrived, the court brats and FYGs emerged from the Manse and filed down its steps. Hob scanned their faces; on the surface these mehrùn were a diverse sampling of humanity descending from many different tribes and nations. But Hob knew that wasn't really true. Every court brat and FYG shared three things in common: magic, money, and heritage. The twelve families represented by this group controlled half of Impyrium's wealth.

Hydes, Jains, Eluvans, Menlos, Hans, Klausses, Chens, Castiles, Yamatos, Palantines, Khans, and Sylvas. Hob eyed them with polite disdain. None of these boys and girls had ever spent a second worrying whether a roof or meal awaited them. Legions of servants catered to every conceivable want. Meanwhile, they got to lord it over those with more talent simply because they belonged to the right family. But Hob imagined many of them didn't see it that way. They probably convinced themselves that they deserved their station, that they'd miraculously earned the wealth, connections, and privilege conferred upon them the instant they were born. His gaze fell upon a chinless Klauss boy mocking a master behind the man's back.

I'd like to see you sit séyu.

Once the Faeregines joined the group, Master Montague addressed the crowd. "We have a busy day, so please pay attention and be on your best behavior. That includes you, Lord Ezra."

Laughter as the Klauss boy reddened. Hob found that he rather liked the master, despite the homunculus on his shoulder.

"The Direwood is not our comfortable Manse," said the master pointedly. "It contains creatures that have had little contact with humans for many years. While most inhabit its remoter regions, there's no guarantee we won't encounter some near the ruins. We have taken precautions, but no amount of planning can overcome willful stupidity."

The master directed a glance at Lord Klauss, before setting off on a path that led around the Manse. The court brats and FYGs followed in chattering cliques.

Hazel passed Hob without acknowledging him whatsoever. This was not a surprise; no one was to know, or even suspect, that a page was tutoring her. Dàme Rascha, however, managed a nod as she conversed with Isabel Faeregine's tutor, a stooped faun named Archemnos. When Sigga strode past, Hob caught an unmistakable twinkle in the agent's eye.

The servants trailed after the young lords and ladies, passing by academic buildings and the school's temple. Along the way, they encountered scholars and students who had actually earned their place here. These individuals—some rather accomplished judging by their ornamented magechains—stepped aside to make room. They watched the pampered lordlings and ladies march past. Many darted sympathetic glances at the master.

Hob trailed behind, trying to decipher Sigga's look of amusement. Was the agent acknowledging he'd penetrated her disguise? Did she suspect he was a spy? If so, why didn't she simply have him arrested? Perhaps she wanted to toy with him, jiggle the lure until Hob led her to bigger fish. What if her apparent blunder this morning hadn't been a blunder at all? What if the Grislander wanted Hob to know she was onto him and goad him into panicking? Anything was possible.

Don't think yourself into knots. She doesn't know anything. You're just a page tutoring Her Highness. If you believe it, so will they. . . .

The academic buildings thinned, replaced by cemeteries and care-taker cottages. Statues lined the path, some so ancient that their faces had nearly worn away. Hob held his breath whenever he passed one by; they reminded him of the harbor boatmen.

Ahead was a wall of mossy stone some thirty feet high and hundreds of yards across. Behind it rose a hedge of trees that disappeared into a canopy of mist. Two guardsmen were waiting by an iron-banded door set into the wall. The master walked ahead to speak with them. All chatter died away as the heavy door was unlocked and heaved open. Even the trees seemed to grow hushed and watchful. No birds called, no squirrels scurried about. Beyond the gate, the path was dark as midnight.

"I don't want to go in there," said one of the FYGs, a gangling Eluvan in a green coat.

Others quickly voiced their agreement.

"Students in the mainstream program spend a week alone in the Direwood before graduating from Rowan," observed the master drily. "You are being asked to spend a single afternoon in the company of fifty classmates. I'm sure you can muster the necessary courage."

A tall, well-looking boy of perhaps sixteen, with a tangle of reddish-blond hair and a trace of beard pushed to the fore. Hob knew him from the handbook: Dante Hyde, nineteenth Earl of Eastmarch, firstborn son of Willem and Eva Hyde, and heir to the house that bore his name. Unlike the other FYGs, he wore a military coat and cavalry saber.

"I'll go first."

Violet Faeregine strode forward with Isabel at her elbow.

"Faeregines go before Hydes," said Violet. "We wouldn't want to upset the natural order."

Dante made a smirking bow. "How very brave of your Impyrial Highness." He nodded at the three Red Branch.

Another page nudged Hob. "This could be good," he whispered.

But no scene occurred. Her Impyrial Highness merely called for Hazel to join them, and the three sisters disappeared into the tunnel, followed by their bodyguards and tutors.

Once the Faeregines entered, there followed a fierce insistence on precedence. Dante and Imogene Hyde went next, followed by a flock of Castiles, Yamatos, and Menlos. After them came the Eluvans, Jains, and Hans, elbowing aside the Chens, Klausses, and Khans who would not allow a Palantine or Sylva go before them.

The servants were also slaves to hierarchy. Oliveiro went in first, followed by two ladies' maids, four valets, and six housemaids. The pages took playful pains to determine who came from the humblest origins and should therefore bring up the very rear. The victor would win a copper from his fellows. Hob liked his chances.

"I'm a bastard from the Sentries," he informed the others.

His neighbor shrugged. "My parents are cousins."

Hob handed over a copper. Once through the door, he found he was in a tunnel formed by dense, interlacing tree branches. The air inside was much warmer and very still. His nose tingled with the scent of pine sap and something else, a musky smell like an animal's den.

Despite years of squeezing down mine shafts, Hob found the tunnel claustrophobic. There was a sinister quality to the trees. Their types were familiar enough—oak and beech, black alder and ash—but their trunks and branches twisted so unnaturally that their forms looked bizarre, even tortured. Hob avoided looking at them.

The group's procession was eerily quiet. The only sounds were muffled footfalls in the carpet of wet, decaying leaves. Mercifully, the tunnel ended at an archway of intertwining yew branches half-strangled with creepers. When Hob stepped through, he almost dropped the basket he was carrying.

The Direwood was gargantuan, far larger than should have been possible for anything contained within Rowan's grounds. It was not merely larger than the school, the Direwood dwarfed the entire Sacred Isle.

Before Hob crumbling ruins stood surrounded by a sprawling savanna hemmed by dark forests and foothills. Beyond the foothills, a chain of snow-capped mountains loomed over the landscape, extending for miles until they disappeared into a misty haze. For a moment, Hob could only stare at them—there were no mountains on the Sacred Isle. A glimmer caught his eye and he gazed upon a nearby lake. Its surface sparkled gold as shafts of sunlight pierced the drifting thunderclouds.

"I'm dreaming," he murmured.

"No, Mr. Smythe, you are not," said Oliveiro. "You are witnessing a wonder of the ancient world." Taking Hob's baskets, he sent him to help the servants hammering stakes for the lunch pavilion. Hob took a spot nearest the master so he could hear what was said.

". . . ruins predate the Cataclysm itself. Back when the Direwood was known as?"

"The Sanctuary," said one girl.

"Very good," said the master. "Can anyone identify that glorious building over there?" He gestured to the remains of a foundation half-submerged in the lake.

"What glorious building?" said Dante Hyde. "It's rubble."

The master frowned. "Use your imagination. Anyone?"

"The Warming Lodge," said Isabel Faeregine, looking up from a sheet of paper.

"Excellent," said the master. "As Her Highness has discovered, your packets contain a map of the ruins. They're also each marked with a number indicating the team to which you're assigned. Take a moment to find your teammates."

The brats and FYGs milled about, forming ten clusters. Hob glimpsed Hazel looking very young in a group whose members Hob recognized from his handbook: Dante Hyde, a pale Jain count, a gorgeous Castile duchess wearing sable, and a springy Han girl who appeared to be Hazel's friend.

"Your teams," the master continued, "will take part in a contest we have devised to test your knowledge of the empire, this school's history, and the creatures that inhabit the Direwood. To win, your team must complete three challenges. These will not require magic, simply attentive and cooperative minds."

"What do we get if we win?" asked Imogene Hyde.

"My esteem," replied the master. "Full marks for the day. And these . . ."

One of his graduate assistants unveiled a lacquered case containing five quart-size jars. Each was filled with a muddy green sludge that pulsed and flickered with blue witchfire. Hob grimaced as a tiny, six-fingered hand emerged from the murk to press against the glass.

"*Homunculi mandragora*," the master announced proudly. "These come from my private stock and are superior to anything you'll find in the Impyria bazaars. Each member of the winning team will receive one, prebonded, as soon as their wings develop."

The atmosphere changed almost instantly. Homunculi were valuable creatures, prized by mehrùn as assistants and familiars. During Hob's Fellowship training, Ms. Marlowe said that some could share their senses or even minor powers with the human to whom they'd bonded. Students who had been gawking at the scenery now paid close attention.

A moment later, the master asked the pages to join the teams. They were to assist, run errands, and carry materials. Hob made straight for Hazel's group. He had no competition; most of his peers found Hazel's presence unnerving. The Castile girl promptly handed him her furs, which he stowed in the pavilion. The master held up his arms and made a final announcement.

"Your clue to the first challenge is in one of your packets. You may begin . . . now!"

"Who has it?" said Dante, looking about the group. The instant Hazel slid a red envelope from her packet, he snatched it away. "I'll be team leader."

"Why you?" said Tatiana Castile.

Dante ripped the envelope open and scanned the clue within. "Because I'm oldest, smartest, and a captain in the Vanguard."

"Hello?" said the Han girl. "Do we get to see?"

He tossed the paper at her and took the map from his packet.

"What's it say, Mei-Mei?" said Hazel.

Mei-Mei pushed a long strand of black hair out of her eyes and read aloud:

"Sons of earth with roofs of turf,
they plied their trades with skill;
with magic and coal, iron and gold
they made gifts for gods and men;
a head of hair, a ship so rare,
a hammer forged of thunder.
To claim your due, follow this clue
to their sacred shrine down under."

"What is that supposed to mean?" said the Jain boy, echoing Hob's sentiments. The clue was gibberish.

"It's pre-Cataclysm lore," said Dante, studying the map. "Old Norse. Dvergar lived here once, descendants of smiths that made things for the gods. You know, Thor's hammer; that ship the Hound sailed to the Sidh . . ."

The Jain boy laughed. "Oh come on. Those are fairy tales. They're useless."

Shading his eyes, Dante surveyed the ruins. "Congratulations, Namdu. You're not just dumb, you're wrong." His ice-blue eyes flicked to Hob. "Keep up, muir. Understood?"

"Yes, milord."

Dante strode off toward the ruins, his saber clanking at his side. The group hurried after with Hob in tow. Dàme Rascha had joined the other tutors under the pavilion, but Sigga followed at a distance, a rangy lioness trailing a herd.

Consulting his map, Dante led them down what must have been a main avenue. The dusty cobbles were worn, the buildings little more than sun-bleached skeletons. Turning a corner, they gave a start as a two-tailed cur gave a braying yelp and dashed off.

"Where are we going?" whined Tatiana.

Dante pointed at a crumbling facade near a withered yew tree. The nineteenth Earl of Eastmarch was not exactly personable, but did seem capable. All Hydes served in the military and it appeared this wasn't mere show like it was for so many FYGs. Ducking under an archway, Hob followed them into the roofless building.

"This was a smithy," said Dante, pointing at some rusted tools. "And the map says it belonged to dvergar. This is definitely the place."

Hazel peered about. "So I guess now we need to find the sacred shrine."

"That will be the forge," said Dante.

"How do you know that?" said Mei-Mei Han.

Dante smirked. "Because the Hydes haven't forgotten how to craft things. Forges are sacred to smiths. You would know that if your family didn't rely on silly Workshop gadgets."

Mei-Mei flushed and slipped something in her coat pocket.

Going to the opposite corner, Hob noticed Hazel was already poking about. Kneeling, she brushed some rubble away and raised a bronze ring. "There's something here."

Dante came over. "Of course. The clue said the shrine would be *down under*. Out of the way."

Hazel glanced sharply at him, but merely brushed the dust from her hands. Hob cleared his throat.

"Beg pardon, Your Lordship, but the princess should be addressed as *Your Highness*."

Lord Hyde spun about with a dumbfounded expression. Had he just been reprimanded by a page? His eyes wandered over Hob, as though finally registering him as an individual and not an anonymous servant. "Do you have any idea who I am?"

Hob bowed. "You are His Lordship Dante Hyde, nineteenth Earl of Eastmarch. And this is Princess Hazel Isis Faeregine, granddaughter of our Divine Empress. She is to be addressed as *Your Highness*."

Mei-Mei clapped a hand over her mouth and glanced at Hazel, who had flushed several shades of pink. Dante continued to stare at Hob, his expression wavering between disbelief and rage.

"Is that so?"

"I'm afraid it is," replied Hob pleasantly. "I'd be obliged if you remembered it."

Tatiana gave a delighted squeal. "And I thought today was going to be boring! Your Highness, you should have this page knighted." Laying her hand on Dante's arm, she spoke in a flirtatious undertone. "And you should simmer down, Lord Hyde. You know perfectly well your manners are appalling. Now, are you going to win me a homunculus or not?"

Dante tore his gaze from Hob and glanced at the pretty Castile girl. With an absent nod, he crouched and yanked the cellar door open. Peering within, he promptly covered his nose. "Something must have died." He turned to glare at Hob. "What are you waiting for?"

Removing his suit jacket, Hob rolled up his shirtsleeves and peered down the trapdoor. A rank, rotting odor wafted up from the blackness.

"I'll need a light," said Hob.

"Can't you conjure one?" said Dante. "Ah, but of course, you're only muir." With a flick of his fingers, he sent a ghostly green orb drifting down the opening. "Be quick."

The orb only gave off enough light for Hob to see his immediate surrounding, so he descended the winding steps cautiously, testing each with his toe. Ten steps. Fifteen. He squeezed past a brittle tree root. The smell was getting stronger.

The final step deposited him in a low room, where Hob had to crouch. At the edge of the orb's eerie light, he saw a forge. As he approached, the smell became overpowering. A dead animal—a badger or wolverine—was decomposing by the bellows.

Sitting atop the forge was a crucible with two scrolls poking out. Dante called down.

"What did you find?"

"Two scrolls," replied Hob.

"Bring them both."

Hob sighed. Cheating was bad; cheating like an idiot was infinitely worse. "Are you certain, milord?" he called.

"Now!" barked Dante.

With a sigh, Hob took the scrolls and squeezed back up the staircase.

"Give them here," growled Dante when Hob had reached the top.

Hazel spoke up. "If we take both, another team won't be able to find their next clue."

Dante broke the seal on one of the scrolls. "Nothing gets past you, *Your Highness*."

Hazel exchanged an incredulous look with Hob. "Two scrolls means only one other team has this challenge," she explained to Dante. "If they don't find a scroll down there, the master will know our team took it."

"That's right," exclaimed Namdu. "We'd be disqualified."

Dante's jaw tightened. For a moment, it looked like he was going to strike Lord Jain, but he merely thrust the unopened scroll back at Hob, who returned it to the forge.

When a thoroughly filthy Hob climbed back out, he found the team had left the roofless smithy and was now bickering in the street.

"It has to be that lagoon by the Warming Lodge," insisted Tatiana.

Once again, Dante consulted his map. "Don't be ridiculous. That's far too obvious. I'd guess Star Lake." He pointed at a distant peak.

"It would take us all day to hike up there," said Tatiana.

Dante sneered. "Afraid you'll get your shoes dirty? No wonder no one takes the court brats seriously."

Tatiana rolled her eyes. "That's exactly my point. It's the weekend. The masters know perfectly well they can't keep us more than a few hours before we throw a fit. Everything will be nearby."

"My family has a dinner across the channel," reflected Mei-Mei gravely. "If I'm not ready by six, my parents will kill me. But they'd kill the masters first."

Tatiana folded her arms.

Dante watched Isabel Faeregine give a triumphant whoop as she emerged from a ruin a few blocks down. "You'd better be right," he muttered.

The group set out for the lagoon beyond the ruins. They passed several teams along the way, some huddled in urgent conversation, others affecting disinterest as they trudged off to their next objective. Too eager to win or too cool to care. Hob felt a stab of pity for both camps. The wonders of the Direwood seemed to be lost on them. His gaze fell upon a herd of wildebeests grazing in the distance.

A vise closed about his upper arm. Hob turned to see Dante's gold-whiskered face inches from his own. The boy's tone was calm but the look in his eyes was murderous.

"Correct or contradict me again, and they'll find you rotting down that hole. Do you understand me?"

"Yes, milord."

Releasing Hob's arm, the boy strode ahead, his hand resting on his saber's pommel. The rest of the group was looking at the lagoon, except for Hazel, who gazed back at the stragglers with a frown on her pale pixie face. Brushing past her, Dante retrieved a pair of oars poking out from some reeds and tossed them into a rowboat beached upon the shore.

"What was that about?" said Hazel as Hob reached her.

"Nothing, Your Highness."

"Get in the boat, muir," said Dante coldly. "The clue says someone has to row to the middle and turn three circles."

"Very good," said Hob. "Would anyone care to come with me?"

Namdu balked. "I heard selkies live in Direwood lakes."

Tatiana peered at the water's wind-rippled surface. "Aren't selkies like mermaids?"

"No," said Mei-Mei. "Strovsky mentioned them last term. Selkies don't look anything like mermaids. They're water beasts."

Wonderful, thought Hob. Tossing his jacket on the grass, Hob dragged the boat into the shallows. Cold water pooled in his shoes, but he didn't care. He was seething over his exchange with Dante. It took all his restraint not to snap an oar in half.

"Wait."

Hob turned to see Hazel stepping carefully down the bank to join him. He helped her into the boat, where she sat almost comically upright with an expression of nervous expectation. Trudging through the muddy shallows, Hob pushed the boat past the reeds.

"Is this prudent, Your Highness?"

"Probably not," she replied. "But I'm not going to let the pages have all the fun. And Sigga's never far." She waved to the bodyguard, who was watching from a different bank. Hob had no doubt that if something went awry, the Red Branch would be at the princess's side in a blink. The agent could probably walk on water.

Pulling himself over the side, Hob figured out how to slip each oar into its lock.

"You don't have much experience with boats," Hazel said, pulling up her hood. Rain was beginning to fall in tiny droplets.

Hob looked over his shoulder to gauge the lake's center. "None, Your Highness. Where I'm from, water tends to be frozen." Pulling on the oars, he tried to mimic what he remembered of the skiff boatman's technique, but still managed to splash water everywhere. The boatman's job was safe.

Hazel did not speak again until they were well away from the bank. "What did Dante say to you just now?"

"Nothing that bears repeating, Your Highness."

"He's vile," she muttered. "All the Hydes are vile."

Hob said nothing. It would not do for a page to comment on such an observation. He focused on rowing and trying not to think of sea monsters. Water would never be his element.

"I think," said Hazel, "this may be the first time I've spoken to you alone."

"I suppose it is, Your Highness."

From the corner of his eye, Hob could see her fidgeting with her rings. "Our conversations in Rattlerafters have been very helpful. So . . . I guess I wanted to say thank you. And for speaking up for me just now."

Hob inclined his head. "You're very welcome, Your Highness."

He rowed in silence while drops began to patter on the water. The rain was cold, but not unpleasant. Hazel hugged her knees.

"We must look silly to you," she said. "Us court brats and FYGs. You've actually done things in your life. We mostly posture and pretend."

"Running an empire isn't pretend."

A smirk. "Ministers and magistrates run Impyrium, Mr. Smythe. Don't act like you don't know. I'd imagine you must think we have it awfully easy."

"No, Your Highness."

"You're lying."

Am I? Hob was not entirely certain. He pulled one oar to straighten the boat. "Most people get to do what they're good at. You have to be good at everything. That can't be easy."

She sat up suddenly. "That's *exactly* what it is," she exclaimed. "The expectations can be so suffocating. There are times I just want to . . ."

She trailed off, at a loss for words or something deeper. Hob glanced up. Hazel Isis Faeregine, granddaughter of the Divine Empress, was gazing over the side with a tiny, almost rueful smile. Hob was on the verge of feeling sorry for her when he remembered who she was and what her family represented.

Today you're Hazel. But someday, you'll harden into a Faeregine. It's only a matter of time.

Still, this was an opportunity. The princess was clearly in need of a friend.

"It's probably not my place to say this, Your Highness, but I have faith in you."

A mirthless laugh. "You're legally obligated to have faith in me, Mr. Smythe. Don't you know I'm a living god?"

Careful, Hob told himself. *You can't win this game today, but you could lose it. Lighten things up.*

"I don't know much about gods, but I do know you've been a quick study in Rattlerafters. I have faith you'll get done whatever it is you need to do. Just keep at it."

He couldn't decide if her nod was one of appreciation or simple acknowledgment that he'd spoken. A moment later, the princess gave a start and spun about to face the shore.

"Is everything all right?" asked Hob, puzzled by her behavior. One would have thought someone had just tapped her on the shoulder.

Hazel did not answer. She looked troubled, as though searching for something in the forest or foothills she could not quite pinpoint. After a few seconds, she faced forward again and glanced over Hob's shoulder.

"That must be it."

He turned to see a small buoy bobbing in the green water. "I guess we'll see if I can turn this thing." Gripping the oars, he pulled one and then both, one and then both, until he'd made three shaky circles.

"Now what?" he asked.

There was a shout from shore. Mei-Mei Han was jumping up and down, pointing frantically behind them. Hob turned to see something rising just beneath the water's surface. It raced toward them, a bow wave forming over a sleek brown head. How big was it? Twenty feet? Thirty? Was it a selkie? Some kind of whale? Hob looked for Sigga. Why wasn't she coming to help? The creature was closing rapidly. The bow wave disappeared as the beast submerged.

CHAPTER 10
THE REAPER'S TOMB

One gallant act is worth a thousand dinner dates.

—Toby the Smee, fabled bon vivant, raconteur, and lothario

"Hold on!" Hob yelled.

The boat gave a jolt as the creature rose beneath it and propelled them toward shore with heart-racing speed. Hob and Hazel clung to the boat's sides, uncertain whether to laugh or shriek as lake water streamed over the sides.

Poking his head up, Hob saw they were already near the reeds. If they didn't slow down, they'd crash onto the shore.

There was a barking laugh as the creature released them and wheeled its great bulk about. Peering over the side, Hob found himself staring into an intelligent black eye set in a seallike face. Rolling onto its back, the selkie flicked something into the boat before submerging. It was a packet wrapped in oilcloth.

"I guess that's the next clue," Hob said, handing it to Hazel.

"Thank you, Mr. Smythe. When I can breathe, I'll open it."

They laughed. For an instant, Hazel seemed like any other girl he might have known in Dusk. The moment was short-lived, however. Already, the boat was drifting through the reeds.

"Do you have it?" called Tatiana.

Hazel held up the packet.

"Woo-hoo!" cried Mei-Mei. "That was amazing!"

"Hurry up," said Dante. "Other teams are on their third challenge."

Hopping out, Hob dragged the rowboat through the shallows up onto the pebbled sand. His uniform and shoes were ruined, but it had been fruitful. A year's worth of Rattlerafters classes would not have yielded what a brief, terrifying trip in a rowboat had just done. Hazel Faeregine trusted him. Hob only wished that fact made him happier.

While Hazel and Mei-Mei opened the packet, Dante loomed over Hob, who was busy pouring water from his shoes.

"You row like a one-armed ostrich."

"Ostriches have no arms, milord."

Dante darkened. "I know they don't, muir. That's the joke."

"Thank you, your lordship. Jokes are always better once they're explained."

Tatiana snorted. Once again, Dante seized Hob's arm. His fingers dug in like talons.

"I don't care for your manner. If you served my family—"

"He doesn't," said a cold voice.

Dante wheeled upon Hazel. "What did you say to me?"

"He doesn't serve House Hyde," she said flatly. "Mr. Smythe serves House Faeregine. And if you don't release him, you're going to learn what that difference means."

Hob was astounded by Hazel's transformation. It wasn't physical— she remained a small albino girl in dripping red robes—but the look of contained anger upon her delicate features was positively unsettling.

Dante let go of Hob. "There certainly is a difference, Your Highness. Your house is dying and mine has never been stronger. There hasn't been anything special about the Faeregines for a thousand years. Everyone knows it but you. It wasn't *Typhon* that went up in flames. It was your whole damn family."

"What does that ship have to do with anything?" said Hazel.

A laugh. "Ask your uncle."

"I'm asking you."

The young earl spread his hands as though it pained him to share such unpleasant news. "Rumor has it Lord Faeregine poured his entire fortune into that ship. Losing one's own money is bad enough, but he lost a lot of other people's too." He tutted. "Wise men don't put all their eggs in one basket. Especially baskets stuffed with gunpowder."

"I don't know what you're on about, but say another word against my uncle and I'll—"

"You'll what?" Dante sneered. "Report me to the empress?"

Hazel took a step forward. A ghost of a smile appeared that did not extend to those rabbity red eyes. Her voice was barely a whisper. "No. But you will dearly wish I had."

Hob had his own doubts regarding the Faeregine mystique, but he could not pretend a chill wasn't invading his bones. He hadn't felt anything like it since séyu when he realized the Cheshirewulf was stalking him. Who was this Hazel?

Namdu broke the tension. "Are we actually going to solve this last clue or stand around arguing? I could use a homunculus."

Releasing Dante from her gaze, Hazel opened the envelope and read the clue aloud.

> "Earthbound Goddess, Winter's Bloom,
> the Reaper sleeps within her tomb.
> Stand within the ancient crown
> that rises from the barrow downs.
> Past Sphinx Rock and by Split Oak,
> you'll find her where the ravens croak."

"Lovely," said Tatiana.

Namdu gazed about the Direwood. "Where's Sphinx Rock?"

Mei-Mei was already studying her map. "I don't see it anywhere."

Hazel folded the clue and tucked it in her coat pocket. "I know where to go. It isn't far."

Dante laughed. "How's that, Your Highness?"

"I've been there before."

Mei-Mei plucked Hazel's elbow. "But you said earlier you'd never set foot in the Direwood."

"I haven't."

With that, Hazel turned and walked west, arms folded as she leaned into the wind. Her teammates looked at one another.

"Well," said Tatiana. "This took a turn for the weird. What should we do?"

Mei-Mei shrugged. "Follow her. Unless someone has a better idea."

The group trailed after Hazel, who was already thirty yards ahead. Pulling on his squashy shoes, Hob glanced back to see Sigga following once again. Bodyguards probably had to walk a delicate line between ensuring one's safety without being too intrusive. The Grislander must have known the lagoon contained a selkie and that the creature wasn't dangerous. Perhaps she'd come to the same conclusion about Dante Hyde.

Despite its fearsome name and reputation, the Direwood struck Hob as more wondrous than truly perilous. Court brats and FYGs lived in mansions and palaces. Of course they were ill at ease in the outdoors. But Hob grew up in rough country. Compared to the Sentries, the Direwood was a game park: wild enough to see some animals, safe enough for lords and ladies.

But that impression began to change as they left the grassy open and climbed a narrow trail into the foothills. Once again, as in the tunnel, Hob sensed a tense watchfulness in the woods. Hazel was plunging ahead, heedless of the branches and brambles. The others, however, proceeded more cautiously.

"Are there wolves in here?" asked Tatiana, flicking a leaf from her shoulder. "This seems like the kind of place that would have wolves."

Dante grinned. "Afraid you'll be devoured, Lady Castile?"

"It would be a tragedy to die before the May Ball. My dress is fabulous. Who are you taking, by the way?"

"Hazel Faeregine, if she'll have me."

The two laughed.

"Shh!" said Namdu, who flinched at every broken twig. Hob found this entertaining until he realized he'd be fetching Lord Jain new trousers if an owl gave an untimely hoot.

"What do you think of all that 'Reaper' business in the clue?" whispered Mei-Mei. "It symbolizes Death, doesn't it? I don't need a homunculus that badly. My family has imps."

"Don't you know anything?" said Dante. "It's a reference to Mina the Fourth. Historians call her the Reaper. Strovsky's always blathering on about her. She has a thousand tombs scattered around Impyrium. I've ridden past one in Eastmarch. Another one must be here."

This explanation did not comfort Namdu, who touched his forehead in a sign against evil. "She's supposed to be the worst one!"

To his chagrin, Hob found that he sided with Namdu. The Reaper was greatly feared in the Northwest, which still bore the scars of her brutality. Whole regions were still uninhabitable, their soil a toxic ash. According to legend, she was even more powerful than Mina I and infinitely more bloodthirsty. The Hauja called her Ankü—Hunger— and would not leave their huts during the winter solstice when her specter was said to walk abroad. That the former empress had been murdered and her body scattered meant nothing to the Hauja. They insisted the Ankü could not be killed, not truly. She would return someday, like some dark comet, to have her vengeance.

"That must be Sphinx Rock," exclaimed Mei-Mei. She pointed to a gap in the trees where a jutting slab of granite vaguely resembled a sprawling lion with a human head. They watched Hazel run her fingertips over it as she passed it by. "Next we need the tree."

They found it some thirty yards past the sphinx, a colossal oak that had been split down the middle by lightning. Through the gap, Hob saw Hazel clambering over a tussocky mound toward another crowned by black standing stones. Hob had come across two similar sites in the Sentries but never approached them. The stones looked evil, like fingers stretching forth from the underworld.

Hob turned to locate Sigga. Through the trees below, he glimpsed the ruins and the lake. But there was no sign of the Grislander.

A bird gave a throaty call from a nearby branch. Hob turned and saw Hazel standing amid the ring of stones. She turned slowly with a composed, inward expression. The others gathered about the mound's base, but none dared climb it. Even Dante's smirk had disappeared, replaced by a look of frank apprehension.

Crawwk!

A raven the size of a cat called from a nearby hornbeam. Another joined it in a noisy flap of wings. Three more called from a withered rowan tree.

Crawwk! Crawwk! Crawwk!

The hilltop was alive with a chorus of raven calls. Dozens of black shapes were settling on nearby branches to peer down with wet pebble eyes. Sharp beaks bobbed as they fluttered their wings and cried out.

Tatiana took a step backward. "What's going on?"

Mei-Mei shrieked as a swooping raven grazed her. The group backed away, crouching and covering their heads as more ravens began diving and wheeling about. But no bird would touch the standing stones or even fly between them. When Hob saw Hazel reach toward the nearest stone, he cried out for her to stop.

The princess did not hear him.

The instant she touched it, the ravens screamed and bolted in a shower of twigs and feathers. An unnatural stillness settled over the forest. Hob broke out in a cold sweat.

No one moved. Hazel appeared to be in a trance. Her fingers still touched the stone, which had begun to hum. The sound was barely audible, but Hob could feel dull vibrations, like an electric current, coursing through the rocks and soil. Where was Sigga?

When Hob turned to look for her, he froze. Something was crouching in the split oak's shadow. For a second, he tried to convince himself the silhouette was simply part of the tree.

But then it moved.

The figure inched forward, rising to its full height as it ducked clear of a branch. It remained shadowed, but Hob could see it wasn't human. It was taller than any man; and when it turned, it revealed a head crowned with broken stag antlers.

Its face was like something from a nightmare. With each cautious step, the features became clearer. Hob discerned a pair of yellow owl's eyes set within a primitive visage that was both goatish and manlike. Matted fur covered a powerful body that was stealing up the hill with unnerving stealth. No one else was yet aware of its presence. As for the beast, it did not appear to care about anyone but Hazel. Its eyes never left her as it crept toward the standing stones.

Was this all part of the challenge? Hob did not think so. Every instinct told him something was very wrong. This was no game.

Hob would have given anything for his Boekka. As it was, he didn't even have a pocketknife. Glancing at the ground, he saw a palm-sized rock several feet away. Just as he reached to seize it, Namdu caught sight of the stag-man and screamed.

The creature gave a hoarse bellow and rushed toward Hazel, scrabbling on all fours. Everyone but Hob scattered and fled from its path. Hob heard the others shrieking, but he couldn't turn back. He ran at an angle with the rock clutched in his fist. Catching sight of him, the stag-man bared a mouthful of yellowed teeth. Hob let the rock fly, striking it solidly on the cheekbone. The beast tumbled in the wet leaves, clutching its face before scrambling back up.

Hazel was still touching the standing stone, oblivious to her danger. Hob and the creature converged toward her. Hob was closer, but the stag-man was faster. Jumping a root, Hob planted his foot on a fallen tree and leaped.

He tackled Hazel at the waist, knocking her flat as something sharp—nails or talons—slashed the back of his unprotected head. An iron grip seized his calf and dragged him backward. Kicking furiously, Hob seized a branch and whipped around to go for the stag-man's eyes. He missed, but gashed its forehead. The beast leaped backward and crouched as though readying for a spring. Its owlish eyes flicked from Hob to something just past his shoulder. With a snarl, it turned and dashed off on two legs through the trees. Its howl echoed throughout the hills.

Panting and bleeding, Hob turned to see Sigga crouching over Hazel.

"Where were you?" he demanded. "Your orders are to protect her."

Sigga glanced at him. "You have no idea what my orders might be, Mr. Smythe. I suggest you contain yourself." The agent raised the princess to a sitting position. Now that Hazel was no longer touching the stone, she blinked dazedly up at the trees.

"She was here," Hazel whispered. "I could . . . hear her."

More howls sounded from the forest's depths. Sigga lifted Hazel like a doll.

"It's time we left, Your Highness." She cocked her head at Hob. "You all right?"

He touched a patch of blood oozing from a small gash over his ear. "Nothing serious."

A twig snapped. Hob turned to see a sheepish Mei-Mei peering with concern at Hazel. The others had also returned. Dante Hyde went straight for a scroll propped against one of the stones. "We still might have a chance."

"How can you think of the contest?" said Tatiana, her face pale and muddied. Leaves and brambles clung to her expensive clothes, but she did not seem to notice. Her eyes never left the woods. "Hazel could have been killed."

Dante cracked the scroll's seal. "She's fine. If anything, we should be upset. She's the one that touched the stone and summoned that thing. Maybe she called it herself. She's a freak."

"Go down to the pavilion," said Sigga curtly.

"I don't take orders from Grislanders."

Sigga shrugged. "Stay here then. I'm sure they'll find most of you in the morning."

Dante gazed uneasily at the darkening sky and the tangled trees. More howls sounded in the distance, answered by drums. Pocketing the scroll, he trotted back the way they'd come, trailed by Namdu and Tatiana. Mei-Mei walked with Sigga and Hazel. Hob came last, one hand on his cut, two eyes on the woods.

Halfway down the hill, Hazel insisted on being set down. While Dante ran ahead with the final scroll, the rest walked slowly through the ruins. Although Hazel was unharmed, she did not appear to know what had happened.

"You said *she was here*," said Mei-Mei quietly. "Who is 'she'?"

"What?" said Hazel. "I don't know what I said. I got dizzy and thought I might faint." She looked at Hob. "Why are you bleeding?"

"It's nothing, Your Highness."

Sigga spoke up. "A creature was prowling near the stones. Mr. Smythe protected you. We are in his debt."

The agent gave Hob a subtle but unmistakable nod of what? Thanks? Approval? He was still curious where Sigga had been when the stag-man appeared. He ruled out negligence—she hardly seemed the type. If her orders weren't simply to protect Hazel Faeregine, what were they? Perhaps she wanted to see what Hob would do when danger threatened, but that seemed a terrible risk to take with the princess's safety. For the moment, however, he could think of no better explanation.

Why had the stag-man wanted to attack Hazel? Had she broken some taboo by touching the standing stones? If so, why would the masters choose such a dangerous location for the clue? And what had caused her odd behavior? It wasn't just the Reaper's tomb; Hazel was behaving strangely well before they reached it.

Hob could make little sense of it all, but it was the first evidence he'd seen that there might be something unusual about Hazel Faeregine. This was just the sort of thing Mr. Burke and Ms. Marlowe wanted to know. He would have to file a report as soon as possible, and be sure to detail the spat between Her Highness and Dante Hyde. If what Dante said was true, the *Typhon* explosion had plunged Hazel's uncle—if not the entire family—into financial ruin.

When the rest of Hazel's team reached the pavilion, most of the other students were already eating. Hob fully expected to see a concerned Dàme Rascha hurry toward Hazel. But he was surprised to find a stiffly formal Oliveiro waiting for him.

"Mr. Smythe, I would like a word."

Confused, Hob followed him to a stand of trees out of earshot.

"Is there a problem, sir?"

Oliveiro glanced at Hob's clothes. "I won't comment on your appearance, for I know some pages were required to perform the messier tasks, but I am extremely concerned by your appalling behavior."

Hob blinked. "I don't understand."

"One of the lords has made a complaint." Turning, Oliveiro bowed to Dante Hyde, who strolled over from the pavilion.

"Sorry to raise a stink, Oliveiro, but I thought you'd want to know one of your own was behaving badly."

Don't lose your temper. Clasping his hands behind his back, Hob stared straight ahead. "May I ask what I did to cause offense?"

Dante gave a disbelieving laugh. "This is what I'm talking about, Olly! The muir doesn't know his place. Always talking back or making smart remarks. You're too soft on them."

Turning casually, Dante struck Hob a vicious blow across the face. Hob fell back a step, his cheek burning and eyes watering. He looked for Oliveiro to intervene, but the underbutler was looking gravely down at his shoes. Dante wiped Hob's spittle from his glove and considered him a moment before drawing his hand back.

"Perhaps one more for good meas—"

Dante's head snapped back as Hob cracked him squarely in the nose. He staggered and fell with Hob atop him. For Hob, the world had turned red. In the moment he wasn't a palace page or Fellowship spy; he was a Hauja who'd sat séyu and sworn to honor the four spirits whose images adorned his flesh. He did not care that Dante Hyde was mehrùn, or that he belonged to one of Impyrium's most powerful families. No one was going to strike him at his leisure. He'd rather die than endure such humiliation.

A strong arm clamped around his neck, choked off his air, and pulled him off. Struggling to free himself, he glimpsed a carabine lying on the grass. One of the guardsmen had him. Tiny spots were swimming before his eyes. He was losing consciousness. A voice cut through the buzzing in his ears.

"Release him."

The guardsman let go and Hob fell onto his hands and knees. Sputtering and coughing, he glanced up to see that Dante had drawn his sword. The earl was pale with rage. Spitting a gob of blood, he aimed a sweeping blow at Hob's head.

Clang!

Hob opened his eyes to see Sigga Fenn standing between them. How she moved so quickly, Hob could not imagine. Somehow the agent had parried the saber with one of her daggers.

"Get out of my way," Dante seethed.

"You will not harm Her Highness's servant," she said. There was no anger or threat in her tone. It was a calm statement of fact.

"He attacked me! For muir to strike mehrùn is punishable by death."

"Only if you press charges," she observed.

"I don't need charges," Dante spat. "I'm pronouncing judgment! It's my right as a Hyde."

Sigga was unmoved. "The Divine Empress pronounces judgment on those guilty of disloyalty. It's her right as a Faeregine."

Dante wiped blood from his nose. "What are you talking about?"

"Your words by the lake," said Sigga coolly.

"You were fifty yards away," he snapped.

"I heard them perfectly, milord."

Dante sneered. "A Hyde's word against some mercenary's from the Grislands? Let's bring the issue before a magistrate."

Mei-Mei Han crept forward holding a palm-sized device whose button she pressed. Dante's voice issued from its speaker: "There hasn't been anything special about the Faeregines for a thousand years. Everyone knows it but you. It wasn't *Typhon* that went up in flames. It was your whole damn family."

Dante's face darkened. "What is that thing?"

Mei-Mei sounded gleeful. "Just a 'silly Workshop gadget.'"

"Still care to insist upon your rights, Lord Hyde?" asked Sigga.

Dante hesitated and glanced at his classmates watching the scene from the pavilion. With a furious scowl, he turned back to Sigga and sheathed his sword. "No," he muttered. "This has all been a misunderstanding."

Glaring at Hob, he brushed grass from his coat and stalked off toward the hedge tunnel that led out of the Direwood. His sister, Imogene, ran after him. Oliveiro looked as though he wanted to crawl under a rock. Straightening his cuff links, he drew himself up.

"Mr. Smythe, that was shameful. Your service is terminated. Go and pack your things."

Hazel came forward with Dàme Rascha. "He will not," she said.

Oliveiro bowed. "Your Highness, I humbly beg to differ. The boy has—"

Hazel spoke softly but there was steel in her voice. "My family will not lose a valuable servant because Dante Hyde is a bully. If anything is shameful, it is a grown man who stands by while a boy is unjustly struck in his presence."

The underbutler opened his mouth and promptly shut it. He looked astonished, as did everyone else. Who was this girl and what had she done with Hazel Faeregine?

Master Montague cleared his throat. "I think we will end the day's expedition here. Mr. Oliveiro, the young man is bleeding and requires medical attention."

Sigga helped Hob to his feet and called over the guardsman who had not choked him. "Escort him to the palace. Lord Hyde may be waiting by the tunnel's exit. If any harm comes to this page, I'll hold you personally responsible."

The guardsman bowed. Sigga walked with them a ways, resting a hand lightly on Hob's shoulder. "Tell the healers to treat it with night-shade."

"Why?" said Hob. "What do you think that creature was?"

"I can't say for certain, but I intend to find out."

"I'll tell the healers," said Hob. "And thank you, Agent Fenn. I'd be dead if you hadn't stepped in."

She looked down at him. "You helped Her Highness. I helped you."

An hour later, Hob was sitting at his desk and trying not to pluck at his stitches. Viktor was also worse for wear and lay in his bunk, nursing various wounds from hall thumper. Hob had not yet told Viktor what happened in the Direwood; his roommate had enough on his plate. Evidently, Viktor and Zeke had lost badly—had not even reached the first marker. Since Zeke was being treated for a concussion, Viktor would have to brave the kitchens alone.

"They'll eat me," he reflected solemnly. "I've always known I'd die a casserole."

"The hags won't eat you," Hob assured him. "You've been sniffed."

This did little to console Viktor, who began planning his last will and testament. Hob was to get his best boots. There was a soft, almost hesitant knock at the door.

"It's open," said Viktor.

Hob turned to see Oliveiro in the doorway.

"May I come in?" he asked.

"Sure thing, Olly," said Viktor. "You're going to help me steal a pie. An underbutler would be a perfect decoy."

"I need to have a word with Mr. Smythe."

Viktor looked puzzled. "You want me to leave?"

"Stay put," Hob said to Viktor. "If you want to fire me again, go ahead, sir. No need for ceremony."

The underbutler looked pained. "Er, no. Nothing like that. I've come to apologize. In a stressful moment, I did what was proper instead of what was right. I deserved Her Highness's rebuke, particularly in light of additional facts that have come to my attention. I hope you can forgive me."

Hob was taken aback, even touched by the man's sincerity. He supposed he shouldn't have been surprised Oliveiro stood by when Dante struck him, obeying mehrùn was all he knew. Getting up, he came over to shake hands. "Of course, sir. No hard feelings."

Oliveiro was visibly relieved. "Thank you. Well, good evening, gentlemen." He glanced about at Viktor's side of the room, which was strewn with pummeled bread, socks, and other pieces of discarded armor. "You might consider tidying up."

"What was that all about?" said Viktor, once Oliveiro had closed the door.

"Nothing," said Hob. "I'm sure you'll hear all about it."

"I gather it's got something to do with that." He pointed at Hob's swollen knuckles and the stitches above his ear.

Before Hob could answer there was another knock.

Viktor groaned. "A guy can't even plan his will." Rolling off his bunk, he opened the door. "Who are you?"

A young, conspicuously formal voice answered. "Does Hobson Smythe live here?"

Hob tried to see who it was, but his roommate was blocking the doorway.

"What do you want with him?" said Viktor suspiciously.

"I have a message."

"Give it here."

"I've been ordered to wait for a reply," said the other party stiffly.

"Well then," said Viktor, "I guess you better get comfy." He shut the door in the visitor's face. "Smug little bugger. What's a Hyde servant want with you?"

He handed Hob a small envelope sealed with black wax. Hob guessed what it contained before he opened it.

His Lordship Dante Willem, Earl of Eastmarch, and Heir to House Hyde, demands satisfaction for a blow struck earlier this day. He will be waiting at the cliffs by Hound's Trench at two o'clock tomorrow morning. The muir may be assured the matter will be settled without magic. Show or be scorned for eternity.

Hob laid the card aside.

"What is that?" said Viktor uneasily.

"A challenge. To a duel."

"You're joking," said Viktor. "What, with that squeaker out there? I'll box his ears and send him off. He can't be ten."

"Not with a page. Dante Hyde."

Viktor's grin faded. "What?" Once again his eyes fell on Hob's knuckles. "Hob, please tell me you didn't sock an earl on the chin."

"More like his nose and teeth."

Viktor slumped on his bed, staring at Hob with an expression that alternated between horror and awe. "You really did this?"

Hob nodded. With his permission, Viktor read the card twice before setting it down. "I don't understand. Nobles don't duel pages. No offense, but you're not even mehrùn, much less a member of a Great House. It's beneath Dante Hyde to fight you. He can just have you hanged."

"He won't press charges."

"Why not?"

Hob did not want to get into the details. "Hazel Faeregine spoke up for me. I'm under her protection, but if I agree to meet Dante in a duel . . ."

"He can have his revenge," said Viktor grimly. "Well, I'll just tell that little twit outside you'll take your scorn with two lumps of sugar."

"No," said Hob, standing in his way. "Where I'm from you don't refuse a challenge. Not ever. You'd be hissed to the grave."

"You're not in Dusk," said Viktor pointedly. "And you're not some lord with family honor to uphold. No one even cares what a page's name is, much less whether he shows up to a duel."

"I'm not afraid of him."

"Then you're an idiot too," retorted Viktor. "Dante Hyde is a psychopath, Hob. He's not just some school yard bully and this isn't his first duel. He's killed people."

"So have I," said Hob softly.

"Well, maybe you did," said Viktor dubiously. "But this isn't some brawl in the Sentries. It's a gentlemen's duel and your opponent's been trained by the best swordmasters in Impyrium. You won't last two sneezes."

"Then you can have my best boots. But I'll need a second."

Viktor looked anxious. "I've never been someone's second in a duel. I wouldn't know what to do."

"You can start by telling the messenger I'll be at Hound's Trench," said Hob.

Viktor pursed his lips. "You're resolved on doing this?"

Hob nodded.

Viktor sighed. "Then I guess I'll be your second. I have only one condition."

"Name it."

"You have to steal a pie."

The two shook hands.

CHAPTER 11

HOUSE BLADES

Prime visited in the night. The uprising was finished.
No ruler of a rebel house would escape the empress's wrath.
Prime would find them all.
—*Impyrium, An Official History, Vol. XI*

It was past midnight when Hazel trudged back to the triplets' tower. Rascha had suggested rest after the Direwood (she was ready to throttle the master, who claimed nothing like this had ever happened before), but Hazel insisted on having their Mystics lesson. She had wanted a distraction after all the excitement and upset. Oddly enough, it proved to be a wise choice; despite her weariness, she had never performed better. Even Rascha found little to criticize.

She could have made the trip to her tower blindfolded. Sixty-seven steps from the art gallery to the library, thirty-three more to their chambers. She eyed the familiar portraits as she passed them: Mina I, Mina V, Mina XIII, and their grandmother Mina XLII. Between each, a sconce illuminated a bust of some long-dead archmage or magistrate. She paused at the final niche where a pen lay on a velvet cushion. Sigga stopped two stairs ahead.

"Everything all right, Your Highness?"

"Fine," Hazel murmured. She tapped the protective runeglass. It rippled red at the pressure. DO NOT TOUCH. "Do you know what this is?"

"I believe it's a pen, Your Highness."

Hazel's breath fogged the glass. "Not any pen. The Demon-Queen Lilith used it to surrender all of Zenuvia to the empire."

Sigga grunted. "The Three-Day War. But I thought that pen was in a museum."

"This is the real one," said Hazel. "My grandmother had it placed here to remind us what our ancestors accomplished. We didn't even have to send soldiers when Zenuvia refused to pay tribute. Mina the Fourth went herself. The Reaper versus a kingdom. And the Reaper won."

"She was formidable."

You have no idea, thought Hazel, staring at the pen in silence. *The Reaper was there today in the Direwood. A tiny part of her deep beneath those stones. All hatred and fury.*

"It's late, Your Highness. You should get some rest."

Nodding, Hazel continued up the stairs to where Omani Kruger, Violet's bodyguard, sat outside the triplets' outer door. He was the second oldest of the Red Branch, a two-hundred-year-old mountain from the Navaché slums with red-brown skin, a silver beard, and the warmest smile Hazel had ever seen. He was said to have over a hundred grandchildren, a fact that struck her as rather horrifying. Assassins should not have grandchildren.

He greeted them pleasantly, but his hand remained on his spear until Sigga relayed some private signal.

"Are you on dawn duty?" said Hazel to Sigga.

The agent yawned. "Omani's the lucky one. Good night, Your Highness."

Slipping inside, Hazel heard Agent Kruger secure the locks behind her. The door was almost six inches thick and brimming with warding spells. Nothing could get past it; no boots, ax, or battering ram.

Tossing her coat on the vestibule bench, Hazel was about to remove her shoes when she noticed firelight peeping beneath the door to the common room. She bit her lip; her sisters were still awake.

The minute she went through that door, Isabel would surely pepper her with questions, but what could she tell her? She had not been entirely truthful with Sigga in the stairwell. In the Direwood, she hadn't merely felt the Reaper's presence; she'd heard the goddess's voice.

It had started by the lake, a faint whisper on the breeze skimming over the grass. Hazel had gotten in that boat not merely to thank Mr. Smythe, but to get away from that ghostly hiss on shore. When she returned, however, the voice had grown stronger. It no longer carried on the wind but flowed like poisoned honey from the Direwood hills. Five simple words that nearly froze her heart.

I've been waiting for you.

The voice had been drawing her forward, luring her like that piper in Uncle Basil's storybooks.

Poking her head into the common room, Hazel saw her sisters sitting by the fireplace, talking quietly and sharing a plate of cookies. Neither was facing the door and they had yet to notice she was home. Slipping off her shoes, Hazel tried to tiptoe around and scoot quietly into her room. She made it three steps before Isabel swiveled about.

"There you are," she said. "I can't believe Rascha kept you up so late after everything that happened. Were you at Tùr an Ghrian?"

Hazel forced a yawn. "Yes, and I'm exhausted, so—"

"Sit down," said Violet, pointing at the couch. "We want to talk with you."

"It will have to wait until morning," said Hazel. "Like I said, I'm tired."

Violet stood. "And like I said, sit down."

Hazel laughed. "Or what? You're going to rub burrs in my hair like you did when we were six?"

"If you're going to act like you're six, I just might," Violet retorted. "Sit down."

"Listen," said Isabel soothingly, "we just want to make sure you're all right. What happened in the Direwood?"

A lump formed in Hazel's throat. She was tired and frightened and in no mood to be interrogated. "I don't want to talk about it right now, Isabel. All I want to do is go to bed."

She turned to go into her room, but Violet strode forward. "Sit down this—"

"Leave me alone!"

As Hazel spoke, the fire roared up, sending a crackling shower of embers onto the hearthstones. Hazel glared at her sisters, who looked stunned by her outburst. Neither spoke as she stormed into her room.

Once inside, she locked the door and tapped it after making an intricate sign with her fingers. It was not precisely the same spell Rascha had taught her last week. Hazel's instincts led her to make some modifications. No more hairpins would be picking this lock.

She went straight for the painting. For the time being, it was hidden behind a large portrait of Mina VII that hung above the fireplace. Mina IV sat comfortably between her great-granddaughter's canvas stretchers. Sliding the painting free, Hazel propped it against the pillows on her bed.

She glared at it, breathing hard. "Was that you talking to me in the Direwood?" she demanded.

The longer Hazel stared at the moonlit image, the more foolish she felt. Did she actually expect it to answer? Slowly, her breathing steadied. Unballing her small fists, she assessed the portrait as a sane person might.

She found it impossible to reconcile that girl with her reputation. Mina IV was responsible for both the greatest and most appalling deeds in history. The young empire was on the verge of dissolution before she came to power. Muir were in open revolt and the Great Houses, who thought little of Mina III, undermined the empress's authority by establishing the Triad, a legislature whose laws openly defied her edicts. Despite her ineffectiveness, Mina III's advisers opposed her decision to abdicate in favor of her daughter. None of them believed that gentle, soft-spoken Arianna could possibly deal with the challenges at hand.

They were mistaken.

The very hour she became empress, Mina IV destroyed the Triad in a storm of witchfire so hot it melted the building's stone into glass.

Everyone inside—every noble who had boycotted her coronation—was burned alive. The act sent a shock wave throughout Impyrium. No one suspected the girl possessed such power, much less that she would wield it in such fashion. Within the week, all the surviving members of the Great Houses prostrated themselves before the Divine Empress and swore everlasting fealty to the House of Faeregine.

Within two years Mina IV had conquered every last outpost of rebellion, leaving trails of blight and desolation that remained to this day. Half the global population died during the purges that would give the empress her fearsome epithet. Not content to merely salvage her empire, the Reaper expanded it by swallowing up Zenuvia and portions of the Grislands. And once this was done, she solidified her dominion with unprecedented feats of magic.

The list was seemingly endless. The Reaper had fashioned the four Otherland Gates, permanent portals to other worlds. It was her magic that ensorcelled the dragons who guard them, her sorcery that held the Shibbolth at bay when the ancient demons sought to enter this world. When her enemies sent assassins to slay her, the Reaper brought forth Prime the Immortal to obliterate them. The power she wielded was both awesome and terrifying. As Hazel mused on these facts, her eyes adjusted to the dark room. The painting's finer details began to emerge, so fine that Hazel fancied a peculiar glint in the eyes of the painting's subject. It imbued the portrait with an eerie, almost lifelike quality. By moonlight that innocent face now looked mocking, even sinister.

I've been waiting for you.

Again, Hazel heard the whisper, but she could not be certain if it was a trick of the mind. She promptly conjured a glowsphere which bathed the room in a cheerful radiance. Once again, the painting's subject was lifeless, her eyes mere daubs of pigment. If there had been a spirit lurking in the canvas, the light had banished it.

Don't be ridiculous, Hazel told herself. There never had been any spirit—just her weary mind projecting her fears. The Reaper was dead, murdered over twenty-six hundred years ago by the Atropos, an assassins' guild working in league with muir revolutionaries. That was the official history. The unofficial history, popular with conspiracy theorists, was that the Faeregines themselves were behind the plot, that the family had secretly hired and equipped the killers in a bid to save the world—and their dynasty—before the Reaper destroyed them both.

It did not matter which version was true: the Reaper was no more. Her body was scattered among a thousand consecrated graves. She was never coming back.

Hazel froze as a knock sounded behind her.

Isabel's voice called softly through the door. "Hazel?"

A second knock launched Hazel into action. Whisking the portrait off the bed, she quickly stashed it behind the larger painting. Isabel was now trying to turn the doorknob. A moment later, something rattled in the lock, but the door refused to give. Hazel felt a twinge of pride as the rattling ceased and the knocking resumed.

"Hazel, please open up. Violet didn't mean to be rude. We're just worried about you. Please come out. Do it for me."

Hazel bowed her head. She couldn't say no; Isabel was always there for her.

"Just a minute," she said, and quickly changed into the nightgown Olo had left on her bed. If she was going to be interrogated, she might as well be comfortable.

She opened the door to find her sister holding out a sugar cookie. "A peace offering," Isabel said.

Hazel took it and followed Isabel into the common room. Violet was now sitting on the chaise beneath a blanket. She scooted in her feet, signaling that Hazel could sit beside her. This was the closest thing to an apology Violet could manage, and so Hazel settled next to her and shared the blanket.

Isabel sat in the nearby rocker. "Let's try this again," she said. "Are you really all right? Mei-Mei said some kind of goat or stag creature tried to attack you."

"I'm fine," said Hazel. "It never laid a finger on me."

Isabel frowned. "No thanks to Sigga, I hear. Where was she?"

"No idea," said Hazel. "All I know is that she was there when I could make sense of things. I'd nearly fainted."

"I spoke with the empress," said Violet. "Sigga takes idiotic risks. She isn't suited to be your bodyguard."

Hazel could not help but smile. "I'm touched, Violet. Last I heard, you didn't think I needed one."

Isabel shot Hazel a pleading look to desist. "And what did Grandmother say?"

Violet gave a dissatisfied sniff. "She is 'perfectly content' with Sigga's performance."

"There," said Hazel. "Can I go to bed now?"

"Not yet," said Isabel. "Something weird is going on with you, and not just today in the Direwood. It's been weeks, and we're going to get to the bottom of it tonight."

"You can start," said Violet, "by telling us what you were doing just now."

Hazel sighed. "Getting ready for bed."

"Not that," said Violet. "What have you been doing with Rascha at all hours, every day since New Year's?"

"Studying Mystics," said Hazel, finishing her cookie.

Isabel nudged the plate on the coffee table toward her. "Come off it, Hazel. I study Mystics. Violet studies Mystics. That's not all you're doing."

"Yes, it is," said Hazel, selecting another cookie. She was starving.

Isabel gave a dubious snort, but Violet held up her hand. "Let's pretend that's true. Why do you suddenly have to binge on Mystics when you're failing everything else?"

Hazel wiped a crumb from her chin. "I am not failing everything else. Montague wrote 'better' on my last essay. He even underlined it."

"Congratulations," said Violet drily. "The point is, why has Mystics—"

"Become an obsession?" said Isabel pointedly.

Hazel groaned. "I knew this day would come. You've finally started finishing each other's sentences."

"Please answer the question," said Isabel.

Hazel closed her eyes, the cookie clutched lightly between her fingertips. She just didn't have the energy to stonewall. If she held out long enough, Violet might get bored and disengage, but not Isabel. She exhaled slowly.

"I have to pass the Mystics exams by our birthday."

"We all have to pass Mystics exams," snapped Violet.

Hazel clarified. "I have to pass *official* examinations. Third Rank."

Isabel chuckled. "Come off it. You're joking."

"I'm not."

Violet shifted, claiming the entire blanket. "If you're going to lie, at least make it plausible. There aren't five hundred Third Ranks in all Impyrium. Rascha's lost her mind."

"Rascha's not the one pushing me," said Hazel.

A pause. Isabel's eyes widened. "The Spider?"

Hazel said nothing. She didn't have to. Who else but their grandmother could impose such a mandate?

Violet turned so that she faced Hazel directly.

"Why would the Divine Empress demand such a task of you?" she asked.

Hazel hesitated. "She thinks I have the Old Magic."

"You're a Faeregine," said Violet coolly. "Of course you have the Old Magic. *Every* Faeregine has the Old Magic."

Oh dear.

Hazel took a deep breath. "I think what Grandmother meant is that I might truly have the Old Magic. That it's not just something our family says. Or pretends."

Violet swatted this notion aside. "Ridiculous. You're no more magical than either of us."

"How do you know?" said Isabel. "We're only allowed to practice magic with our tutors. It's been years since you've seen Hazel do anything."

"Maybe so," said Violet. "But I don't recall her being some prodigy at fairy lights."

Isabel scraped a cookie's fudge with her upper teeth. "People thought the Reaper was muir until she was our age. Her mother almost disowned her. Archemnos says some talents don't emerge until you're fully grown."

"Maybe for some," said Violet. "I've had the Old Magic since birth. Why do you think Grandmother chose me to succeed her?"

Isabel considered. "Reverse alphabetical order?"

There was no point telling Violet that her claims were absurd. While there were many powerful sorceresses among the Faeregines, Rascha believed the last to truly possess the Old Magic was Mina XXV, a beloved ruler whose subjects called her the Monarch. She was the last Faeregine empress to perform truly rare and powerful magic before numerous witnesses. Like the butterfly for which she was named, the Monarch's reign was beautiful and brief. Mortemagia claimed her at seventy.

"Listen," said Hazel wearily, "I don't want to argue. You asked what I've been doing and I told you. Frankly, I feel better that you know. And now, I'm going to bed."

"Not so fast," said Violet. "I want a demonstration."

Just like the Spider, thought Hazel. "You're not empress yet, Violet, or have you forgotten?"

An acid stare. "I will be, Hazel. Or have *you* forgotten?"

An uncomfortable silence ensued while rain pattered on the roof.

"I thought we were going to play nice," said Isabel. "By the way, I'm hurt that neither of you has congratulated me on winning the master's challenge. I had half a mind to name my homunculus Haziolet. Maybe Viozel, but now . . ."

Violet made no attempt to laugh. "Our names don't go together. They never have."

Hazel ignored the barb. "Congratulations, Isabel. My team got all tangled up."

"I'll say you did," said Isabel. "I can't believe Dante had the nerve to say those things about our family. Such lies!"

Hazel observed that Violet had gone very pale. Apparently, Isabel noticed too.

"What's the matter?" asked Isabel.

Violet blinked as though jolted from some private nightmare. "Dante wasn't lying."

Isabel made a face. "Oh, what does he know? Dante's a pig. No, forget that—pigs are too good for him. He's a mosquito. Revolting and useless."

"Careful," said Violet. "You might end up wedding that mosquito."

Isabel's grin froze. "Don't even joke about something like that."

Violet rubbed her temples. "I wish I was. Hazel's not the only one with a mandate. I have to sit through briefings with bankers, magistrates, military advisers, house patriarchs. The empress is teaching me how to rule. That's how I know what Dante said about Uncle Basil is true. It's also how I know Dante's father inquired about your marriage rights." She gave her sister a sympathetic glance.

Isabel smacked the table. "Never! I'm not even sure I like boys, much less Dante Hyde."

"It has nothing to do with what you *like*." Violet sighed. "It has everything to do with whatever arrangement the empress and Lord Hyde reach. Your involvement may be required."

Isabel looked truly horrified. "How is Lord Hyde in a position to require anything of us?"

Violet fixed her sister with a hard look. "Because our brilliant uncle invested millions of the bank's solars on *Typhon*. Lord Hyde's rallied the stockholders and they're demanding a change of control or restitution from our family coffers. Even more humiliating, Uncle

Basil personally borrowed money to buy mountains of silk that went up in flame."

"Can't the Spider just take care of it?" said Isabel. "We must have enough treasure to cover Uncle's losses."

Violet laughed. "Most of it's already committed. These aren't the old days, Isabel. We need to find who's responsible and make them pay, or we'll have to pay with whatever assets the family has. Like it or not, *you* are one of those assets."

Isabel looked stunned.

"But the newspaper said the explosion was an accident," said Hazel.

"Of course it did," said Violet wearily. "That's what we told them to report. But nobody actually believes it. You should hear the arguments behind closed doors. Absolutely vicious. Uncle Basil's practically begging Grandmother to declare war on the Lirlanders. He's convinced the demons are behind *Typhon* and the crimes at the Lirlander Vault. You both heard Lord Kraavh on New Year's. He was openly hostile."

Isabel gave a sudden cackle. "I can't be sold off like some broodmare. I'm second in line for the throne. No potential empress has ever gotten married."

Violet's response was measured. "Times have changed. In the past, we never had to do anything like that. We also never had to consider surrendering the bank or Lirlander Seals."

Isabel blanched. "That couldn't actually happen."

"Everything is on the table," said Violet pointedly. "And if Grandmother can settle this mess by marrying you off, she will."

Violet rose from the chaise and stretched. "Try to look on the bright side. Dante's handsome, rich, and—unlike the other FYGs— he has something like a spine. I almost feel sorry for that page." She covered a yawn. "And now I'd better go to bed. Lady Sylva's picking me up at nine. We're going cross channel to ride in a motorcar." She glanced at Hazel. "Thanks for sharing your 'big secret.' You must feel very special."

With that, Violet disappeared into her room. Once she'd locked the door, Hazel toppled facedown on the chaise.

"Why is she like that?" she groaned. "It's like she's incapable of ending a conversation without a teensy dig. For a minute she was almost . . . human."

"Which minute was that?" quipped Isabel. She took another cookie and eased down onto the bearskin rug by the chaise. "Is that true what you said about the Mystics exams? Third Rank and all that?"

Hazel remained facedown. "Yes."

"How is that possible?" said Isabel. "Third Ranks have to be able to shadow walk and hydeshift and a million other things I can't fathom. Can you actually do those things?"

"I'm trying," said Hazel. She was intensely private where her magic was concerned. Discussing it made her feel exposed and vulnerable. Even with Isabel.

"I'd love to see you do something," said Isabel. "Can you conjure a scrying orb?"

"Sometimes. You need perfect concentration and Rascha says I'm 'drifty.'"

"Forget it." Isabel sighed. "I just wanted to see my future husband get skewered. Not that there's any real chance of it."

Hazel peeped over the armrest. "What are you talking about?"

"I thought everyone knew, but I guess you've been off with Rascha." Isabel picked bits of cookie from her hair. "Dante challenged that page to a duel and the page accepted. Not very bright, but undeniably plucky. Cute too, in a muirish kind of way."

Hazel tried to remain calm. "When is the duel?"

"Two o'clock at Hound's Trench. Everyone's sneaking out for it. Horrible weather, but I wouldn't mind watching through a scrying orb."

Hazel twisted toward the grandfather clock. Not yet one. She jumped up from the chaise.

"What are you doing?" said Isabel.

Hazel had already retrieved her shoes. "I have to stop this. Hob won't stand a chance."

"Who's Hob?"

"The page," said Hazel, turning pink. "I know him. He's been tutoring me on the Muirlands. He's why I'm doing better in Montague's class."

Isabel stared. "A *page* is tutoring you?"

"Yes," said Hazel irritably. "He's not just a page. He's brilliant."

Isabel clucked her tongue. "That's why you spoke up for him. I'd wondered."

"Yes. And I'm not going to let Dante murder him."

"You can't interfere with a duel," said Isabel. "Not even the Spider meddles with them. It's custom."

"Custom is stupid," snapped Hazel. "Hob's just a page. He doesn't know what he's gotten himself into."

"Then he shouldn't have accepted."

"He's too proud," said Hazel. "He's clawed his way up from nothing, Isabel. No money, barely any family. He's hunted Cheshirewulfs! He taught himself history and mathematics and placed first in the Provinces. Do you know how hard that is? I won't let someone like that be butchered by Dante Hyde."

"He'll have a fighting chance," said Isabel. "Dante won't use magic. It's blades only."

Hazel gave her sister a contemptuous look. "Dante's brilliant with a sword. Hob's probably never even held one. Even if he had Bragha Rùn, he . . ."

Isabel waved a hand in front of her eyes. "Hello?"

Hazel seized her sister's hand. "That's it!" she exclaimed. "That's what we'll do. We'll give him Bragha Rùn!"

Isabel extricated herself from Hazel's grip. "You've lost your mind. Let a page use Bragha Rùn? It's the best blade in Impyrium."

"Exactly!" said Hazel, hopping excitedly. "No one's ever lost with it!"

Isabel continued looking at her as though she'd gone insane. She calmly reminded Hazel that Bragha Rùn was not so much a sword as a holy object crafted from priceless materials and riddled with ancient enchantments. Setting its inestimable value aside, there remained the pesky fact that Bragha Rùn was the Faeregine House Blade.

This last point reminded Hazel of something, a tale or poem she'd read. Hurrying to a bookcase, she snatched up a book containing children's versions of popular Faeregine stories. She rifled through the pages and held it up in triumph.

"Look!"

Isabel stared at the colorful illustration, one of their early favorites. It showed an armored man standing over a vanquished foe. "And your point is?"

"Precedent," Hazel declared. "Mina the Fifteenth allowed Lord Branwen to fight with Bragha Rùn on her behalf."

Isabel whacked Hazel on the head. "She was empress."

"She was a Faeregine," Hazel retorted. "Any Faeregine has a right to Bragha Rùn. And if one Faeregine was able to lend it, then it follows another can too."

Isabel groaned. "Branwen was championing the empress! This isn't anything like that."

"Hob protected me in the Direwood," said Hazel. "When Dante was being Dante, Hob insisted that he call me *Your Highness*. When they fought, he was defending Faeregine honor." This last part stretched the truth a twinge (the altercation had more to do with Hob's honor than the Faeregines'), but Hazel didn't care. There was nothing wrong with a white lie in a just cause.

Isabel took the book from her. "This sounds like it has more to do with a boy than family honor. I'm not letting you give our House Blade to a servant, Hazel. The Spider would have us whipped."

Hazel lifted her chin. "I'd rather be punished than sit by and do nothing."

"Well, aren't you noble," said Isabel sarcastically. "Let me ask you another question, O Righteous One. Let's assume we actually pry Bragha Rùn from its keeper—a detail you seem to have overlooked. But let's say we've got it and hand it over to this page, a boy you admit has probably never held a sword. Are you with me?"

Hazel nodded.

"Splendid," continued Isabel. "So what happens if our brave little page gets slaughtered? Have you considered that? No one wielding Bragha Rùn has *ever* been defeated, Hazel. That's its mystique. That's why no one ever challenges Faeregines to duels. Think of what Violet was saying just now. Our family has enough troubles without newspapers reporting that our invincible House Blade is no longer invincible."

"But he won't lose," said Hazel. "I'm sure of it. Hob's tough, Isabel. Really tough. You saw him. He'd have beaten Dante bloody if that guardsman hadn't grabbed him. He might be inexperienced with a sword, but that's where Bragha Rùn evens things out. It can parry or cut through anything. They say you even move faster when you're wielding it!"

Isabel would not budge.

"Fine," said Hazel. "Let me ask *you* a question for a change."

"Dazzle me."

"If Hob wins, would you have to marry Dante?"

Isabel opened her mouth and promptly shut it again. "No," she conceded. "He'd be dead or disgraced. His father would probably disown him if he lost to a muir page."

Hazel curtsied. "I rest my case. Anyway, I'm getting Bragha Rùn. With or without you."

Isabel cocked her head. "And how do you intend to get past Omani? You know he won't let you leave here."

Hazel went to get her coat. "If you want to see some magic, here's your chance."

Tom struck one o'clock as the sisters slipped inside Hazel's bedroom, now bundled up for the rainy trek to Hound's Trench. Hazel's pulse was racing. She knew she was doing the right thing, knew it as surely as she'd known anything in her life.

Oh, but if something went wrong! Even if everything went smoothly, there would be consequences. But the alternatives were worse. She was sneaking out of the palace in the middle of the night to lend a servant the Faeregines' ancestral blade. She was insane.

But she was also alive, more vividly and deliciously than she could remember. If she distilled her twelve years into a single moment, it could not possibly rival this giddy, terrified elation. The world seemed new.

"Whatever you're going to do, hurry up," hissed Isabel. "I'm having second thoughts."

"Okay, okay! Shut the door."

When it was closed, Hazel waved a hand at her little fireplace. Golden witchfire roared up within it, projecting their shadows upon the walls. She paced back and forth, thinking through her options. This was not the time for improvisation. Raw sorcery could yield the most powerful results, but it was too unpredictable, especially with Isabel present. Hazel's Mystics repertoire was limited, but those spells would be more reliable. The incantations and outcomes were well documented. Far less risk.

But which spell?

She eliminated any that required rare components—no time to gather those. And it would have to be something that would allow Isabel to join her. . . .

"I've got it!" she exclaimed. "Take my hand."

Isabel did so hesitantly. "What are you going to do?"

"Stonecrawl," said Hazel. "I read about it last week. Raszna discovery. Ninth century."

"I don't care who invented it. What does it do?"

"It makes us semicorporeal in stone. We can sink through the walls down to Founders Hall. Then we can make our way to the throne room. That's what should happen, anyway."

"What do you mean 'should'? Haven't you done it?"

"No." When Isabel tried to pull her hand away, Hazel held firm.

"It will be okay. There's nothing tricky about the verbalization or gestures. I just need perfect concentration or we'll be entombed. Instant death."

"Perfect concentration?" cried Isabel. "Didn't Rascha say you were 'drifty'?"

"Did she? I wasn't paying attention."

"That isn't funny."

Hazel squeezed her sister's hand. "Isabel, relax. This is what I do . . ."

Casting her gaze at the fire, Hazel let her mind slip into that beautiful, abstracted state where her magic flowed most freely. Coaxing the fire's heat toward them, she felt its energy loosen their particles, so when the proper words were spoken, their bodies could trickle through stone like flour through a sifter. With her finger Hazel drew the runes of earth and air, of iron so they might sink, of spirit so they might float, of will so they might emerge whole and unscathed. Once this was done, she led Isabel to the wall beside her bed and spoke the incantation. Translated into common Impyrian, it had an almost jaunty sensibility:

> *"Through rock and stone*
> *My flesh and bone*
> *Shall rise and sink with ease,*
> *So lithe, so light, so merry and bright*
> *Like a cork upon the seas."*

With a firm grasp on Isabel, Hazel walked straight into the wall, pulling her sister behind her.

It was like stepping into sludge. Everything grew hazy, but Hazel found she could breathe, and even see through the surrounding stone as though it were cloudy gelatin. Far below, she could make out dim pinpricks of light in orderly patterns—Old College streetlamps.

Hazel took two sluggish steps forward and then turned around so they'd have a better view of their destination. And with that, the sisters began to sink.

And sink.

And sink . . .

Progress was agonizingly slow, a foot per second at best. Given the tower's height, the trip should have taken some eight minutes, but that didn't account for the snaillike detours around windows and archways. They'd be hard-pressed to retrieve Bragha Rùn and reach Hound's Trench by two o'clock. Hazel tried not to dwell on this, tried not to picture Hob marching over rainy grounds to his death.

One thing at a time. Concentrate.

Some fifty feet below, Hazel saw the massive braziers outside the entrance to Founders Hall. Two guardsmen were posted nearby. The girls couldn't simply pop out next to them—particularly as one was busy picking his nose. Men were disgusting! Hazel tugged Isabel toward a staircase where they could exit unseen.

As they inched along, Hazel reflected that "Stonecrawl" should have been called "Stoneooze." Their destination was tantalizingly close, but she could go no faster. The staircase was empty at present, but what if somebody came along? Just a few more seconds . . .

Hazel ended the spell the instant they'd stepped entirely out of the wall. Solid once again, the sisters took deep, grateful breaths. Isabel mopped sweat from her forehead.

"I just discovered I'm claustrophobic," she gasped.

"You did great," Hazel whispered. "We don't have much time, so we make straight for Bragha Rùn. Agreed? If anyone stops us, you do the talking. You're bossier."

Isabel grinned.

Smoothing their coats, the two walked briskly down the final stairs and rounded the corner. Instantly, the two guardsmen snapped to attention. The princesses walked right past them, their footsteps echoing in the vast corridor.

Maybe they won't say anything, thought Hazel. A second later, she winced.

"Your Highnesses?" called one of the guards.

Isabel stopped and turned. "Yes?"

The soldier bowed. He looked nervous, as well he might. Impyrial Guardsmen never addressed members of the royal family. Not unless they were spoken to.

"I'm sorry, but shouldn't you be accompanied by Agents Rey and Fenn?"

"We have a private and pressing engagement," Isabel replied.

"Of course, Your Highness. But I must ask you to wait while I contact my superior. There are protocols."

Isabel drew herself up. "What is your name?"

He saluted. "Private Sarcosa."

"Tell me, Private Sarcosa, do protocols permit the picking of one's nose while on active duty?"

"Of course not, Your Highness."

Isabel held up her thumb and forefinger. "And what about flicking the proceeds into a thirteenth-century vase?" She mimicked his technique.

The man turned a sickly gray.

Isabel ceased her demonstration. "Spare us a lecture on protocols and we'll skip the one on hygiene. If you're concerned about our safety, you may escort us to the throne room."

Shifting his carabine, the guardsman fell in step a few paces behind them. No one else challenged the pair as they marched through the palace's vast but eerily quiet halls.

The throne room stood empty except for several imps. The sisters made for an alcove of polished black marble.

"Stay here," Isabel commanded their escort. "Better yet, fetch two horses and have them waiting in the winter gardens."

He demurred. "Your Highness—"

Isabel repeated her flicking motion. Private Sarcosa departed on his errand.

"Nicely done," said Hazel. She wasn't overly fond of horses, but every Faeregine learned to ride at an early age. On horseback, they could reach Hound's Trench with time to spare. All they needed to do now was claim Bragha Rùn from its keeper.

The girls paused before the alcove's arch where a phrase was chiseled in pre-Cataclysm Latin:

PRIMUS ULTIONIS

Isabel exhaled. "*Vengeance first*. That always gives me shivers."

"It's supposed to," Hazel whispered. "Have you ever crossed the threshold?"

"No."

Hazel peered within. Bragha Rùn's keeper was straight ahead, just fifteen feet away. "Ever seen him move?"

Isabel shook her head. "No. I'm not even sure 'he' is a he. It might not even be alive. Maybe it's a Workshop machine."

The "*it*" in question was Prime the Immortal, eldest of the Red Branch and arguably the most feared being in all Impyrium. No one but the sitting empress knew Prime's identity; none but the empress could command it. Hundreds of rumors surrounded Prime, but all assumed its origins preceded the Cataclysm. Some whispered it was wicked Cain; others swore it was the angel that slew the firstborn sons of Egypt. The most popular theory was that Prime was an incarnation of the Hound, a demigod who departed this world before the empire was founded. Gazing at the shiny black visage before them, Hazel decided Prime was a mirror. Whatever you feared most, you'd find staring back at you.

The figure standing within the alcove might have been a museum exhibit—an eight-foot smoothly muscled statue of pure obsidian. No face. No features save the Red Branch insignia on its inner wrist. It was bent at the waist, leaning forward as though to present Bragha Rùn to a petitioner. One hand grasped the dragon-pommeled hilt; the other supported its blade.

"Run in and get it," Isabel urged.

Hazel wavered. "What if there's an alarm?"

"Prime *is* the alarm," said Isabel. "As long as you're a Faeregine, you have nothing to worry about."

"Let's go in together."

Isabel steadfastly refused. "No chance. As long as I don't help, I can claim I tried to stop you. I'll be in enough trouble as it is."

Far off, Old Tom chimed one thirty. Isabel pinched her. Hazel swatted her hand away.

"I'm going!"

Inching her way to the threshold, Hazel eyed the gleaming fiend. There really was nothing to fear. She could even make out a sprinkling of dust on Prime's feet. A deep breath steadied her nerves.

Hazel inched into the alcove, her eyes fixed on the giant before her. Bragha Rùn was just a few feet away, its gilded scabbard gleaming under the soft lamplight. She glanced anxiously at the massive fist closed about the weapon's hilt. The blade looked anchored in place, utterly immovable. It reminded her of one of Uncle Basil's tale about a sword in a stone. Would Hazel have to free it somehow?

Prime loomed above her, still and terrible in his faceless grandeur. Hazel's trembling hand took hold of Bragha Rùn's scabbard. She gave a tentative pull, but Prime did not let go. Hazel pulled harder, but the sword did not budge. What was she supposed to do? Pry each finger off the hilt?

Isabel gave a hiss behind her. "Look up!"

A hole was opening in the center of Prime's torso, a cavity some six inches across and perhaps eighteen inches deep. It looked like a lamprey's mouth lined with row upon row of jet-black teeth. Beyond them, something wet and faintly luminous was pulsing like a heart.

"Something's in there," she whispered. "I—I think I may have to reach in."

"Well, what are you waiting for?" said Isabel.

"There are about a thousand teeth!"

"Well," said Isabel. "Try not to touch them."

"You're a help," Hazel muttered. Removing her coat, she pulled up her sleeve. For once it was a good thing she was so skinny. Assuming she was careful, she should be able to avoid those hideous teeth without too much trouble.

You can do this, she told herself. *One. Two. Three . . .*

Hazel slid her hand within the hole, trying desperately to keep steady. Inch by inch she advanced. All was going well until she was nearly up to her elbow. Then, like a slow spring had been released, the hole closed about her arm. Hazel froze as hundreds of needlelike points came to a gentle halt against her skin. One sudden move and they'd cut her to ribbons.

"It's got me," she whimpered.

Isabel came forward, but the instant she crossed the threshold, the pressure on Hazel's arm increased.

"Stop!" she cried. "Go back. It's not hurting me, but I think it will if you try and help."

Isabel retreated at once. "Can you pull your arm out?"

Hazel tried, but the teeth were angled inward. Her hand could go farther in but not back. Holding her breath, Hazel pushed forward and tried her best to ignore the sensation of razors dragging lightly over her soft skin. Just a few more inches . . .

At last, her fingers pierced what felt like a thin membrane. Her hand plunged into a cold, viscous substance. Hazel could sense life in it, a dull current that made her fingertips tingle. Seconds later, the cavity's teeth retracted so that its walls were smooth as glass. With a shuddering exhale, Hazel removed her arm to find her hand perfectly clean and dry.

"Well done," Isabel whispered.

Something moved in Hazel's peripheral vision. The hand that gripped Bragha Rùn's hilt was opening like a flower. Prime was giving it to her.

She did not need to be asked twice. Snatching the blade by its scabbard, she dashed out of the alcove, her face a rictus of pure terror. Once she was safely out, Isabel started laughing.

"What's so funny?" Hazel demanded.

"Y-your face." She tittered. "You look like you're trying to poop!"

Hazel scowled. "Shut up. You're the poop!"

But Isabel only laughed harder, doubling over into teary hysterics. Whenever Isabel was terribly frightened or distraught, she was apt to start giggling. It was just her way of relieving stress. Nevertheless, Hazel never sat by her at funerals. She tugged Isabel by her scarf.

"Come on," she said. "The horses should be ready."

A black charger and a dappled-gray stood outside by the camellias. The guardsman held them by their reins, trying to look professional despite the rain dribbling off his helmet's visor. Isabel managed to compose herself and thanked the private.

He bowed. "Allow me."

Hazel was grateful for assistance, for the horses were far larger than any mount she'd ever ridden. She pressed Bragha Rùn to her chest as Private Sarcosa lifted her into the gray's saddle and shortened the stirrups before turning his attention to Isabel.

Hazel tucked the House Blade inside her coat. It was awkward but not impossible, for Bragha Rùn was a rather short sword. It measured only thirty inches and was fashioned in the style of a Roman gladius, with a narrow crossguard and a straight, broad blade. Hazel thumbed the weapon's pommel, felt shallow notches scratched in the dragon's head. Her smiled faded.

The gravity of what they were doing suddenly hit home. The thrill of sneaking out, of stonecrawling, and taking Bragha Rùn had sugar-coated reality: they were riding to a duel where someone might die.

"Ready?" said Isabel, taking up her reins.

Hazel exhaled and gave a nod. Pulling up her hood, she turned the gray about.

The girls cantered north on the ancient road that traced the eastern shoreline. Below them, the harbor was fogged in, its ships and maze ghostly silhouettes as the rain poured down. Hound's Trench was over a mile away, past ancient monuments commemorating the Siege of Rowan.

The Hound was said to have made the trench during that very battle, striking the earth with his spear so that it split apart and swallowed his enemies. While few actually believed this (Cataclysm earthquakes offered a more likely explanation), there was no denying Hound's Trench was an odd place. It cut into Rowan's shoreline like an ax wound, a jagged chasm that extended well inland. Nothing grew nearby, and the wind seemed to wail when it blew through its blackened canyons. It was a perfect setting for ghost stories.

Or a duel.

Ahead, Hazel saw dozens of figures illuminated by torches thrust into the ground. A belyaël's eerie notes carried over the wind. Someone must have brought a kitsune or glynfaun, for the belyaël was a notoriously difficult instrument for humans to play.

Hazel now made out the musician—a fox-like kitsune—along with several imps among the many court brats and FYGs. The crowd was beginning to form a ring. At its center, Hazel could see Dante frowning, arms folded as Imogene spoke into his ear. Where was Hob?

Everyone turned as the Faeregine girls arrived.

"Isabel!" exclaimed Luca Yamato. "What are you doing here?"

Isabel swung off her horse. "Came to see the fun."

Imogene hissed a final word to Dante and strolled over. She did not bother wearing a hat or hood, but let the cold drizzle fall on her silvery-blond braids. She gazed up at the dismal night.

"I thought the sun was supposed to rise whenever Faeregines stirred. What happened?"

"Sun's running late," said Isabel. "Hold my reins and keep a lookout."

Imogene offered a withering smile. "Very kind of you to support Dante, but you might have stayed in bed. This won't last long. It's not worthy of Volsifer."

Volsifer was the Hyde House Blade, a fearsome claymore with an ivory handle and glowing runes down its jet-black blade. It was twice as long as Bragha Rùn, but light enough that Dante could wield it one-handed. He was doing so now, executing a series of flashy maneuvers on the pretense of warming up.

"Quite the butter scraper," said Isabel. "What's the page using?"

Imogene laughed. "I'm not really sure what to call it."

She pointed to some rocks near the cliff edge. Hob was sitting at the edge of the firelight. He was gazing at Dante, but he looked like his mind was a million miles away. Another page stood beside him, tall with a mop of yellow hair. In the shadows at Hob's shoulder squatted a burly hag holding what looked like a long-handled spade or cleaver.

"That's not fit for a duel," said Isabel.

Imogene sniffed. "We finally agree on something."

Dante thrust Volsifer into the damp earth. "Seconds come forward."

Hazel dismounted as the gangly page and Andros Eluvan, Dante's second, met in the middle of the forming circle. Clutching Bragha

Rùn under her coat, Hazel squeezed in between Isabel and Gretchen Klauss. The belyaël trailed off into silence.

Owyn Menlo stepped in to preside. At nineteen, he was the oldest FYG, a perpetual student who preferred his leisure to academics.

"Lord Eluvan," he said, bowing, "and, well, I guess I'll just call you 'page.'" No bow. "Are your principles ready?"

The seconds acknowledged that they were.

"And does either wish to withdraw or issue an apology?"

Neither did.

Hazel tugged her sister's elbow. "When should we . . . ?" She pointed to the blade hidden in her coat.

Isabel leaned close. "Just before they start. It will throw Dante off."

"Splendid," Owyn continued. "Lord Hyde has agreed to forego magic, so the matter will be settled with blades only. By custom, only death, surrender by a principle, or forfeiture by his second can bring the duel to a close. Is that understood?"

The seconds bowed. Hazel crossed her fingers. Perhaps Dante would withdraw once he saw Bragha Rùn. He was a bully and bullies were often cowards when faced with greater strength. And nothing— not even Volsifer—was Bragha Rùn's equal.

"Let's have the principles," called Owyn. There was a smattering of cheers and boos.

This is disgusting, thought Hazel. People were acting like the duel was nothing more than a party, an excuse to sneak out to Hound's Trench.

Everyone, that is, except Dante. There was nothing jubilant in that cold smile. Hefting Volsifer, he rested the huge blade upon his shoulder and waited for his opponent.

There were gasps and titters when Hob appeared. The page had removed his shirt and shoes and walked into the ring wearing naught but black breeches. To Hazel's astonishment, she saw that Hob's chest and shoulders were heavily tattooed. Ezra Klauss aped his steps, capering and hooting. Hob glanced at him as if he were an insect. Ezra's grin faltered.

Isabel leaned close. "If I knew muir tutors looked like that, I'd have gotten one ages ago."

Hob came to a halt before Dante. He was younger and a few inches shorter, but Hazel did not get the impression he was at a physical disadvantage. Instead, it looked like a young wolf sizing up a greyhound.

"Bit more than you bargained for, eh, Imogene?" said Isabel.

Imogene acted unconcerned. "The page is well built—what of it? Volsifer doesn't mind cutting muscle. That cleaver looks like it came from your kitchens."

Hazel had to agree. Maybe that's why the hag was present. It was time to even things up. Clearing her throat, she tried to forget that she hated public speaking.

"One moment," she called out.

Everyone turned.

"Er, yes, Your Highness?" said Owyn. "You wish to say something?"

"I do," said Hazel, trying not to hyperventilate. "I've . . . well, I've just come to realize that dueling is vile, even if there's an even match. But how can we pretend there's even a smidgeon of honor in what we're about to witness? Look at what the page is wielding!"

Several of the FYGs sniggered. Hob merely gazed at Hazel with an inward expression.

"It's more than a disgrace," said Hazel passionately. "It's murder."

This broke Dante's glowering silence. "Enough! I won't have my name sullied. The muir accepted my challenge and chose his weapon. It's not my fault that's the best he could lay his hands upon."

"It isn't."

Hazel brought out Bragha Rùn, holding the sword up so that all could see the famous blade. Its name meant "red death" in the demon tongue. Indeed, the gladius was red, from its red-gold pommel to its crimson blade forged from enchanted lymra. According to legend, there was nothing Bragha Rùn could not cut, pierce, or slay. The blade was even said to impart the matchless prowess of the gladiator for whom it was named. It was a weapon fit for a god.

The crowd was silent. The blade made a dull ring as Hazel slid it from its scabbard and presented it to an astonished Hob. He took it tentatively, offering her a questioning glance. She gave a slight nod. Clutching the scabbard, she returned to the circle and prayed Bragha Rùn would have the desired effect.

Imogene was furious. Spittle flew as she confronted Hazel. "Letting a *servant* wield your House Blade? Your family has finally sunk into the sewer!"

Hazel folded her arms. "Thanks for keeping it warm."

Owyn Menlo's gaiety had dwindled. "Dante," he said earnestly, "do you still want to do this? There's no shame in withdrawing . . . to that." He gestured at Bragha Rùn.

Yes! Hazel urged silently. Withdraw so this farce can end without bloodshed. You can nurse your pride at home.

Dante stared at Bragha Rùn, whose blade reflected the guttering torches. Hundreds of feet below, waves crashed upon the rocks, funneling into Hound's Trench with a drumming moan. In the firelight, Dante's features betrayed a subtle interplay of emotions: fear, doubt, even defiant anger. Hob stood motionless, his gaze leveled on his opponent. Coming forward, Andros Eluvan whispered in his friend's ear. Dante's face darkened. He shook his head savagely.

Andros frowned and turned to Owyn. "You said a second is allowed to forfeit on behalf of his principle?"

Owyn nodded.

Dante jabbed a finger in his second's chest. "If you do, our friendship is ended. I will come for you myself!"

Andros held up his hands and withdrew. "Have it your way."

Turning back to Hob, Dante drew himself up. His expression was wild, bloodthirsty. Hazel's hope for a peaceful conclusion vanished.

"I do not withdraw," he growled. "I don't care what you wield, muir. You die this day."

Hob did not reply. The crowd's merriment waned in the cold drizzle. Glancing round the circle, Hazel saw nothing but apprehensive faces. The Castile twins looked like they might be sick. Even Isabel was fidgeting. Hazel took her hand and squeezed it fiercely. She had counted on Dante being a rational coward. Evidently he was neither.

Owyn cleared his throat. "Are you ready?"

Both boys nodded.

Owyn backed out of the circle. "Begin."

Immediately, Dante went on the attack. Striding forward, he feinted a jab before spinning about to bring Volsifer screaming at his opponent's head. Hob sprang back, nearly slipping on the wet ground.

Again, Dante closed, this time holding Volsifer like a fencer's rapier.

He flicked his wrist, the movement so sudden that Hazel caught only the flash of torchlight on the blade. Hob grunted with pain, backing away as blood streamed down his forearm. One of the Castile twins turned away.

Crouching low, Hob feinted and swept Bragha Rùn at Dante's midsection. The attack was quick but inexpert; he might have been swinging a cudgel. Dante parried it easily and nearly beheaded Hob on the counterattack.

Hazel almost wished the kitsune would resume playing her belyaël. The duel was a horrific sight, but its sounds were almost worse: shuffling steps, the shrill ring of steel, the hoarse gasps of its combatants.

There had been eight passes thus far and two facts had emerged: Hob was extremely agile; and he had no chance of defeating Dante Hyde in a sword fight. Blood now flowed from three wounds to his left arm and knee. His face remained grim and focused, but he was clearly favoring his uninjured leg as he circled away from his skillful opponent.

"Coward," hissed Dante. "Stand and figh—"

Hob slipped. Rushing in, Dante brought Volsifer down like a thunderbolt.

But he'd been tricked! A boulder jutted from the earth behind Hob and he used it as a backstop to plant his foot and dive low at his opponent. Volsifer swept harmlessly over him, sparking as it cleaved the stone. Dante toppled backward into the mud as Hob tackled him around the waist. Imogene cried out as her brother flailed about on his back, one hand on his weapon, the other on Hob's wrist. A sword like Volsifer was useless at close quarters; the

Faeregine blade was made for it.

But Bragha Rùn was pointed skyward. The two were at a stale-mate, Dante gasping as he strained to prevent Hob from reversing his weapon.

Crack!

Hob brought Bragha Rùn's pommel down on Dante's nose.

Crack! Crack!

Two more blows in quick succession. Dante turned his head, reveal-ing several broken teeth. Hazel could not breathe, could barely look as the two struggled. Dante was beginning to panic. He twisted about, frantically searching the crowd as he tried to keep Hob's weapon at bay. The instant he found Imogene an understanding passed between them. Dante shut his eyes.

Imogene pointed at Hob and whispered, *"Ayin!"*

A flash of phosphorescent light burst like a mortar before Hob's eyes. He recoiled, rolling off Dante and clutching his face with one hand. Isabel whirled on Imogene.

"You can't do that!"

"Do what?" said Imogene coldly.

"Stop the duel!" Isabel shouted. "The Hydes cheated!"

Imogene ignored her. "Finish it, Dante!"

Owyn was flustered. He began to speak, hesitated, and was silent as Dante scrambled to his feet. Hob backed away, gasping and holding Bragha Rùn at arm's length. He made tentative stabs as though grop-ing for an unseen opponent. Blood trickled from glassy, unfocused eyes. Dante circled like a shark.

Hazel looked on, almost literally paralyzed with terror. It was like a waking nightmare; she saw what was occurring, wanted to stop it, and yet her body was completely unresponsive. She wanted to cast a spell—*needed* to cast a spell—but her mind was numb. She glanced about at her classmates.

Why didn't someone stop the fight?

Dante swung Volsifer. There was a hideous clang as Bragha Rùn was knocked from Hob's grasp. Weaponless, Hob tried to sidestep but found Volsifer pressed against his ribs. Leering like a madman, Dante dragged its point across his opponent's stomach, raising a thin line of blood. Hob raised his head and gazed blindly at Dante. Hazel had never seen a more contemptuous smile.

"You're soft as cake, mehrùn," said Hob. "Don't ever forget that."

He spat at Dante's feet.

Hazel turned away, horrified for Hob and ashamed at her impotence. What was the point of studying magic if you couldn't use it when it mattered most?

"He forfeits!" cried a frantic voice.

Hazel turned to see the blond page, Hob's second, bolt into the circle. "Mr. Smythe forfeits! He withdraws, he surrenders—whatever you wish to call it. He's out!"

"Hold!" cried Owyn, waving his arms. "The duel is ended! Honor has been satisfied and Lord Hyde is the victor."

Dante looked tempted to cut the blond page in half. Instead, he turned back to Hob. The earl's voice was thick through broken teeth.

"One good turn deserves another, eh, muir?"

Using both hands, he struck Hob full in the face with Volsifer's pommel. The page dropped and lay motionless in the mud, limbs splayed like a discarded doll's.

Hazel saw Imogene step on Hob's throat as she congratulated her brother. Recovering her senses, Hazel hurried into the ring and knelt by Hob.

His face was a bloody ruin. Nose shattered, left eye hidden by a grotesquely swollen cheekbone. He was alive, however. Breaths came in wheezing whistles through a chipped tooth.

"Is he dead?" whispered a boy.

Glancing up, Hazel saw the other page. "He's unconscious. You did the right thing to forfeit. He never would have surrendered."

"He's my roommate. I know how stubborn he is."

"Should we move him?" said Hazel. She knew nothing about nursing or healing spells.

"Step aside," said a quiet voice.

She turned to see Sigga Fenn. The agent looked far from pleased. Hazel scooted over immediately.

Crouching over Hob, the Red Branch ran her long fingers over his chest, tapping his heart and humming softly. Leaning close, she spread his eyelids and peered at his pupils. "We have to get him to the healing ward," she muttered. "He'll live, but he might not be so pretty."

Hazel half sobbed out of relief for Hob and guilt at everything she'd done. "I know I shouldn't have gone out without you. I'm sorry."

The Grislander's green, almost luminous eyes surveyed her thoughtfully. "Do it again and you can find another bodyguard, Your Highness. Do we understand each other?"

Unable to speak, Hazel merely nodded.

A breathless Isabel grabbed Hazel by the shoulder. "Look!"

When Hazel waved her away, Isabel spun her about so forcibly that she almost toppled over. Hazel looked up, bewildered. To her astonishment, she saw that her sister's face was tear streaked. Isabel *never* cried.

"What's wrong?" Hazel gasped.

Isabel let out a whimper. "We're dead. . . ."

She held out her hands. Within them, Hazel saw only a muddied gold hilt and jagged pieces of metal. Bragha Rùn was broken.

CHAPTER 12
THE CONVALESCENT

History tells you what happened.
Economics tells you why.

—David Menlo, archmage (17 P.C.–72 A.C.)

Five days later, Hob squinted through his bandages as he composed a letter in the palace's healing ward. It was a large room with lots of windows and sunlight and flowering rowan trees where cardinals nested and chirruped. Instead of Faeregines, its paintings depicted pastoral landscapes. As Hob scratched away with his pen, there was a grunt from the neighboring bed.

"Ready when you are."

"Just a minute," Hob muttered. Setting down the pen, he flexed his fingers and read the letter over.

3014, March 21

Dear Ma,

This is my eighth letter and I haven't heard back, but you're probably busy, or mad. Don't be mad. You always said a soul has to find its own way in the world. I'm finding mine. Hope what I left is helping. You could move come summer. Anything's better than renting from the Danes. . . .

　You wouldn't believe where I am. The empire's a grander, stranger place than I ever imagined. I'm doing fine, so don't worry. Write when you can. You can send letters to the Stock & Trade Servant School, 111 S. Fells, Market District, Impyria. They'll forward it on. Give Anja a hug and my fishing pole (the one with red tape). She could try Miller's Pond when the mayflies hatch. Say hi to all, especially Mole and Bluestripe.

Satisfied, he folded the paper and slipped the letter in a waxed envelope so it would survive its journey to the Sentries. By the time mail arrived in Dusk, most of it had been drenched or opened.

"It needs stamps," said Hob's neighbor, the private.

"I plan to win them off you," said Hob. "Ten points each?"

"Let's make it five to teach you a lesson."

"Done."

Hob maneuvered so he could reach the arcadia board between their beds. He inspected the game's four platforms and checked to ensure all was proper.

"What's the objective?" he asked. Arcadia offered five objectives and each required different strategies. His neighbor's disfigured face twisted into a grin.

"Conquest."

"Works for me," said Hob. "Your move."

Turning the little hourglass, his opponent jumped his centaur down a level so that it was square with Hob's dragon. An aggressive play, too aggressive so early in the game. Hob slid his jinn next to an unclaimed tower . . .

Half the hourglass's sand remained when the guardsman conceded defeat. He stared at the board in disgust.

"Good game," said Hob.

"That wasn't a game," the soldier grumbled. "It was dissection. What do I owe?"

"Let's see," said Hob. "I've still got my dragon, afrit, centaur, sorceress, and both hampersprites. One hundred and five points, so . . . twenty-one stamps."

A groan. "Revenge?"

Hob agreed provided the soldier coughed up the ten stamps needed to mail his letter. These were passed over. Once Hob affixed them, he put the letter aside and scooted his bed back to its place.

"What about our game?" said the guardsman.

"You need time to recover your spirits," Hob joked. "And I have work to do."

The older boy scoffed. "What work? You're a page on bed rest."

Hob drew the curtain between them and slipped his Impyrial handbook from the box of personal items Viktor had brought him.

He transmitted messages to the Fellowship using the spypaper on the inside back cover but he received replies on a different page. These appeared amid a dense paragraph that listed diplomats and blended with the surrounding text. The last he'd received was before his injuries, but another was due. He turned to page 213.

Many people took great risks to place you in the palace. They did not do this so you could fight an idiotic duel that endangered your life and drew unwanted attention. We are extremely displeased. Lower your profile and resume quiet progress toward your goal. Failure to do so will force us to take steps we would rather avoid. Intelligence gleaned from page duty is helpful, but your priority is information regarding HJ's magical capabilities. You will report everything you hear or observe. We fear you are not being wholly forthcoming . . .

Hob reddened, feeling some of the accusations were unjust. He'd reported everything he'd witnessed in the Direwood: Hazel's argument with Dante, her dreamlike trek to the Reaper's tomb, and the appearance of that horrifying stag-man. What else was he supposed to say? Hob had no idea what had drawn Hazel to those stones, or what her capabilities might be. Her Highness never discussed magic, and Hob was reluctant to press the issue after the debacle at Hound's Trench. He felt fortunate that they'd still be meeting to discuss the Muirlands.

In fact, they would be meeting that very afternoon. A zephyss from Dàme Rascha had inquired if he was well enough for a short session; Her Highness had a test on economics that week. He did not need to stir. They would come to him. Closing his eyes, Hob tried to recall everything he'd studied for Provinces: financial principles, means of production, regional industries . . .

Shortly before five o'clock, one of the moomenhovens wheeled Hob's bed into a private room and changed his dressings. All of the ward's nurses were moomenhovens—plump, matronly beings, almost entirely human but for their cow legs and tails. Despite his initial misgivings, Hob had discovered they were gentle creatures, tireless in service of their patients.

Hob leaned over the bed rail for a glimpse of the nurse's shins. "Thank you, Suusa."

She smiled shyly. Moomenhovens were mutes and nearly identical save for the spotted patterns on their legs. Once she'd brought in two extra chairs, Suusa took her leave.

Her Highness arrived right on time, accompanied by Dàme Rascha and Sigga Fenn. Lowering her hood, Hazel offered a somewhat anxious greeting and asked how he was doing.

"Better each day, Your Highness." He cleared his throat. "I'd like to thank you for the other night. I'm deeply sorry about your family's sword."

"Oh," said Hazel, turning pink. To Hob's surprise, she looked almost embarrassed by his apology. "The sword wasn't your fault," she began, glancing at Dàme Rascha. The vye shook her head in answer to some unspoken question. Hazel seemed inclined to argue, but Dàme Rascha gave a warning chuff. Hob quickly changed the subject.

"When did you get this?" He pointed to the bat-like creature clinging to Her Highness's cowl.

Hazel grinned. "This is Merlin. Master Montague had an extra homunculus and gave it to me as a reward for speaking up on your behalf. He said I showed backbone."

Hob leaned forward on his bed. The creature was smaller than his hand and resembled a minuscule person with glistening blue-black skin and delicate, membranous wings. He was fast asleep and breathing rapidly, eyelids fluttering as though deep in a dream. Despite being newly spawned, the creature's wrinkly grimace made him look like a toothless old man.

Hazel stroked its glistening head. "Isn't he beautiful?"

Hob managed a noncommittal grunt. "I suppose we should dive in. What's the topic?"

The princess groaned. "Money—the most boring subject ever. I think I've got the theory, but Montague likes it when I apply them and use examples. That's where you come in."

"Understood," said Hob. "Tell me what you know and we'll go from there."

Sighing, Hazel rattled off what she'd memorized concerning currency types and their values before trying to explain—semicoherently—that the Bank of Rowan did *something* to manage how much money was in circulation to help Impyrium's economy.

"How was that?" she asked.

"Not bad," said Hob. "But even the theories aren't going to help you understand how the economy really works."

"What do you mean?"

"There's almost no Impyrial currency circulating in the Northwest. Not even in bigger settlements like Wulfast."

"Why?"

"The banks hoard it. It makes it more valuable, Your Highness."

"But the values are set," said Hazel. "My textbook says what they are."

"In real life, Impyrial currency's much more valuable than what it says in your book," said Hob. "There's lots of demand, but banks only release very little."

"But why do they do that?" said Hazel.

Hob considered how best to explain. "There's a woman in my

village named Mother Howell who told me there's really just a few things to understand about money, and then you can figure out the rest. The biggest one is supply and demand."

"The master mentioned that," said Hazel. "But he assumed we all knew what it meant. He didn't give examples. I don't understand it."

Hob pointed at the water pitcher his nurse had left. "What would you pay me for that?"

Hazel gave it a puzzled look. "Nothing. I can get water whenever I want."

"What if you couldn't? What if this was the only water left? What's it worth then?"

"Well, everyone needs water," said Hazel slowly. "If there isn't any, I guess that would make the pitcher priceless."

Hob nodded. "That's supply and demand. It usually sets something's price. Now, what if I told you water was scarce, but I had lots in a secret reservoir? Should I sell it all at once?"

The princess considered a moment. "If you did, the price would go down. But if you sold small amounts at a time, you could keep the price high."

"How high?"

The princess shifted Merlin. "As high as people were willing to pay, I suppose."

"Exactly," said Hob. "And that's why banks hoard currency in the Muirlands. If I borrow ten solars from a bank, it will cost me thirty solars worth of goods to get the coin to pay it back. Most people never get out of debt."

"If banks are so expensive, why do people use them?" said Hazel. "Can't they just barter instead? Master Montague said bartering was common throughout the Muirlands."

"People do," Hob replied. "No one in my village pays each other with coin—too valuable. We exchange furs or fuel, little nuggets of silver, even labor. But you can't barter with tax collectors or banks. They only accept official currency."

Hazel was deep in thought. She turned suddenly to Dàme Rascha. "Is that really how it works? It doesn't seem fair."

The old vye cleared her throat. "I do not know, Your Highness. As Mr. Smythe says, theory and practice may differ throughout the land. But I cannot imagine your uncle would approve banks hoarding currency that muir are required to use. It would seem unethical."

Hob kept a straight face. This was *exactly* what the Bank of Rowan had been doing for centuries. It was amazing how little these people knew about the institutions keeping them in power. Ignorance was no excuse. They were part of the system, complicit in its injustice.

As they discussed this, Hob could not help but wonder if the Fellowship was misusing him. Hazel's naïveté showed how Impyrium's problems went much deeper than the individuals who comprised the royal family. Its laws existed to benefit a tiny sliver of the population. Perhaps things had been different under Mina I, but that was three thousand years ago. Impyrium was corrupt now, rotted and stinking to its core. It seemed a waste to spend so much time and energy trying to assess the princess's magical capabilities. There was real work to do.

Putting these reflections on hold, Hob continued the lesson and discussed further concepts like interest and risk versus reward. Mining provided plenty of the examples.

"When I started to work," he explained, "I had to borrow against future wages to buy my gear. The interest was high, so I wanted to pay off the debt as quickly as possible. To do that, I volunteered for jobs with hazard pay."

"What's hazard pay?" said Hazel.

"An example of risk and reward," said Hob. "Some jobs are more dangerous than others, so the miners who do them demand more money. If I did blasting or worked near the Grislands, I could double my pay. But I had to be smart. Some jobs were worth the risk, others weren't."

"How did you know which to take?"

Hob shrugged. "Instinct. Talking to old-timers. If the foreman was too quick to sweeten the pot, I never volunteered. Those were sucker gigs."

"Er, what's that?" Hazel asked.

"Apologies, Your Highness. It's slang for a job only a very foolish person would accept."

Hazel turned to Dàme Rascha. "We're on a sucker gig."

The vye gave a series of barking growls that might have been her closest thing to a chuckle. Indeed it was, for she pinched the princess and scolded her for making an old lady laugh. It was touching to see the affection between them. Hob suddenly missed his mother and Anja.

"Do you have any other questions, Your Highness?"

The princess put away her notebook. "Your injuries. How are they healing?"

Hob pulled up his gown sleeve to show her the neat stitches in his left shoulder. "Some aches and pains, but they're mending." He ran a finger over a large black tattoo. "This has seen better days. My mother will never forgive me."

"I meant to ask you about those," said Hazel. "I hadn't realized you had such markings. Do all muir have them?"

"No. These are Hauja symbols. They're my mother's people. Hauja boys receive these if they survive séyu. The shaman refused to give me mine, so my mother inked them herself."

"What are they?" asked Hazel.

Hob opened his gown, baring his torso. The princess blushed, but he pretended not to notice. "Hauja worship twelve spirits. Once a boy sits séyu, the shaman chooses three to guide him in life." Hob pointed to each, starting at his right shoulder. "Fenmaruq is the Wolf, Vessuk the Salmon, and Kayüta the Fox."

Hazel peered closely. "I couldn't see them clearly with all the patterns. They're lovely. Why did your mother choose those spirits?"

Hob looked down. "She believes the Wolf gives me strength, the Salmon my will, and the Fox my wits."

"And what about that?" she said, pointing at the gashed tattoo. "It looks like a bird."

"That's Morrgu," he answered. "Every boy gets her. When I die, the Raven will ferry my soul to its resting place. If I've honored my guardians, she'll take me to my ancestors. If not, my soul goes into the Void."

"Do you believe that?" asked the princess.

Hob gave an unconvincing smile. "I try not to. Breaking the Faeregine House Blade is probably a one-way ticket. I still can't believe that happened."

Hazel turned to Dàme Rascha. "He needs to know the truth. This isn't right."

"Your Highness," the vye warned.

Hazel turned defiantly back to Hob. "You did not break Bragha

Rùn, Mr. Smythe. You've never even held it."

"I don't understand," said Hob. "You gave me a fake?"

"No," said Hazel quickly. "Well, yes. But I had no idea it was a forgery. I took the sword directly from Prime's hand."

"So where's the real one?" said Hob.

The princess ignored her tutor's growl. "We don't know, which is the only reason my grandmother wasn't harder on me and my sister. If it weren't for us, the empress wouldn't know it was missing. Unfortunately, it's been ages since the real Bragha Rùn was used. The sword could have been stolen years ago."

The vye had heard enough. "Your Highness, we do not know the sword was stolen. We know only that it was not in Prime's keeping. You would do well not to spread rumors."

"Come on," said Hazel. "Of course it was stolen!"

"Only a Faeregine can claim Bragha Rùn from its guardian," the vye retorted. "You are accusing your own family of theft. I am sure there is another explanation."

Hob's mind raced back to the moment he'd taken hold of the legendary blade. He hadn't known what to expect, but he certainly hadn't expected it to feel so ordinary. But it was not his own reaction to Bragha Rùn that puzzled Hob. It was his opponent's.

"I think he knew," he said softly.

"You think who knew what?" said Hazel.

"Lord Hyde," said Hob. "He knew the sword was a fake. That's why he agreed to go through with the duel—he knew it wasn't the real Bragha Rùn."

Sigga cocked her head. "What makes you believe that?"

"I was watching him closely," said Hob. "When he first saw Bragha

Rùn, he was genuinely surprised. But then I caught something else. A sly look, like he knew it couldn't help me. All that posturing of whether to go through with the duel was just to make himself look brave. Lord Hyde always meant to fight."

Hazel whirled to face Rascha. "I knew it! The Hydes are behind all of this—the vault, *Typhon*, and now Bragha Rùn. It all makes sense!"

"It does not," said the vye stiffly. "And you should not be discussing these things in front of outsiders."

Sigga Fenn laid a hand on the vye's arm. "This outsider has valuable insights. I'd like to hear more of what Mr. Smythe has to say on these matters."

Hob hated the agent's eyes. They were like a damned cat's, inscrutable and mocking.

Just tell the truth.

He gave an apologetic shrug. "No insights, really. Just a hunch from reading Lord Hyde's face. Looking back, I'd bet anything he knew that wasn't Bragha Rùn."

"It's more than a hunch," said Hazel excitedly. "It's proof. Which house spends the most on Lirlander Seals? The Hydes. Which house has been suing for control of the bank since *Typhon* blew up? The Hydes. If Bragha Rùn goes missing, who has the best House Blade? The Hydes!"

The princess was delighted with her deductive powers. Dàme Rascha furrowed her craggy brow.

"Your Highness, every one of the Great Houses would like to see your family lose control of the Lirlander Seals and the bank. And you forget that a Hyde could not have taken Bragha Rùn from Prime. Only a Faeregine could."

"There are hundreds of minor Faeregines," said Hazel. "Maybe the Hydes bribed one and—"

"Enough!" snapped Dàme Rascha. "I will not have you flinging about half-formed accusations. The Lirlanders are far likelier suspects in the vault and the *Typhon*. You assume Bragha Rùn is somehow related to these events, but there's no evidence to support this. These conjectures are irresponsible."

The vye folded her arms. Hazel looked mutinous, but Sigga Fenn continued gazing at Hob. "Any theories, Mr. Smythe?"

Hob glowered at her. "Why are you asking me?"

The agent smiled. "I like to read faces too."

"Sigga," said Hazel crossly, "you sound like you're accusing him. But what do you think, Mr. Smythe? I would like to know."

"Honestly, I haven't any idea if these events are connected or who might be behind them. But my neighbor would agree with Dàme Rascha about the vault. He thinks it was the Lirlanders."

"Who's your neighbor?" said Hazel.

Hob scratched the bandage covering his left eye. The wound itched terribly. "Private Marcus Finch. He was on duty that night at the Lirlander Vault. He's the guardsman who survived."

Hazel pointed at the ward. "And he's right out there?"

"Yes, Your Highness. In the far corner."

The princess stood at once. "I want to speak with him."

Dàme Rascha rose almost as quickly. "Your Highness, I cannot advise this. The empress and your uncle have people looking into these matters. It is not for you to play detective."

Hazel shoved her books into her bag. "It's been months, Rascha. No one's discovered anything. Talking to Private Finch can't hurt.

Anyway, I have my own reason for wanting to find out if the Hydes are responsible for any of this."

"And that is?" said Rascha.

"Let's just say I don't want Dante Hyde for a brother-in-law," said Hazel, before turning back to Hob. "Do you think Private Finch would speak to us?"

"I'm sure he'd be happy to," said Hob. "He's very dutiful. He's crushed he can't serve in the guard any longer."

"Why can't he?" asked Hazel.

Hob searched for a diplomatic answer. "The Impyrial Guard has strict physical requirements. Private Finch no longer meets them."

"Oh," said Hazel, looking troubled. "Well, I'm sure he's doing the best he can."

The soldier was dozing when the moomenhovens rolled Hob's bed back into place. The ward was not crowded, but the nurses screened off their corner so Her Highness would have some privacy.

"Marcus," he hissed. "Wake up, eh?"

The guardsman stirred, slid up to a sitting position against the headboard's rails. "What's up? Time for our game?"

"Later," said Hob. "Someone wants to meet you."

"Who?"

"A noble."

"Which house?"

"One of *the* nobles," said Hob significantly.

"Now?" hissed Marcus. "I haven't brushed my teeth."

"Don't think she'll care. She just wants to ask you some questions. About New Year's."

Marcus gripped his bed rails. *"Not the empress!"*

Hob shook his head, which seemed to relieve his neighbor. The private sipped some water and tried to smooth what remained of his hair. Hob signaled Suusa to fetch the visitors.

"Private Finch," said Hob. "Allow me to present Her Highness Lady Hazel Faeregine, along with her tutor, Dàme Rascha, and Sigga Fenn of the Red Branch."

Marcus sat up as the three slipped between the screens. The former guardsman tried to salute but Hazel insisted it wasn't necessary.

"You're very good to see us on short notice, Private Finch. I trust our people are looking after you," said Hazel. Her words were perfectly courteous, but she did not look Marcus in the eye. The instant she glimpsed his almost fleshless, noseless face, she averted her gaze.

He looks this way because he was guarding your family's vault, thought Hob irritably. *Don't make him feel like a freak.*

"They take good care of me, Your Highness," said Finch. "With luck, I'll be discharged by summer and can return home."

"And where is home?" said Hazel pleasantly, still inspecting the floor. Hob simmered. This was not the Hazel at Hound's Trench; this was a Faeregine princess visiting the troops for a photo op.

"Thystle, Your Highness. A village west of New Halifax."

She nodded. "I imagine it's very pretty there. I'm sorry to intrude, but I wonder if you could share what happened that horrid night."

"Of course, Your Highness. But I've already told everything I remember to the guard captain and Agent Harkün."

"I would be very grateful," said Hazel.

Private Finch spent the next twenty minutes rehashing what he remembered. He'd clearly done so many times, for he moved seamlessly from one event to the next. He began with his reassignment from harbor patrol, the appearance of the imposters, the arrival of Lord Faeregine, and their realization that a crime was under way. His account was dispassionate until the attack. Then his emotions began to fray and Marcus reached frequently for his water.

"The vault door was opening," he said quietly. "Sergeant Beecher ordered me to take Lord Faeregine to safety. We ran. The sergeant fired off a few shots and then there was a scream. Horrible scream, I'll never forget it. There was so much light from the vault. A shadow was on the wall. The vye was chasing me. I turned to fire, but it was too late. I was knocked out cold and woke up here. Didn't even get to attend Sergeant Beecher's funeral."

"You admired him," said Hazel.

The private nodded. "He was a soldier's soldier, Your Highness. If he hadn't bought us a bit of time, I don't think your uncle or I would be here. I owe him my life."

He pointed to a photograph on his nightstand. Hob had assumed the man was a relative. He hadn't realized it was the murdered sergeant. The Impyrial Guard had few like him anymore; Beecher actually looked like he'd fought a campaign or two.

"He has a kind face," said Hazel. She picked up the one beside it showing a handsome young man. "And who is this?"

Finch hesitated. "I—I'm afraid that's me, Your Highness. It was taken the day I heard I'd made the Guard."

The princess set it down and exhaled slowly. "My deepest apologies, Private Finch. I should have recognized you at once."

Hazel finally looked upon Marcus and did not turn away. No patrician benevolence remained. There was only a girl whose eyes shone with compassion.

"No apologies necessary, Your Highness," said Marcus. "I hardly recognize myself either. Don't feel bad. My face is gone, but my hands still work. My dad's a cobbler. I can work in his shop."

The princess could only nod, for her eyes were rapidly filling with tears. Private Finch tried to lighten the mood with a laugh and what passed as a grin for one without lips.

"This won't do. You've come for answers, not a pity party. What else can I tell you?"

Hazel recollected herself. "Are you certain it was a vye that attacked you? Some mehrùn are capable illusionists."

The soldier gestured at his face. "This wasn't done by an illusion. No, Your Highness, it was either a vye or some other kind of shape-shifter. I've always heard demons can change their forms. Personally, I think the imposters were Lirlanders."

"It's a popular theory," Hazel acknowledged. "I'm curious why so much light was coming from the vault."

"The Lirlander Seals," said Private Finch. "Each one's very bright. There must be hundreds in the vault."

"Why aren't they on actual ships?" asked Hazel.

Dàme Rascha spoke up. "Every Seal in circulation has a twin that is kept in the vault. The two are magically tethered, Your Highness. Disabling one, disables the other."

"Clever," said Hazel. "No one can just buy a Seal at auction and sail off forever. If they don't return it, we can just turn it off by disabling its twin in the vault."

"Correct," said Dàme Rascha.

"So why didn't the thieves take any?" said Hazel. "I mean, we were just talking about supply and demand. A set of paired Seals would fetch a fortune."

"There wasn't time, Your Highness," said Private Finch. "When the imposters opened the door, we were already raising the alarm. And the Seals are the size of shields. A person couldn't just walk off with a few."

"Then how were they supposed to make off with any Seals to begin with?" said Hazel.

This stumped the private. "I don't know, Your Highness. The thieves didn't bring anything with them. All I do know is that they looked just like Lord Faeregine and Dr. Razael."

Hazel nodded, but she looked puzzled. Hob could relate. He got the impression there were far deeper currents swirling about these matters than he could even guess. Perhaps the attempted theft at the Lirlander Vault hadn't been a theft at all; perhaps it had been a diversion . . .

Bragha Rùn.

Hob stifled an exclamation. The vault break-in could have been made to deflect attention from the real crime—the theft of Bragha Rùn. If the Hydes were behind recent events, their strategy was paying off handsomely. In the past few months, the Faeregines had been publicly embarrassed, suffered a significant blow to their finances, and learned that their House Blade was missing. Individually, each one benefited the Hydes; together they were an outright coup. Even better, the Lirlanders made ideal scapegoats for the vault break-in and the *Typhon* explosion.

Despite his excitement, Hob recognized there were holes in his theory. If what Dàme Rascha said was true, only a Faeregine could have taken Bragha Rùn from Prime, which would mean that a Faeregine had betrayed the family. And why the murder of Dr. Razael? What would have been the point of killing her? More problematic was the break-in itself. It would only serve as a diversion if it was discovered, and it was only discovered because Lord Faeregine arrived while the imposters were inside the vault. Why was he even there? Was he involved somehow? Hob doubted it. No one had suffered more from recent events than Basil Faeregine. The vault break-in had damaged his reputation and, if Dante Hyde was to be believed, *Typhon* had sunk his fortune.

By now, Hob's head was spinning.

Slow down. You can't report conspiracy theories to the Fellowship.

Hazel asked several more questions. A few concerned the vault, the rest had to do with Private Finch. She thanked Marcus for his loyalty to her family and the sacrifice he'd made on her uncle's behalf. Hazel's interest in his recovery and future plans appeared to be genuine. Before leaving, she promised to visit Private Finch again. Hob believed she would. So did Private Finch.

"I used to think the princess was some kind of demon," the soldier muttered once their visitors had gone. "The way she looks, all those rumors. Shows what I know. She's the prize of the whole bunch. Her uncle's never once looked in. Just sent a note and a bit of money."

"She's a good person," said Hob. His simple answer belied the complicated thoughts and feelings that were simmering underneath. The world wasn't as black-and-white as he wanted it to be.

"How do you know her?" said Finch.

Hob looked up. "What? Oh, I wouldn't say I know her. We talk now and again about life in the Muirlands. She studies them for school."

"Yeah? And how'd you get the job?"

"Just lucky," said Hob. "You up for a game?"

Finch thumped his bed railing. "Yes, sir. It's my turn for a bit of luck."

Once he'd set up the arcadia board, Hob proceeded to lose in steady fashion. He wanted Finch to win back his stamps, but Hob would have lost regardless. His mind was not focused on the game but on conspiracies and luck.

His response to Finch's question had been a joke, but it made Hob think. Luck had certainly played a role in putting him with Hazel Faeregine, but it was hardly the only factor. The Fellowship had been fortunate that Dàme Rascha poached Hob from Lady Sylva, but they had also made countless maneuvers to steer events toward that outcome. And they had done so with the cooperation—willing or not—of a Great House. It was conceivable the Fellowship could be working with other Great Houses on other schemes. Hob recalled his journey on the Transcontinental, and Burke's great interest in newspaper stories concerning the Lirlander Vault. Was the Fellowship involved somehow? Could they be in league with the Hydes to topple the Faeregines?

If so, what was each party hoping to gain? Surely, each had to realize the other would turn upon them after they'd defeated their common enemy. They were diametrically opposed. After all, the Fellowship did not want to replace the Faeregine dynasty with a Hyde dynasty—they wanted to shatter Impyrium's very foundations. Hob's instructors had been very clear: *all* mehrùn were the enemy, *all* mehrùn were responsible for muir oppression. The entire system had to go. The Great Houses were little better than the royal family. From what Hob had seen of the Hydes, they might well be worse when it came to muir rights. He couldn't imagine Mr. Burke or Ms. Marlowe aligning themselves with such people.

As Finch gloated over his winnings, Hob found himself hoping the Lirlanders were to blame. It would simplify things and dampen his misgivings that he was a bit player in a game he did not fully understand. The Fellowship was demanding more information, but Hob was reluctant to share anything until he'd thought this through more carefully. He wanted to know what he was working toward and with whom. The Fellowship's last message disturbed him. It was unquestionably a threat: *Behave and report or else.*

Why were they so eager to learn about Hazel Faeregine? She was a kid, after all, though not much younger than Hob himself. And the more Hob saw of the princess, the more she surprised him. He never imagined she would be the type of person to take risks for someone else, much less a servant. Twice she'd stood up for him when it would have been far easier to do nothing. And she'd just shown real empathy and compassion for Finch. Hob did not believe Hazel was anyone's enemy. If he uncovered that she was powerfully magical, so what? Weren't all Faeregines supposed to be? What did the Fellowship intend to do with that information? Hob felt a pit begin to grow in his stomach.

Two moomenhovens came to prepare Hob for his nightly moonbath. Removing his bandages, they spread a glutinous salve on his wounds and face—even his chipped tooth. They then wheeled him to an adjoining room where a lift raised his bed until he was positioned beneath a runeglass dome. High above was a gibbous moon. When its light fell upon him, his skin began tingling as the salve's tiny lunasects wriggled to life.

He tried not to dwell on thousands of magical organisms leeching and chewing, burrowing and regurgitating as they repaired his flesh and even bone. Hob regretted his curiosity since his first night in the ward. Sometimes it was better not to know how something worked.

Hours passed before he was returned, clean and drowsy, to the main ward. Finch was snoring softly, the arcadia board untouched to commemorate his victory.

When the nurses had gone, Hob drew the curtain around his bed and reached for his handbook. Opening it to page 213, he found the Fellowship's message had faded, replaced by the list of diplomats. Flipping to the inside back cover, he stared at the blank buckram before tracing a reply with his finger.

Nothing to report.

CHAPTER 13
THE PHANTASIA GROTESQUE

I was born a poem, became a song,
and shall die as laws bound in calf.
I wish I'd stayed a poem.

—Mina I (9 P.C.–144 A.C.)

March would not go easily. Its gales whipped about Tùr an
Ghrian, making the tower creak and sway like a flagpole.
Hazel stood at a window, watching whitecaps move in formation across the harbor. Not even the boatmen were out. Two trade
galleons lay at anchor, bright Lirlander Seals on their prows.

Hazel mopped her forehead with a sleeve. Her mouth was dry
and her bones ached. Rascha had never pushed her so hard. No more
progressions; the vye was dragging her from the sunny shallows into

Mystics' murkier waters. The feats Hazel had been attempting were not only challenging, they frightened her.

The vye's staff rapped the malachite floor.

"Again, Your Highness."

"I can't, Rascha. I'm too tired."

"Because you are resisting. Changing shape requires an open mind. Stop clinging to Hazel Faeregine."

"But I *am* Hazel Faeregine."

Rascha wanted her to let go, to open doors in her awareness, but Hazel was afraid of what might be lurking on the other side. She had not heard any whispers since the Direwood, but she was becoming obsessed with the Reaper's portrait. Every night, she took the painting from its hiding place and stared at it by candlelight. The likeness both comforted and repelled her. She could no longer go to bed without completing her little ritual.

"That is only a name," her tutor insisted. "You are matter and energy, a spark of awareness. You can assume whatever form you wish."

Hazel turned to less existential concerns. "Then why do I have to become a *pig*?"

From her seat by a hearth, Sigga chuckled and nudged a piece of tangerine at Merlin. Hazel's homunculus accepted it gratefully, holding the segment with its wingtips.

"Human and pig anatomy are similar," Rascha answered. "It is the simplest transformation, and a useful one. I myself have had occasion to use it."

As she finished the sentence, Rascha's wolfish figure sank toward the ground. Robes pooled about her feet as the vye became a bristly black hog.

"I know you can do it," said Hazel. "I'm the one who can't. I don't have enough power."

The hog shifted again, flesh rippling, robes rising as it became an aged vye once again. Bending slowly, Rascha retrieved her staff. "You have power in spades. What you lack is focus and a willingness to let go. Try again."

Trudging back within the ring of megaliths, Hazel balled her fists and shut her eyes. She pictured the pig she'd like to become: a cute pink ball with a curly tail.

"I'na morphos soo'ar," she whispered. *"I'na morphos soo'ar . . ."*

"That's it," said Rascha. "You must see like a pig, hear like a pig, even smell like a pig . . ."

Hazel giggled.

"Focus!" Rascha barked.

Hazel's smile vanished. She listened dutifully as her tutor encouraged her piggy alter ego to shiver in the windstorm, tamp the earth with cloven feet, root in damp pine needles, scratch her side against rough tree bark.

But other impressions were invading Hazel's mind. It was no longer a pig she pictured, but something huge and dark, ragged and feathered. She did not smell damp pine but ash, blood, and boiling sap. The surrounding forest was ablaze, its heat and energy feeding the fires within her. But still she was ravenous.

Hazel's skin was growing uncomfortably snug. Her breath came in shuddering gasps, filling her lungs with air that tasted strangely metallic. Unlike Rascha's pig transformation, she wasn't shrinking down to four legs, but getting taller on two. Pain shot through her shins and feet as they began to lengthen. The ragged figure in her mind's eye was coming closer. Firelight flickered on a face that was a patchwork of bone, beak, and flesh. It was coming for her, coming for all of them. With a supreme burst of will, Hazel wrenched her gaze away.

Opening her eyes, she staggered and grabbed hold of a heavy brazier to regain her balance. For several seconds, she could do nothing but gasp for breath as the pains in her legs subsided.

"I give up," she croaked.

"Give up?" scoffed Rascha. "You're not even trying! Cease these theatrics and let go. Convince yourself that you are a pig!"

"But I'm not a pig!" cried Hazel. "I've never spent time with pigs. I don't know how they sniff or scratch or root or run. I'm using my imagination for everything and . . . other stuff creeps in. It would be easier if I had experiences to draw on, but I have no experiences. I've lived my entire life on this island."

A pause. "If you cannot change shape, you cannot pass the exams."

"I know," said Hazel. "No one knows better than I do."

The vye stiffened. "The empress is depending on you. You owe her your best effort after that foolery with the House Blade. There are worse punishments than mucking out the stalliana stalls. She was lenient with you."

"She was," Hazel admitted. "But will she be as forgiving with you?"

Dàme Rascha sat heavily on a carven bench and motioned for Hazel to sit beside her. "Is that what this is about? You are afraid for me?"

Hazel nodded. "You're the one who suffers if I fail. It terrifies me."

Rascha tutted. "At my age, threats and punishment mean very little. They do not frighten me, so do not dwell upon them. All I care about is seeing you become what you could be."

"And what is that?"

"The greatest sorceress since Mina the Fourth."

It was the last thing Hazel wanted to hear. "I don't want to be anything like her," she said quietly. "Besides, the Reaper was much more powerful than I am. She was a god."

Rascha leaned forward on her staff. "People thought that girl was muir most of her early life. Her power came later. And you doubt your own too much. Remember what Lord Kraavh said to you before the *Typhon* exploded."

Hazel recalled her conversation with the demon, his paralyzing and almost hypnotic aura. "He said I shone."

The vye nodded. "On some nights you shine brighter than any being I have seen. Brighter even than the gate dragons. Old Magic is in you, but you keep it locked away. That is where you and the Reaper differ. She reveled in her power."

Hazel had not told the vye about the whispers she'd heard in the Direwood, much less the monstrosity she'd just glimpsed while trying to transform. Rascha reported regularly to the Spider and Hazel did not want that information circulated. Not yet, when she herself didn't know what to make of it. Who knew how it would be interpreted?

"We end things here," said Dàme Rascha. "You have time for a quick supper, but no more. The phantasia begins at nine."

Hazel was relieved. "How is Mr. Smythe getting there?"

"He will come with me as my servant."

"But he's supposed to be a guest," said Hazel.

The vye had enough arguing. "Your Highness, that is the best I can do. Your sisters will be there. Perhaps the empress. Is this really the battle you wish to fight?"

Hazel knew her protests would be pointless, particularly if her grandmother was attending—she would never allow muir to sit in the royal box. But it did spoil her plans somewhat. She'd wanted to give Hob a special treat to celebrate his recovery and thank him for helping her ace Montague's latest exam. The master particularly liked her essay comparing economic theory and practice, and even shared a portion of it with the class. Isabel had been impressed, Violet astonished, and Imogene Hyde looked like she wanted to vomit. Each reaction was deeply gratifying. And so, Hazel was a little disappointed with the evening's arrangements. Only favored servants attended events like phantasias, but it still wasn't the same as being a guest.

Supper was brief, seared scallops and greens taken in the triplets' common room. Violet had already left, intending to dine with Lady Sylva and some of her friends. Isabel was there, however, arguing with Olo about which dress to wear.

"I like the turquoise," she said.

The maid disagreed. It was her opinion that the neckline plunged a bit too far. Her Highness was now a young lady . . . there were *considerations*. Hazel glanced down at her bony, tubular form. She wouldn't mind some considerations.

Isabel called to her homunculus on the ottoman. "What do you think, Pamplemousse?"

Hazel thought it rather unkind to have named him "grapefruit," but it was Isabel's favorite word from an ancient language. And the homunculus did not seem to mind. He looked up from his dish of blueberries. For a newly spawned being, his manner was shockingly mature.

"Is this really a question? The turquoise."

Olo hissed, tossing aside the conservative gray. The maid had not taken to Pamplemousse, who was not shy of voicing his views on matters of dress and decor—areas Olo considered her turf. She was more tolerant of Merlin, but only because Hazel's homunculus said nothing whatsoever. Hazel nudged him off her gown, so she could hold it up to the light: yellow silk embroidered with mother-of-pearl. Pamplemousse glanced over.

"You'll never pull it off, my dear. Not with your coloring."

Hazel could not say whether she pulled off her dress, but she did like what Olo had done with her hair. She admired it as the coach rolled down to the inlet where the Faeregines moored their yachts. Her fine white tresses were parted at the side, smoothed with a bit of cream, and pinned with a gold barrette. She was sleek as a selkie, in sharp contrast to Isabel's unruly mane. Isabel snatched Hazel's mirror to fix the lipstick Olo had refused to apply.

"I hate boats," she murmured.

"I think it's called a clipper," said Hazel.

"It won't care what it's called if I'm sick all over it."

Pamplemousse's head poked up from her furs. "Mind the shoes."

Isabel had dressed him in a purple velveteen suit that could accommodate his wings. Hazel thought it was ghastly. Merlin wore sensible tweeds.

Sigga opened the door and Isabel's bodyguard, a ruddy, side-whiskered Red Branch named Matthias Rey, helped them out. At the end of the ramp, *Vesper* bucked on the rough black sea. Clutching a railing (she'd never liked wearing heels), Hazel greeted the captain who escorted them into the cabin.

Mercifully, the voyage would not be long. *Vesper* was over eighty feet long, but she was built for summer regattas, not skipping over harbor chop.

"So, how does he look?" said Isabel, declining hors d'oeuvres from a crewman.

"Who?" said Hazel, knowing perfectly well who she meant.

"A certain page."

She affected surprise. "Him? Oh, he's fine. Lunasects can work miracles on minor wounds. Even his tooth is fixed."

"I heard he might be there tonight," said Isabel.

"Is that so?"

Isabel rolled her eyes. "Stop pretending. Archemnos heard Rascha making the arrangements. I think it's nice you invited him."

A weight slid off Hazel's shoulders. "I thought it was only right after everything that happened, but I know Violet won't approve."

Isabel put up her feet. "Who cares? She still isn't speaking to me for 'embarrassing the family,' but if it weren't for us, no one would know the real sword was missing. I say we're heroes!"

Hazel grinned. She could march to the gallows so long as Isabel was with her. Cheery irreverence was a tonic. She set Merlin on the windowsill. Outside, the night was brilliantly clear, the wind having driven the clouds inland. High above, Draco lashed a sapphire sky.

The voyage was only five miles, but it required them to navigate the harbor maze. Their destination was one of the many islands dotting the channel between the Sacred Isle and Impyria. Most housed naval bases, but the largest—the Île des Rêves—was dedicated to the arts.

Sitting atop the island was a grand concert hall whose spiraling white curves resembled a nautilus. Hazel had always loved the building's elegance and vast sculptural spaces. Of course, her previous visits were only for ordinary concerts. This would be her first phantasia.

Three phantasias were staged each year, but the spring Grotesque was by far the most popular. Not only did it herald an end to winter's doldrums, the Grotesque was reputedly stranger and more shocking than summer's Pastorale or autumn's Melancholia. The Spider forbade the triplets to attend any before their twelfth birthday. Dozens of yachts and several transport barges already surrounded the Île des Rêves. They belonged not only to Great Houses, but also to minor nobility, magistrates, and merchant princes. Phantasias were open to any with the means to afford a ticket, which was to say very few.

The Faeregines had their own docks, and Captain Whelk did a splendid job of navigating *Vesper* to the port. Once the vessel was secured, Hazel and Isabel followed their bodyguards down the ramp where the press was waiting. The girls did their best to ignore their questions.

"Isabel, is it true you want to be Divine Empress?"

"Where's Violet? Is there a rift in the family?"

"Is Lord Faeregine really stepping down as bank director?"

Hazel ignored Isabel's tug and stopped. "What?"

The man who'd shouted the question elbowed aside the competition. His beefy face broke into a snarky grin. "Evening, Your Highness—Gus Bailey from the *Busy Bee*—is it true your uncle's been forced from his post? That your family is losing control of the bank?"

Hazel recovered from her initial shock. "I have no idea what you're talking about." She and Isabel continued through the gauntlet of security as chamber music wafted from the hall.

Mr. Bailey kept pace with them. "No worries, Your Highness, no worries. Just dish on this nugget. Are you sweet on a page named Hobson Smythe?"

Hazel walked swiftly ahead, her face burning in the cold. Isabel had stopped, but all she wanted to do was get inside, to shut out the laughter and catcalls that followed her. She was used to pushy journalists and impertinent questions, but this struck a different kind of nerve. Of course she wasn't "sweet" on Hob—the notion was ridiculous—but it was just the kind of story that would make life impossible. Who would spread such a rumor?

She knew the instant she spied Imogene Hyde chatting with Tatiana Castile, Rika Yamato, and a few other court brats in the cavernous entry hall. They were standing by the bar, a sinuous stretch of redwood beneath floating glass sculptures. Several feet away, Lord Willem Hyde was holding court with the Castile and Yamato patriarchs. Imogene's mother was absent, but Dante stood at his father's elbow, a youthful version of his balding sire. Catching sight of Hazel, Imogene beamed and beckoned for her to join them.

Hazel ignored the invitation and allowed a servant to take her coat. Isabel stormed in a moment later.

"Idiots," she seethed, shaking off her coat. "At least Matthias flung that reporter's notebook into the harbor. Are you all right?"

"Fine," said Hazel. "I think Imogene started the rumor."

Isabel glared at the girls by the bar. "Of course she did."

Someone called Hazel's name. She turned to see Uncle Basil approaching with an entourage of ministers. He looked slimmer and more cheerful than when Hazel saw him last. Sending his guests ahead, he stopped to embrace his nieces.

"You look beautiful, both of you. I know I have to say these things, but it's true."

"You look dashing yourself," said Isabel.

Their uncle appraised them again, this time with a wistful air. "Only yesterday you were gummy, hairless creatures and now you're attending your first phantasia."

Before he could leave, Hazel tugged his elbow and lowered her voice. "A reporter said you were stepping down from the bank. Can that be true?"

His face darkened. "Who said that? Was it that man from the *Bee*?" Hazel nodded.

"I've had enough of him," he muttered before glancing at Hazel and softening his tone. "Don't let such rumors upset you. I'm not going anywhere. Our family still controls the bank. Our family will *always* control the bank."

"Yes, Uncle."

"Good," he said, kissing the top of her head. "I'll see you two in the box. And don't think I've forgotten about my mermaid, you thief. I want her back."

Isabel watched him go. "What was that about? What mermaid?"

"*The Little Mermaid*. I borrowed-slash-stole it."

Isabel linked her arm with Hazel's as they made their way through the glitterati. "I never liked that story. What's so charming about an amphibious stalker? If you ask me, she was creepy . . ."

The pair debated this all the way to the royal box. It was the largest and centermost suite on the grand tier with a commanding view of the stage, orchestra pits, and (most important) the audience. The box was already half-full, mostly with minor Faeregines from the mainland. Every relation—no matter how tenuous or distant—got to sit in the royal box once during his or her lifetime. They promptly stood when Hazel and Isabel entered.

The girls offered polite smiles, but made straight for Dàme Rascha and Archemnos, who had taken seats in the second row. Hob and the other servants stood at attention along an aisle.

"Sorry," she whispered, coming up to him. "I thought this would be, you know, fun. But it looks more like work."

Hob smiled. "Not at all, Your Highness. Do you remember Mr. Grayson?"

"Yes, of course," said Hazel, glancing at the page who had been with Hob at the duel. "How nice to see you again."

He bowed.

Isabel beckoned from the pair of seats she'd claimed in the first row. "Come on!"

Hazel's sister was eager to begin spying on other patrons, a favorite pastime going back to their first recitals. Already, she and Pamplemousse were scanning the hall for interesting subjects. Sitting next to her, Hazel let Merlin dangle his tiny legs over the railing. He craned his neck to observe his fellow domanocti settling like starlings on a special perch near the ceiling.

"Scandal sighted," Isabel whispered. "By the woodwinds. I believe—yes, there he goes again—that Lord Martin is squeezing that woman's bottom."

The girls snickered. Isabel scanned the boxes on their tier belonging to other Great Houses. She raised her glasses. "Duke Eluvan is really letting himself go."

Pamplemousse took a peek. "That's not a duke; it's a monument."

Meanwhile, the orchestras were warming up. A bassoon's warbling note rose above the fray. Isabel swiveled about.

"I didn't know Montague was here."

The girls doubled over with laughter, but Pamplemousse was not amused. "I'll ask you not to disparage my maker."

"How does that work?" asked Hazel, recovering herself. "I mean, you're only a few weeks old and you already know so much."

"Alchemy," replied the homunculus. "We all get drops of this or that. I fear your Merlin received too much antimony."

Merlin said nothing, but scratched his ear with a wingtip.

"When do I get to see through your eyes?" asked Isabel.

Pamplemousse patted her arm. "Soon, my dear. The bonding process takes time. No self-respecting familiar hands over powers on the first date."

Lights dimmed as chimes signaled the performance would begin. Below, patrons streamed through the doors as ushers guided them to their seats.

"Did you get a program?" asked Hazel.

"There are none," replied Isabel. "Only the performers know what's in store. Dr. Phoebus composes each Grotesque while he's in a trance."

The lights dimmed further as musicians ceased their warm-up. Most of the seats were now filled, including the Lirlanders' box. Hazel saw Lord Kraavh, his eyes three luminous slits. A feeling of tense expectation settled over the vast hall. Hazel peeked at Hob, but he was watching the door.

The royal chamberlain's tenor called out, "Her Radiance, the Divine Empress Mina the Forty-second."

Hazel and thousands of others stood as the Spider, accompanied by Violet and two bodyguards, made her way down the aisle. As usual, her grandmother eschewed elaborate costumery for a simple outfit in Faeregine red. She wore no makeup or jewelry save the Impyrial crown perched atop her balding head. In the stage spotlight's glare, her face looked like a death mask. Her expression was drawn and rigid with thin lips set in a widow's grimace. She might have been a corpse but for her eyes. They were very much alive—sharp and black, shrewd as a jeweler's. No one in the royal box was spared their attention as she shuffled down the steps. Her gaze lingered longest on Hazel.

Everyone remained standing until the empress was situated. Laying a translucent hand on Uncle Basil, the Spider gave her son a loveless kiss as he eased her into her seat.

Isabel leaned close. "She looks so frail."

Hazel nodded as they sat. She had been thinking the same. It was one thing to view a goddess upon a golden throne, but quite another to watch an arthritic crone inch down some stairs. Everyone would be speculating how much time the Spider had left. A year? A month? Hazel pitied Violet. She would be empress soon.

There was a brilliant flash before the hall plunged into darkness. Several people in the audience cried out. Hazel gripped Isabel's hand.

"Is this part of the performance?"

Isabel's response was strangely muted. "I—I don't know."

Hazel felt blindly for Merlin, but he seemed to have disappeared. Waving a hand before her eyes, she saw nothing, felt nothing—not even the chair beneath her. She might have been suspended in ink. Even the sound of her breathing had vanished. Something was systematically smothering her senses.

A subsonic humming began, deep and slow. Its vibrations crept up Hazel's body. Gradually, her heart adjusted to its slow, primitive beat.

Thump-thump . . . thump-thump . . . thump-thump.

Another vibration set Hazel's molars tingling. She had not let go of Isabel's hand, but she could not feel her sister's warmth. There was only the Sound, and it seemed infinite.

Her mind was floating. How long had she been sitting here. Hours? Days? How many heartbeats? Everything had gone numb.

Suddenly, she smelled lilac. Just a hint, but it brought a flood of memories. She was playing in a garden under the summer sun. A woman sat nearby, staring out at the sea. She was not yet forty, pretty but careworn with thick black hair that whipped in the breeze. Hazel noticed a signet ring on her finger. A plump little boy brought over a beetle he'd found. The woman gave an obligatory smile before looking at Hazel.

"Cover up, Arianna, you're starting to burn."

Boom!

Hazel cried out as a jolt shook the hall. Kettledrums were roaring, accompanied by thunder sheets and discordant bells. Hazel writhed in her seat, disoriented and frightened.

The drumming subsided as lights appeared before her eyes, blossoms of purest color that gamboled about, marvelously alive and tragically ephemeral. They left an aching void when they faded. Would Hazel ever see anything so beautiful again? Why had she ever taken such wonders for granted?

Drums returned: louder, faster, predatory. They reminded her of the Direwood. Did singing accompany them? Hazel thought she heard a chorus of faint ethereal voices.

Boom!

Another jolt and the concert hall returned. The dim stage was crawling with grossly elongated figures. The silhouetted forms squirmed and intertwined, swaying up like serpents poised to battle or mate. The spectacle was revolting yet spellbinding.

Isabel tapped her shoulder and pointed up. Hazel's jaw dropped. Onstage, the dancers' movements appeared abstract. Upon the ceiling their shadows were pantomiming a story.

Hazel tried to fathom how such chaotic movements could project such precise and complex shadows. Was it magic or sheer artistry?

More instruments joined the fray. One orchestra played melodies, the other jarring cacophonies. Often, it seemed they were trying to shout over one another. But every so often the sounds converged, creating harmonic nodes of such beauty that Hazel could hardly breathe.

The dance was building toward something. The music took on a nightmarish quality. Roving spotlights shone on the nemone dancers, illuminating their bizarre, fantastic forms.

Nemones were technically human but it was hard to believe. For thousands of years they had been bred to create extremes of balletic line and form. The result was hairless, androgynous beings who moved with uncanny, almost jointless fluidity. Some stood eight or nine feet tall, with three-foot necks and sleekly muscled limbs. They spent their entire lives on the Île des Rêves, cared for by servants. Dr. Phoebus might compose and conduct the phantasias, but the nemones were the star attraction.

Hazel turned to see how Hob was enjoying the performance. To her dismay, he stood perfectly rigid with an expression of contained revulsion. Her heart sank. She'd wanted to dazzle him, show him something of royal life the way he'd been sharing his experiences in the Muirlands. Maybe phantasias and nemones were an acquired taste.

The orchestras fell silent so that only a single musician remained playing. Applause sounded and Hazel turned from Hob to see a spotlight shining on a kitsune in flowered robes plucking a red belyaël.

Reisu was the most famous musician in Impyrium, a being whose gifts (two extra arms and sixteen extra fingers) gave her a unique ability to manipulate the instrument's many strings and slide beads.

But extra fingers were not needed for the piece she was now playing. Its simple notes were discordant and menacing. Onstage, the nemones backed away as something rose through the floor.

The huge figure was vaguely anthropomorphic. Was it a beast? A bird? Hazel could not say, but it must have required several nemones working together beneath some kind of feathered pelt. Its form looked unsettlingly familiar. The creature was pulsing, shaking, straining against its chains. Strange shadows now danced upon the walls. Hazel rested her chin on the railing. What was that thing?

A child-size figure flitted onstage wearing what looked like the Faeregine crown. It circled the mountain of feathers, soothing and stroking it. The other nemones were growing wild and agitated. The crowned figure tried to order them about, to conduct their patterns, but the leaping dancers knocked it to the floor. The figure retreated to center stage where the quaking black mound was tethered. Isabel whispered in Hazel's ear.

"I think the feathered thing's supposed to be the Reaper."

Hazel nodded. She suspected as much when the crowned figure had appeared. Mina III had been a weak ruler, which might explain why she was portrayed as a child.

When the tiny dancer placed its crown atop the hulking figure, there was an explosion of light and sound. Bursting its chains, the Reaper drew herself up and up, dwarfing even the tallest nemones. They retreated as bright green flames radiated from her, spilling over the stage and racing up the walls. The audience applauded the first-rate illusion.

But not Hazel. She watched in dry-mouthed horror as the monstrosity prowled about the stage. Periodically, it would rush at one of the nemones and engulf it in a frenzied shaking of black feathers. When the Reaper moved on, its victim had disappeared and it had grown larger.

The music grew wilder. Below, Dr. Phoebus was slashing left and right with his batons. Were his works really based on visions? The Reaper reigned over two thousand years ago. Why was she the subject of this Grotesque? Had the Reaper's Direwood whisperings somehow reached or influenced Dr. Phoebus?

Onstage, the nemones formed two rings that rotated in opposite directions around the monster. With their long, undulating movements, they appeared to glide rather than step.

Their beguiling patterns had a purpose. A sword was being passed among them, its presence visible to the audience but not to the bloodthirsty goddess. Whenever she appeared close to discovering the blade, its holder would flip it to another dancer with astounding skill and dexterity.

Flickering green flames were turning gold. The Reaper's search became frantic. The nemones scattered before her, darting just out of reach, passing the sword so quickly Hazel often lost track of it. The Reaper spun about. It lunged at a dancer, only to find it empty-handed . . .

I've been waiting for you.

The stage vanished as the ghostly whisper sounded in Hazel's mind. She was no longer sitting in a concert hall, but dozing in a hammock. Someone was shaking her and none too gently. Hazel cracked an eye open. A teenaged boy stood over her holding a half-shuttered lantern.

"Cap'n wants coffee."

Hazel was shocked to hear herself make a reply. "Make it yerself, Ratter. I just turned in."

"Ya turned in three hours ago. Up, or I cut ya down, Danny."

Why was he calling her Danny? When Hazel didn't move, Ratter held a small blade to one of the taut ropes suspending the hammock. Hazel scrambled out to find she was already dressed in canvas clothes and cheap, sturdy shoes. Steadying herself against the ship's roll, she staggered to a little washbasin. The bleary face blinking in the mirror was not her own.

She was a boy!

There was no mistaking it. Hazel Faeregine was a disheveled, drowsy boy no older than eight who looked like all he wanted was to crawl back in his hammock. Yawning, he snatched a cap with *Polestar* stitched on its wool in white thread. Snugging it down over his mousy brown hair, he glared up at Ratter before making his way to a tiny kitchen where he proceeded to grind little brown beans and heat a kettle of water.

Another whisper: *The world has been waiting for us.*

A sudden jolt shook the ship. Hazel crashed into a bulkhead, knocking the kettle off the stove as cooking utensils rained down. Boiling water scalded her hand; she fumbled for a dish towel. Panic set her heart fluttering. She gazed about, frightened and confused. What was happening? She gave a cry as the ship ground to a shuddering halt.

Cries sounded from on deck, followed by a scream that froze her marrow. Dropping the dish towel, she huddled in the corner, a mouse too frightened to move. Heavy footsteps raced past. A hoarse shout aft—the captain calling for all hands.

A cannon fired, its roar rattling the galley. Others followed, seemingly at random. The din was enormous. There were more screams. Hazel clamped her blistered hands over her ears. Someone burst in—the older boy from earlier. Ratter was deathly pale. He clutched a carpenter's mallet and hissed at Hazel to get below, to hide anywhere she could—

Timbers exploded as something swept through the galley, obliterating its upper half like matchsticks. Ratter was gone; he might never have existed. Hazel remained huddled in her spot. Icy rain pelted down upon her. She looked up to see a roiling black sky. Something had sheared the roof clean away.

You see what we are facing.

Something sinuous rose up to fill Hazel's view, a thorny tentacle lit from beneath by a phosphorescent shimmer. It was huge beyond imagining, even bigger than the masts. It swayed up toward the clouds, curling back like a great whip. When it began to descend, Hazel shut her eyes and recited a prayer she'd never heard before.

It is time to let me in.

Hazel gave a violent start. She was back in the concert hall, clutching Isabel's hand. Kettledrums were thundering, shaking the very seats. Onstage, the Reaper had its back turned to a nemone, who suddenly revealed the sword it was hiding. The blade flashed like fire as the nemone brandished it once . . . twice. . . . The Reaper whirled about just as the stroke fell. The blade plunged deep into its heart.

Whoosh!

The Reaper burst into hundreds of live ravens, screaming and cawing, wings flapping as they wheeled about the concert hall and soared out slender skylights. The flames chased them out, vanishing with a mad crash of cymbals.

Lights came on for the first intermission. The audience applauded and began to file out. Isabel whooped.

"That was amazing! What do you think, Pamplemousse?"

"I've done better productions myself."

"Oh fie." Isabel laughed. "You're not even a month old—" She broke off as she caught sight of Hazel, who sat rigidly upright while sweat poured off her stricken face. "Hazel, you don't look so good."

"I think I'm going to be sick," Hazel whispered.

"Maybe you should get some air," Isabel suggested.

Hazel nodded and rose from her seat. But the instant she stood, her legs wobbled and the room began to spin. Hazel reached out to stop herself from falling into the aisle, when she suddenly felt someone's hands on her waist setting her upright.

"It's all right. I've got you," Hob whispered in her ear.

Steadying her, he handed her off to Sigga, who sat Hazel against one of the pillars. Hob remained nearby, shielding her from view as Rascha and Sigga tended her. The anxious vye touched her wrist to Hazel's forehead.

"No fever. How is your stomach?"

"Okay," Hazel gasped. "I just got light-headed."

Dàme Rascha's brow furrowed. "Phantasias can have strange effects on sensitive natures. You've had enough for one night."

Hazel nodded. Isabel's face appeared.

"How is she?"

"Her Highness is going home," said Rascha. "Do you wish to come with us?"

Isabel did not—not once she'd been assured Hazel was fine. The Grotesque had three acts and she was not about to miss more pyrotechnics, stabbings, or shambling horrors made of live ravens. She would sail back on *Hippocamp*. Pecking Hazel on the cheek, she hurried out to socialize with their classmates.

Hob and Sigga helped Hazel up. Her head was clearing, but she remained woozy. She glanced down at the empty stage. In the orchestra boxes musicians were changing reeds and talking quietly with one another. It might have been intermission at any symphony or opera. Hazel began to feel enormously foolish. Had anyone else seen what was happening aboard that ship? Were hallucinations just part of the phantasia?

While Hob ran off to fetch their things, Hazel made her way slowly up the aisle. Half the box had emptied, but the Spider remained in her seat, surrounded by attendants. As Hazel passed, the Spider locked eyes with her before gesturing for Dàme Rascha to approach. The vye knelt so that the empress could speak softly into her ear. With a curt nod, Rascha returned to Hazel's side.

"What was that about?" said Hazel, blinking as they stepped into the bright entry hall.

"Nothing, Your Highness. Your grandmother merely asked if Mr. Smythe was the young man who fought the duel against Lord Hyde."

Hazel frowned. "Why did she want to know that?"

"I could not say, Your Highness."

They descended the staircase, Hazel holding the smooth glass railing as Sigga trailed behind them. Hob was already waiting below. As he helped Hazel into her coat, she heard someone call her name. Looking up, she saw Imogene and several court brats lining the balcony.

"I guess the rumors are true," Imogene called. "Have fun, you two!" She blew a kiss. The other girls howled with laughter.

Hazel turned and walked out of the concert hall, past the paparazzi, and down to the dock where *Vesper* was waiting. Within five minutes, its crew had them sailing back toward the Sacred Isle.

Hazel sat in the cabin, gazing out at Impyria's distant lights. She couldn't bear to look at anyone for fear she'd burst into tears. Those whispers; that scene aboard that ship. Hazel's stomach was twisted into icy knots. When Captain Whelk came in to check on his passengers, Hazel asked if she could have a word. Ignoring Rascha's quizzical look, she went to his cabin. Sigga followed, but remained just outside.

"Did you want to steer the ship, Your Highness?" he asked. "It's been a few years, but I daresay you remember how."

"No," she said. "Nothing like that. I was curious if you know a ship called the *Polestar*?"

His cheerful face brightened. "I do indeed. My wife's brother serves aboard her. First mate. Beautiful vessel—one of the old Hadesians."

Hazel could barely find the words. "And . . . is she at sea?"

The captain shook his head. "She's refitting off Malakos, Your Highness. Won't set sail for at least a week."

Hazel breathed for what seemed the first time since the phantasia had begun. Thanking the captain, she returned to the others and reclaimed her seat by the window. The evening had hardly gone as planned, but at least she hadn't just witnessed an actual catastrophe. Dàme Rascha came to sit beside her.

"What was that about?"

"Nothing," said Hazel. "I was curious about something."

"You're upset," the vye observed. "Is it the Hyde girl?"

"No. Please drop it." Hazel closed her eyes.

Dàme Rascha was good at many things, but reading emotional cues was not one of them. Despite her good intentions, she could not truly empathize with Hazel's feelings. Vyes didn't get frightened or embarrassed, at least not in a human sense. Hazel wished she could be more like Hob. He'd faced lots of challenging, even brutal situations without fainting or going to pieces. Where did that kind of toughness come from? Were some people just born with it or was it something you could acquire?

She saw his reflection in the window. He was sitting across the cabin near Sigga, fingers laced, his eyes on an antique globe bolted to the floor. Hazel spoke to his reflection.

"You could have stayed, you know."

His eyes met hers in the glass. "Thank you, Your Highness. I had enough too."

"You didn't like the Grotesque?"

A pause. "It was an experience."

Turning away from the window, she leaned against Rascha's shoulder. "That's funny. I'm always telling Rascha I need more experiences—normal experiences, not like phantasias. Would you believe Île des Rêves is the farthest I've ever traveled?"

Hob pointed across the channel. "The world's greatest city is right over there. Why doesn't Master Montague take your class? You're studying the Muirlands after all."

Hazel laughed. "He probably hasn't left the Sacred Isle for thirty years. Once masters make it to Rowan, they cling like barnacles."

"Why don't you take a trip yourself?"

Rascha stiffened. Hazel was about to say *I'm not allowed*, her automatic response to mainland invitations. It was the quickest way to stop the conversation. But this time something stopped her.

Why couldn't she visit Impyria?

She was a princess, not a prisoner. For twelve years she'd stayed put on Rowan, chained partially by royal custom, but also because she often preferred to stay in her room with a good story or spell book. Her sisters had visited the mainland. Not often, but they'd both done it. Upon reflection Hazel felt like a rabbit that had spent its life in an unlocked cage, too timid to hop out into the meadow. The revelation was so startling, it distracted her from the deeply troubling things she'd seen and heard during the Grotesque. She turned to Rascha.

"Could we?" she asked.

"What? Visit Impyria?"

"Yes."

"Absolutely not. Far too dangerous at present. Wouldn't you agree, Agent Fenn?"

To Rascha's annoyance, Sigga did not agree. "Her Highness would need to be disguised, but I don't see any harm in a daytime visit. Perhaps she'll stop sneaking out at night."

"That was one time!" said Hazel.

But Dàme Rascha stood her ground. "After your birthday," she said. "Until then, we need every minute and we're losing a week to the May Ball and Midsummer. After your birthday, I promise we'll take a vacation. Perhaps you'd like to visit the Witchpeaks."

"Oh come on, Rascha," Hazel pleaded. "I can't wait until my birthday. I'm hitting a wall now. Maybe Impyria will inspire me, give me more experiences to draw on. Couldn't that be *useful?*" she added significantly. She could not discuss her magical studies in front of Hob.

"And if it isn't?"

"Then we've wasted one day. Even if a visit doesn't help our task, I'll see lots that I can use for Montague's class."

"*Master* Montague," her tutor corrected.

Whenever Rascha started nitpicking, Hazel knew victory was within reach. She snuggled up next to her tutor. "Please, Rascha? One tiny field trip." She gently arranged the vye's shawl.

Rascha sighed and gazed down at her affectionately. "A child wants a toy."

Hazel grinned. "But a very sweet child. And a very educational toy."

"Very well," said Rascha. "I will consult the empress. If she approves, you may go." She turned to Hob. "You. Boy."

He looked startled. "Yes?"

"You know the city?"

"Some districts better than others."

"Good," said Dàme Rascha. "This was your idea so you will come too. You can show Her Highness all the muirish things. And if anything goes amiss, you'll be at hand so I can kill you."

Hob smiled.

The vye did not.

CHAPTER 14
TOURISTS

What strange phenomena we find in a great city,
all we need to do is stroll about with our eyes open.
Life swarms with innocent monsters.

—Charles Baudelaire, Pre-Cataclysm poet (192–146 P.C.)

Two weeks later, Hob ate buttered toast at a corner table in the servants' dining room. Despite its underground location, sunlight filtered through mirrored light shafts, illuminating the windows and brightening the space. In the neighboring kitchens, hags could be heard singing (and swearing) as they went about their work.

Given that it was eight thirty on a Sunday morning, the dining room was nearly empty. Those on duty had already eaten; those who were not elected to sleep. Thus Hob was able to scavenge almost an entire newspaper from remnants discarded by the early risers. The front page was missing but it was far better than the usual pickings. On most days, he was lucky to get the advertisements.

And so he nibbled toast and luxuriated with almost all the empire's news at his fingertips. As Hob turned the page, he heard a playful voice.

"Well, Mr. Smythe, I see you're taking your ease."

The voice belonged to Maeve Poole, a maid from the Skeiner Isles. The two worked many of the same shifts and had become friendly. Hob pushed out a chair for her to sit, but she held up a silver tray.

"Can't. Lady Ferrina likes her breakfast hot and prompt. You playing thumper later? Karina and I were thinking of coming. I hear you're the one to watch."

"Not today. Working."

She glanced skeptically at his wool suit and cap. "Not in those clothes you're not."

"Heading across the Channel."

Maeve's freckled face clouded. "With a certain princess?"

Hob finished his toast. "You know I can't answer that. Faeregine business is private."

"Especially hers," she chided. "Rumor's true then?"

"What rumor?"

The maid batted her dark lashes. Hob set down his coffee.

"You've been reading Gus Bailey," he said. "You know better than to trust that smudger. He's gutter trash."

"Well," said Maeve, "someone agrees with you. That's just where he turned up."

Hob cocked his head. "Come again?"

She nodded at the ironed newspaper on her tray. "Gus Bailey's dead. They found him last night behind the *Bee*."

"What happened?"

"Someone cut his throat for 'im." Hob's mouth fell open. Maeve laughed and tossed him the paper as she headed for the door. "Read all about it—Lady Ferrina never bothers."

Hob nodded good-bye, still processing the news. He had nothing but disdain for Gus Bailey, but he didn't like hearing anyone had been murdered. Perhaps he shouldn't have been surprised. The man made a living irritating the rich and powerful. Mosquitoes that buzzed too loud got swatted.

He flipped the newspaper over, but it was not the Bailey headline that got his attention but the one in extra-large type splashed beneath the masthead:

POLESTAR LOST AT SEA
Galleon disappears off Malakos. Lirlanders suspected.

Eyewitness accounts suggest that *Polestar*, flagship of Thaler & Company's trading fleet, was lost with all hands in the early morning hours off Malakos. In addition to lost cargo, the *Chronicle* regrets to report that several notable persons were aboard . . .

Hob's jaw tightened as he read the list of mehrùn and minor nobles who had booked passage on the ill-fated ship. No mention whatsoever of the numerous crew who also lost their lives. Of course not; they were just muir. He returned to the article.

Coastal fishermen report the ship sank within minutes of passing the warning buoys marking demon waters. Despite overnight storms, the galleon's Lirlander Seal was clearly visible. She was sailing southwest when she came to an inexplicable halt. According to witnesses, the beacon shook violently before bobbing up and then disappearing into the sea. Experts speculate that the vessel possibly broke in two before sinking.

Initial suspicion falls on the Lirlanders. Given the moderate seas, few natural hazards could sink a ship of *Polestar*'s size and refurbished condition. No icebergs have been sighted in the area and the waters contain no hidden rocks or shoals. If the Lirlanders are to blame, the incident would represent a blatant violation of the Red Winter Treaty, which guarantees safe passage to any ship bearing a Lirlander Seal. Ambassador Kraavh has issued a statement denying any wrongdoing by his people. Lord Kraavh, who has been confined to his embassy since the recent *Typhon* explosion, was unavailable for further comment. That incident remains under investigation . . .

Hob scanned the rest and gave a low whistle. Wars broke out over things like this. He wondered what the Fellowship's position would be on a conflict between Impyrium and the Lirlanders. It would undoubtedly weaken the Faeregines and Great Houses, but it would also cost thousands—if not millions—of muir lives. And that was assuming Impyrium was victorious. What if the Lirlanders triumphed? Life under the Faeregines might seem like paradise compared to a world ruled by demons.

Taking his dishes, Hob headed into the kitchens, where the hags were busy mixing, mashing, slicing, and dicing under Bombasta's watchful eye.

During the past few months, he had grown strangely fond of the hags whose terrifying exteriors masked more endearing qualities. Yes, they were foul and brutish, but they could also be generous, funny, and fiercely loyal to those they deemed sufficiently haggish.

Hob had earned haggish status not only for dueling Dante Hyde but also for having "the stones" (Gorgo's delicate term) to court a Faeregine princess. Whenever he denied this, the creatures would simply brandish their beloved tabloids as if they constituted unimpeachable evidence. And while the hags openly wagered when Hob would be executed, they honored his temerity. He was a moron, but he was *their* moron.

Dropping off his dishes, he headed to the beverage station, where Bombasta was waiting. "Well, well, it's Mr. Smythe. Or should I say Lover Boy? How ya like your coffee?"

"Black."

She filled a thermos. "And I like my money shiny. You bring it?"

"How good are the seats?"

The hag shrugged and screwed on the thermos cap. "No clue, but my produce feller hooked me up and he's a big supporter. Never shuts up about it. Blah, blah, blah, GOAL!"

"All right," said Hob. Reaching in his pocket, he produced four demilunes.

Bombasta shook her greasy head. "Six."

Hob closed his hand. "We said four."

The hag leaned as close as her belly would allow. "And I'm telling ya six. Call it a service fee."

"Do you realize who you're shaking down?"

A greasy thumb and forefinger pinched his cheek. "A nice little page who's gonna find two more silvers."

"Sigga Fenn."

The hag's grin vanished. "You're yanking my haunch."

"Nope. It's her money."

"Fee's waived." When Hob opened his hand, the hag took only three coins. "So there's no misunderstanding, eh? Good lad."

Handing Hob the thermos, Bombasta hunted for the tickets in her voluminous shirt. Her efforts yielded a moist and crinkled envelope that he accepted without comment.

He left the kitchens, continuing down the many ramps and steps that led to Rowan Harbor. At the guard station, he was searched and his possessions cataloged. Since the discovery that Bragha Rùn was missing, everyone departing the Sacred Isle was searched. While a guardsman went through his pockets, Hob realized how eager he was to set foot on the mainland. He had not been back since taking up service in the palace. Many servants only made the trip once or twice a year. Some hadn't left in decades. Satisfied, the guardsman stamped Hob's papers and and he was authorized to leave the Sacred Isle.

Authorized to leave.

For a boy who'd grown up in the Sentries, this was a chilling concept. Aside from the occasional tax collector or census taker, Duskers had little contact with Impyrial officials. The Northwest was too wild and sparsely populated for the authorities to bother with them. But here it was different; almost everything required paperwork and permission. Even Hazel Faeregine—a direct descendant of Mina

I—required official permission to leave her home. That Her Highness received it was irrelevant. A lenient jailer was still a jailer.

Breathing deep, Hob emerged into the bright April morning. Spring had arrived. Its scent was in the salt breeze, its song in the gulls gliding on the currents, screeching and diving into briny pools. The beach's sand was gray and damp, glinting with shells and strewn with kelp. His shoes squelched with every step, leaving soft impressions the tide would wash away that afternoon. The thought struck him as sad somehow, but Hob supposed they were all just beachcombers on a one-way stroll. Even the Faeregines.

He'd brought no coat, only a wool cap and scarf that fluttered behind him as he walked to the cove where the royal boats were docked.

As Hob walked along the beach, he passed a group of monks in golden robes, meditating on the wet sand. One stood in the shallows, chanting and scattering handfuls of rice. Many religious delegations came from all over Impyrium to visit Faeregine tombs or behold various relics. Hob guessed the monks were paying homage to Ember. Some believed the Father of Dragons still slumbered beneath the Sacred Isle, and that the beast's awakening would herald a second Cataclysm. Hob did not share this view.

At the checkpoint, he showed his papers to one of the guardsmen and ignored the man's grunt of recognition. Apparently soldiers read tabloids too. The man waved him ahead.

"Stay away from *Mariner*," he warned. "Captain's got her on alert after what happened to *Polestar*."

Hob continued on, gazing at the trade galleon in question. Sailors and cranes were unloading crates from her holds and deck.

A Lirlander Seal shone like a ghostly sun beneath her bowsprit. Hob could not get over the ship's size. The harbor tugs and yachts were toys in comparison. He recalled the newspaper account of the *Polestar*'s disappearance. What could possibly tear such a vessel in two?

He was the first to reach the rendezvous spot. Sitting on one of the pier's benches, he watched birds circle the lighthouse on Kirin Point. Within its shadow stood the Lirlanders' embassy, a structure resembling a crown of black coral. A barricade blocked the coastal road to its doors. Just offshore, a pair of Impyrial warships lay at anchor. He would inform the Fellowship of their presence.

Hob wondered how many more reports he would ultimately write. Over the past few weeks, he had come to the realization that he was a good teacher and a poor spy. He was too proud, too quick to defend his honor in situations where muir were not supposed to have any. Professional spies didn't fight duels or find themselves in gossip pages; they were bland, forgettable collectors of available intelligence and clever procurers of intelligence that was *not* readily available. It was this last quality that differentiated spies from mere informers and Hob had failed miserably in this regard. His reports on Hazel Faeregine had been limited to her strange behavior in the Direwood, her dizziness at the phantasia, and the fact that she worked late every evening atop Tùr an Ghrian. None of these provided any real insight into her magical capabilities.

He had made casual inquiries into her magic, innocent little questions about what she was working on, what Tùr an Ghrian was like, and so forth. Yet they never yielded anything more than a sharp reminder from Dàme Rascha that he would confine his lessons to the Muirlands.

And those would soon be at an end. Hob was perfectly aware that Hazel's grades were the only reason he had not been fired. They had improved significantly, and not just in Montague's class. Still, Hob knew he only had so much time to gather information until the school year ended and he'd be shown the door. If he was lucky, Oliveiro would give him a reference and a bribe to go quietly. The Fellowship would be disappointed—perhaps even angry—but Mr. Burke would find another use for him.

As time ticked past, Hob grew troubled. Several yachts had come and gone. From high above, Old Tom chimed the hour. Nine o'clock. Nine thirty. Still, no Hazel. Hob confirmed with a patrolling guardsman that he was at the right pier. It was nearly ten when an elderly banker in a gray suit asked him the way to pier seven.

"This is it," said Hob, glancing at the two young clerks that accompanied him.

"Good," said the banker complacently. "Apparently the illusion is effective. Come along, Mr. Smythe."

Hob cocked his head. "*Sigga?*" he whispered.

"Rascha," replied the banker curtly. "Don't gawk, boy. You did not think we would venture out undisguised, did you? Come."

Getting up, Hob followed them down the pier, trying to guess which clerk was Sigga and which was Hazel. Rascha led them not to a yacht but to a little sloop whose captain was dozing with a cat on his lap. He cracked an eye as Rascha stood in his sun.

"You Yezdani?" he said. "If so, you're late."

"Yes," said Rascha. "Thank you for waiting."

The man spit tobacco juice over the side. "It's your money. Come aboard. Try not to scratch the paint."

He laughed at his own wit. What little paint the *Spritely* had was faded and peeling. As they walked down the gangplank, the captain barked orders at a barefoot girl playing jacks in the bow. She scowled and got up to unmoor them.

The boat eased into the harbor. Through the cabin's dirty windows, Hob watched as the captain steered them toward some boatmen bobbing in their skiffs. One took up its oars to guide them through the maze. The younger of the clerks—a small red-haired boy of ten or eleven—came to stand near Hob.

"Sorry we're late. I was having second thoughts."

Hob stared. "Your Highness?"

The clerk nodded. The other one, a dusky teenager, pushed aside some newspapers and sat on a bench. "You'll get your own illusion once we're off this tub."

"Agent Fenn?" said Hob.

"At your service."

Hazel's eyes wandered about the cabin. "Speaking of tubs . . ."

Rascha sat heavily next to Sigga. "You wanted real experiences, Your Highness. The *Spritely* is the cheapest fare to the mainland. She's popular with servants and tradesmen."

Hazel nudged aside a sandwich crust. "I miss *Vesper*."

The four sat in the cabin as the little sloop followed the boatman through the shadowed maze. It was far easier to get out than in, but Hob noticed the route they took was different from the one used on the night he'd attended the Grotesque. He would never grow used to the maze's towering walls and smothering mists.

The sun returned when they left the maze. Sailing south, they rounded its outer walls and headed west toward Impyria. Water sprayed over the bow as *Spritely* skimmed the waves. Turning from the window, Hob did a double take.

"What's wrong?" asked Hazel.

"Your disguises are gone," he said, looking from one to another.

"They're not," said Sigga matter-of-factly.

"But I can see you," Hob insisted. "You're not a boy in a gray suit anymore. You're Agent Fenn plain as day."

"That's not what the captain or that girl see," Sigga replied. "Since you know it's a disguise, the illusion gradually loses its effect on you. But others see it." She took out a small folding mirror and angled it toward him. "Look at us in there."

To Hob's amazement, the banker and his clerks continued to live in the looking glass. The hairs on Hob's arm stood up.

"Mirrors intensify illusions," Sigga explained. "They always show the false image. Even to those who know better."

Hob left the cramped cabin to get some air. On deck, the captain hummed a bawdy shanty. The cat now sat by the young girl, who had resumed her game of jacks.

Hob went to the starboard rail. Looking north, he could just make out the Île des Rêves, its concert hall a white seashell on a bed of black rock. The island had no other buildings that Hob could see. He wondered where the nemones lived. Looking down, he watched his shadow racing over the sea. A taller one joined it.

"Are you feeling all right?" Sigga asked, coming to stand by him.

"Just needed air," he replied. "I really don't like boats."

"You wouldn't. You're a Sentries boy."

He nodded.

"I was just thinking about your village," she said. "Dusk came up in my security memo."

Hob turned. "Is everything okay? Were there raiders? My mother and sis—"

Sigga waved off his concern. "Nothing like that. No, there's an Impyrial dig site nearby. The archaeologists returned and discovered that someone made an unauthorized visit."

Hob tried to keep calm. "I heard about that site. Someone trespassed?"

She nodded. "They even destroyed its guardian. The archaeologists found a rifle all twisted up in the golem's hand. A Boekka." The agent paused, gazing thoughtfully at the waves. "You had a Boekka, didn't you? You used it to hunt that Cheshirewulf."

"Everyone in the Northwest uses Boekkas."

Sigga grinned like a jackal, hungry and clever. The Grislander was showing through.

"Oh, I'm not accusing you of anything," she said. "This happened sometime after mid-October. Your records say you enrolled at Stock & Trade's in July. Unless you can teleport, you couldn't possibly have been at the dig site."

Hob tried to keep his mouth from twitching. "I'm glad you did your homework."

Sigga drummed her fingers. "Of course, there's always a chance your records were falsified. It's happened before and you're certainly smart enough. Did you falsify your records, Mr. Smythe?"

Hob met her gaze. "No."

"Very good."

Her tone was such that Hob couldn't tell if she was satisfied by his answer or complimenting his performance. The Grislander glanced sideways at him.

"Ever been to Whitebarrow?"

The question was so out of the blue that Hob merely stared at Sigga a moment. Whitebarrow was a ruin in the high Sentries, not far from the pass that led into the Grislands. Most Duskers assumed it had been some kind of burial or religious site, but none could say for certain. Whoever raised its mounds and stone structures had left long before even the Hauja settled those inhospitable lands.

"What does Whitebarrow have to do with anything?" he asked.

"Have you been there?" she repeated.

"Near it," he admitted. "I passed by its cairns on séyu. But I never set foot in the actual ruins. No one does. It's supposed to be haunted."

"Someone visited," said the Grislander simply. "And fairly recently."

"Okay," said Hob. "Why is that so disturbing?"

Sigga was studying his face closely. "The archaeologists found a recent blood offering atop the highest cairn. This is disturbing, Mr. Smythe, because Whitebarrow was built to honor the Shibbolth. Have you heard of them?"

Hob searched his memory. "The Shibbolth are demons, aren't they?"

"Correct," said the Grislander. "Ancient demons that remained in their own realm during the Cataclysm. Unlike the Lirlanders and Zenuvians, they viewed Astaroth as an upstart and refused to serve him."

"So, they're like another tribe?" said Hob.

"More like another race," Sigga replied. "The Shibbolth are older than the Lirlanders. Since they never served Astaroth, they were never conquered by humans and haven't spent millennia confined in the mortal world. Some would say they are purer demons, untainted."

"You almost sound like you admire them, Agent Fenn."

This made her laugh. "I wouldn't be the first. Once, there were cults that worshipped the Shibbolth as gods. The worst was a group of necromancers called the Coven. They're the ones who built Whitebarrow."

"I've never heard of them," said Hob. "Is there a reason you're telling me this?"

She tutted. "No need to get defensive, Mr. Smythe. I merely thought you should know what we'd found. If I had family in Dusk, I'd want to warn them. Necromancers prey on humans and your village is the closest settlement to Whitebarrow."

Hob felt sick. "You think they're in danger?"

"I hope not," said Sigga. "The offering at Whitebarrow might have been a hoax or an isolated incident. After all, the Coven was stamped out centuries ago. I'd still alert those I care about."

"I'll write to them tonight," said Hob. "What should I say?"

"To be vigilant," Sigga replied. "Necromancers can be difficult to detect because they hide within living hosts, but I'd tell your mother to be wary of any recent arrivals in Dusk. If she's suspicious of someone, she should watch to see if they linger near burial sites. Necromancers are drawn to death. It enhances their power."

Hob nodded. "Anything else?"

From her pocket, Sigga produced a slim vial filled with a greenish liquid. Hob peered at it, for it appeared to be bubbling.

"What is that?"

"A special poison," said Sigga. "Harmless to ordinary humans, lethal to necromancers. It incinerates the host's body they're inhabiting. I'll make you a deal, Mr. Smythe. You drink this and I'll give you a second vial you can send on to your mother."

Hob gave an uneasy laugh. "You think I'm a necromancer?"

"Not really," said Sigga. "But a necromancer can pass as just about anyone—even a child."

Hob peered warily at the potion. "You're certain that won't hurt me?"

She handed it to him. "Let's just say I'm optimistic." As Hob took the glass tube, he had a sudden urge to fling it into the sea. Was he really going to drink some mysterious potion? It might very well be dangerous. Then again, he imagined refusing to drink it might be more so. Turning his back to the cabin, Hob tossed back the vial's impossibly bitter and even greasy contents. The first time he tried to speak, he nearly retched.

"That"—he wheezed—"was unbelievably disgusting." Wiping his mouth, he glowered at Sigga. "How long 'til I explode?"

She patted his shoulder. "No explosions, Mr. Smythe. Apparently, that's the body you're meant to have. I'm glad. I'd have hated to say good-bye this way."

The Red Branch handed over a second vial. "I hope your mother puts it to good use. Let's move on to happier topics. I trust you got the tickets?"

Hob patted his jacket pocket. "Four seats, midtier. Should be decent."

Sigga held out her hand for the change, nodding with approval at the number of coins. "Thank you, Mr. Smythe. I hope Her Highness enjoys this day. I know I am."

She returned to the cabin. Hob spent the next hour in an anxious state. Her story of necromancy at Whitebarrow was troubling, but his main concern was the discovery of his Boekka at the dig site. Mr. Burke had promised Hob that no inquiries into his background would turn up anything suspicious. His paperwork passed muster, but what if Sigga had someone make inquiries in Dusk itself? Most Duskers would stonewall Impyrial questions, but someone would talk eventually. Angus Dane would be more than happy to tell the authorities that Hob had been there through the New Year.

What did Sigga truly suspect? The agent was not broaching these topics by chance. She was playing with him, spooking him on purpose. To what end? She could have him arrested any time she liked. Was Sigga hoping he'd lead her to bigger game? He needed to stay calm and think things through. The Fellowship would have experience in these matters. He would contact Mr. Burke as soon as it was safe. Gazing ahead, Hob saw they were nearing the long, curving seawall that sheltered Impyria's harbor. The *Spritely*, along with other ships, was making for the southernmost gap. Hob walked back to the captain.

"Why are we coming in so far south?"

The man pointed to colored flags fluttering atop the seawall. "Scrag's End's safest today. Rough currents."

Hob returned to the cabin where Hazel was sitting beside Dàme Rascha. She stared straight ahead, her upper teeth caught on her lower lip. He noticed she was wearing a tiny smudge of pink lipstick. He'd never seen her wear lipstick before, not even at the phantasia. And those little silver earrings were new. So was the camel hair coat. One hand stroked Merlin; the other gripped the strap of a smart little purse. She looked like a girl on her first day of school. He'd almost forgotten Her Highness was disguised by an illusion until he caught her reflection in the opposite window. It showed an anxious clerk sitting beside a scowling banker.

The banker spoke. "Feeling better, boy?"

He glanced at Dàme Rascha. "Yes, thank you. The captain says we need to come in from the south, so we'll be sailing by Scrag's End. Perhaps Her Highness might want to see it."

The princess frowned. "What is Scrag's End? It's not one of the districts."

"It's an unofficial district," said Hob. "Technically, it's not in the city limits. It's—"

"The slums," said Sigga bluntly.

"And why would Her Highness wish to see slums?" said Rascha.

"I thought the idea was to see how people live in the outside world," said Hob. "Scrag's End is part of it. A bigger part than many realize."

The vye offered a baleful glare. "Are you lecturing me?"

"Of course not," said Hob. "I'll see if we can sail around—"

Hazel hopped to her feet. "I want to see it. The whole point of today is to have new experiences. Besides, it can't be that bad."

They smelled Scrag's End well before the *Spritely* slipped past the massive seawall. Its reek carried on the wind, a miasma of raw sewage, dead fish, and concentrated humanity. On deck, Hazel promptly produced a handkerchief and pressed it tightly against her nose.

When it came into view, Hazel stared in astonished silence. Scrag's End couldn't be seen from most parts of Impyria. It was tucked away, separated from the city by walled cliffs crowned with watchtowers. A makeshift city of tents and shacks sprouted in their shadow like toadstools. Most were made of wood, scrap metal, even bits of sailcloth. Many hundreds were piled atop one another, ten or even fifteen high on makeshift scaffolds. Space was so scarce that the settlement overflowed onto the sea in networks of rafts and houseboats. They rose and fell on the swell like clumps of seaweed.

Dàme Rascha chuffed. "Not the introduction to Impyria I would have wished."

Hazel was spellbound. "How many people live there?"

Hob couldn't have guessed. The distant figures teemed like maggots on a carcass, thousands upon thousands of human beings climbing the scaffolds, peering out from shacks, relieving themselves in the very water where others fished or bathed.

"A hundred thousand," said Sigga. "Give or take. Sometimes a fire destroys it, but they always rebuild."

"Why?" said Hazel. "I mean, why don't they live in the city? Or go someplace else?"

Sigga shrugged. "If they could, they would. Some are sick, some have no money, some have lost their wits. Plenty are hiding. From the law, or something worse. Everyone in Scrag's End has a story. Except the kids. They're just unlucky."

"Have you been in there?" asked Hazel.

"Twice."

"And did you stay long?"

A pause. "No, I tracked down my targets and got out. Had to burn my clothes." The Grislander narrowed her eyes and called back to the captain. "Larboard bow."

He called back. "Got 'em."

"What?" asked Hazel.

"Pirates."

Sigga pointed to two galleys flying fanlike sails. They were several hundred yards away, but Hob saw they were packed with men, some lining the decks, others pulling on oars.

Hazel laughed. "*Pirates?* We're not in a story. There can't be pirates in the capital's harbor."

"No patrols come down here," said Sigga. "Any boat off Scrag's End will snap up something if opportunity presents. We're small enough to look interesting."

Hazel's expression suggested she still refused to believe such things could occur in broad daylight. "Are we in danger?" she asked. "Are they going to—what's the term?—*board* us?"

The Grislander looked amused. "No, Your Highness, we're not the ones in danger. If they come too close, I'll be boarding them."

Spritely changed course, sailing parallel to the shore. Pursuit lasted another ten minutes. When it was clear they would not catch her, the pirates ceased rowing and the galleys fell off, coasting along like reef sharks.

They left Scrag's End behind, passing several buoys before rounding a point that revealed Impyria proper. Hazel stood near the bow, Merlin perched on her shoulder as they passed ironworks and warehouses, shipping piers, and little cliffs dotted with homes belonging to merchants and sea captains. The ships moored or docked in this section of the harbor were huge—great galleons and barges, some flying Lirlander Seals, others outfitted for coastal work. Hazel pointed to the stern of a yellow xebec.

"She's based in Ana-Fehdra! It says so right there."

"That's right," said Hob. "If that's home, what do you think she'd be carrying?"

"Spices," said Hazel at once. "They're Ana-Fehdra's chief export— particularly jinn pepper and sweetseed."

"And what might Ana-Fehdra want in return?" Hob prodded.

The princess wrinkled her nose. "Grain?" she ventured. "Didn't some kind of insect ruin the last two harvests?"

Hob pointed to the where workers were stacking large sacks onto pallets.

"Ha-ha!" she crowed. "I knew it! I'm practically a seer!"

The princess's enthusiasm was contagious. Hob could not help but smile as she gripped the rail, leaning this way and that to see each ship and guess what it might be carrying or what its next destination might be. She turned to Hob, her eyes aglow.

"There must be thousands of them," she said excitedly, "sailing all over the world this very minute. I had no idea. It's all so enormous."

"Commerce powers the empire, and the empire is vast," said Dàme Rascha. "You see why the Lirlander Seals are so important. None of this happens without them. You understand now?"

Hazel nodded, then pointed at the highest cliffs. "That's the Grand Temple!"

"Yes," said Dàme Rascha. "Rather larger than the palace's. If we'd arrived earlier, we might have attended services."

"But we're much too late," said Hazel quickly. "What's that?"

Something hidden by the Grand Temple's spires now appeared within view—a red zeppelin tethered by ropes to an inland building they could not yet see. Three white letters were stamped on the balloon's side: IEC.

Hazel sounded it out. "Yech? What does that mean?"

Hob stifled a laugh. "Impyrian Euclidean Club. There's a match this afternoon."

"Euclidean Football?" said Hazel. "Isabel is always going on about it. Rowan students play it."

"This is the professional league," said Hob. "Best players in the world."

Hazel turned to Dàme Rascha. "Can we go?"

The vye did not spoil the surprise. "Our schedule is full. We will be touring several districts before visiting the museums. There's a porcelain exhibit I want to see."

Hazel gazed wistfully at the balloon. "Porcelain sounds most interesting."

But nothing could dampen her mood for long. There was too much to see, even from the harbor. Hazel stood in the bow as the captain sailed for a dock near the Dragon Pier, where the shrouded boatmen waited to ferry visitors to the Sacred Isle.

She watched with delight the foul-mouthed banter between the young mate and a grizzled salt who caught the rope she'd tossed and tied *Spritely* to the pier. While Dàme Rascha paid the captain and made arrangements for their return, Hob, Sigga, and Hazel stepped onto the dock. No one paid them any notice. Hob reminded himself that they weren't seeing a Faeregine princess but a pair of young clerks and a palace page on leave. Sigga led Hob behind a newspaper stand and murmured something before tapping his forehead with two fingers.

"You're no longer Hobson Smythe," she muttered. "For the rest of the day, you'll answer to Peter. I'm Isaac. Her Highness is Billy. Dàme Rascha is Mr. Yezdani. Got it?" She held up her folding mirror that showed a boy with tousled blond hair and brown eyes. When Hob blinked, so did the stranger in the glass. He shivered.

They joined the others as Rascha handed Hazel some crisp Bank of Rowan notes.

"Your allowance. Use it wisely."

Hazel beamed. "Oh, I will. I will!"

They spent the next fifteen minutes trying to dissuade Her Highness from purchasing every trifle from the merchant stalls lining the piers. She was particularly set on a velvet painting of a pink unicorn leaping over the word *Impyria* in flowing script. It was perfect, she declared, absolutely *perfect* for a spot between her bedroom windows. Dàme Rascha quietly informed Her Highness that a priceless self-portrait by Mina VII currently occupied that space. The vye also pointed to a dozen identical paintings in nearby stalls. Hazel put away her money, but not without a rueful glance at the unicorn.

They elected to walk up Wyrm's Way, pausing now and again so Dàme Rascha could catch her breath and Hazel could take in their surroundings. Shading her eyes from the sun, she gawked at the snaking path that Ember had made long ago.

"It must be a two hundred feet wide," she remarked.

Wheezing slightly, Rascha gave a cough and sat on a nearby bench. "No description can truly do dragons justice. The Lirlander Seals were made from Ember's lesser scales and yet I've seen some that you could sleep upon. Talysin is smallest of the gate guardians, but even he is huge beyond reckoning. You will see for yourself come June."

"Don't remind me," said Hazel, watching a colorful food cart trundle past.

Hob mused on what he'd just heard as they climbed the rest of the way. Apparently, Her Highness was making a special trip in June to the Otherland Gates. Hob knew of them from tales his mother passed down from her shaman father. There were four of them, mystic doorways to other worlds that the Reaper—or Ankü as his mother called her—created at the height of her power.

According to Hauja beliefs, only one doorway at a time could exist between two worlds. By creating permanent portals, Ankü prevented her enemies from opening others, for she feared they might seek the aid of some god or spirit to challenge her. Once her gates were complete, nothing could enter or leave the mortal realm without passing the dragons she had set to guard them. To the Hauja, the Otherland Gates were abominations—artificial dams that disrupted the natural flow between worlds.

Once atop of Wyrm's Way, the group craned their necks at the Grand Temple, closed their ears to the Caterwauls, and headed toward the Market District. Twice, Sigga had to steer Hazel out of the path of a trolley or carriage. Her Highness was too busy grinning with idiot delight at the crowds and street performers to notice little things like traffic.

They went as far south as the Artisan District, turning up the main avenue to walk past the city guilds—large brick buildings whose stained-glass windows depicted their trades: stonemasons, ironworkers, shipwrights, weavers, cartwrights, glassblowers, silversmiths, clockmakers, carpenters, shoemakers . . .

Hazel stopped at a demonstration where a blind woman had set up a loom. A crowd had gathered, marveling as the woman selected different colored yarns, working with uncanny nimbleness and precision. She'd put out a hat to collect tips, leading some spectators to suspect a scam. Their hunch was correct; their focus was being misplaced.

While these skeptics studied the woman's face or waved their hands to see if she'd notice, the weaver's accomplices—two boys no older than five—relieved the unwary of their purses. Hob quietly pointed this out to Hazel.

"Pickpockets!" she exclaimed.

Poof!

There were three flashes of sulfurous smoke as the boys and weaver vanished. In their place were three red-capped lutins—elfin creatures with an insatiable love of gambling and mischief. They dashed through the crowd, cackling madly and clutching their eponymous hats. The victims gave chase, shouting for the guard as the tiny thieves darted down an alley.

The excitement kept Hazel in a breathless chatter until they stopped for lunch. The vye chose an outdoor café where three districts intersected. It was like a confluence of rivers with merchants, officials, and mystics flowing from their respective districts to form an eclectic mix of muir, mehrùn, and nonhumans. A troupe of actors strolled past, their faces powdered for the matinees. Hazel watched them go before turning to Hob.

"How can you stand it?" she asked.

Hob swallowed the bread he'd been chewing and reminded himself she was a fellow clerk and not to address her as a princess. "How can I stand what?"

She lowered her voice. "Serving on the Sacred Isle when you could live here." She pointed to some balconies draped with flowervine. "You could rent an apartment. That one's even over a bakery. There is so much life here, so much excitement. It'd be such fun!"

Hob was tempted to inform Her Highness that the apartment's monthly rent was probably five times a page's annual salary. But he reflected that she'd spent her entire life on an island where servants looked after every need. Money was an abstract concept. When Dàme Rascha had given Hazel the banknotes, she had to confirm what they were. Her cluelessness about money was almost charming. Besides, he could make a more salient point.

"That building's mehrùn only," he said.

Hazel stared at it. "What? How do you know?"

He pointed to a four-pointed star engraved on the doorway's lintel. Hazel squinted at it.

"Is that really what that means? It's on lots of windows."

Dàme Rascha cut in. "An old law. Some businesses choose not to serve muir. It goes back to the Revolt of 1619."

Hazel frowned. "Why haven't I learned about this in class?"

The vye spread her hands. "The masters cannot address every edict and custom. They must focus on the important ones."

The princess set down her chopsticks. "Half a billion people live in Impyrium and most are muir. How is that law not important?"

Dàme Rascha shot Hob an irritated look. "Most muir don't live near mehrùn. I doubt many even know the law exists."

Hazel gave a disbelieving laugh. "An unjust law's acceptable because lots of people don't know about it? That doesn't make any sense."

"We're attracting attention," Sigga muttered, taking a last bite of fish.

It was true. More than a few of their fellow diners were looking with curious disapproval at the table with the outspoken clerk. One patron got up to speak with the manager.

Wiping her mouth, Dàme Rascha leaned forward and spoke in a simmering undertone. "If the law is good enough for the Divine Empress, it is good enough for me. And for you. And for everyone else in the empire."

The vye left money on the table and motioned for them to get up before the manager approached. Once they had crossed the street, Dàme Rascha turned to Hazel.

"You must be more discreet," she cautioned. "You could be arrested for saying such things."

Hazel turned to Hob and pointed at the bakery. "What would happen if I walked in that shop?"

"They would tell you to get out."

"And if I refused?" said Hazel.

Hob did not like the look on the princess's face. Her expression was growing eager and self-righteous, a dangerous combination when you had no idea what the consequences might be. He glanced at Dàme Rascha, who clearly wished him to provide a bland response.

"The owners would be within their rights to call the guard," he said mildly.

Who would beat you bloody before dragging you in front of a magistrate, he thought privately. *If you're lucky, they'll seize everything you own and deport you to the provinces. If they decide to make an example of you . . .* Hob was glad Her Highness would finally recognize what those pervasive stars meant, but this did not need to go any further. Not today, anyway.

"Not worth the trouble," he added lightly. "Bad view and I hate the smell of fresh bread. Besides, the Mystics District is right this way." It was a pathetic shift, but it was enough to make Hazel smile.

Soon she was asking more questions and seemed to have forgotten all about the stars. Hob noticed the same tendency after they passed Scrag's End. The squalor had truly appalled Her Highness, but her horror was put aside when more scenic delights came into view. Was she that shallow or simply overwhelmed by experiencing so many things for the first time? Things she hadn't known existed or were even possible?

As they walked through the Mystics District, broad avenues gave way to twisting lanes filled with little shops and apothecaries offering alchemical ingredients, minor spells, and enchanting services. Those at street level looked seedy—tourist traps as opposed to places where one might procure serious magic.

Such places did exist. The Fellowship told of secret establishments where one could retain the services of powerful sorcerers or purchase items of singular provenance and potency. But these were not the kind of places that hung wind chimes by their doors. Apparently, one accessed them far above (or below) street level and only by special appointment.

It was soon clear Hazel found the district disappointing. She stopped at a peddler's stall and examined one of the many scarabs arrayed on blue silk. The proprietor resembled an old Hauja but for the tattoos beneath his eyes; only Hauja women inked their faces.

"You've good taste," he said approvingly. "Hang that charm over your bed and no evil spirits will trouble you."

Hazel peered at it. "This isn't magical. It's not even silver."

The man snatched it away, baring filed teeth and making wild hand gestures. Hazel laughed.

"What are you doing? Are you trying to curse me?"

"Begone before I set my ghoul upon you!"

She peered at the brindle sausage snoring in his doorway. "Is the ghoul a pug?"

More curses as the man scooped the dog into his arms. Startled from sleep, it gave him a fractious nip before baring its tiny teeth at Hazel.

Dàme Rascha quickly hailed two rickshaws and told the satyrs pulling them to take them to the Garden District. Sigga accompanied Hazel. Dàme Rascha rode with Hob. The vye ignored the satyr's complaint that they were heavier than they looked and would be charged accordingly. Once they were under way, she turned a stern gaze upon Hob.

"Your task is to instruct my charge on the Muirlands, not fill her head with nonsense concerning muir rights."

"I simply explained what the star meant."

"You knew perfectly well what you were doing," said the vye. "Do you think me ignorant? You always manage to point out problems: banks keep muir in debt; muir cannot travel; muir innovations are constrained; important jobs are off-limits."

"With respect, do you wish me to lie?" said Hob. "How can she understand the Muirlands if she has no idea what life is actually like for most of its people?"

A pause. "You will confine yourself to basic facts and techniques for memorizing them. You are not to discuss controversial subjects. Do you understand?"

"Perfectly."

The vye fell into an agitated silence. Hob looked out at the stately buildings they passed in the Magistrate District. Straight ahead, past the Impyrial museums and gardens, the giant red balloon hovered over the Coliseum Athletica. Crowds of people streamed toward the stadium, many wearing Ferropolis gray or Impyrial red.

A large hand patted Hob's knee. He turned to see Dàme Rascha's wolfish face. "You are a good boy," she said stiffly. "My charge has learned much from you. You make the lessons matter to her. And you improve her spirits. That pleases me. But you cannot interfere with her duties to the empire."

When they passed beneath the Garden District's archway, Dàme Rascha told the rickshaw driver they would get out. She gave Hob a conspiratorial look. "Now, I will have my little joke."

As the vye paid the drivers, Hazel turned about, taking in the museums and reflecting pool, the flower gardens and parterre. Impyria's gardens could not compete with the Sacred Isle's for lushness or rarity, but their scale was unrivaled.

Dàme Rascha steered Hazel toward the nearest museum, a colonnaded monstrosity. Its banners advertised several exhibits, including one on twelfth-century porcelain and glazing techniques. The vye pointed to it.

"The tour is three hours long and then we go home."

Hazel eyed the red zeppelin above the stadium.

Rascha followed her gaze. "What? You'd rather watch a frivolous game?"

"It's okay," said Hazel. "Look at all those people. It's probably sold out."

At Rascha's signal, Hob produced the four foil-stamped tickets. Hazel blinked at them.

"I don't understand . . ." She turned to Rascha with delighted shock. "You tricked me!"

The vye's old eyes twinkled. "You may thank Agent Fenn. The tickets are her gift."

Sigga shrugged off Hazel's thanks. "You need a holiday. Besides, Ferropolis is my team. Come on, or we'll miss kickoff."

The four walked briskly through the gardens, joining thousands on their way to the match. Hazel gazed about at the flags and colorful outfits, covering her ears when they passed by drummers and fife players.

The coliseum loomed ahead, an enormous structure of limestone and red marble ringed by halos of witchfire. Roaring chants could be heard within, accompanied by horns and the rhythmic stamping of countless feet. Hazel looked both thrilled by the pageantry and overwhelmed by all the noise and activity.

By the time they reached their seats, she could scarcely breathe. Far below on the emerald pitch, the team captains were shaking hands. Hob and Sigga sat on the outside with Hazel and Dàme Rascha in the middle. Her Highness turned to Hob.

"So, what's happening? How does this the game work?"

"Pretty straightforward," said Hob. "The team that scores the most goals wins."

He was practically yelling as the teams took the field and the crowd worked itself into a frenzy. "What's a goal?" she screamed. Hazel listened intently as he explained the basics.

"They can't touch the ball with their hands?" she asked.

"No, mostly they use their feet."

"But that's silly."

"It's the rules."

"So many rules," she groaned, before becoming thoroughly flummoxed by the concept of offsides. Hob tried to explain, but not even shouting sufficed when Ferropolis kicked off.

He fell silent as the incandescent ball blazed a fiery arc over the field. Players from both sides tried to position themselves under it. As it plunged to earth, however, great waves suddenly rippled across the field, as though an invisible giant was shaking out a carpet.

Some players toppled like tenpins, others kept their feet, battling one another to take control of the ball as the enchanted field heaved and churned. Hazel shrieked and laughed, seizing Hob's wrist in her excitement. She let go abruptly, cheering as Impyria's midfielder took control of the ball and raced downfield. He feinted left, tangling a defender's foot as he spun right to close upon the goalie and—

The stadium groaned as a wave of turf broadsided him like a rhino. He went somersaulting over the grass to land in a crumpled heap. Leaping over the submerging wave, the goalie cleared the ball to a defender. It was all too much for Merlin, who retreated inside Hazel's coat.

Hob watched the match with fierce attention, marveling at the players' athleticism and dexterity. It wasn't natural, of course (each player was a mystic skilled at amplifying their physical capabilities), but it was breathtaking to watch human beings run faster than Cheshirewulfs or leap fifty feet over rippling walls of turf. Players passed and shot with such power, the glowing ball was often a blur.

Ferropolis scored first, a fifty-yard bullet whose phosphorescent trail showed its curving path. Hazel cheered wildly. Minutes later, Impyria answered on a header from a player thirty feet in the air. Hazel clapped and tried to imitate the ear-piercing whistle of a nearby fan.

"You can't cheer both teams," Hob shouted as Impyria's supporters broke into song.

"Why not?"

"You've got to pick a side," Hob insisted. "You stick with your team."

"Poo on that!" she cried, and joined the Impyrian fight song. Merlin hooted.

The two were still hooting and singing when the match ended ninety minutes later. Impyria had defeated Ferropolis 5–4. Sigga was unhappy, but the stadium shook with a celebratory fervor as they filed down the ramps and past the colonnades.

"That was marvelous," Hazel croaked, her voice quite gone.

Dàme Rascha agreed, looking up at the sky, a blaze of orange and pink. "I'll get a carriage," she said. "We meet *Spritely* at six thirty."

"We've still got time yet," said Hazel. She walked over to a cart where a vendor was stamping medallions with the match's date and outcome. "We'll take four," she said eagerly.

She watched with delight as the man placed the copper disks on the press and pulled a lever. She chose four distinct ribbons and proudly paid the man with a banknote. The vendor thought it was his lucky day until Sigga insisted on change.

"Yes, I forgot they have different numbers," said Hazel, thrusting the bills in her purse. "No matter. I've never had such fun."

She gave each of her companions a medallion, selecting the blue ribbon for Hob and the green for herself. Sigga placed the red one around her neck. She looked strangely moved.

"Thank you."

"You're welcome," said Hazel. "I just hope I still have enough for that painting."

Dàme Rascha sighed and steered the princess through the gradually thinning crowds. Hazel, not remotely ready to go home, stopped to buy some fried dough dipped in honey and brown sugar. She promptly declared they were the best things she'd eaten in all her life.

"Why don't we have these?" she asked Rascha earnestly. "They're much better than those fruit tarts. I'm going to make inquiries."

Streetlamps changed from green to red as they reentered the Magistrate District. The avenues were broad, the buildings huge with marble statues flanking their entries. Rascha pointed to the behemoth ahead on their right.

"The Bank of Rowan."

"What are all those people doing?" said Hazel.

She pointed to a crowd gathering at its steps, standing behind a line of Impyrial Guardsmen holding carabines across their chests. A few held signs, some were shouting.

"Protesters," said Sigga. "I think people want answers about that ship."

"What ship?" asked Hazel.

"A trade galleon disappeared off Malakos late last night," said Sigga. "From the reports, it sounds like Lirlanders might have attacked it."

Hazel blinked slowly, as though the news was not merely upsetting but had shaken something deeper. "What's the ship's name?" she asked softly.

"*Polestar*," said Sigga, surveying the growing crowd. "We should get going."

The Grislander led them across the street, past the stock exchange. They'd reached the Workshop museum when Dàme Rascha noticed something was wrong with Hazel.

Her Highness was crying.

She stood in the middle of the sidewalk in her camel hair coat, clutching her souvenir medal, her shoulders shaking with silent sobs. Rascha quickly ushered her to the side, in front of the museum's plate glass window displaying a silver motorcar.

Hob was baffled why the princess was so upset. He tried to come over but the vye, who had practically enveloped Hazel, waved him away. Hob glanced to see if Sigga would yield any clues as to what was wrong, but the agent was busy watching the crowd and those hurrying past them to join it.

The number of protesters was growing quickly. Dozens were now hundreds. Isolated shouts were becoming angry chants. There was a tension in the air, an electric charge that the crowd seemed to both generate and feed upon.

Hob climbed onto a streetlamp's pedestal for a better view. From this perspective, the protesters looked like a hive of agitated bees. Their swelling ranks were a sea of surging, jittering motion. By contrast, the guardsmen were a motionless red wall, stoic and unblinking. The nearest protesters were just feet away, separated by low barricades.

This won't end well.

He scanned the crowd to see if any protesters were carrying anything resembling a weapon. His eyes fell upon someone he knew.

Badu Gabriel, his friend from Fellowship orientation, was brandishing a sign and shouting himself hoarse. Other familiar faces emerged, spaced at remarkably even intervals throughout the crowd. Some had been in Hob's own cohort; others he recognized from the hallways and dining halls. The Fellowship was here in force, and its members appeared to be the primary agitators.

The spectacle excited Hob, who felt a little envious. This was what he thought he would be doing when he signed up for the Fellowship—confronting authority and making his voice heard. Badu and the others were making a visible, tangible difference while Hob was tutoring a sweet and harmless princess about the Muirlands.

Hob hopped off the pedestal, worried that someone might recognize him and say something. His fears were unfounded, however. A glance at the museum window reminded him that he was still disguised by Sigga's illusion. Dàme Rascha was still kneeling by Hazel, who clung to her tutor like a child stirred from a nightmare.

Hob turned as the protesters erupted in a frenzied chorus of angry shouts. Files of Impyrial Guardsmen emerged from the bank's great doors to escort some men down the steps. Even at a distance, Hob recognized Lord Faeregine. Hazel's uncle was accompanied by a dour Lord Hyde, Lord Yamato, and another man—a civilian—who wore a brimmed hat and topcoat.

Lord Faeregine waved genially to the crowd as though they were staunch supporters and not a mob calling for his head. Hazel had realized her uncle was there. Leaving Rascha's side, she went to stand by Sigga and watched him try to make a statement. It was no use: the crowd's shouting drowned out what he was trying to say. He gave up after the second try.

Meanwhile, the guardsmen by the barricades were moving the protesters back, clearing the way for an enormous black carriage to pull in front of the bank. A handful of protesters refused to move until they discovered the carriage was pulled by a team of stallianas.

There was a stampede as protesters rushed to get away from the creatures, which tossed their manes and bared their teeth. Once the lords and the civilian were safely inside, the carriage's driver cracked his whip and they raced ahead, heedless of the people in their path.

Sigga pulled Hazel back from the curb. The stallianas raced past with wild eyes, cinders sparking from their hooves. Hob stood fast, his eyes first on the monstrous horses and then on the carriage window. A man was looking out. He and Hob locked eyes before he drew the curtain across. The carriage disappeared down the avenue as Hob's companions hurried over.

"Are you crazy?" snapped Sigga. "You could have been killed."

"Sorry," said Hob. "I . . ."

Gunfire sounded behind them, followed by screams. Hob tried to turn, but Sigga already had a firm grip on his collar as she herded them all into an alley. From there, the Grislander led them on a brisk flight down a number of backstreets until they were in a quieter, residential neighborhood. She hailed a passing carriage and ordered the driver to take them to Dragon Pier.

No one spoke as the carriage made its way steadily down toward the water. Hob was almost numb. He avoided looking at Rascha, who was glowering at him from the opposite seat. She had been against the trip from the start, and threatened to hold him personally responsible if anything went wrong. Hob imagined that dragging a weeping princess away from riots and gunfire probably qualified. The vye looked like she wanted to murder him.

He prayed that neither Badu nor anyone else had been hurt, and listened in vain for the sounds of additional gunfire. Above all, Hob tried not to think about the man who peered out the carriage window, the man whose gaze lingered on him. Despite Sigga's illusion, he had known who Hob was. His eyes had flashed with surprise and recognition the instant they caught sight of him. The man had not been Basil Faeregine or one of the other lords. It had been the civilian, the gentleman in the hat and topcoat. It had been Mr. Burke.

CHAPTER 15
ECHOES

A wise man asks where he comes from;
a wiser man tries to forget.

—Muirlands proverb

It was past ten o'clock when Hob returned to his room. Thankfully, Viktor was working a night shift. Hob liked his roommate, but he rarely shut up and Hob needed quiet to process all that had happened.

He laid his jacket over his chair and kicked off his shoes. Removing the medallion, he studied it a moment, touched by Hazel's joy when she'd given it to him. He was still baffled by what could have caused such an abrupt and dramatic change in her spirits. It was not merely the sight of some protesters—Her Highness's tears started well before things turned ugly. Was she simply reacting to news of a missing ship?

If so, the intensity of her distress was puzzling. Hazel merely wasn't upset, she was traumatized.

For his own part, Hob was shaken by his conversation with Sigga aboard the *Spritely* as well as his glimpse of Mr. Burke in Lord Faeregine's carriage. Hob intended to write his mother about Whitebarrow that very night, but he suspected a Fellowship message would be waiting for him in his handbook. He was not disappointed.

Fancy seeing you there.

A chill settled over Hob as he stared at the page. The message left no doubt that Mr. Burke had recognized him. Hob had no idea how the man had seen through Sigga's illusion. Had he also identified the others?

But Hob's biggest questions centered on Mr. Burke's companions. What had he been doing with Lord Faeregine and the other lords? Ever since his duel with Dante Hyde, Hob had wondered if the Fellowship was involved in grander schemes involving other Great Houses. Today's sighting appeared to confirm those suspicions. Hob knew he was a pawn on someone else's board. He did not mind so long as he understood the game and believed in its objective. But the board was turning out to be far larger than he had supposed. Today, he realized he didn't know who all the players were. He was not even certain what game he was playing.

This frightened him. It also made him feel like a fool, no better than those conned by lutins outside the weavers' guild. It was clear that Sigga was manipulating him for her own ends. Was the Fellowship playing him too? All his life, Hob had been the smartest person in the room. Not anymore.

But what to do?

He wasn't sure he should tell anyone about Sigga's cat-and-mouse game. If the Fellowship thought she was onto him, would they come to his aid or cut him loose for fear he'd lead her to them?

Before he could answer Mr. Burke, a second note appeared:

I'm surprised you did not tell us you would be visiting the capital with Her Highness. Are you committed to what we're doing? Do you believe in a free Impyrium? In equal rights for muir?

"Of course I do," Hob muttered angrily. He scribbled a hasty reply:

I believe in the cause. But I don't like being in the dark. I'm not the only one keeping secrets.

He flipped back to the other page, feeling anxious and defiant. Several minutes passed before a reply appeared.

A conversation is overdue. Tomorrow you will receive a zephyss requiring you to visit Old College. Behind the Rose Chapel there is an empty caretaker cottage. The door will be unlocked. Go down to the cellar.

Mr. Burke's offer was more than Hob had expected, or even wanted. At present, the idea of venturing down into a cellar with Mr. Burke was a little frightening. For all the Fellowship's talk of brotherhood and camaraderie, they would not permit a compromised operative to damage the organization. In the Sentries, you didn't let frostbite spread—you amputated.

He wrote back, insisting on a more public setting.

The reply read:

Impossible. I must come to you and the cottage is our only option. We are not upset with you. On the contrary, it's time we shared more about our initiatives. I would also like to talk about your father. Will you come?

Hob read the message again, digesting it slowly. Refusal would effectively sever his ties with the Fellowship and mean he'd forego whatever chance he might have to learn what really happened to his father. At best, he would be alone and friendless; at worst they would seek to silence him. Hob was frustrated, but he still believed in the Fellowship's core mission. He even suspected that taking Hazel Faeregine to Impyria might have helped the cause.

Her Highness had a good heart and was, by nature, inclined toward justice. The protest had frightened her, but it also showed that people were serious about change, that Scrag's End and those four-pointed stars were not merely unpleasantries on a tour. These were real issues that needed to be addressed. Hob was confident that the visit would continue to make an impression.

The Spider would be dead soon, and the triplets represented the dynasty's future. If Hob could win Hazel over, perhaps she could influence her sisters and push for change. There was an opportunity here. Hob could not turn his back on the Fellowship now—he needed more time, not more enemies. Besides, if Mr. Burke or the Fellowship intended to harm him, they would find a way, cellar or no.

He stared at the page a full minute before scrawling a reply that said he'd be there. Once that was done, he composed a long letter to his mother and set it aside with Sigga's green vial. Viktor had friends in the mailroom. Hob would have him send it express.

The zephyss arrived shortly before ten the next morning. Hob was already at his post in the palace reception hall where he spent most mornings. Since dawn, bankers and emissaries had been arriving to discuss recent setbacks to trade. Things were getting worse.

Another galleon had sunk. Unlike *Polestar*, there were no witnesses to *Stormprow*'s fate, but her splintered figurehead and several crates had washed ashore in a fishing village near the port where she was overdue. The news spread like wildfire. All across Impyrium, galleons were turning back or refusing to leave port. If more followed suit, trade would sputter to a halt and the empire would be facing a full-blown catastrophe. Incidents like yesterday's riot would become commonplace. Throughout the busy morning dignitaries were whispering and muttering, forming little cliques as they waited for an audience with the Lord of This or Minister of That.

From what Hob could overhear, people fell into two camps: those who favored war with the Lirlanders, and those advocating alternative trade measures. One gentleman wondered why they should bother braving demon-infested seas when zeppelins and flying machines could transport cargo through the skies. The Workshop possessed the requisite technology and materials. If only the empress would ease some restrictions . . .

"Mr. Smythe."

The speaker was Chalmers, fifth underbutler, a sixtyish man with a perpetually harried air. A zephyss hovered by his ear like a glowing bumblebee. It was not Hob's turn to run a message, and thus Chalmers beckoned him with a frown. One did not become fifth underbutler by deviating from a well-ordered system. Hob crossed the room.

"Yes, sir?" he said.

"You've been requested," said Chalmers sourly. "Master Strovsky has documents for you to deliver in Old College. You know where his office is?"

"Yes, sir."

"Off with you."

Hob left, ignoring the envious glances from the other pages. Errands meant movement, a break from standing rigid in a smoky room surrounded by self-important boobs.

It was drizzling outside, but Hob welcomed the fresh air. He half trotted through the blooming gardens to the little wooded pathway connecting the palace grounds to Old College.

The campus teemed with students and scholars swathed in shawls and robes. They strolled along pathways or stopped to chat beneath the boughs of budding trees, hugging spell books against their chests. Hob sensed none of the crackling tension that plagued the palace. Rowan had been a school long before the island played host to Divine Empresses. It had its own rhythms, and they were slow and stately, steeped in traditions that had nothing to do with trade or high politics.

The cottage was behind Rose Chapel, past a small cemetery of weathered headstones. It sat near a little brook, tucked among some birch and evergreens. It looked to have been out of commission for some time. Several windows were broken and its paint was peeling.

Hob stopped and scanned the woods, mindful of every bird or creature scurrying in the undergrowth. Hazel was in class and Sigga Fenn would be with her, but there was always a chance the Grislander would have someone else watching him. He saw nothing but squirrels, heard nothing but rain pattering on the branches.

Hob entered the cottage quietly, a hand in his jacket pocket. It gripped a paring knife he'd borrowed from the hags that morning. He'd agreed to come to the meeting, but he wasn't going to come unarmed. The knife wasn't much of a weapon, but it was better than nothing, and Hob could not carry anything more conspicuous. The blade was short but shaving sharp.

The cellar door was off the kitchen next to a broom closet. Hob opened it silently and inhaled the smell of damp earth. The stairs were dark, but he made out a dim flickering at the bottom, as if a candle or lamp were burning.

Hob wiped sweat from his palms, irritated by his fear. He didn't bother putting the knife back in his pocket. Mr. Burke would just have to be offended. Of course, that assumed he was even here. Everything the man said might have been a lie. There was always the chance no explanations awaited him in this cellar. Instead of answers, Hob might find an assassin waiting to remove a Fellowship spy whose loyalty was in question.

Closing the door behind him, Hob felt his way down the steps, his attention fixed on the flickering light. When he reached the bottom, he found Mr. Burke sitting at a small worktable by an oil lamp. The man spied the knife. A glint of amusement shone in his lively eyes.

"Is that for me, or a piece of fruit?"

"I'm not really sure," said Hob.

Mr. Burke sighed. "This is all my fault. I've debated when to have this conversation ever since that night in Dusk. I was afraid it would be too much, too soon, but I can see I was mistaken." He gestured to the other chair. "Please sit down and let me explain."

"Not yet," said Hob. "How did you recognize me in Impyria? Are you mehrùn?"

"Of course not," said Mr. Burke. Tilting his head back, he touched a finger delicately to his pupil and removed a translucent lens. "This was made for me by a Workshop defector who tired of Impyrial restrictions. You may have heard that mirrors can strengthen illusions. Well, that's true—to a point. Once an illusion has been reflected too many times, its effect is negated entirely. My friend's ingenious lens does just that on a very small scale. I only wear one, which allows me to perceive what is real and what mehrùn wish me to believe is real. Both have their uses."

He reaffixed the lens and blinked rapidly. "Any more questions?"

"Yes," said Hob. "What happened to my father? No more talk until you tell me."

Mr. Burke clasped his hands. "You want straight answers, so here you are. Your father was executed for treason at Hound's Trench on November 16, 3001."

For a moment, Hob was stunned. He had not anticipated such a blunt response.

In many ways, his life was a patchwork quilt. Some of its squares were perfectly vivid, if not always pleasant. Those having anything to do with his father were largely blank and so Hob filled them in himself. According to his imagination, Anders Smythe of the Impyrial Guard had fallen in battle with Lirlanders or giants. In other versions, he wasn't even dead but exploring fantastical lands or other worlds. In Hob's favorite, his father hadn't even been a mortal man—he was Kayüta the trickster in human guise. That was the wonderful thing about not knowing the facts: the truth could have been anything.

But not anymore. All the gods, giants, and glory were replaced by a blackened gorge on a gray winter day. Anders Smythe hadn't even been executed by firing squad, as was a soldier's due. He'd been tossed down a hole, like garbage.

"You should sit, lad," said Burke gently. "I know it's hard. Dates and details make it hit home. Do you want to know more, or have you heard enough?"

Hob sat so the oil lamp flickered between the two of them. "No point turning back now."

Mr. Burke gave an approving nod. "As I told you, your father came from Novaslo. His family were serfs. He ran away after killing a mehrùn who had murdered his father. Once he joined the Fellowship, Ulrich rose quickly. When we heard rumors of ormeisen in the Northwest, I picked him to help me acquire it."

Hob had heard of ormeisen, or "dragon iron" as others called it. Legend held it could only be found where true dragons had been born. Old miners loved to convince greenhorns that hunks of ordinary schist were worth a king's ransom.

"I thought ormeisen was an old wives' tale," said Hob.

"No," said Mr. Burke. "It exists—or at least it did. Few dragons remain in the world. All but one of their birthplaces were discovered long ago, but the ore has been mined from them, and no one has seen ormeisen for centuries."

"What happened to it?"

"Ormeisen is highly magical," said Mr. Burke. "If properly crafted, weapons made of dragon iron can harm immensely powerful beings— even those of the Old Magic. As you can imagine, such weapons would be priceless for the Fellowship, or any who fought against such foes. When an ormeisen blade was used to assassinate the Reaper, her successor confiscated all the ormeisen in Impyrium. It didn't matter if your very House Blade was made of the stuff. You surrendered every scrap or Prime the Immortal paid you a visit."

"But someone discovered the final dragon's birthplace?" said Hob.

"We thought so," replied Mr. Burke. "Rumors spread that scholars had traced Hati the Black's origins to the Sentries. Your father and I infiltrated the Impyrial Guard and joined the detachment that was sent there. The campaign was brutal, the winter beyond anything I could have imagined. We would have died if a tribe had not sheltered us."

Mr. Burke slid several photographs across the table. The first showed himself and Hob's father wearing guard regalia, unshaven and wind-burned in the Sentrics. They were high above the timberline, the world stretched out in miniature beneath them. In the distance, Hob made out Bear Lake. Others showed Private Smythe ice fishing and constructing a shelter.

"Let me guess," said Hob. "You lived with the Hauja."

Burke nodded. "We gave them enough food and fuel oil to suffer us for a few months. But they weren't happy when a young private and the shaman's daughter took to each other."

Hob could not return the man's smile. Mr. Burke obviously thought he was sharing a charming anecdote about Hob's parents. He could have no conception how much pain and hardship stemmed from that ill-fated romance.

"Did you find what you were looking for?" Hob asked, uncertain if the question was meant for Mr. Burke or himself.

"Did we find ormeisen?" said Mr. Burke. "No. The mission was a disaster. Avalanches and mountain giants wiped out most of the regiment. Your father and I decided our best chance for survival was to separate from the other soldiers. After weeks in the wild, we made it to the village where your mother had gone when the Hauja banished her for carrying a skänder child. Your father was overjoyed to be reunited with her, and to meet his son. He wanted to remain in Dusk and raise you, but Ulrich had a strong sense of duty and knew our work was not finished. He promised your mother he would return before you started school, but the Fates had other plans."

Hob sat very still and watched the flame dancing on the lamp's wick. If he spoke, tears would come. It had been so long since he let himself cry, he wasn't sure he'd be able to stop.

Mr. Burke looked upon him with sympathy. "You never got to know your dad, and that's a hard thing for a boy. Few of us get to choose how we die, but we all can choose how we live. Ulrich died fighting for a noble cause. Most men die fighting gout."

"So, what happened," said Hob, wiping his eyes, "between Dusk and Hound's Trench."

"Your father was a superb soldier," said Mr. Burke. "So good, that we decided he should stay in the guard where he was sure to rise. Ulrich returned to our regiment and maintained he was the expedition's lone survivor. I went on to the capital and focused on growing businesses to fund the Fellowship's initiatives."

He paused as Old Tom sounded the hour. When Hob glanced at the stairs, Mr. Burke assured him that the underbutlers would not be expecting him for some time.

"As we hoped, Ulrich did very well," he said. "He was promoted twice within the year and was selected to accompany the empress on her annual pilgrimage to one of the Otherland Gates. That year, they were paying homage to Graazh, the dragon who guards the way to Nether. Normally, no one but Faeregines remain once the gates have been opened, but the priests allowed a guardsman to stay and assist the empress's daughter, who was heavy with child. That very night, Elana Faeregine went into labor."

"She had the triplets," said Hob.

Mr. Burke learned forward, lowering his voice as though the cellar walls were eavesdropping. "The only witnesses to what happened next were the Divine Empress, Ulrich Doyle, and Graazh himself. Your father saw something he should not have, and it cost him his life. This is why I've been reluctant to divulge everything. The truth is dangerous."

Hob mastered his dread. "No more secrets. I want to know it all."

"Her Highness had only been expecting twins," Mr. Burke continued. "Elana was still alive when the first two arrived. But a third baby came after—a tiny puling thing, pale with colorless eyes. Its first breath was her mother's last. The empress had been tending the twins, but when she heard Elana cry out, she discovered what had happened. Ulrich said her mind snapped. She declared the child an abomination and would have killed it, or cast it 'back into the Nether' if your father and Graazh had not intervened."

"The dragon intervened?" said Hob. "What did they do?"

"Your father restrained the empress and kept her a safe distance from Graazh, who snaked round the child. The dragon guarded the infant even as it devoured Elana's body."

Hob was horrified. "It *ate* Hazel's mother in front of her?"

Mr. Burke nodded. "When the empress regained her senses, she told the priests and priestesses an interesting tale. She had not tried to kill the baby but embraced her as a blessing from Graazh, who had honored Elana just as Ember the Great had honored Mina the First. These were wondrous omens—unmistakable signs that a Golden Age was upon Impyrium." The man laughed bitterly. "The priests believed it, of course. They're willing to believe anything if it's sufficiently grand and mysterious. But the Spider still had a problem."

"A witness," said Hob.

"Correct. She accused your father of trying to murder the child and had him arrested for treason. He was bound and returned to the Sacred Isle to be executed at Hound's Trench."

Anger and disgust stirred in Hob. He pictured his father sitting in a dark cell, waiting for an executioner to march him off to a grimmer fate. Hound's Trench was accursed. A soul could find no rest there. Hob struggled to keep his voice steady.

"How did you learn what happened?"

"Ulrich was a clever man," said Mr. Burke. "All condemned prisoners are entitled to confession. When he penned his, it contained a coded portion that told the real story of what happened at the Nether Gate. The high priest saw nothing amiss and gave the scroll to his acolyte to dispose of. That acolyte was one of our people."

Hob nodded slowly. "So, the Spider murdered my father."

"Yes," said Mr. Burke. "For the unpardonable sin of saving a baby from its grandmother. But Ulrich's death was not in vain. We learned a great deal from his note. It has value to this day."

"How's that?" said Hob.

Mr. Burke held up a hand. "My turn for a question. I want to know what's made you so suspicious of the Fellowship. Ms. Marlowe and I have sensed for some time that you've been holding back. Why didn't you tell us you were accompanying Her Highness to Impyria?"

Hob stared at the table. "I've felt for a while that I don't know what's really going on with the Fellowship—that we're involved in more things and with more people than I'd have guessed. All this business with the Lirlander Seals, the missing House Blade, seeing you with those lords yesterday." He glanced up. "I don't like being in the dark."

"I see," said Mr. Burke. "And you think it is your right, as a new recruit, to be informed of all initiatives? Forgive me, Hob, but doesn't that strike you as rather presumptuous?"

The man did not sound angry so much as legitimately perplexed by Hob's attitude. Hob had to admit that it did not sound very good when put that way.

"Listen," said Mr. Burke, "I have big plans for you. But you have to be patient and trust us. At this moment, we have thousands of brave souls risking their lives in hundreds of operations. Only two people know about them all."

"You and Ms. Marlowe?" said Hob.

Mr. Burke nodded. "Some are intelligence operations or recruiting efforts; others are purely humanitarian missions. As we speak, the Fellowship is smuggling food to muir in Ana-Fehdra. The local 'nobility' have commandeered everything that remains in the public granaries. Those villages would starve without us, and we're rather busy trying to ensure others don't as well. I'm sorry, lad, but we can't debrief you on every initiative to ensure it meets with your approval."

"Fair enough," said Hob. "Is it all right if I ask about one?"

"Aye," said Mr. Burke. "I think that can be managed."

"Lord Faeregine?" said Hob. "What were you doing with him at the bank?"

"I've known Basil for years," said Mr. Burke. "I represent an investor group that has quietly acquired a significant stake in the bank. Basil's always been incompetent, but with *Typhon* he reached new heights of greed and stupidity. He overextended himself and now owes the bank, Lord Hyde, and several others a great sum of money."

Mr. Burke gave a pitying sigh.

"Poor Basil. No one hates settling a debt more than a nobleman. The wealthier the man, the more established the family, the less he feels a duty to honor his obligations. In his mind, only someone who is inexcusably ill-bred would insist that he settle up."

"How convenient," said Hob.

Mr. Burke chuckled. "The Great Houses have mastered the art of making you feel like you're part of the club when they need something, and showing you the door once they have it."

"So Lord Faeregine's weasling out of his debts?" said Hob.

"He's trying. Basil's offering lands, art, favors, titles—anything but cash."

"Don't those other things have value?" asked Hob.

Mr. Burke scoffed. "The land's tundra, the art's junk, his word's worthless, and the titles are meaningless. A Faeregine House Debt would be something, but only the empress can authorize such measures. No, Basil's in a tough spot. He owes too much to people he can't ignore."

"You, Lord Hyde, and Lord Yamato."

"Among others," said Mr. Burke. "And if you think a Hyde is going to let a Faeregine off the hook, you haven't been paying attention. Lord Willem is set on usurping control of the bank. Yamato wants to divide up the Lirlander Seals."

"And what do you want?" said Hob.

Mr. Burke grinned. "To extract maximum value from the situation. Lord Hyde wants my support. So does Lord Yamato. And Basil? He'd give me anything to bail him out."

"So what are you going to do?"

"No, I want to see that brain work. What would you do in my place?"

Hob considered several moments. "I'd wait. The longer you hold out, the more they'll worry you're going to make a deal with one of the others. You can keep raising your price."

Mr. Burke inclined his head. "Precisely. There is a method to our madness, Hob. We are gaining leverage over the Great Houses— leverage we can apply at critical moments. Lady Sylva had no choice but to accommodate us when it came to that dinner party. When we heard she wanted to get rid of her husband's parents, we helped ensure that would happen. She's now the youngest matriarch of a Great House, free to revel in her status—so long as she does what we want, when we want it. House Sylva now belongs to the Fellowship. And when the time is right, so will the Hydes and Yamatos."

Hob was impressed. "It's like arcadia," he mused aloud. A poor player focused on game pieces; a good player focused on patterns. The Fellowship was taking systematic control of the board while the Great Houses were busy chasing figurines. "You're dissecting them."

"Indeed," said Mr. Burke. "I don't blame you for being suspicous, Hob. Paranoia is common in our profession. But the Fellowship cannot function without trust, and trust requires an element of faith. You are a vital piece in an intricate mechanism. You have your job; others have theirs. If you stop doing your job to question what all the other pieces are doing, the mechanism will break down. This brings us to your mission."

Hob braced himself for a rebuke, which, he now admitted, was probably justified.

"I apologize for our impatience," Mr. Burke continued. "Your task is a difficult one and you were thrown into it with relatively little training. That you've maneuvered your way into Her Highness's inner circle is remarkable."

The word "maneuvered" struck a distasteful chord with Hob; like he'd been manipulating Hazel and taking advantage of her kindness. They weren't "friends" in any usual sense of the word, but there was a bond. He shifted uncomfortably in his chair.

"You've grown fond of her," Mr. Burke observed mildly. "Not surprising. You've been on your own, surrounded by enemies. It's only natural you'd begin to identify with them."

Hob sat up straight. "Hazel Faeregine is not our enemy. She's more interested in muir rights than you know. The only thing she's guilty of is being born into the royal family—a family where she'll never wield real power. I don't understand why we're so interested in her."

"There is power and then there is *power*," replied Mr. Burke. "Her

Highness takes her magic rather seriously if she spends every evening locked in Tùr an Ghrian."

"Every student at Rowan studies Mystics," Hob retorted.

"I see," said Mr. Burke. "And did these other students slip into a trance and march off to a Reaper tomb? Did a fomorling appear and attack them?"

Hob's brow crinkled. "Are you talking about the stag-man?"

"That 'stag-man' was a fomorling," Mr. Burke explained. "They're a race of lesser giants, thought to be an offshoot of the ancient Fomorians. Fomorlings are almost extinct themselves. The few that remain tend to be sighted near Reaper tombs."

"Why is that?" asked Hob.

Mr. Burke tended the lamp which had begun to sputter. "I can't say for certain, but I think they keep vigil to ensure she remains at rest. The Reaper nearly exterminated them." He set the lamp back on the table and wiped his fingers with a handkerchief.

"Incidentally, what do you actually know of Mina the Fourth?"

Hob's response was like a school recitation. "Born Arianna Faeregine in 308. Ruled from the age of fifteen. The most magically gifted Faeregine, surpassing even Mina the First. She created the Otherland Gates, crushed the Great Revolt, and expanded the empire to its present borders. Assassinated in 401 A.C. Her ashes are scattered across hundreds of burial sites called Reaper tombs."

"Rather encyclopedic," said Mr. Burke.

"Thank you."

The man shook his head. "It was not a compliment. Facts are mere trivia if you don't bother to think about them. You just described a woman who opened portals to other worlds, pushed the boundaries of magic, and expanded her family's domain."

"And?"

"Don't you think it's odd the Faeregines leave her in little bits and pieces all over the globe? The locations of Reaper tombs are well known. Why hasn't some empress collected her remains and brought her home?"

Hob had no idea.

"Can you tell me where to find the Reaper's memorial?" said Mr. Burke.

He suddenly reminded Hob of Oliveiro. "I don't know," he confessed. "I haven't read anything about it."

Mr. Burke gave him a significant look. "That's because it doesn't exist. Have you ever come across her portrait in the palace?"

Hob considered. The palace was filled with countless artworks, and yet he could not recall any paintings or sculpture of Mina IV. There was not even one to accompany her abbreviated entry in his handbook. Even the face of her caryatid in the grand entry hall was blank. None of the others were like that.

"No," he muttered. "I haven't."

"Omissions can be telling," said Mr. Burke. "Why do you think the Faeregines downplay Mina the Fourth's existence? Practically obliterate her?"

"I don't know."

Mr. Burke dropped his voice to a whisper. "Because the Reaper *terrifies* them. Some powers are too great for the mortal realm, Hob. Their very presence unbalances things and threatens our survival."

"Everyone knows the Reaper was a monster," said Hob. "What does this have to do with Hazel Faeregine?"

Mr. Burke cocked this head. "Are you familiar with the concept of reincarnation?"

"Sure," said Hob. "It's when a spirit's reborn in another body. Some religions believe in it."

"In a few seconds, you might too."

From his case, Mr. Burke removed a picture frame that he held up to Hob.

"Behold."

At first, Hob was merely confused. Behind the frame's glass was a faded black-and-white photograph of a thin, pale girl, laughing as she ran from a little boy who was chasing her through a garden. Hob brought the photo closer. If her hair had been lighter, he might have been staring at Hazel Faeregine.

"What is this?" he said uneasily.

Mr. Burke leaned back against a post. "This is a photograph of Arianna Faeregine, taken a few years before she became Mina the Fourth. We think a court artist used it as a reference for a painting that was destroyed when Mina the Fifth outlawed her mother's image. Fortunately, a very brave person managed to save this, lest future generations forget what evil can look like."

For a full minute, Hob sat in the cold, damp cellar and stared at the photograph. The room was so quiet, they might have been two shades in a tomb. The girl's smiling face certainly didn't look evil. Her delighted expression was exactly like Hazel's when she'd seen her first Euclidean soccer goal. Hob glanced at the toddler chasing after her.

"Who's the boy?" he asked.

"Her younger brother, the Prince Maximillian," said Mr. Burke.

"He was killed the following year in a failed bid to assassinate their mother. They say Arianna never smiled again."

Hob gazed sadly at the little boy. He couldn't have been older than three. Time and again, Hob had to remind himself that he was *not* looking at Hazel Faeregine. And every time, he fought a convulsive shiver. At last, he cleared his throat.

"It's a coincidence," said Hob. "Lots of the Faeregines look alike."

Mr. Burke propped the frame against the wall. "Then explain why you're as pale as Her Highness."

"I never said it wasn't uncanny."

Mr. Burke gave a wry chuckle. "Hazel Faeregine isn't some commoner who 'happens' to resemble a historical figure. We're talking about a girl born by an Otherland Gate on All Hallows' Eve. A girl whose unforseen arrival resulted in two deaths—her mother's and your father's. A girl who bears no resemblance to her living relatives but is nearly indistinguishable from Arianna Faeregine. If the likeness is merely superficial, why did Her Highness sleepwalk to a Reaper tomb? Why did she suffer a fit during a phantasia depicting the Reaper's assassination?"

"That doesn't prove anything," said Hob. "I almost had a fit myself."

Mr. Burke was having none of it. "Hob, you are a rational person. No rational person could possibly require more proof to believe something deeply disturbing is at work."

Hob glanced again at the photograph. "But I know Her Highness. She's not a monster."

"Neither was Arianna Faeregine," retorted Mr. Burke. "By all accounts, she showed almost no magical ability until adolescence.

Everything changed after Maximillian's death and her first pilgrimage."

Returning the photograph to his case, Mr. Burke looked at Hob very seriously. "My ambition is not only to achieve equality for muir but to do so with a minimum of bloodshed. Within two years, Impyrium will have an impressionable new ruler. By that point, we will control most of the Great Houses, several key institutions, and a number of population centers. Her Radiance will have no choice but to accept our proposals."

"You're going to leave a Faeregine on the throne?" said Hob.

"For a time," said Mr. Burke. "Radicals may embrace violence but the common man detests it. If we try to tear everything down overnight, we'll spur our enemies into desperate measures while alienating the very people we are trying to help. We must be strong, wise, and patient. Within a generation, muir will have all the same rights as mehrùn and the aristocracy. Within two generations, there will be no aristocracy."

A boyish grin appeared on Mr. Burke's face. He thumped the table with his fist.

"We're smarter than they are, Hob. We're better organized, and we have a deeper purpose than simply protecting a title or lifestyle. After centuries of oppression, we are almost in position to win this game. Can you even imagine?"

Hob was not certain he could. He wanted to, but the idea that such an outcome might actually be attainable was so jarring and foreign, he struggled to envision it. It occurred to Hob that he'd joined the Fellowship because he wanted a connection to his father, and he believed in the righteousness of their struggle. He'd given very little thought to actually *winning* that struggle. Deep down, he'd never believed it was a realistic possibility. But Mr. Burke was making it sound like victory wasn't merely attainable, it was imminent.

Mr. Burke's next words, however, were spoken in a grim tone that recalled Hob sharply to the present.

"It's all for naught if Hazel Faeregine is what we fear," he said. "She won't just win the game, she'll incinerate the entire board. The world is still recovering from the first Reaper. It won't survive a second."

Rising from his chair, Hob paced about the cellar. "You're planning to kill her. Don't pretend you're not."

Mr. Burke knit his fingers and spoke in a measured voice. "An assassin is in place but I haven't given the order to strike. Not yet. I have been waiting for more information, Hob. If you do not provide it, I will have to assume she cannot be saved."

Hob abruptly stopped pacing. "Wait. There's a chance to save her?"

"We have our own scholars when it comes to magic," Mr. Burke explained. "They believe there are two possible explanations for Her Highness's resemblance and behavior. The first is that she is truly the Reaper reborn. If so, she must be killed. The second theory is that Hazel Faeregine is an innocent girl being possessed by some other entity, possibly even a fragment of the Reaper's spirit. If that is the case, an exorcism might save her."

Hope flashed, but Hob wasn't biting yet. "What if it's neither? What if I'm right and she's just a girl?"

Burke gave Hob a meaningful look. "We both know that isn't true."

"Then why bother to see if Hazel can be saved?" said Hob. "You don't care about her as a person."

"Several reasons," said Mr. Burke. "Despite what you may think, I am not a cold-blooded murderer, Hob. It matters very much to me if I'm ordering the death of an innocent victim, especially a child. The other reasons are purely practical. Assassinating a member of the royal family would trigger a massive response. It would enrage the empress, unify the Great Houses, and set our timetable back years. In addition, if Her Highness is truly sympathetic to the injustices we face, she could be a valuable ally for the reforms I envision. I have no intention of taking her life needlessly."

Hob had to acknowledge that this made sense. No good would come of letting his emotions get the best of him. He sat back down. "What do you need me to do?"

"What I need," said Mr. Burke, "is the information we asked for when we chose you for this mission. My scholars must have an understanding of Her Highness's studies and magical capabilities. Only then will we know what we are dealing with. If you cannot paint a clearer picture, we will have to assume the worst."

"I understand," said Hob. "I'll get you what you need."

"I hope so," said Mr. Burke. "Time is scarce. Her Highness is now twelve. In a few months, she will go on her first pilgrimage and her powers may fully emerge. Is there anything else you can tell me?"

"I've never sat in on her lessons or seen her do any magic," said Hob. "I just know that she has some big task or test to complete by her birthday. Dàme Rascha said they would take a vacation once it was over."

Leaning back, Mr. Burke folded his arms and contemplated the lamp's flame.

"This is valuable information," he said. "The Spider is the only person who could impose a task of real significance on Her Highness. With Her Highness spending so much time in Tùr an Ghrian, it certainly involves magic. All this urgency and pressure. The Spider's pushing her granddaughter, trying to accelerate something while she can still influence it . . . I think she knows what Hazel might be. In fact, I'd bet on it."

"But the Faeregines themselves disavow the Reaper," said Hob. "Why would the empress be trying to create a second one?"

"I couldn't say," said Mr. Burke. "Rulers see the world differently than we do. Mina the Fourth's legacy may frighten the Faeregines, but you cannot deny that she saved the empire and enabled her family to sit the throne for another twenty-five hundred years. The Reaper was a forest fire. She razed Impyrium but rejuvenated the dynasty. You need to find out what Hazel Faeregine is doing."

"I'll find a way," said Hob. "Is there something specific I should be looking for?"

"No," said Mr. Burke. "Report *everything* you see or hear, no matter how mundane it might appear. Do not filter, analyze, or interpret. That's the scholar's job."

"Understood," said Hob. "But I need help with Sigga Fenn. She doesn't believe I'm just a page."

He went on to explain what the agent told him about the Impyrial dig site, the rifle found with the golem, and her concerns about Whitebarrow. At this last piece of information, Mr. Burke actually laughed out loud.

"Sigga Fenn accused you of being a *necromancer*?"

Hob reddened. "Not exactly. She just made me drink that potion as precaution. I don't think it's funny. My mother and sister live near Whitebarrow."

"I apologize," said Mr. Burke, but eyes were still twinkling. "It's natural you'd be concerned, but don't lose sleep over Whitebarrow. That was my doing."

Hob stared. "I don't understand. Whitebarrow was a Fellowship initiative?"

"Another of Ms. Marlowe's brilliant ideas," replied Mr. Burke. "When I was embarking for the Northwest last autumn, she suggested I plant a little seed atop Whitebarrow. Apparently, it's blossomed. The Faeregines are paranoid when it comes to necromancy. If the Red Branch thinks an old enemy like the Coven is resurfacing, so much the better. They'll go off on a wild-goose chase while we go about our work."

Hob felt the tension drain from his shoulders. He didn't even mind that he'd have to send another express letter to tell his mother that it was a false alarm.

"So it's just a diversion."

"Of course," said Mr. Burke, "there are only twelve members of the Red Branch. It helps to spread them thin. Back to Sigga Fenn. Has she actually accused you of anything?"

"No," said Hob. "But I can't pretend I'm not scared."

"Naturally," said Mr. Burke. "But keep in mind she's made up her mind you're not a direct threat to Her Highness. If she hadn't, you'd be dead. But it's clear she thinks you're working for somebody. She's trying to spook you into switching sides and coming to her for protection. Common tactic." He picked up the paring knife and thumbed its edge. "Apparently, she's doing a fair job."

Hob flushed. "Like you said, it's easy to get paranoid."

Mr. Burke looked oddly emotional, as if Hob's suspicions had wounded him.

"The Fellowship's a family, lad. We won't betray you and I know you won't betray us. Besides, you're Ulrich Doyle's boy." Reaching into his coat pocket, Mr. Burke handed Hob a folding knife with a handle of polished horn. "I found this among your father's things—he never carried it for fear he'd be taken. The Doyles didn't have much, but that's been passed down through six generations. You're lucky seven, eh?"

Hob turned the knife over. It was a toy really, a child's knife to do some whittling. But for Hob, who'd been rejected by the Hauja, this link to his father's people was priceless. He didn't care that a tear was trickling down his cheek. He studied the handle closely, discerned six sets of initials carved in a column. He'd add his later.

Mr. Burke clapped his shoulder. "Thank you for coming and being frank with me. We're this close, Hob, and your role is vital. Do your job. I'll worry about Sigga."

Wiping his eye, Hob glanced at the steps. "What if she had me followed?"

"She didn't."

"How do you know?"

Mr. Burke laughed. "Because I had you followed. Don't be offended—standard procedure. We've had this cellar for thirty years. Losing it would be most inconvenient."

As Hob left, he reflected how much had changed in the past hour. The revelations concerning Hazel were frightening, but Hob felt like he was facing them with a strong sense of purpose and support. He hadn't realized how truly isolated he'd been feeling. Mr. Burke's visit rekindled his sense that he was a part of something that was not only going to improve this world but perhaps even save it.

When it came to Hazel, Hob flatly refused to believe she was the Reaper reborn. There was something else at work, some spirit or demon that was preying upon her. He was determined to save her, just as his father had when she was born. Hob was not deeply religious, but he did not believe such things were mere coincidence. The gods must have had a grander purpose.

He was about to slip out the cottage's back door when he realized he'd left the hags' knife behind. Turning about, he hurried back down to the cellar.

"Sorry. I forgot—"

Hob stopped dead on the stairs. The space beneath him was dark and eerily quiet.

"Hello?"

He turned slowly about, peering into the blackness. There was no light. No sound. No trace of Mr. Burke.

CHAPTER 16
LINGUA MYSTICA

Mystics play sheet music; sorcerers compose symphonies.

—David Menlo, archmage (17 P.C.–72 A.C.)

Hazel awoke with a cry. For a minute, she simply lay still in the darkness while sweat cooled on her skin. Merlin had flown from her pillow to take refuge on her dresser. The homunculus peered at her with concern, his eyes glowing softly in the darkness. Sitting up, Hazel kicked the damp covers off and tried to catch her breath. Outside, a moonless night showed that dawn was far off.

She'd had the nightmare three times since the Grotesque. In it, Hazel was flying low over an ocean that boiled in her wake. The night was dull red and starless. Crystalline towers rose from the sea like huge antennae. They cracked and shattered at her approach, falling into the sea like ice shearing off a glacier. A headland loomed on the horizon, crowned by a city of black basalt. Banners whipped in the gales, showing a crescent moon entwined by hemlock. Queen Lilith's standard: the flag of ancient Zenuvia. The city's massive gates were opening and an army was marching forth, horns blaring. And then Hazel's shadow fell over them—huge and black and ragged. Ten thousand faces looked up and knew their doom had come.

Hazel was no longer frightened; she was angry. Scooting off the bed, she stalked to the fireplace and drew a sigil in the air. She'd created a new hiding place for the portrait, a stash that neither her sisters nor Olo would ever discover. Green witchfire roared in the hearth, its garish light filling the bedchamber. Crouching down, Hazel thrust her arm into the fire. The flames pained her, but they would not burn or blister her flesh. Her fingers reached what they sought. Snatching the portrait from the fire's midst, she practically flung it against a chair. Smoke curled from the canvas and gilded frame. Its young subject gazed placidly at Hazel.

"Get out," Hazel growled. "Get out of my mind."

It was not a child's voice that Hazel heard but an aged woman's. Something had warped her vocal cords, twisted and stretched them until she barely sounded human.

I'm not in your mind, girl. You're in mine.

Hazel balled her small fists. "I'll tell. I'll tell Rascha."

An almost silent laugh. *You'll tell no one. Least of all her. Poor Rascha. She should have known better than to push you . . .*

"You did that!"

Are you certain?

Hazel stood panting. In truth, she was not sure what had happened with Rascha earlier that week. They had been working away in Tùr an Ghrian when the vye wanted to practice telepathy. Twice, she tried and failed to get into her pupil's mind, but either Hazel or the Reaper would not let her. On the third attempt, the vye suffered a seizure and collapsed. She was recovering, but had not left her bed in days.

Rascha would want you to practice. Shall we start with Progressions?

Hazel stood before the painting with her arms crossed. Behind her, the witchfire took whatever shape her mind commanded, one after another. Each one was perfect, its contours as smooth as molten metal.

Faster, whispered the voice.

The shapes became a blur, like riffling through a deck of cards. The forms were not just coming more quickly, they were increasingly complex. Geometric shapes, organic shapes, crystalline shapes, monstrous shapes . . .

Enough. You're ready.

The witchfire died slowly away. The room was dark once again.

"For what?" Hazel whispered.

Transformation, child. Isn't that what Rascha would want?

Hazel nodded dully, ignoring Merlin, who was flapping about in agitation. Closing her eyes, she pictured the piglet she'd tried so many times to become—pale pink with white whiskers and floppy ears. Nimble little trotters and . . .

That's it.

Opening her eyes, Hazel held up her hand. Her small fingers were slowly fusing together, forming a hooflike shape. Her heart raced with joy. Matter was malleable! Hazel didn't have to become a mere *pig*. She could become something else . . . anything she wished!

The piglet Hazel had been envisioning vanished, replaced by something huge and dark, baleful and feathered. Her hand began to tremble uncontrollably. Flesh began to bubble like boiling dough.

Pain shot through Hazel's other hand. Glancing down, she saw that Merlin had sunk his needlelike teeth into her palm. She tried to shake him off, but the tenacious little creature would not let go. He clung desperately to her hand, nipping the flesh until she finally flung him straight up. He tumbled head over wing and landed on the chandelier in a jingling of crystal.

"What are you doing?" Hazel demanded.

The homunculus was busy scrambling for a better hold. Once he was settled, he gave a soft, inquisitive hoot. Hazel glared at him a moment, furious that he'd broken the spell. She shook her unbitten fist at him.

"Really, Merlin. I've half a mind—"

She stared in speechless horror at the deformity protruding from her sleeve. Hazel's hand was no longer human. It resembled a pig's foot, but one that had been charred and blackened. A gleaming black talon poked through one of the cloves, which had begun to split like an overheated sausage.

Hazel tore her gaze away to look about the room. Daylight was streaming through her windows. The sky outside was a pale peach. Hazel did not understand how time had passed so quickly. Something was happening outside—a commotion of some sort. Opening her window, she heard a yowling din. Every dog in Old College seemed to be barking and braying.

Shutting the window, Hazel locked it and grabbed the portrait of Arianna Faeregine from the chair. As always, she vowed this was the last time she would ever look at it. Conjuring the witchfire, she stuffed it back into the hearth. When the flames vanished, so had the painting.

Turning from the fireplace, Hazel glanced miserably at her hand. Could Rascha set it right? She planned to visit the vye later in the day. With a grimace, she pulled her sleeve over the disgusting sight. What would have happened had Merlin not distracted her? She looked up to see the homunculus peering suspiciously at her from the chandelier.

"Oh, Merlin," she cried. "Please come down. I'm so sorry. I wasn't myself."

The creature inched forward, gave another hoot, and fluttered down. He settled on her shoulder and stretched his leathery neck like a preening turtle. Hazel scratched beneath his chin.

"Well"—she sighed—"sun's up. We might as well face the day."

She emerged from her room fifteen minutes later, wrapped in a fluffy, oversized bathrobe with conveniently long sleeves. Her sisters were already sitting down to breakfast in the common room.

"Did you feel it too?" said Isabel, sitting by the open window.

"Feel what?" said Hazel.

"Earthquake," said Violet from behind her newspaper. "Why do you think the dogs are all barking? They're more sensitive to these things."

Hazel sat down, careful to keep her hand covered and beneath the table. "I didn't feel anything. It couldn't have been very big."

"Ha!" said Isabel. "It could have been a catastrophe and you wouldn't stir. You sleep like the dead."

"You mean she *looks* like the dead," said Violet, peering over her paper. "Those circles are ghastly, Hazel. Use some lemon juice."

Isabel sighed. "There's nothing better than Saturday mornings at this time of year. No class, no services, warm enough to open a window yet cool enough to enjoy a fire. If it weren't for you two, I'd be in paradise." Sipping her juice, she reached for a strip of bacon.

"By all means gobble up more bacon, Isabel," said Violet. "It's not like we have a ball coming up. Oh wait, we do."

Isabel claimed the bacon. "So, we're supposed to starve ourselves while men can plump into selkies. We get fat; they get 'substantial.' You should outlaw corsets when you're empress, Violet. Or at least make men wear them too."

"I second the motion!" called a voice from the breadbasket.

Violet lowered the newspaper.

"Don't be ridic— Ew!"

She swatted the paper at Pamplemousse, who promptly scrambled out of the pastries. She took aim again, but the homunculus was surprisingly nimble, given the state of his belly. He ducked, causing Violet to nearly strike Merlin, who toppled backward off the table. Without thinking, Hazel reached out to catch him, exposing the hand she'd been keeping hidden. Violet dropped her newspaper.

"What is *that?"*

Hazel tried to make light of it. Setting Merlin on the table, she helped herself to bacon. "It's my hand," she said breezily. "I had a little accident."

Isabel's jaw had become unhinged. "What happened?"

"I was trying to shape change," said Hazel. "And I . . . well, I didn't quite manage."

"What were you trying to become?" said Isabel.

Hazel tried to wriggle it. "Isn't it obvious?"

Violet continued to stare at the blocky wedge of semicloven flesh. "Is that a *pig* hand?"

"Technically, it's a pig foot," said Hazel, strangely pleased that Violet could tell.

"And you're eating *bacon?*" exclaimed Isabel. "You're a cannibal!"

Hazel snorted, which only made Isabel laugh harder. Violet was not amused. "Why are you trying things like that when Rascha's sick?"

"I wanted to see if I could," said Hazel defensively.

Isabel poked it with a chopstick. "It's so puffy," she said gleefully. "Can you feel that? Ew! Is that a *talon?*"

"Yes," said Hazel, snatching her hand away.

Violet smoothed her newspaper. "Turning into pigs, being tutored by pages. You do our family too much honor, Hazel."

"Come off it, Vi," said Isabel. "It's incredible that Hazel could do that. It's not perfect, but I can't transform at all. Can you?"

"That's not the point," said Violet.

"But that *is* the point," said Isabel. "The Spider expects her to qualify as a mystic in six months!" She turned to Hazel. "How's it going?"

Hazel glanced at her porky extremity. "Okay, if I was trying to qualify as a First Rank. Third Ranks have to transform into mammals, birds, and reptiles. I've got a long way to go. But this is progress, I guess."

Violet smirked. "Of course it is."

Isabel's face darkened. "How hard would it be to say 'congratulations'?"

"I'm sorry," said Violet. "I'm somewhat distracted by the fact that four more ships have disappeared and I'm attending a war council this afternoon. But congratulations on becoming a partial pig, Hazel. You're an inspiration."

"Four more ships?" said Hazel. "When did that happen? The last I heard about was *Stormprow*." She scanned the headlines. "Why isn't there anything about it in the papers?"

"Because we're paying outrageous bribes to keep it quiet," said Violet stiffly. "The demonstrations in Impyria are already getting out of hand. If people knew the truth, we'd have daily riots across the empire."

"Are we going to war with the Lirlanders?" asked Isabel.

Violet tossed the paper aside. "I don't know. The Lirlanders deny they've broken any laws. I don't know how Lord Kraavh can lie so brazenly. It's obvious the demons are sinking the ships, Seals or no Seals. He's testing us and Uncle Basil is frothing. He already blamed them for *Typhon*."

"What does the Spider say?" said Isabel.

Violet almost laughed. "She doesn't say anything. She just listens to her counselors and glares at everyone with those shark eyes. I think she's getting senile. Why else would she be so interested in Hazel?"

"Enough, Violet," said Isabel. "Do you think she'll step down?"

Violet sniffed. "Lady Sylva thinks I could force her to. Impyrium needs strong leadership and Grandmother might be too old to provide it."

"You should *not* be discussing these things with Lady Sylva," said Isabel heatedly.

"And who should I talk about them with?" retorted Violet. "My sisters? One's becoming a pig. The other's busy flirting with Andros Eluvan."

"Lady Sylva's not your friend," said Isabel pointedly. "Every time you see her, you start talking about the Workshop. She's working for them. If you don't see that, you're blind."

Violet glared at her twin. "It must be nice to think the world's black-and-white and you've got all the answers. Has it occurred to you that we might need the Workshop's support? That maybe I *want* to talk about the Workshop? Perhaps they could be useful in a war with the Lirlanders, if it comes to that?"

"We've slapped down the Lirlanders before," said Isabel.

"When?" laughed Violet. "Two thousand years ago? Mina the Sixteenth was a confirmed sorceress. She had real power over them. The Spider isn't even a proper mystic."

"Isn't she a Fifth Rank?" said Isabel.

Violet rolled her eyes. "Don't be stupid. She can barely light a candle. In the old days, not one Promethean scholar was less than a Fifth Rank. Do you know many Fifth Ranks we have now?" She held up three fingers. "None are Faeregines, by the way, and one hasn't been seen in twenty years. And if the best Hazel can do is turn one hand into a taloned pig foot, then, yes, we might need the Workshop."

Isabel looked stunned. "I—I didn't know."

Hazel looked down. The Spider's mandate to her now took on clearer meaning.

"Now you do," Violet snapped. "So the next time you want to assume I'm just an idiot, perhaps you'll stop to consider that I might have information that you don't. Sometimes, more than I'd like to know . . ." She looked near tears.

Isabel laid a hand on her sister's arm. "You're going to burst if you keep all this bottled up. We can help."

Violet did not seem to hear her. She stared at her cold green tea. "The Spider's dying," she said quietly. "I'm not inheriting a crown, I'm inheriting a war." Her eyes fell on Hazel's misshapen hand. "What are you wearing to the ball?"

"I don't know yet," said Hazel. "I'm trying on some dresses after my Muirlands review."

The future empress rose from the table. "Pick an outfit with gloves. We can't afford to look ridiculous."

"Well," said Isabel, "at least her hand shows we can do powerful magic again."

Violet paused. "No. It shows we can't." Slipping into her bedroom, she closed the door behind her.

Hazel and Isabel were quiet after their sister had left, each lost in their own thoughts. Even Pamplemousse refrained from comment and inhaled a muffin instead. Suddenly, everything seemed darker, more dangerous. The May Ball was an important event—not only a holy day to celebrate the sun's return but a commemoration of the date a sorcerer struck the first blow in mankind's Great War against the demons. Still, given everything that was happening, Hazel wondered if it should be canceled or postponed. There was a knock and Olo entered to clear their breakfast away. Hazel darted her hand back inside her sleeve. Isabel shook her head.

"If you're going out, you'd better borrow my mittens."

An hour later, Hazel left the triplets' suite, dressed and mittened for the day. Sigga was waiting outside and the two made their way down the tower's steps.

While Hazel had known things with the Lirlanders were tense, she hadn't really believed that outright war was on the horizon. And yet Violet was attending a council. The Spider could declare war with the Lirlanders that very day. And what would it mean if she did? There had not been a major rebellion during Hazel's lifetime, much less a war. The only war she'd ever seen was in that terrible dream she kept having. She glanced at her mittened hand.

Never again, she told herself. *You must keep her out or you'll go mad.*

As she and Sigga reached Rowan's grounds and climbed the steps to Old Tom, Hazel's thoughts shifted from a spectral past to an earthier present. Since their visit to Impyria two weeks ago, she had been thinking quite a bit about Hob.

The day they had spent in the capital was one of the best and worst in her life. She had never even attempted to explain why she had become so upset when they encountered the bank protesters. What was she supposed to say? That she had foreseen the *Polestar*'s disappearance and witnessed the Lirlanders destroying the ship through the eyes of a doomed cabin boy? Hob would think she was insane. She had not confided anything to anyone—not even Rascha or Isabel.

But she *wanted* to tell Hob. There was something about him that made her feel safe in his presence. Not physically safe, but safe from judgment. Secure. Hob was a serious boy and could even be intimidating, but he also exuded decency. His first instincts were to listen and to help, not to judge or laugh or recoil. Hazel wished there was someone like him among the FYGs. Then they could actually speak to each other in public.

Instead, she found herself taking roundabout routes through the palace in the hope of crossing paths with him on page duty. Sigga— bless her—never said a word when Hazel suggested nonsensical detours or stopped to poke her head into some hall or gallery. Most of the time, she found nothing but dour ministers, but there were occasions when she spied a certain page standing at attention. If he caught sight of her, Hob would offer a tiny nod and a ghost of a smile before his face resumed a detached, stoic expression. Hazel adored these "chance encounters," but a copy of his schedule would be handy. She was starting to look like a lost dignitary.

This wasn't Hazel's first crush, but it was her first on anyone remotely her own age. When she was six, she'd fallen in love with a guardsman named Captain Hutchens, a man so handsome Hazel told her sisters he was "sparkly." Isabel still teased her about it.

But Hob was different. Hazel actually knew him, had spent many hours in his company. She felt like they understood each other ever since they'd exchanged glances at Lady Sylva's dinner party. If it was not for him, she would not have explored Impyria's chaotic splendor, laughed at lutin tricksters, or marveled at Euclidean soccer. And she never would have beheld Scrag's End; understood those four-pointed stars; or felt the raw, simmering anger of those protesters. Hob was her bridge to the wide world beyond the Sacred Isle, a landscape teeming with beauty, joy, and tragedy. Hazel ached to see more of that world someday. And what's more, she knew who she'd choose to come with her—a tattooed page from the Sentries. Life was odd.

Hob was already waiting in Rattlerafters, his uniform pressed to perfection.

He bowed. "Good morning, Your Highness. Hello, Agent Fenn."

"What tortures have you devised?" asked Hazel, removing her coat and laying it over a chair. From what she could see, each table had an unlabeled map of a Muirlands region.

"Nothing too bad," he assured her. "I thought we'd start with geography. You said the master's a stickler."

This was true. Hazel's exam was less than two weeks away, and she'd heard horror stories about Montague's finals. Apparently he gave his students nothing but blank maps on which to label regions, duchies, cities, major industries, and all kinds of insidious details. Hazel would need to ace the final to pass with honors and satisfy the Spider.

"You'll need to use a pen, Your Highness," said Hob. "You might want to take those off."

He gestured to her mittens.

"Oh," said Hazel. "These. I've been freezing all morning. I'll just keep them on."

Sigga took a chair in the back as Hob quizzed Hazel on the Caspian Steppes. Clutching a pen in her mitten, Hazel tried to label its major duchies, but managed only half.

"Remember," said Hob. "Never Look Under the Bed Past Midnight . . ."

The mnemonic device helped Hazel recall "Unterlyn" but that was it. She abandoned the map and looked at the accompanying note cards. Hob took the first and flipped it over.

"What is the region's primary crop?"

"Rice," said Hazel.

Hob shook his head. "Think about where it is on the map. The steppes are too arid and too far north. Try again."

"Corn?" she said hopefully.

Hob put the note card down. "Wheat. Let's try another. What's the largest nonhuman presence in the region?"

"Goblins," said Hazel confidently.

"What tribe?"

"I remember that," said Hazel, recalling a woodcut from her book. "The Black Jodhpuri. They ride red mules and wear those cute little pants. They're the region's biggest traders."

"Good," said Hob. "Tell me who rules Midvolgha and why that person's important."

Hazel searched her memory. She thought she was prepared, but now everything she'd studied seemed jumbled. "I don't remember." She sighed.

"It's okay," said Hob. "Lord Tristrym is the Duke of Midvolgha, which is the ancestral seat of power in the steppes. He enforces the law and collects Impyrial taxes. He's responsible for the population, which is . . . ?"

Hazel scrunched up her face. "Thirty thousand?"

"Four million."

Hob abandoned the remaining note cards and had Hazel move to another table. He gestured at its map. "The Rowana subcontinent. You should ace this."

But Hazel did not ace it. Other than Impyria, the map's duchies and other cities had become indistinguishable blobs. She stared at them, intensely aware of her audience and the seconds ticking past. Inside her mittens, her hands were sweating profusely.

"I'm drawing a blank," she said softly.

"Start with something you know," said Hob.

Clutching the pen in her mitten, Hazel scrawled "Impyria" along the coast.

"And what's the big city to the north?" Hob coaxed.

Hazel closed her eyes. She knew it, she really did. Big port and fishery. Lots of shale rendering. Periodic trouble with centaurs—some treaty was signed in 2819.

She sank into the nearest chair. "I don't know. I don't know what's wrong. I guess I've forgotten all this stuff. Maybe we should try another time."

"No," said Hob firmly. "You haven't forgotten. And we're not postponing. What's wrong?"

Hazel could only shrug. She felt ridiculous and confused. Tears were threatening, and that only made her feel even more foolish. Hob sat in the chair across from her.

Closing her eyes, Hazel exhaled. "I don't know. I'm tired. I'm worried about Rascha. She's never been sick like this. Not ever."

"She'll get better," said Hob.

Hazel nodded, but the truth was she wasn't certain. Dàme Rascha had served the Faeregines for many decades, had even tutored Hazel's mother when she was a girl. The vye was very old. One day, her Rascha would die.

"I can't do it," she muttered. "You should just give up on me."

Hob shook his head. "Not today. Not tomorrow. Not for all the gold in Impyrium."

Hazel gazed at the boy across from her. His jaw was set, his arms folded, his gray-green eyes level with her own. He looked utterly immovable. She loved and hated him for it.

"You're very stubborn, Mr. Smythe. It's annoying."

He grinned. "I've been told. But I have an idea, Your Highness. Care to hear it?"

"Very well," said Hazel.

"Let's switch things up. I've spent three months talking about my world. Why don't you tell me about yours for a change?"

"My world?" said Hazel. "But you live here. You see it every day."

Hob considered a moment. "True," he said. "But I'm not mehrùn. I've always been curious what it would be like to be able to do magic. Is it as fun as I think it would be?"

Hazel sighed. "It used to be. Magic used to be my favorite thing in the world. It wasn't just 'fun.' It was beautiful."

"So, what changed?"

Hazel swiveled to look about the library, at its dusty books and shuttered windows. Everywhere but Hob. She wasn't supposed to discuss magic. "This is pointless. We're supposed to be reviewing the Muirlands."

"We are," said Hob. "We're just coming at them from a different direction. Sometimes a person needs to stop chopping wood and sharpen their ax."

Hazel groaned. "Is that some sort of Hauja proverb?"

"No," he said. "But that would probably sound better. I actually heard it from Mother Howell back in Dusk. She had a lot of common sense. A lot of wood too."

Hazel laughed in spite of herself. "All right, Mr. Smythe. We will 'sharpen my ax,' whatever that means. Lead on."

"You were saying magic is beautiful," said Hob. "What did you mean? Were you talking about its effects or something else?" Hob rested his elbows on the table and looked at her attentively.

"It's not the effects," Hazel answered slowly. "It's more like a beautiful puzzle. For thousands of years, people have been trying to find its pieces and see how they all go together. That's what Lingua Mystica is: the latest version of a never-ending puzzle. I wish I could explain it better."

Hazel rose and started pacing. Hob was right. It was good to abandon the Muirlands for a few minutes, to engage in something that stirred her deeper passions. She closed her eyes.

"Picture an invisible harp," she said. "It's huge, big as the world. Muir can't see it, but mehrùn can sense its presence and play some of its strings. What you call a spell is really a song, a sequence of notes played on this mystical harp. The more gifted the mystic, the more beautifully they play."

"Makes sense," said Hob. "So, what makes it a puzzle?"

"A person doesn't play this harp with her fingers," said Hazel. "She plays it with language and intent. All words have power, but some have more than others. Lingua Mystica has over two thousand different words just for *fire*—words from any language you can imagine. Each has its own applications. For one spell, Aramaic might suit. Latin or Dryad might be better for another. Changing a single word in an incantation might mean you should change the others. Not all combinations are effective. It's like chess or arcadia—there are theoretically millions of available moves, but only a few you'd actually make."

"People must write down combinations that work," said Hob.

"Of course," said Hazel. "Mystics have been doing that forever. That's what spells are. What's exciting is that better versions exist— they just haven't been discovered yet."

"So, how do discoveries get made?" said Hob.

Hazel warmed to the conversation. She knew Rascha wouldn't approve, but it felt good to talk about a topic she knew so much about.

It reminded her that she really was an expert in something.

"Three ways," she explained. "The most common is when mystics improve known spells by tweaking little things like syntax, reagents, and hand gestures. Sorcerers try to break new ground, but with only one or two of them in a generation, success is rare. And every thousand years or so, a virtuoso comes along who not only plays something new but reaches strings no one knew existed. They're the explorers, the ones that really expand our understanding. Those are people like Mina the First. The only being to approach metamagia—theoretically perfect magic—was Astaroth, and that led to the Cataclysm. But he wasn't using his own magic. He was cheating."

"What do you mean?" said Hob.

"He had an artifact," said Hazel. "The Book of Thoth, which contained every truename. They're the sacred words of creation, and allowed Astaroth to reshape the world however he wished. Thankfully, it's gone now—Impyrium's first archmage used the book's magic to place it beyond reach. It's too dangerous to have such knowledge concentrated in one place."

"So even I have a truename?" said Hob.

"Of course," said Hazel. "Everyone does. Everything. Without a truename, there's nothing to anchor you in the world. You would have no essence, no spirit or soul."

"The Hauja believe something like that," said Hob. "The shamans say even rivers and rocks have a spirit. Is that the same as their truename?"

Hazel nodded.

"What if you speak something's truename?" said Hob. "Does that call it?"

"It can," said Hazel. "But there's more to a truename than simply its letters and the sounds they make. The power is only unleashed when the name is used by someone who has the strength and will to master what the name belongs to. That's why magical beings, like the Lirlanders, keep their truenames so secret—they fear another will use it against them."

"If they're so secret, how can mystics ever learn what they are?" said Hob.

Hazel laughed. "Truenames aren't random. The type of being, their birthplace, their lineage, all sorts of things can play a role in what their truename might be. Mystics and scholars do endless research trying to gather all this information. The thing that makes sorcerers so powerful isn't how much magic they have—it's their instincts. A really gifted sorcerer might be able to guess your truename just by looking at you long enough."

Hob raised his eyebrows. "Could you guess my truename?"

"I never said I was a sorceress," said Hazel. "Even if I was, I would never do such a thing. It's not a game, Mr. Smythe. Your truename is your truest, most personal, and vulnerable essence. With it, I could bend you, break you, change you, bind you . . . anything I wished."

"But those are all bad things," said Hob. "Can't you do good with truenames?"

"That's a controversial topic," said Hazel. "There are some who think we should use truenames to change and improve the world. Others insist they are a sacred gift from our creator, that they are precisely as they should be. By meddling, we corrupt their intended purpose."

"What do you think?" said Hob.

"I think they were wise to hide the Book of Thoth," said Hazel.

"Dàme Rascha says it takes many to build a temple, but only one to destroy it."

"Now, *that* could be a Hauja saying," said Hob. "It's funny, when I came to the Sacred Isle, I thought magic would be everywhere. But other than the maze and the Direwood, I feel like I haven't seen very much."

Hazel couldn't believe how insensitive muir were.

"But magic's all around you," she explained. "There are spells thousands of years old woven throughout the Sacred Isle, particularly here on the school grounds. Enchantments of protection and warding, spells that amplify the magic that's performed here. But it's Old Magic, stronger but more subtle than fairy lights and fireworks. Part of the reason Astaroth brought about the Cataclysm's earthquakes was to destroy Rowan. Everything else fell into the sea, but the school is still here. Old Magic protects it."

Hob looked amazed. "And you can sense this magic?"

"Of course," said Hazel. "Sometimes, I can even sense who made it. I can always tell Mina the First's work. Her signature's unmistakable."

"Really?" said Hob. "Like a pissing post?"

"I have no idea what that means, but it sounds revolting."

"Bad example," said Hob quickly. "There are lots of dogs in Dusk and they're always interested in who's been where."

"Hmm," said Hazel. "I'd say it's more like one artist recognizing another's work. There's an elegance to Mina the First's magic that's absent from Mina the Second's. Mina the Third's is a mumble, but Mina the Fourth's is like a scream. She used fewer words but in stranger combinations than anyone else. Her spells are like a poem you don't fully understand but somehow changes the way you see the world."

"If you know what their spells say, can't you re-create them?" said Hob.

Hazel smiled. "Every day you walk past hundreds of paintings in the palace. How many could you replicate?"

"Not a one."

"It's the same with magic," said Hazel. "Mystics can admire another caster's technique, but it doesn't mean they can do it themselves. If it did, there'd be lots of Tenth Ranks instead of just one in all of history. More goes into a spell than just the words. There's the caster and components—even context. A spell cast on Midwinter might be more potent than if cast at another time. There are countless factors. That's why people spend their entire lives studying it. That's the beauty I was talking about."

Hob had an inward, almost wistful expression. "It's amazing," he said simply. "Could you show me something?"

Sigga spoke up from the corner. "Your Highness, I don't think Dàme Rascha would approve."

Hazel glanced apologetically at Hob. "She's probably right."

"Fair enough," said Hob. "I was just curious. Even a glimpse of fairy lights."

Hazel hesitated. Explaining magic's principles to someone reminded her how much she loved it. She wanted to show Hob a little of what she could do, but the idea also made her feel anxious. Glancing at him, she felt her heart do a cartwheel. Surely, a *little* spell couldn't hurt—something she could do in her sleep.

"You must never tell anyone," said Hazel. "Promise me."

Hob raised his eyebrows at her sudden intensity, but nodded. "I promise, Your Highness."

"Very well," said Hazel. "Anyway, you don't even need to be First Rank to do this one and it can't hurt to practice the basics. This spell's called *bibliosk*. It's popular with librarians."

Raising her mittens, Hazel spoke the incantation, substituting the Akkadian word for "name" instead of the conventional Greek. Instantly, the books in Rattlerafters shot from their shelves. Hob took cover as leather tomes and paper pamphlets zoomed about, rearranging themselves in reverse alphabetical order. Within ten seconds, the last book had squeezed into place and scooted its spine flush with its neighbors.

Hob coughed and waved at the air, which was thick with swirling dust. His face broadened into a grin, and then into outright laughter. Hazel found herself laughing too.

"Incredible!" he crowed.

Hazel tried to look modest. "Like I said, it's an easy one. I'm sure every mehrùn on the Sacred Isle can do it."

"By the gods," said Hob, gazing about, delighted. "You practically just snapped your fingers. If I were you, I'd be doing magic all the time."

"It's tempting," said Hazel. "But that's why there are schools like Rowan. Using magic unnecessarily—'rogue magic' as some masters call it—is considered vulgar and even dangerous. Magic always has a cost. And it carries risks."

With a deep breath, Hazel removed her mitten and held up her disfigured hand. She'd felt vulnerable many times in her life, but this moment was different. She could not say why, but she wanted Hob to see it.

Sigga hurried over. "When did this happen, Your Highness?"

Hazel plucked a bit of mitten lining from the talon. "Early this morning," she said. "Don't worry. I'm sure Rascha can put it right." She shot Hob an anxious glance. How would he react to something like this?

His smile had faded, but he did not recoil or look repulsed. His expression was one of concern. "How does something like that happen?"

"I was trying to change shape," said Hazel. "When I'm tested, I have to demonstrate that I can become all kinds of animals. And I was trying . . . well, I was trying to become a pig."

He gave the talon a puzzled look. "Is that much harder than performing the *bibliosk*?"

Hazel laughed weakly. "Rascha would say no. She would say there's no fundamental difference. That's why she gets frustrated with me."

"But if you think there's a difference, then there is one," said Hob. "Even if it's just in your head. What makes *bibliosk* so easy for you?"

Hazel exhaled and gave a little shrug. "I don't know. It's just a fun little spell."

"Isn't turning into a pig fun?" asked Hob.

"Of course not," said Hazel, getting flustered. Hob had a way of asking simple questions to clarify issues that once seemed hopelessly complex. It was useful when it came to the Muirlands. But this was magic they were discussing. It was infinitely more personal. Hazel wasn't sure she wanted to go down this path.

Hob repeated the question, his expression open and expectant. Hazel swallowed hard and shut her eyes.

"If I can't transform, I can't qualify as a Third Rank. I'm running out of time. I'll be thirteen in October."

"But you're going to pass," said Hob. "Make 'Third Rank' or whatever."

Hazel held up her pig trotter. "You think so?"

He waved it off. "A detail. You already know everything you need to transform. Just like you know everything to ace Montague's exam. It's all in there."

Hazel's throat grew tight. "Then why can't I do it?"

"You haven't given yourself permission."

She laughed weakly.

To Hazel's surprise, Hob didn't bat an eye. "I'm dead serious. Failure scares some people so badly they forget what they're even trying to do. They're not trying to succeed at something; they're just trying not to fail. There's a big difference. I saw it on séyu and at the Province exams. *Bibliosk* was easy because you weren't afraid of the outcome and could just be in the moment. You even had fun with it." He leaned forward. "It's time to believe in yourself, Your Highness. Give yourself permission not just to succeed but to be great."

Hazel retreated a step. Hob was too intense, too serious right now. What he said made her afraid. What nonsense! People didn't give themselves permission to be great. Greatness came from . . . She frowned. Where did it come from?

Being a Faeregine came with all kinds of expectations. Hazel had been conscious of them all her life, and they were almost always coupled with fear—fear of failure, rejection, or ridicule. She'd never conceived of greatness as something that could be joyful, a mind-set or a state of being. It was simply a daunting standard. Of course, Hazel wanted to be great—who didn't?—but had she ever given herself permission? She supposed she hadn't. After all, granting permission required her to believe she had value, something worthy to contribute.

But did she? Violet didn't think so. Neither did the court brats. Isabel might, but she also regarded herself as Hazel's champion. A sudden realization flashed in her mind.

No one else's opinion mattered.

It was so simple, one of those things a consoling parent might say, and yet it contained a fundamental truth. The entire world could believe in Hazel's greatness but their faith was meaningless if she didn't believe it herself. Conversely, the world could dismiss her ambitions, but it didn't matter as long as Hazel believed in their possibility. Greatness not only started with her, it could not begin anywhere else.

Hazel blinked. She did not know how long she'd been standing there, only that tears had traced two paths down her cheeks. Hob had not moved. Neither had Sigga. Above them, she heard the clicks and groans of Old Tom's clockwork. Hazel gazed at her deformed hand.

She didn't need to say the incantation aloud; it wasn't necessary for magic affecting one's person. She simply spoke the words in her mind and focused her intent.

It was like unraveling a complicated knot by tugging gently at one end. Instantly, her thumb and fingers separated and lengthened to assume their rightful proportions as the talon retracted and disappeared. She wiggled her fingers, not in disbelief but in giddy delight. A few hours ago, the task had been hopeless. Now, it came as naturally as breathing.

Hazel gazed at Hob and Sigga in turn. A grin spread across her face as she now envisioned a pink piglet, smooth and round as a bolster.

Suddenly she was sinking. The table, the chairs, everything was rising around her as though they had grown very large or she had grown very small. Straight ahead, Hazel found herself looking at Hob's pants and shoes. He was getting up, hurrying around the table. Hopping nimbly over her clothes, Hazel heard a panicky squeal.

Did I make that?

She bolted toward Sigga, whose form no longer appeared as subtle shades and gradations, but flattened shapes of white and black. Red, greens, and blues remained, but the rest of the color spectrum had muddied. Sigga was crouching for a better look at her. Squealing wildly, Hazel darted past her and rounded a bookcase that smelled strongly of oak, dusty parchment, and floor wax. She could smell the domovoi who cleaned in here, even detect traces of those who'd handled nearby books. Her questing snout conveyed so much information it more than compensated for the loss in vision.

"Your Highness," said Sigga. "Are you all right?"

Of course she was all right—she'd just changed into a pig! With a merry squeal, Hazel raced up and down the stacks, reveling in her speed and nimbleness. Hob was grinning, trotting to try and catch sight of her before she rounded another stack.

What a day.

Hazel wanted to race all over Old College, root in the hummocky woods, snort defiance at the masters, and shake her tail at them. And Rascha! Dàme Rascha would leap out of bed when she learned Hazel could shape change. Hazel couldn't wait—she had to tell her instantly! All she had to do was change back and . . .

Hazel skidded to a panting halt by her clothes.

She was naked! Pig naked.

"Well done!" said Hob, clapping.

Hazel bolted away. Yes, she was a pig, but she was a naked pig and she didn't want Hob to see her. She shook with mad laugher at the absurdity of it all. There must be a modification to ensure one's clothes would change with you. If not, the Mystics examinations were going to be rather awkward.

Racing to the library's back corner, she darted inside an empty cabinet just as Old Tom began chiming. Turning about, she nosed the sliding door shut as the bells boomed above. Darkness enveloped her as she transformed, gasping and panting, back into Hazel Faeregine. Slight as she was, she was cramped and folded in upon herself. Beads of sweat trickled down her ribs as she waited for the chimes to cease.

"Sigga?" she called at last.

A boot thumped the cabinet door. "Your Highness?"

"Would you be so good as to fetch my clothes?"

Sigga's response was admirably restrained. "Of course."

"Wonderful," said Hazel. "Mr. Smythe?"

His response came from across the room. "Yes, Your Highness?"

"I wonder if we could reschedule the rest of our review. I need some time to . . . collect myself."

"Of course."

Thank you!

Another thought occurred to her. If she was going to be stuck inside a cabinet, she might as well ask a question she could never say to his face.

"Eh, one more thing," she called.

"Yes?"

Hazel screwed her eyes tight. "Would you consider coming to the May Ball?" she blurted. The rest came in a breathless, rapid tumble of words. "You'd have to come as a servant, which I know isn't quite fair, but I hate these kinds of things and I'd . . . well, I'd feel better knowing I had a friend there."

A pause. "I'd be honored."

Hazel gave a piggish squeal. Duly mortified, she curled up and waited for him to leave. Seconds later, a familiar voice seemed to whisper in her ear.

All we need now is the dragon.

CHAPTER 17
THE MAY BALL

*The hags have invited me to a sacred feast
where I am to be the guest of honor.
The brutes have accepted me as one of their own
and academia shall reap the rewards . . .*

—Recovered journal of Dr. Ezra Planck,
cultural anthropologist.

On the afternoon of the May Ball, zephyss after zephyss zoomed down the servant hallways, their jingling accompanied by opening doors and the tromp of well-polished shoes. The palace was overflowing with distinguished guests who required a small army of maids, pages, and valets. There were clothes to be ironed, pets to be walked, errands to be run, and egos to massage.

As Her Highness's personal attendant, Hob was spared these

summonses. Viktor was not, and had already dashed off to bring tea and toast to a Lord and Lady Vensu visiting from Pearl Bay. Tossing his jacket on the bed, Hob opened his handbook to find a message from the Fellowship:

Relay anything noteworthy from this evening, particularly anything to do with HF or the Cirlanders. Do not worry about Sigga Fenn. Her queries into your background have been intercepted. Jor truth, equality, and a free Impyrium.

The tone of the Fellowship's communications had softened since Mr. Burke's visit, particularly once Hob passed along specifics regarding Hazel's magical studies. In that report, he'd told the Fellowship that Her Highness was tasked with qualifying as a Third Rank mystic, and described in detail the spell she'd performed. He also took pains to convey how she'd talked about the magical works of others, how she could sense who had created what. Hazel had referenced the Reaper's style, but she talked about Mina IV as though she was any other historical figure. While Mr. Burke had told him not to analyze or interpret, Hob could not help but think it was a promising sign.

Hob did not enjoy sharing these discoveries. He had broken his promise to Hazel and exploited her trust to gain the information. His actions were dishonorable, but he reminded himself that he was only trying to protect her from those who might assume the worst. Hazel was no Reaper reborn, and if there was some spirit or evil force at work, he would help her get rid of it. It wasn't her fault she'd been born a Faeregine any more than it was his fault he'd been born a bastard.

Slipping on his jacket, Hob checked his appearance in the mirror.

Oliveiro had dropped off a gold emblem that would give him access to the ballroom. When he tried to pin it to his lapel, however, the backing snapped. Picking up the broken piece, he stifled a curse and sucked his bleeding thumb. He was due any minute in the ballroom.

He ran down to the kitchens where thirty-seven hags were busy cooking and screeching at the fauns who would be serving their creations upstairs. The creatures had every tool imaginable, some for cooking and others for more nefarious purposes. They were sure to have some glue. Plunging through a cloud of steam, Hob almost collided with Gorgo, Bombasta's mutinous deputy.

The hag stood atop a little stool peering into a cauldron that she stirred with close attention. She did not look up; a flare of her nostrils told her who was at her elbow.

"Evening, Lover Boy."

"Hey, Gorgo. Got any glue?"

"Left drawer. Grippy stuff. Don't get it on ya."

Hob found the tube amid various junk, fingernail clippings, and what looked disturbingly like a shriveled ear. Squeezing out a drop, Hob glued the backing and held it fast.

"Thanks," he said, giving the cauldron a second glance. "Er, what is that?"

"Keep it down," she muttered. "It's a potion."

Hob was intrigued. "Can you do magic?"

She nodded proudly. "I'm a sorceress. And a true Shrope, unlike that cow Bombasta. This'll teach her to put on airs."

Hob stared at the bubbling concoction. Looking furtively over her shoulder, Gorgo added a pinch of powder and cackled. "For extra oomph!"

"Gorgo, please tell me that isn't poison."

"Nah," she said ruefully. "Just a tummy rumbler."

Hob grimaced. "It makes you go to the bathroom?"

"Like a volcano!" She tittered as she ladled some into a vial. "Take some, eh? Oliveiro gets too high and mighty, put a splash of this in his wine. It'll learn him."

"Really, Gorgo, I don't need . . ."

But the hag insisted, pressing her creation upon Hob until he decided it would be rude and perhaps even dangerous to refuse. Slipping it in his pocket, he hurried out the swinging doors, saluting the hags who jeered his departure. From the kitchens, he wound his way up the staircases until he reached the entry hall.

He arrived to find nobles from across the empire streaming toward the ballroom's double staircase: tattooed witches from the east; dark royals from Afrique wearing colorful robes; skänder nobles with green coats and silver court swords. A party from Zenuvia passed bearing Queen Lilith's moon and hemlock standard. Mehrùn and demons, Elder vyes and fauns—even a group of centaurs wearing flowered wreaths. May Day was sacred not only to humans.

If people back home could see this.

Hob nearly laughed. The spectacle before him would have sent Duskers sprinting to their root cellars. But Hob was enchanted. The nonhumans lent the procession a dreamlike magnificence unlike anything he'd ever seen. He watched a group of faerie folk skim past like shimmering dragonflies.

"Move," barked a guttural voice.

An arm thrust Hob back so forcefully he nearly toppled over. Regaining his balance, he found himself looking into the bright yellow eye of an oni. The demon was no taller than a man but thrice as broad, wearing embroidered robes whose delicacy was incongruous with its ox-sized head. Great tusks protruded from a black beard crackling with electricity. The oni did not give Hob a second glance, but bulled ahead, bellowing for all to make way for Lord Kraavh.

An assortment of imps followed, carrying Lirlander banners and scattering moonflowers before the ambassador. The very air seemed to warp and shimmer about Lord Kraavh. Hob found he could scarcely breathe, much less move until the demon passed.

He watched, spellbound, as the Lirlanders proceeded up the staircase. Hob knew Lord Kraavh wasn't the only rakshasa in existence, and that rakshasa were not even the most feared among the Lirlanders. It was hard to imagine how mankind had conquered such beings.

Hob gazed about the vast hallway, at its pillars and ancient frescoes. What if the Faeregines hadn't mastered the demons and driven them beneath the sea? What would the world be like? Would humans still even exist?

He contemplated this as he left the main procession and took a shortcut through a courtyard. Far above the palace spires, a warm and tranquil twilight was settling into evening.

Seeing his pin, a guard waved him through a side entrance. The ballroom was like an enormous jewelry box: rich reds and pale gold with a map of the empire painted upon its vaulted ceiling. Hundreds of tables were arranged around a gleaming dance floor where an orchestra was playing. Faeregines were seated at the head, their tables flanking a dais where the Spider would sit. The empress had yet to arrive.

The triplets were present, however. Hob saw Violet and Isabel conversing with the archmage. Hazel was seated nearby with Dàme Rascha, who was finally up and about. Hob picked his way through the crowds, giving a wide berth to Mr. Dunn, the head butler.

"Mr. Smythe, what a pleasant surprise."

The voice came from a nearby table. Hob gave an inward groan as he turned to see Dante Hyde. The earl was seated with his family and other members of their house. Hob bowed stiffly.

"Yes, milord?"

Dante addressed his parents. "This is the page I was telling you about. The one I want."

Lord Willem Hyde was a powerful-looking man with a fringe of graying yellow hair and eyes like pale glass. Like Dante, he wore a cavalry saber.

"So, you're the muir bastard that attacked my son."

Hob's face assumed a stony expression. "Yes, milord."

Lady Hyde's contemptuous gaze wandered over Hob. "Why does this animal still possess a head?"

Her husband sipped his wine. "He's under Faeregine protection, my dear. No matter. He'll belong to us soon enough."

Dante leaned forward. "He'll belong to *me*. The page brawls like a savage. I intend to show him how a gentleman duels."

Hob bowed. "I must confess that duels are fought differently here. Where I come from, one's sister isn't permitted to take part. Is that a common tactic, milord, or your own stroke of genius?"

Dante flushed scarlet and shot an anxious glance at his father. He was on the verge of a furious retort when a hand came to rest lightly on Hob's shoulder.

"Her Highness is expecting you."

Hob had never been so happy to see Sigga. The Grislander did not bother greeting the Hydes as she led Hob away from their table.

"You're late," she muttered.

"Sorry. I was busy being threatened."

Sigga cocked an eyebrow. "Great Houses don't often waste their venom on junior servants. Are you sure you're just a page, Mr. Smythe?"

"If I'm not, I'm underpaid."

The assassin smiled and peeled off to have a word with Agent Kruger, Violet's bodyguard. Hob continued to Her Highness's table and stood alongside Olo and the other family servants. Hazel turned.

"Mr. Smythe, so happy you could join us."

Hob bowed. "Good evening, Your Highness. Dàme Rascha, I'm pleased to see you're feeling better."

The vye nodded her thanks.

"Rascha's on the mend but now Isabel's banged up," said Hazel. "Fell off her horse this morning."

Indeed, Hob spied Hazel's sister leaning on a pair of red crutches as she spoke with the archmage. He hadn't noticed from across the room, for the crutches matched her gown.

As for Hazel, she wore a dress of rose gold that shimmered like fish scales. Her white hair was up, arranged beneath a pearlescent tiara with the Faeregine harp in gold. The emeralds on her necklace could have purchased a barony.

Isabel hobbled over and whispered something in Hazel's ear that brought a look of dismay. Setting Merlin on the table, Hazel leaned back for a better view of Violet.

Her Impyrial Highness was still talking with the archmage. There was no denying Violet's beauty, but it was remote, like a sculpture in cold marble. At the moment, however, she looked surprisingly anxious as the archmage directed her attention to an enormous crystal sphere that hovered high above. Gazing up at it, she gave an infinitesimal shake of her head. The archmage noddedand led her to the empress's dais.

Hob was confused. Was the Spider not coming?

He was not the only one to notice. A ripple of chatter was drowning out the orchestra. Hundreds of curious faces had turned toward the dais. Hob glanced at Hazel, who was having a hushed though heated conversation with Isabel. She shook her head until Isabel pointed at her crutches and hissed something. Evidently, she made her point. Slumping low, Hazel gave a resigned nod and glanced miserably back at Hob.

"I have to dance," she mouthed.

Hob's shrug assured her that it was a ball; everyone had to dance. Hazel shook her head.

"In front of everybody . . ."

Another you'll-be-fine shrug.

". . . with Dante!"

Hob sneezed to convey his disgust. Hazel tried to smile but merely looked nauseated.

"Do you know how to dance?" said Hob.

Her stare implied that she knew how to dance perfectly well, thank you very much. Palace life entailed many receptions and balls. She'd probably been pirouetting since she could walk.

Their conversation ended as Faeregines from near and far descended en masse upon the nearby tables. Hob recognized many from his handbook. These extended members of the clan boasted many lofty titles but little responsibility. Several were mystics or held administrative positions; most spent their days in idle luxury on vast estates. Without the Spider's imposing presence, the Faeregines looked soft.

Hob felt he was seeing precisely what Mr. Burke had been talking about. Faeregine strength used to reside in their magic. Now the family depended on institutions they controlled. Break their hold on the bank and the Seals and you broke the dynasty. He studied Basil Faeregine sitting to Violet's left. His lordship was reading a note a servant had just handed him. His face curdled.

More bad news.

A bell chimed. The room fell silent as Violet Faeregine rose to address them.

Hob had to admire the princess's composure. Despite her nerves a few minutes ago, she now stood tall and straight. Her voice rang throughout the ballroom.

She spoke in Old Impyrian. Hob understood little, but he gathered it was a recitation. Periodically, she gestured at the crystal sphere far above them. Her audience was silent; not even the lutins or domanocti stirred. Hob surveyed the many tables and the ancient families surrounding them. How many schemes was this nest of vipers hatching? And how many involved the Fellowship?

He spied Lady Sylva standing by her husband. If not for her, he wouldn't be here. Hob wondered if her efforts to forge a friendship with Violet Faeregine were to further House Sylva's ambitions or purely a Fellowship directive. Of course, the lady was a Yamato by birth. Maybe they were involved.

Parsing these possibilities gave Hob a headache. There was something so exhausting and sordid about the way these families lived. They were the wealthiest, most powerful people in the world, yet they spent their days consumed with rivalries. What good was a palace if you never got a good night's sleep?

The princess was reaching the end of her address. She raised her hand at the crystal sphere, her voice clear as a trumpet.

"Sol Invictus!"

Unconquerable sun, Rowan's motto going back to ancient times. As she spoke these words, the sphere erupted with light, a blinding brilliance that filled the hall before condensing into a ball of churning witchfire.

"Sol Invictus," replied the guests, raising their glasses as the orchestra began to play a slow, waltz-like number. The lights dimmed and a spotlight shone on Hazel. Resigned to her fate, she walked with her chin up, shoulders back to the middle of the dance floor. Once there, she assumed a proper pose and awaited her partner.

Heads turned to the Hydes. The flustered chamberlain beckoned for Dante to rise, but the young earl smiled modestly and declined. His sister was shaking with silent laughter. Their parents looked placidly on, neither amused nor displeased.

Hazel remained in the spotlight, a small and solitary figure frozen in the ludicrous attitude of a lady awaiting her suitor. The orchestra continued playing; Dante Hyde remained in his chair. The audience began to squirm.

Basil Faeregine abruptly popped to his feet and strode onto the floor. Despite his troubles, his lordship cut an elegant figure with his silver hair and tailored suit. Bowing low to his niece, he asked if he might have the privilege.

Many applauded as the two began to dance; others cast stony looks at the Hydes and turned their backs to them. Family rivalries were acceptable; humiliating a young girl was not. Dante Hyde had overstepped the bounds. He watched with a scowl as Hazel danced a truly elegant waltz. Instead of looking foolish, she looked every bit a Faeregine princess.

The piece wound to a close. Bowing once again to his partner, Lord Faeregine escorted a beaming Hazel back to her table. As the applause died down, the orchestra began playing a new number and pairs made their way to the dance floor.

A breathless Hazel was aglow with excitement. Isabel thumped the floor with her crutch.

"Well done!"

"Indeed," said Basil Faeregine. "I had no idea you were such a fine dancer, young lady. Very light on your feet."

Hazel leaned into him. "I had a good partner."

"Well," he said, "let's have a celebratory toast before your dance card fills up."

As Lord Faeregine left to fetch refreshments, Hazel sat back down with Isabel as people came over to pay their respects.

"The Hydes were always tactless," sniffed a matronly cousin. "You handled yourself very well, my dear. I wish your grandmother had been here to see it. Where is the empress?"

Isabel cut in. "Taking a well-deserved rest. Her May Day duties began before dawn. I think my sister fills her seat admirably."

She gestured to Violet, who was sitting atop the empress's dais looking more like an ornament than a hostess. Hob actually felt sorry for her.

"She does indeed," said the great aunt. "A lovely— Oh!"

Lord Kraavh's shadow fell over the table. The cousin mumbled an excuse and fled as Sigga seemed to materialize over Hazel's shoulder. The rakshasa bowed. His deep voice had an unearthly resonance.

"An elegant turn, Your Highness. I haven't seen you since the *Typhon* mishap. You're coming into bloom."

Hazel craned her neck at that fearsome face. "Thank you. You are well, I trust?"

The rakshasa gazed about. "Merely grateful to escape the embassy. I'm not accustomed to being confined in my own home."

Basil Faeregine returned with a lemonade for Hazel. "You're fortunate you're not in prison," he said angrily. "Another galleon went down off Ankura. This time, some of the crew survived. They've all sworn it was Lirlanders."

The ambassador spread his hands. "If intruders sail into our waters, we cannot guarantee their safety."

Lord Faeregine darkened. "Those ships are under Impyrial protection. They bore Seals."

"So you keep insisting."

"Of course they did. Why would a ship cross Lirlander waters without one?"

"An excellent question, but one you should ask their captains."

Lord Faeregine's face darkened. "Their captains are dead. Are your people so intent on war?"

Three green eyes narrowed to glowing slits. "If the Faeregines desire war, then there will be war. But we will not be the ones to break the treaty." The demon turned to the royal dais. "Where is the Divine Empress?"

"That's not your concern."

"Tell Her Radiance I desire a meeting."

Lord Faeregine straightened. "I'm not your errand boy. Send one of your imps."

The ambassador turned his attention once more upon Hazel. "A pleasure, Your Highness. You are not only the most intriguing member of your family you are also its most courteous. Good evening."

Hazel inclined her head. The demon continued on his rounds, stopping to speak with the Hydes. Lord Willem and his family stood at once to pay their respects.

"Of course they would," muttered Lord Faeregine. Finishing his champagne, he glanced down at Isabel. "How's the leg, O valiant horsewoman?"

"Broken," said Isabel. "Once I've sat here awhile looking chic, I'm off to take a moonbath with those revolting lunasects." She turned to Hob. "What's it like?"

"Not too bad, Your Highness. More tingly than painful."

She groaned. Her uncle took notice of Hob.

"You're the young man who dueled with Dante Hyde."

Hob confessed that he was.

Lord Faeregine chuckled. "I had no idea we employed such bruisers among the pages." He clapped Hob's shoulder. "You'll get him next time, eh?"

"I'm hoping to avoid future trips to the healing ward, sir. Incidentally, Private Finch is safely back home."

"Who?"

"Marcus Finch, milord. From the Impyrial Guard."

Lord Faeregine offered the smile favored by well-bred persons when they had no clue what you were talking about. He promptly turned to greet a member of the foreign council, and the two stepped away for a private conversation. Meanwhile, a handsome boy approached to ask Hazel for a dance. Dàme Rascha promptly shooed him away.

"Rascha," said Hazel, once he'd gone. "That was rude."

The vye was in no mood to be contradicted. "He's a Tallow," she growled. "His family's fortunate to attend, much less ask for a dance with the empress's granddaughter."

Isabel gazed about the ballroom. "Oh, I don't know. These boys from Houses Minor aren't so bad. I'm tired of the FYGs. They're such duds and they practically share a chin." She turned to find a FYG standing by their table. "Oh, hello, Andros. I wasn't talking about you. Your chin's a land mass."

Andros Eluvan rolled his eyes. "Whatever you say, Isabel. Since you've managed to hobble yourself, I thought I'd ask Hazel for a dance."

"Ah," said Isabel. "Better check with Rascha. She just turned away a Tallow and he was much better looking."

Ignoring the jab, Andros bowed to Hazel and held out his hand. When Dàme Rascha made no objection, Hazel accompanied him onto the dance floor. As they melted into the crowd, Hob silently wished Andros would trip and fall on his face.

Are you jealous?

Of course he wasn't jealous! He was happy for Hazel. She was doing well in her classes, transforming into piglets, and now enjoying herself at a ball. These were not only good things, they made all the Reaper talk seem increasingly far-fetched. *Jealous?* The idea was ridiculous.

Hob became aware that Isabel was watching him. She gave a knowing grin.

"I knew it."

Dàme Rascha turned to her. "You knew what, child?"

"Nothing," she replied innocently. She held out her hand as Pamplemousse landed in a flap of membranous wings. The homunculus plucked irritably at his waistcoat.

"I told you it was tight."

"You poor thing," Isabel teased. "Perhaps Mr. Smythe will fetch us an ice while we abuse the dancers. I think he could use a diversion."

Hob made for one of the many bars situated about the vast ballroom. A crowd of servants was gathered around it, fetching various libations for their masters.

A voice whispered in Hob's ear.

"Two months and you're my property. You can't imagine what I'm going to do with you."

Hob turned to see Dante leering down at him.

"Good evening again, Lord Hyde. You don't have to hang about the bar like a servant. Let me get you something."

Dante was not amused. "Did you hear what I said, muir?"

"Yes. You want 'to do things with me.' I'm flattered, but surprised His Lordship wants to socialize with the help."

Dante leaned closer. "That tongue will be the first to go. Then your feet . . ."

Hob feigned disappointment. "Where's you imagination? Where I'm from there are folk that'll stitch your eyes open."

The earl grinned. "There's an idea. Perhaps I'll—"

"Can I be of service, Lord Hyde?"

The boys turned to see Oliveiro standing by, the very image of the sober professional. Judging by his expression, it was clear he understood the nature of their discussion.

"No need," said Dante pleasantly. "I was just telling your boy here how I like my drink."

Oliveiro glanced at the half-empty glass in the earl's hand. "Mr. Smythe will bring another to your table."

"I'll be waiting."

Once Dante withdrew, Oliveiro fixed Hob with a stern gaze. "What was that about?"

"Nothing," said Hob. "He just came over to say hello."

The underbutler frowned. "Once you deliver Lord Hyde's beverage, you are excused for the evening."

"But Her Highness—"

"I'll explain to Dàme Rascha. There's to be no more trouble with the Hydes."

Hob's jaw tightened. "I didn't start this."

Oliveiro clasped his hands behind his back. "No, Mr. Smythe, I don't believe you did. But that is neither here nor there. Deliver his drink and take your leave."

"Very good, sir."

Several minutes later, Hob had three ices, Pamplemousse's juice, and Dante's drink on a salver. He delivered Lord Hyde's first, leaving a puzzled maid to set it before His Lordship. Hob glided away without comment and returned to the Faeregine table, where he served Isabel's ice and Pamplemousse's juice. Hazel was just returning from a dance and went straight for one of the ices.

"Is this for me?" she asked.

"One for you," said Hob. "And one for Dàme Rascha."

Pamplemousse swatted Merlin away from his drink. "Took long enough. In my day—"

"You're only two months old," moaned Isabel.

The creature scowled and set upon his juice, lapping it up with a long, forked tongue. Hazel spooned her ice.

"I'm so glad that first dance is over."

"You were great," said Hob.

"No thanks to Dante Hyde," she muttered. "Leaving me to stand there like an idiot. I swear I'm going to get him. I just need to think of something sufficiently dreadful."

Hob pretended to give this some thought. "We could put something in his drink," he said quietly. "Nothing dangerous—just something to ensure a highly public *accident*."

Hazel almost swooned. "That's perfect! Let's do it."

"Consider it done."

"Okay," she said eagerly. "When?"

"How about five minutes ago?"

She blinked. "Five minutes ago? I don't . . ."

Hob gave her a significant look and an expression of horrified delight blossomed on Her Highness's pale features. She peered furtively at the table where Dante was busy flirting with Tatiana Castile. The glass was nearly empty.

"Did you really?" she whispered.

Hob nodded before addressing her in a formal tone. "Your Highness, Mr. Oliveiro has excused me for the evening. With your permission, I will take my leave."

"Yes," she said quickly. "Yes, of course. Good night, Mr. Smythe. And thank you!"

With a bow, he made for the exit, avoiding eye contact with the Hyde table. Passing a gauntlet of guardsmen, he slipped from the ballroom and descended the double staircase.

Hob knew he'd done something rash but it was worth it. He'd

never hated anyone—not even his mother's family—as much as he despised Dante Hyde. And he wasn't just striking a blow for himself, he was striking one for Hazel. His real regret was that he wouldn't get to see the proverbial fireworks in person.

When Hob reached the servant quarters, he found the pages' wing unusually quiet. Most were on duty; the rest had to sit about in their uniforms should they be needed. Several were playing cards in the little common area. Hob said hello but did not linger to chat. He wanted a nap before the after-party game of hall thumper. He and Viktor were on a winning streak.

Viktor wasn't in. Opening the little window, Hob sat on his bed and pulled off his dress boots. Music wafted in from the ballroom far above. It reminded him that the Fellowship wanted a report as soon as possible. His attendance had been brief, but he'd seen plenty of interest. With Viktor out, he might as well report while the details were fresh. Lying on his cot, he opened the handbook and took up a blunt toothpick.

Empress did not attend; VF presided. Looked nervous when told she would have to light crystal "sun" during ceremony. Believe archmage did it. Open hostility between BF and Kraavh. Ship sunk off Ankura. Some crew survived—insist Lirlanders attacked. Kraavh said ships trespassing. BF says demons have broken treaty. War seems imminent. Separate note—Dante Hyde threatened me. Says I will "belong" to him in two—

There was a commotion in the hallway: running footsteps and a chorus of shouts. Did someone call his name? Hob slipped the handbook under his pillow just as someone hammered on his door.

"What?" he called.

The door shattered.

Splinters pelted his hands and arms, some piercing the skin. No ordinary blow or kick could have done that. This was magic. Hob peered through the dust. Dante Hyde stood panting in the doorway.

"You put something in my drink."

Hob rose slowly from his bed. He didn't bother arguing; it wouldn't have mattered if he were innocent. Dante's skin had a waxy sheen. Beads of sweat trickled steadily down his forehead. Drawing his sword, he staggered into the room.

"I'm going to kill you . . ."

Yanking the blanket from his cot, Hob flung it at Dante's face and bolted for the door.

As he hoped, Dante swatted the blanket aside, providing a window for Hob to dart past him. But Dante recovered and shouldered Hob into the doorjamb with such force the two crashed to the floor. The saber's point grazed Hob's stomach as he scrambled to his feet and stumbled out of the room.

A dozen pages were in the hallway, staring in speechless astonishment. Viktor was among them. Hob waved them away.

"Get out of here. Fetch the guard!" he yelled.

Dante staggered into the hallway, clutching his saber and looking murderous. "That's right," he rasped. "Fetch the guard with their guns. They're little muir maggots just like you."

All the boys ran except for Viktor. Hob's roommate looked petrified but stood his ground. Dante looked amused.

"Are you going to be a hero?"

When Viktor didn't answer, the earl pointed at his feet. *"Ignis."*

Viktor's shoes burst into bright flames. With a cry, he dropped to the floor and tried to remove them. Hob rushed over and pulled them off, singeing his hands in the process. The boy's socks had already burned away; the skin beneath was smoking. Viktor gripped Hob's shoulder.

"Run!"

Dante laughed. "That's right, boy. Run."

Hob tried, but his body had trouble obeying. Dante had cast some sort of hex that caused his muscles to feel horribly sluggish. Running was impossible; even walking was like wading through mud. The best Hob could do was back away, and even that took surprising effort.

Dante stepped over Viktor, clutching his saber with one hand and his belly with the other. He wasn't well, but he wasn't nearly as sick as Hob assumed he would be. Perhaps Gorgo's potion only worked on hags. Dante's face twisted into a leer.

"Still think you're my equal?"

Hob continued backing away. He reached the junction of the boys' and girls' wings. If he could get to the stairs . . .

"You're just some half-tamed savage," said Dante hoarsely. "My family's been ruling Impyrium for millennia."

"You should tell the Faeregines," said Hob.

"They're finished. I'm going to butcher their servant in their own house and they won't say a word. We own the Faeregines, which means I own you. . . ."

Fortunately, Dante was the sort who always had to have the last word, which was tremendously helpful when one was trying to stall. All Hob had to do was argue.

"You don't own me," he said.

"But I do! You're going to be my puppet. I'm pulling the strings now."

The earl jerked his hand and an invisible force yanked Hob off his feet. He dangled in the air like a marionette. When Dante released him, he fell in a heap. Gasping, Hob made for the nearby staircase.

"Crawling like a worm," Dante observed. "Compared to you, I'm a god."

It was an impressive statement. Unfortunately, it ended with a thunderous belch that left the speaker in dry heaves.

"Very godlike," grunted Hob, seizing the railing.

Dante wiped spittle from his lips and pointed a finger. "*Ignis!*" he croaked.

A wave of heat billowed over Hob's face, but it was no worse than opening an oven door. Perhaps the potion was taking effect, or perhaps Dante had tapped out his stores of magic. Hob didn't really care so long as he still had a face.

Hob reached the landing and descended another flight. Despite his peril, he could not help but recognize the situation's absurdity. This had to be the slowest chase in human history. He took another laborious step.

"Why can't we just be friends," he wheezed. "I think we have a lot in common."

"We have nothing in common!" yelled Dante.

"You know that hurts my feelings."

An enraged Dante redoubled his efforts. He staggered down several steps before coming to an abrupt halt. A warbling gurgle sounded from his stomach.

"Better find a privy," said Hob. "Don't worry. I'll wait."

Dante gave a convulsive shiver. "I swear I'm going to kill you. . . ."

At last, Hob reached the servants' dining room. "Why aren't you using Bragha Rùn? Everyone knows you stole it. Did you sell it already?"

Dante smirked. "No one's selling that blade. Not 'til the assassin's done his work."

Hob's smile vanished. "What are you talking about? What assassin?"

Dante lurched nearly within striking distance. His voice was a rasping hiss. "The assassin that's going to murder your girlfriend. I hear he's already in position."

Keep him talking. "You're making that up."

Dante shook his head. "Overheard my father. The order could come any day. Too bad you won't be able to warn her . . ."

The saber whistled past Hob's nose. Stumbling backward, Hob crashed through the swinging doors to the kitchens. Dante rushed after him, grinning madly as he held the sword inches from Hob's face.

"Any last words, muir?"

Hob propped himself on his elbows. "A question."

"Let's hear it."

"Have you ever been sniffed?"

Dante blinked. His uneasy gaze traveled about the kitchen, taking in the burly figures that stopped what they were doing to regard the stranger. Bombasta broke the eerie silence.

"Who the bloody hell is you?"

Dante straightened. He was so outraged at being questioned in such a manner that he failed to notice a hag sidling casually behind him. "I'm Lord Dante Hyde, you disgusting brute. Earl of Eastmarch, heir to House Hyde, and—"

"A roast!" squealed the hag.

Dante shrieked as she wrenched him off his feet. In a flash, the hag had pinned his arms and flung his saber in a nearby sink. While

Dante flailed, other hags rushed forward with kitchen twine. They fell upon the earl in a frenzy of activity. He reappeared moments later trussed as neatly as a rib roast. His shrieks soared into falsetto range.

Sobbing and pleading, he offered gold and even houses to the many hags now rubbing him with butter. His entreaties fell upon deaf ears; hags did not listen to their food. They merely passed him down the line where others waited with herbs and spices. At the far end, Gorgo was tending the oven while Bombasta sharpened a cleaver.

Tempted though he was, Hob decided he could not actually let the hags devour Dante. Getting to his feet, he found his spell had been broken. He quickly made his way to Bombasta.

"Happy May Day, love," she said. "Nice gesture to bring us supper. Was feeling peckish."

"About that supper," said Hob. "You can't eat him."

"Rubbish! He's a strapping lad. Plenty of good meat there."

"He'll make you sick."

Bombasta wrinkled her nose. "How's that?"

"I spiked his drink."

Gorgo slammed the oven shut. "You gave him Bombasta's potion?" she cried.

Bombasta wheeled on her. "Whatchoo mean *my* potion?"

Gorgo fled into a nearby pantry. With a sigh, Bombasta dumped out her tankard and considered the well-seasoned earl now being transferred to a roasting pan. "Oi!" she shouted. "Hold up, girlies."

The assembly line ceased. Thirty-five hags turned their beady eyes upon their chief.

"Let 'im go," she grumbled. "Meat's no good."

The kitchen hags looked at Hob. They weren't angry so much as disappointed. Two seized the roasting pan by its handles and dumped their quaking supper on the floor. Bombasta jabbed a finger in Hob's chest.

"You owe us an earl."

Before he could reply, Oliveiro burst into the kitchen with four guardsmen at his heels. The underbutler's eyes found Hob before he noticed the hog-tied lord on the kitchen floor.

"Get away from him," he ordered.

The hags gave their meal feisty, unrepentant looks as they shuffled off in their clogs. The soldiers helped Lord Hyde to his feet and Oliveiro cut away the twine. Dante was apoplectic.

"I'll have all your heads!" he shouted. "Every last—!"

His eyes shot wide.

Gorgo's potion had finally kicked in.

Moments later, Hob stood in quiet amazement. He had not realized a human stomach could expel its contents from so many places, and with such astonishing force. Even the hags were horrified. They had scattered to the far corners as Bombasta bellowed for mops.

A nonplussed Oliveiro retrieved a hand towel and calmly wiped his face. He did not offer one to Lord Hyde, who remained in a crouched attitude, looking stunned and appalled.

"Well," said Oliveiro. "I'm reasonably confident I will never forget this May Day. Mr. Smythe, return to your quarters."

This snapped Dante from his trance.

"Your page poisoned me!"

"Do you have proof?" said Oliveiro.

Dante was incredulous. "It's all over you!"

Oliveiro tutted. "Perhaps your lordship overindulged. Such strong drinks are a bit much for a young man. Even an earl."

"How dare you! I want him arrested!"

"Do you indeed?" said Oliveiro. "Given your lordship's literal and figurative position, I assumed you'd wish to handle this privately. From what I gather, you—a guest of Her Divine Radiance—trespassed into the servant quarters, destroyed property, assaulted one page with magic, tried to murder another, and emptied your bowels in her kitchens. Am I missing anything?"

"He offered me an estate!" cried a hag indignantly.

The underbutler frowned. "Attempted bribery." He cocked his head inquiringly. "Shall we press the issue, milord, or would you prefer fresh clothes and discreet transportation?"

His lordship chose the latter option. Turning to Hob, Oliveiro ordered him back to his room before he and the guards escorted Dante out the kitchen's back entrance.

Hob found Viktor in their room, tending to his feet while a pair of domovoi removed twisted hinges from the doorframe.

"How are they?" asked Hob.

Viktor rubbed salve into his toes. "Crispy, but I'll live. You?"

"I'm fine," said Hob, slipping his handbook into a towel. "I'm sorry you got involved. I'll be right back—just going to clean up. I'm covered in Lord Hyde."

He ran down the hallway to the pages' bathroom and ducked into a stall. Once inside, he locked the door and scribbled a hasty note to the Fellowship.

DH just attacked me. Am all right. He boasted of an assassin—over-heard his father. Said order's been given for HF. Is that true?

He flipped to the page that would display incoming messages.

"Come on," he whispered, tapping it impatiently. "Simple yes or no."

What if they said yes? How was Hob going to warn Sigga? Should he tell her himself or leave an anonymous note?

A message arrived. The words surfaced one by one, overwriting the list of diplomats.

> *Boy is a fool who overheard outdated conversation. No order needed. Scholar does not believe HJ is what we feared. Stay course. I will deal with Hydes.*

Hob almost whooped aloud. It was the best possible answer he could have received. No assassination order had been given, and none was coming. Hazel was just Hazel, after all. If she was sick or plagued by some malignant spirit, they would find a way to help her. It might take time, but he knew she could become an invaluable ally and smooth the transition to a more just Impyrium.

Leaving the stall, he went to the sink and splashed some cold water on his face. He would not have wanted to be Dante Hyde at this moment, not for all the gold in Eastmarch.

Viktor and his glistening feet were lying atop his bed when Hob returned to their room. He had not bothered to pick up or sweep aside any of the broken wood, and simply lay among the splinters with a dazed look on his face.

"Are you all right?" said Hob.

Viktor nodded dully. "Yeah. But maybe you should think twice before tweaking someone like Dante Hyde. He could have killed you. Or me. Or any other page that got in his way."

"I'm sorry," said Hob. He'd been so eager to prank Dante he'd never stopped to consider it could endanger his friends.

"Please tell me it was worth it," said Viktor, flicking a splinter off his pillow.

"I don't know if it was worth it," replied Hob thoughtfully. "But it was pretty good."

While the domovoi hung a new door, Hob cleaned the room and shared what transpired with the hags and Dante's digestive system. Viktor shook with laughter.

"I can't even stay mad. They'll send you packing, but no one can say you didn't go out with a bang. Pages around the world will erect statues in your honor."

Hob tried to laugh, but Viktor's words tied his stomach in a knot. He had been so preoccupied with Dante and Hazel that he had not stopped to consider what was going to happen to him. Of course he would be fired. He gazed around the little room. He would miss it, and Sunday breakfasts in the dining room, and the rowdy games of hall thumper. Gods help him—he would even miss the hags.

And then of course, there was Her Highness. Teaching Hazel about the Muirlands had given Hob a chance to exercise part of his brain he never thought he'd use again. He looked forward to their sessions and, truth be told, he looked forward to seeing her.

Their friendship wasn't like his friendships back in Dusk. And it wasn't just because Hazel was a royal or even a girl. She understood and challenged Hob in a way his old friends never could. Hob knew what Mole would be in twenty years. Any given night a dozen Moles could be found in Mother Howell's. But he had no idea what Hazel Faeregine would be someday. Neither did she. And that was exciting.

There was a knock. Oliveiro stood on the threshold, pretending not to notice the room's state of destruction. "Mr. Smythe, I wondered if you would join me for a cup of tea."

Hob said he would be very happy and steeled himself for the inevitable. He followed the underbutler down the hallway and up a flight of steps to the suites where the underbutlers lived. Unlocking a door, Oliveiro stood aside for Hob to enter.

Oliveiro's rooms were small but very neat, with a window offering a view of the May Day fireworks over the lighthouse at Kirin Point. A cat was dozing on a chair. Scooping it up, Oliveiro resettled it on a cushion by the radiator and gestured for Hob to sit. While Oliveiro boiled water on a little stove, Hob studied the portraits and photographs arrayed upon the walls and bookcases. The nearest showed a mustachioed gentleman with dark skin and thick white hair. The man's stern, almost fierce expression reminded Hob of the shaman.

"My great-great-grandfather," said Oliveiro. "Head butler in his day. Devoted his life to the Faeregines. Never even left this island. He was, you might say, a natural servant."

Handing Hob his tea, Oliveiro settled in an armchair.

"I realize you have special duties with Her Highness, but technically you fall under my authority. And I can say—without exaggeration—that no page in living memory has wreaked so much havoc in so little time. You are *not* a natural servant, Mr. Smythe. You are a natural catastrophe."

"I'm sorry to hear it, sir."

Oliveiro gave him a frank look. "Did you put something in Lord Hyde's drink?"

Hob met his gaze. "I did, sir."

The underbutler nodded. "I see. Well, it grieves me to say this, Mr. Smythe, but I must relieve you of your page duties. Your service is terminated."

Hob began to rise, but Oliveiro held up a hand.

"Please sit, Mr. Smythe. I'm not quite finished with you."

"What else is there to discuss, sir?"

"Your future."

"Why should you care about my future, sir?"

"Because you're an able lad who has repeatedly defended Her Highness's honor."

Setting down his tea, Oliveiro rose and gazed out the open window. "Like I said, you're not a natural servant, Mr. Smythe. I've never met anyone less temperamentally suited for the job. But that doesn't mean I think poorly of you. On the contrary, I'd like to help you find a more fitting profession."

"That's very kind of you, sir. What did you have in mind?"

"Have you thought about being a soldier?" said Oliveiro. "I have some contacts. With some luck, and a few more inches, you'd make the guard someday. The pay isn't terrible, and you have shown a certain aptitude, shall we say?"

Hob thought of his father's patched and faded coat. *Like father, like son.*

"Would that appeal to you, Mr. Smythe?"

"I don't know," said Hob. "Are they hiring?"

Oliveiro beckoned Hob over to the window and pointed down at the fleet of warships crowding Rowan Harbor.

"I think they may be."

CHAPTER 18
THE INTERVIEW

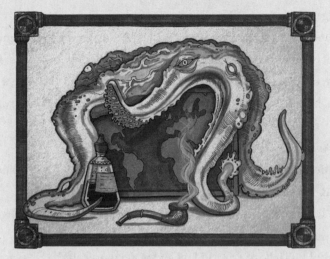

Everything we hear is an opinion, not a fact.
Everything we see is a perspective, not the truth.

—Marcus Aurelius, Pre-Cataclysm ruler (1892–1823 P.C.)

The distinctive crackle of gunfire filtered through Hazel's window. The volleys began at dawn and came at regular intervals. Now and again, she could even hear the drill sergeant barking. The noise was irritating, but nothing compared to the roar of ship cannons. Those would begin at noon, as they had each and every day since the May Ball two weeks ago. A staggering six more galleons had disappeared since the celebration. By Impyrial decree no ships were to enter Lirlander waters. Those already at sea were ordered to the nearest port.

Hazel knew the Lirlanders were sinking those ships. It wasn't an iceberg or reef she had glimpsed in that vision of the *Polestar*'s final moments, it was a tentacle the size of Old Tom's clock tower. The image still haunted her, as did the ship boy's terror. Many times she debated whether she should tell Rascha, her uncle, or even the empress what she'd seen. But she could not bring herself to do it. There were other witnesses now; no one doubted that the Lirlanders were responsible. Coming forward would only invite questions she was not prepared to answer.

Not quite yet.

Merlin stirred as Hazel glanced at the fireplace. The little homunculus could sense when his master's will was weakening.

"Don't worry," said Hazel, scratching his wing. "I haven't forgotten my promise."

Still, Hazel eased out of bed and walked over to the fireplace. She crouched before it in her nightgown, staring at the hearth's blackened stone. The itch to retrieve Arianna's portrait had never been this strong during daylight. Merlin flapped about her like an injured starling.

"All right," said Hazel, waving him away. She stood and went to look out the window. The sky was overcast, with great blotches of dark gray. A galoshes and umbrella kind of day. Hazel went to her armoire. Olo was off today and Rascha adamantly refused to participate in Hazel's errand, so she would have to fend for herself. As she perused her options, her eyes fell upon a square of paper propped on one of the shelves where she kept her jewelry boxes. It was the note someone had slipped in *The Little Mermaid* on New Year's Day. Rascha made Hazel keep it to remind her the world was a dangerous place. She picked it up, holding the paper by its edges.

Spiders weave and Spiders lie
in wait for easy prey,
but we can spin a web ourselves
and catch you any day.

With love,
the Butcher, the Baker, the Candlestick Maker

Such a strange note. Such strange names. There was something inherently creepy about ancient nursery rhymes. Whenever she read the note, she was tempted to throw it out. But she never did—it would only make Rascha angry.

Once she had dressed, she went into the common room, where she found Violet at a window, nibbling toast and watching the regiments far below. It was Saturday, but Violet was dressed formally. She was always formal now. And serious. Hazel set Merlin on the breakfast table.

"Good morning."

Violet made a face. "Do you have to put him there?"

Hazel shrugged. She was tired of tiptoeing around Violet. Isabel came bustling out of her room, still brushing her black tangles. Violet glanced at her boots.

"You're going riding?"

"Why not?" said Isabel. "My leg's good as new."

"It's going to rain."

Isabel peered out at the sky. "I'll chance it. Why don't you come? We can race to Kirin Point."

"I can't," said Violet. "There's a war council. And you aren't to go anywhere near there."

"Why not?"

"It's right by the Lirlanders' embassy."

"Are they going to chase me on seahorses?" Isabel said, laughing. "I can outride them any day."

Violet closed her eyes. "Just do what I tell you to do. For once."

Isabel took a piece of toast. "And why would I start doing that?"

"Because we're declaring war this afternoon."

"What?"

Hazel and Isabel had exclaimed in unison. The latter dropped her toast.

"It's not official yet," said Violet. "But it will happen at today's council. Two more ships were attacked last night. Grandmother's been biding her time, but she can't hold off anymore. The evidence against the Lirlanders is overwhelming. Protests are breaking out all over Impyrium. Martial law's been declared in Ana-Fehdra. If we don't act, there will be a revolution. We have no choice."

"What happens if we declare war?" said Hazel. "Lirlanders live below the sea. We can't march an army against them."

"No," said Violet. "We'd tear up the Red Winter Treaty and summon them using truenames. Or try to. Rulers like Prusias are too powerful to call against their will, but the Promethean scholars think we could bind some of the lesser lords within summoning circles. They're already inscribing them."

"And then?" said Hazel.

"We hold them hostage," said Violet. "The Lirlanders will have to make peace and reparations, or surface to fight a war."

"What do you think they'll do?" said Isabel.

"Fight," said Violet. "And why not? They outnumber us mehrùn."

"But we have lots of soldiers," said Isabel. "And our navy—"

"Is useless," Violet interrupted. "Our weaponry is outright primitive. I'm told our ship's cannons were popular centuries before the Cataclysm."

"Doesn't the Workshop have anything useful?" said Isabel.

"We don't allow them to develop anything useful!" snapped Violet. "Do you remember telling me how wise Grandmother has been to keep the Workshop on a short leash? That advanced technologies threatened mankind's existence? Well, hooray for us. We've done such a good job restricting it that we're in no danger of destroying ourselves. Others can do it for us." She shook her head in disgust.

"No one's going to destroy us," said Hazel quietly.

Violet looked at her. "How reassuring. Are you going to fight the Lirlanders, Hazel?"

"If it comes to that."

"Ah, yes," said Violet drily. "I forgot you're our secret weapon. A taloned pig foot would wreak havoc upon the demons. Let's pray we don't have to call upon you."

Hazel stared at her. "I think that would be wise, sister."

"Back to reality," said Isabel. "If the Lirlanders have become stronger than we are, why haven't they revolted before?"

"The Red Winter Treaty was signed in the presence of Mina the First," said Violet. "She shattered Prusias's crowns. She helped defeat Astaroth. And she was merciful to all who surrendered. The oldest Lirlanders regard her as a sacred being. They believe a terrible curse will befall them if they break the treaty."

"But they've already broken it," said Isabel.

"Lord Kraavh insists they haven't," said Violet. "He says they haven't attacked a single ship bearing a Lirlander Seal. It's nonsense, of course. They all had one."

There was a knock and Sigga entered the room. She bowed to Violet and Isabel before turning to Hazel.

"Are you ready?"

"Where are you two going?" said Violet.

"Master Montague's office," said Hazel. "I want to see if Mr. Smythe can get a job at Rowan."

Violet slipped the Impyrial signet ring on her finger. "Well, that's perfect. I'm attending a war council while Isabel goes horseback riding and you find work for an unemployed page."

"If you want to abdicate, I'm right here," said Isabel.

Violet strode past Sigga to the vestibule, where her bodyguard was waiting. "Don't tempt me."

Hob was waiting for them on a bench beneath an elm in Old College. It was always strange seeing him out of uniform. He wore a dark suit of decent quality, but made for colder weather. He did not see them right away, for he was busy watching a regiment shooting at targets along the cliffs. Once he caught sight of them, he popped to his feet and removed his cap.

"Good morning, Mr. Smythe," said Hazel.

"Good morning, Your Highness. Where's Dàme Rascha?"

"Taking her ease. She doesn't quite approve of this excursion."

"I see," said Hob.

Sigga was surveying the regiment. "How's their aim?"

"Fair enough," said Hob. "Don't like those carabines, though. No range. I can't see why they bother with them."

"Carabines are easier to handle," said Sigga. "Range isn't as important for a guardsmen as the rate of fire."

"A rifle's plenty fast," said Hob.

The Grislander turned to Her Highness. "What time is Master Montague expecting us?"

"Nine o'clock."

The agent glanced up at Old Tom, which showed a quarter to. "Your Highness, could you indulge me for a few minutes?"

Hazel was intrigued. "Of course."

She and Hob followed as Sigga made for the drill instructor, a sergeant wearing a crested helmet and crimson coat. Upon seeing them, he held up his hand for the soldiers to hold their fire. He bowed low to Hazel.

"A pleasure, Your Highness. What can I do for you?"

"Who's your best marksman?" asked Sigga.

The sergeant didn't hesitate. "Private Carver."

"We'd like to see Private Carver fire three shots as fast as he can at the target."

The private was in his twenties and, like almost everyone in the guard, a perfect physical specimen. At his sergeant's command, he faced his target and brought up his carabine.

Crack, crack, crack.

Three shots, three small puffs of smoke on the distant target. The private lowered his weapon, looking satisfied.

"Do you have a proper rifle, Sergeant?" said Sigga.

Hazel did not know the difference between a carabine and a rifle until the sergeant retrieved another gun from a case. It had a longer barrel.

"Just this one," he said. "But it's not really a soldier's weapon. I use it for hunting."

Sigga glanced at Hob. "Have you ever used one of these?"

Hob looked at the gun. "It's not a Boekka, but it's close enough. What am I doing?"

Sigga merely smiled and turned to the sergeant. "I'll wager five lunes the boy can shoot this rifle faster and more accurately than Carver and his carbine."

The sergeant smiled like one who's just heard a bad joke. When it was clear Sigga was serious, his amusement dwindled. Evidently, he found the proposal insulting.

"Carver's a professional, Agent Fenn. I'd be taking your money."

"Let me worry about that."

The sergeant glanced at Hazel to see if she disapproved of the contest. She did not. On the contrary, Hazel found firearms rather interesting. Not in themselves—blasting holes in things held little appeal—but for the fact that they were the most muirish objects she could think of. They were taboo for mehrùn to use, but muir seemed to prize them above all else.

The sergeant set the terms. Sigga agreed to all, except the distance. She said Hob would fire from an additional fifty paces farther away. The entire regiment broke into disbelieving grins.

If the wager made Hob anxious, he did not show it. Throughout the exchange he remained stoic, his eyes fixed on Sigga. He appeared more interested in why she proposed the wager than the wager itself.

Once the bet was made, he took the unloaded rifle and examined it. He slid the bolt mechanism back and forth and pressed his finger lightly on the trigger as though gauging its sensitivity. He looked up at the sergeant.

"Can I take a practice shot? It's been a long time."

The sergeant turned to Private Carver, who said the boy could have ten if he pleased. But Hob only loaded four rounds into the cartridge before marching off another fifty paces.

The spectators moved well off to the side while a fresh target was set up. Taking up a stance, Hob brought the rifle slowly to his shoulder.

Crack!

Hazel turned much too late to see anything. One of the guardsmen elbowed his neighbor. "Missed."

They watched as Hob examined the rifle a second time. The sergeant chuckled. "A poor craftsman always blames his tools."

Again, Hob brought the rifle to his shoulder and took aim. This time, Hazel glued her eyes to the target's red circle.

Crack-crack-crack!

The shots rang out so fast it was like firecrackers going off all at once. A single puff of smoke rose from the target's center and dissipated on the breeze. The sergeant applauded.

"Well," he said genially. "He's uncanny quick, Agent Fenn, but accuracy matters. Carver hit the target three times. The lad only hit it once."

"Let's see the target," said Sigga.

A guardsman fetched the paper. The sergeant held it up, revealing three overlapping holes that formed a shape like a clover. He turned to look at Hob, who was walking toward them with the rifle on his shoulder.

"Who is that boy?"

Sigga smiled. "Exactly who I thought he was."

"I don't follow."

"No need to, Sergeant. Pay up."

While the unhappy sergeant scrounged the coins, Hob shook

hands with Carver, who was admirably gracious in defeat. As he returned the rifle, he exchanged a curious, almost defiant look with Sigga. Hazel got the impression the two were playing some private game.

The rain, which had threatened all morning, finally began to fall. The drops were light and rather pleasant as the three left the regiment and walked toward Old Tom. Hazel was still processing the extraordinary display of marksmanship she'd just witnessed.

"Sigga, how did you know Mr. Smythe could shoot a gun like that?"

"A hunch, Your Highness. They found a golem not long ago at a dig site in the Sentries. Someone fired five rounds into it with a rifle—a Boekka—before they blew its head off. That's not interesting. What's interesting is that the shots were grouped uncommonly tight and penetrated to the exact same depth."

"What does that mean?" said Hazel.

"All five were fired in a fraction of a second. Only a gifted marksman could do that."

Hazel laughed. "Mr. Smythe, have you been shooting golems in the Sentries?"

"Impossible, Your Highness," said Sigga. "Mr. Smythe was already in Impyria when this occurred. But I suspected he could shoot. The Sentries are dangerous country and its people learn to handle guns at an early age. And don't forget Mr. Smythe once killed a Cheshirewulf. With a creature like that, there are no second chances. You shoot fast and straight or you die. Guardsmen are mostly city boys who learned to shoot for sport. I had no doubt our Mr. Smythe would win. Incidentally . . ."

The Grislander paused at Old Tom's steps to drop four of the coins in Hob's palm. He did not pocket them right away.

"What's this for?" he asked.

"A rainy day. Soldiers earn a pittance."

"Mr. Smythe doesn't have to be a soldier," said Hazel. "He can be a teacher."

Sigga handed over the fifth coin.

Old Tom was quiet. The only people they passed were a few graduate students and scholars, who used weekends as a quiet opportunity to further their research. Master Montague's office was on the third floor, at the end of a long hallway lined with portraits.

He answered on the second knock, pipe in hand. To Hazel's astonishment, he was dressed in a blue sweater, gray trousers, and shoes that looked suspiciously like slippers. She'd always assumed masters wore their robes day and night, never removing them even to bathe.

The master took out his pipe and bowed. "Good morning, Your Highness. Agent Fenn." He looked inquisitively at Hob, who introduced himself.

The master said he was very happy to meet him and stood aside, admitting them into a large office whose walls were lined with cluttered bookcases and ancient maps. The air was heavy with the smell of exotic plants that overflowed from hanging pots or loomed in corners like spiny reptiles. Along the far wall, Hazel noticed an array of cages, terrariums, and alchemical equipment.

A hoot came from Hazel's pocket and Merlin clambered out. With a flap of his wings, he circled the room and alighted atop a bookcase, where another homunculus reclined like a drowsy cat. The master laughed.

"I see your charge is thriving."

"I hope so," said Hazel. "I'm not really sure. He doesn't speak, but Isabel's never shuts up. I've been a little worried something was wrong."

"No," said the master, closing the door. "Your Merlin is exactly as he ought to be. He and Lady Isabel's specimen received different solutions during their development. But I assume you didn't come to discuss homunculus breeding, Your Highness. What can I do for you?"

At his invitation, Hazel sat in one of the chairs before his mammoth desk. She had worked out what she wanted to say beforehand, but the master often left her flustered. Sitting across from her, he knit his fingers and chewed his pipe stem. Like the Spider, he too was comfortable with silence.

"Well," said Hazel. "As you know, I had some trouble with your class . . ."

She went on to explain how Hob was a palace page who tutored her on the Muirlands.

"I see," said the master. "Well, your arrangement was unorthodox but not unproductive. You've made great strides, Your Highness. I'm very pleased with you."

Hazel flushed pink. Perhaps the master was not so horrid after all. "Thank you. But the reason I wanted to talk with you is because Mr. Smythe is no longer a page. He's looking for a new position, and I think he'd make a fine addition here."

The master's bushy eyebrows rose. "At Rowan, Your Highness?"

"Yes, sir."

"In what capacity?"

"I don't know," said Hazel. "Perhaps he could assist you. I think he'd make an excellent teacher someday."

Those eyebrows climbed even higher. The master glanced at Hob and then back to Hazel with the air of a man weighing how best to explain something that should not have to be explained. Hazel shifted uneasily. Perhaps this had been a mistake.

"I have four research assistants," said the master. "I selected them from hundreds of qualified applicants. While I commend your desire to help Mr. Smythe, Rowan could not possibly offer him work in an academic capacity. If he wishes to be a kitchen boy or servant—"

"But he's smart," said Hazel. "Really smart. He just needs an opportunity."

"Don't we all," said the master, but not unkindly. "Why doesn't Your Highness employ him?"

"I spend much of my time studying Mystics," said Hazel. "Mr. Smythe can't help me with that. But he could help you, Master Montague."

The master sighed and turned his attention to Hob. "Where's home, Mr. Smythe?"

Hob spoke up. "The Northwest, sir. A village in the Sentries called Dusk. Most people haven't heard of it."

The master nodded. "Are you Hauja?"

"My mother is, sir."

"Interesting," said the master. "I don't suppose you have their tribal markings."

"I do," said Hob.

"So you've sat séyu."

Hazel was impressed the master knew so much about a tribal people who lived so far away.

"Yes, sir," said Hob.

The master tamped a pinch of tobacco in his pipe. "Someday, I'll have to hear the tale. I'm quite familiar with the Sentries, Mr. Smythe.

If I were thirty years younger, I'd be there now. There's been a find of tremendous importance."

Hob cleared his throat. "Oh?"

The master's eyes twinkled with boyish enthusiasm. "They've found Vancouver, and not too far from where I predicted. Evidently, my theories on Cataclysmic drift have some merit."

"I'm sorry, but what's Vancouver?" said Hazel.

The master rose and brought over one of the maps. It was like a distant cousin to the world Hazel knew—like and yet not alike. He pointed to a coastal dot on a vast continent.

"Vancouver is a lost city from the Cataclysm, Your Highness. Until recently, scholars believed the civilizations of that time simply vanished. But earthquakes have uncovered ancient cities entombed under rock, oceans, even mountains. Some are hundreds, even thousands of miles from where they once stood."

Sigga spoke up. "You're aware this information is classified."

The master looked mildly amused, as if he was too old to possibly care about obeying rules he considered arbitrary or stupid. He shrugged.

"I'm an archaeologist, Agent Fenn. My study is historical fact, not transparent fictions." He looked at Hob. "Tell me, Mr. Smythe, do people in Dusk believe human civilization began with Impyrium? That everything before was simply a dark age?"

"Of course not," Hob allowed. "I've seen Pre-Cataclysm films. I heard music played once on a machine like that one." He pointed to the master's phonograph. "But no one talks too much about it. You'd get in trouble." He hesitated. "Someone told me that human beings once stood on the moon. Is that true?"

Hazel almost laughed, but the master nodded gravely. She was astounded. For her, the Pre-Cataclysm world was like gravity; she knew it existed but rarely gave it much thought. It was so long ago.

"Why aren't people told the truth?" said Hob.

The master sighed. "Contrary to what some believe, it did not begin as a conspiracy. Muir were more susceptible to the spells that brought about the Cataclysm. When Astaroth wiped civilizations from the map, he also wiped people's memories. As far as most muir were concerned, the world had *always* been the way he ordered it. They recalled nothing of the past."

"But mehrùn could remember," said Hob.

"Yes," said the master. "The mehrùn living then were less affected. And to my knowledge, they told muir the truth. But few believed them. Eventually mehrùn decided it was pointless, even cruel, to keep trying. It was like correcting a senile relative. Over time, these little white lies took on their own life and were accepted as facts. Today, even mehrùn discount the idea of sophisticated Pre-Cataclysm civilizations. They've become almost mythological, but not because of some grand scheme to mislead the masses."

"But the Cataclysm happened thousands of years ago," said Hob. "Shouldn't people have rediscovered what was lost or forgotten? Why aren't we back on the moon?"

"Ah," said the master. "That aspect is intentional—particularly where technology is concerned. Astaroth was a terrible enemy, but some believe his actions saved us from a disastrous course. When he was defeated, many wanted to resume that course and remake the world as it had been. Rowan's leaders did not. Do you know who David Menlo was?"

"Impyrium's first archmage," said Hob.

"And chief adviser to Mina the First," said the master. "David Menlo did not think human judgment could keep pace with human innovation. Since the Pre-Cataclysm Renaissance, groups like the Workshop had been pushing the boundaries of science, and making ever more dangerous discoveries. When the archmage drafted the Red Winter Treaty, he forbade technologies that he believed would ultimately destroy mankind. Divine Empresses have enforced these prohibitions, much to the Workshop's frustration."

"Then why is the Workshop allowed to exist?" said Hob.

"They are a signatory to the original treaty," said Master Montague. "The Workshop is protected. If they were not, Mina the Second almost certainly would have destroyed them. She was far less tolerant than her mother."

"So people will never fly to the moon," said Hob.

"No," said the master. "But they continue to walk the earth. A worthy trade-off."

"If you say so, sir."

"You don't agree, Mr. Smythe?"

Hob shrugged.

The master tutted and pointed for Hob to take a seat. "No, Mr. Smythe, that will not do. In my classroom, if you disagree, you have an obligation to dissent. You don't think these prohibitions wise?"

Casual conversation was at an end. The master now exuded that combative intensity Hazel witnessed so often in his classroom. Hob frowned slightly as he sat in the chair.

"How can I answer that?" he said. "I don't know what those technologies were. I have no idea if the dangers they posed justify the restrictions that were put in place."

"What are your reservations?" said the master. "Speak freely, Mr. Smythe."

Hob glanced briefly at Sigga and Hazel. "Mehrùn can use magic. Muir can't. You might say technology is our magic. The restrictions impact muir much more than mehrùn. If muir couldn't remember what life was like before the Cataclysm, then they had no choice but to accept what mehrùn said about technology and its dangers. Some might say it's a pretty convenient explanation for a policy that's held muir back."

"Held them back? Or held them down?"

Hob considered. "Is there a difference?"

The master grunted. He looked to be enjoying the exchange. "What kind of education do you have, Mr. Smythe?"

"Little formal education, sir. But I did place first in my Province exams."

The master exhaled a curl of smoke. "Did you indeed? Well, that's two things we have in common."

"And the other, sir?"

"I'm muir."

Hazel almost slid out of her chair. Rowan was the world's pre-eminent school of magic. How could one of its leading academics be muir? The master chuckled.

"I take it, Your Highness, that you did not know? You look as stunned as Mr. Smythe."

"But you're a Montague," said Hazel.

"I am," said the master. "But we're not all mehrùn. I doubt any house is. Nature hates being too predictable. In any case, my being a Montague would have little bearing on my magical capabilities. I was adopted."

Hazel gestured at the beakers and retorts, the cages, and shelves stocked with rare herbs.

"But you breed homunculi. Dàme Rascha says you're one of the best. How can you do that and not be able to do magic?"

"I like to think I can do magic in my own small way," said the master. "It merely comes from ingredients rather than my person. Homunculus breeding is entirely alchemical."

Hazel saw an opportunity. The master was being polite, but he would soon thank them for stopping by and show them the door without offering Hob a position. She had to keep things alive, extend the visit by keeping the master engaged. Homunculi were just the thing.

"Could you give us a demonstration?" she asked. "I know nothing about it, and you're regarded as an expert. I'd love to know why Merlin and Pamplemousse are so different."

The master looked pleased. Rising, he invited all three of them to peer at a row of glass beakers fed by tubes. The liquid inside was cloudy, but Hazel could see hints of twisted, fibrous roots. She'd studied very little of potioncraft and alchemy. Rascha considered them lesser arts.

"This is a new batch," said the master. "You start, of course, with mandrake root. Its substance serves as the creature's body. Many factors can influence how each homunculus develops—from the mandrake's harvesting to ingredients added at various phases. Merlin's mandrake was unearthed with a silver spade on Samhain's moonrise. Your sister's was pulled by hand at midnight and trimmed with a copper blade. You see how different they are."

"Like night and day," said Hazel. She pointed to the retorts whose simmering mixtures fed vapors or condensation droplets into the beakers. "What are these?"

The master gently tapped a tube that had backed up. "The contents vary by specimen. With some I aim for intelligence, others for longevity, others for swiftness. Even established formulae can yield different results. People have been breeding homunculi for ages, but it's still more art than science. Like the Lingua Mystica, there so many variables, it never gets boring."

"When did you start breeding them?" said Hazel.

"Around your age," he reflected. "Perhaps younger. I started because I wanted to compensate for being muir. It's a good hobby for an obsessive like myself. And it's safer for muir to breed homunculi than mehrùn."

"Why is that?" said Hob. He was looking intently at the equipment: the labeled jars of chemicals and herbs, butterflies and hummingbird wings, lunestones, and skeletonized chameleons.

"Homunculi are parasitic," the master explained. "They require magic to survive and thus feed on the mehrùn with whom they're bonded. Eventually, the mehrùn can sense what the homunculus senses, see what it sees—even speak through it. Some mystics can channel spells through their homunculi, although this is rare. The relationship is symbiotic."

"Merlin's been feeding off me," Hazel said, turning to Hob with what she hoped looked like a sinister smile. Hob's eyebrows lifted.

"Don't frighten the boy," said the master, chuckling. "You know Merlin absorbs far too little magic for you to notice. It's no more harmful than if a lizard came to sit on your lap to keep warm. It needs the heat and you're no worse for wear. But there can be exceptions, which is why it's safer for muir to breed them. Every so often, you can get one of these."

The master went over to a large terrarium that was on its own table and covered with a black cloth. As he reached for some leather aprons, he nudged the cover, which revealed a glimpse of dazzling light. Sigga stepped in front of Hazel.

"What's in there?"

"A homunculus, but a most unusual specimen," he said. "Not to worry, Agent Fenn. It can't escape its cage. It's probably not even aware we're here. You're welcome to wear a protective apron, but this glass is impermeable. It can't feed on you."

"I don't think this is wise, Your Highness," said Sigga.

"No," said Hazel. "I want to see. I'll wear an apron."

The apron was extremely heavy; thick brown leather lined with lead plates that hung almost to the floor. Even after Hazel put it on, Sigga stood in front of her. Hazel peered round the agent as Hob and Master Montague lifted the cover.

Brilliant white light flooded the office. Hazel squinted, then dug through her purse for her tinted spectacles. As she put them on, the master leaned a pane of smoked glass against the cage so they could see what was inside. Hob promptly recoiled.

"*That's* a homunculus?" he exclaimed.

The master nodded. "A very rare one, as I said. Not a breed so much as a mutation. As you can see, its size and shape differ greatly from the norm."

To Hazel, the creature inside the case resembled a bloated, muscular starfish some four or five feet across. The creature had six—no seven—fleshy arms flopped or splayed against the glass. Each was covered with what looked like warty tumors and round suckers that pulsed and aspirated. One arm was undulating, its tip probing for an opening. As it moved, Hazel noticed its flesh camouflaged to blend with its surroundings. Toad-like eyes appeared in a dozen places, their lids opening in unison. They were round, milky, and seemingly blind.

"Don't let its sluggish demeanor fool you," said the master. "These creatures are voracious. Only yesterday, a mystic kindled the lune-stones inside." He pointed to a bed of rocks that were giving off the brilliant light. "Normally they'd shine for decades, but this cage will be dark as a coffin by Monday. And still the creature's half-starved. A virtual antidragon."

"What does it have to do with dragons?" said Hob.

"A dragon's aura is so powerful it can alter or amplify existing magic," the master replied. "Their auras can even enchant nonmagical objects. This homunculus does the opposite; it devours magical energy at a prodigious rate. Left undisturbed, this one could drain a powerful mystic in a matter of days. Fascinating creature, but it must be handled with precaution."

Hazel was feeling uneasy and called Merlin to her. She had assumed those milky eyes were blind, but she was now getting the distinct impression that they were focused on her—and only her. The creature's tentacles were moving more rapidly, poking and probing about the cage's surface. She heard an almost inaudible whisper deep in her mind.

Get away from it.

"I assume it's regulated," said Sigga to Master Montague.

"Of course," he replied. "If a breeder produces one—these occur quite by accident—they're required to register them. Selling one is forbidden."

"It would be safer to destroy them."

"Too valuable," said the master. "If dragons are magic, these are antimagic. Both offer invaluable opportunities to study mystic energy, but this fellow is a bit more approachable than Hati the Black. Unfortunately, homunculi like this dwimorleech mutation are exceedingly rare. The Raszna have one in Arcanum, and there was an immature specimen in the Workshop's biological museum, but it was—"

"Stolen."

They turned to Hob, who was peering through the glass. "I read it in a newspaper," he said. "Five creatures were stolen from the Workshop's biological exhibits: a vampiric mnemonculus, a Zenuvian shrike, a common bray, an embryonic wyvern, and a dwimorleech. No leads. No arrests."

"Do you have a photographic memory?" said the master.

"Pretty close," said Hob.

"Many scholars would kill to have your gift, Mr. Smythe."

Hob broke out in a grin. "You don't have to kill me, sir. Just give me a job—"

Thunk!

Hazel shrieked as the dwimorleech launched its heavy body against the cage. Tentacles slapped violently as it tried to escape like an octopus gone berserk. The glass did not crack, but the cage was rocking from side to side. The creature's eyes remained locked on Hazel.

Sigga had Hazel in the hallway in less than two seconds. Within the office, Master Montague was shouting at Hob to wedge the cage against a bookshelf while he got the cover. More slapping sounds, coupled with a piercing, high-pitched chittering that caused Hazel to clamp her hands over her ears.

The painful sound stopped within a few seconds. Hazel opened her eyes to see Sigga blocking the doorway. Within the master's office, the lunestones' radiance had been veiled. Jarring slaps subsided to dull thumps and then stopped altogether.

A moment later Master Montague and Hob came into the hallway. She had never seen the master at such a loss. He wiped sweat from his brow with a handkerchief.

"Your Highness, please accept my deepest apologies. In six decades of breeding homunculi, I've never seen anything like that. That dwimorleech has never moved faster than a tortoise. I don't know what got into it. I am terribly sorry if it gave you a fright."

"It's not your fault, Master Montague," said Hazel.

He glanced anxiously at Sigga. "I'm not sure Agent Fenn would agree with you."

"That thing is gone within the hour," said the Grislander. "If you want to study it, you can do so in the archives behind reinforced runeglass and with armed guards."

"Yes, of course," said the master. "You must believe I had no idea."

"I do," said Sigga. "That's the problem." She turned and sent an ice-blue zephyss racing down the hallway.

Hazel removed her apron. "Thank you for your time, Master Montague. Dwimorleeches aside, it was a very pleasant visit. I realize Mr. Smythe may not be a typical candidate, but I think you'd do well to find something for him."

The master eyed Hob with approval. "Well, he certainly kept his head just now, and from what I can tell it's a good one. Let me give it some thought. There wouldn't be anything until the next term, but I'll do what I can. Where are you living?"

"Still in the palace," said Hob. "They're giving me a few weeks to find a new situation."

"Given your latest incident with Lord Hyde, I'd say that's rather generous."

Hob looked horrified. "You know about that, sir?"

"I might be an academic, but I do enjoy my gossip," said the master, smiling. "An underbutler, kitchen hags, and a Faeregine princess are an unusual mix of allies. If such an eclectic group is making efforts on your behalf, it speaks well of you. And I've known Dante Hyde since he was six. Alas, we failed to make a dent there."

Old Tom began chiming ten o'clock.

"Well," said the master, "thank you for the visit, Your Highness, and for bringing the young man to my attention. I will be in touch."

"So will I," said Sigga. "Guardsmen will be here any minute to remove that creature. You will give them your full cooperation."

The master bowed just as they heard boots coming up the stairs. Six guardsmen appeared and marched down the hallway. While Sigga gave them instructions, Hazel cast a suspicious eye on Merlin.

"Don't get any ideas from that mutant, Merlin. You're being fed quite enough. And I better get some of your powers soon or I'm going to revisit our bargain. I won't put up with freeloaders."

The creature hooted and nuzzled her cheek. Stroking his wing, Hazel mused on the dwimorleech. She had never before encountered something that so clearly wanted to devour her.

She tried not to dwell upon it as she and Hob followed Sigga down the hallway. The agent looked irritated.

"What's the matter?" said Hazel.

"Academics have no sense," Sigga muttered. "That thing should never have been sitting in an office. It would be dangerous if it got out, even more dangerous if it fell into the wrong hands. You'd think the master would have taken precautions when a dwimorleech was stolen from the Workshop." She shook her head. "Some other genius is probably raising krakens in the school's swimming pool."

Hob remained quiet until they'd descended Old Tom's steps. The rain had stopped, but the sky had grown darker. The quad was empty except for the regiments firing at their targets.

Thrusting his hands in his pockets, Hob looked Hazel in the eye.

"Thank you, Your Highness. You didn't have to vouch for me."

Hazel did her best to sound breezy. "Don't be too flattered. I'm just trying to get rid of you."

He pulled on his cap and grinned. For an instant, Hazel felt like she was glimpsing a younger Hob, one who had yet to start mining or sit séyu. She liked knowing he was still in there.

"Oh, I know," he said. "But no one's ever done anything like this for me." For a moment, words failed him. "I won't forget it."

"You're very welcome, Mr. Smythe."

The three walked east toward Tùr an Ghrian, stopping by the tower's base to gaze out at the sea. Over the ocean, the sky was the color of slate and rumbled with distant thunder. Below, the harbor teemed with warships. They were black and predatory, with witch-fire burning on their decks and the flags of both Impyrium and the Faeregines flying from their masts.

To the north by Kirin Point, the Lirlander Embassy looked dark and abandoned. The road leading to it was barricaded. Five warships were moored nearby, their cannons leveled.

A light caught Hazel's eye. A merchant galleon with a Lirlander Seal was moving slowly across the harbor as a skiff guided it toward a pier. Bells pealed as dockworkers made ready to receive it. Hazel's gaze returned to the blazing white Seal. They were at the heart of all this trouble; they were why Violet was in council at this very moment.

What's wrong with the Seals? Why aren't they working?

The regiment fired another volley.

"Did you learn anything new today, Mr. Smythe?" said Sigga.

Hob turned from watching the soldiers. "What?"

"About the Cataclysm, buried cities, forbidden technology. The reasons why things are the way they are."

"I guess I did. What did you learn, Agent Fenn?"

"A bit about dwimorleeches. I already knew the rest."

Hazel frowned. What was going on between them? Some inside joke or game was under way. She would ask Sigga about it when they were alone.

"You know," said Sigga, "there are sniper units in the guard. Specialists. You're good enough. I could put in a word."

Hob looked seriously at her. "I've shot two people," he said. "Two men in a raiding party that attacked Dusk a few years ago. If anyone deserved to die, they did, but I still have nightmares about it. I don't think I could take a life on someone else's orders."

Sigga smirked. "I guess I have learned something else, Mr. Smythe. You're sentimental."

Hob side armed a stone far off the cliffs. "Maybe I don't want to end up like Private Finch."

Private Finch. Hazel recalled her visit with that poor soldier missing half his face. She pictured the photographs upon his table—one of the deceased Sergeant Beecher, the other of the handsome young man he used to be. And she'd asked him who it was! She cringed inwardly. Rascha had been right—it wasn't for Hazel to play detective. Still, something had always bothered her about the private's story.

Why hadn't those thieves taken any Seals?

It wasn't just that they hadn't stolen a Seal; they hadn't brought anything to smuggle them out. Why would criminals go through all that trouble only to overlook a detail like that?

A moment later, Hazel's heart skipped a beat.

CHAPTER 19
A STOWAWAY

There is nothing more deceptive than an obvious fact.

—Sherlock Holmes, Pre-Cataclysm detective (fictional)

Hazel exclaimed so suddenly a bee might have stung her. Merlin sensed her excitement and trembled like a mouse.

"Are you all right, Your Highness?" asked Sigga.

Hazel wasn't sure. Her mind was racing, arranging bits of information, and testing their fit.

"When did you read that article?" she asked Hob. "About that theft in the Workshop?"

"January."

"Did it say when the theft took place?"

"December."

Hazel's eyes widened. She turned back to the galleon.

"What is it, Your Highness?" said Sigga.

"We've always assumed the imposters tried and failed to steal some Lirlander Seals," she said breathlessly. "But what if they weren't? What if their mission actually succeeded?"

"What mission, then?" asked Sigga.

"To smuggle something *into* the vault," cried Hazel. "Something small—something that could drain the magic inside. Remember what Rascha said? The Seals in the vault are linked with Seals on ships so we can control them from here. If one in the vault stopped working . . ."

"So would its twin at sea," Sigga muttered. The agent stared down at the trade galleon. Hazel had never seen the Grislander look so astonished.

"You think the stolen dwimorleech is in the vault?" said Hob.

"Yes!" cried Hazel, hopping up and down. "Think about it. Private Finch said the imposters didn't bring anything large enough to carry any Seals they managed to steal. But they could have been hiding something. A dwimorleech was stolen just weeks earlier. Master Montague said it was immature, which means it was probably easy to conceal. Once the imposters snuck it into the vault, they could leave it behind to feed in peace and quiet. If that creature has been draining what's inside the vault, then ships have been crossing demon waters with deactivated Seals. Lord Kraavh has been telling the truth. The Lirlanders may have attacked those ships, but they haven't broken the treaty!"

"But wasn't the vault inspected after the break in?" said Hob.

"It was," said Sigga. "But that was to ensure nothing had been taken.

If the dwimorleech was small, the imposters could have hidden it anywhere."

"And we just saw that those creatures can camouflage themselves," said Hazel.

Sigga nodded, but looked preoccupied. Hazel's gaze swept over the warships surrounding the Lirlanders' Embassy.

"There's a war council going on right now," Hazel said impatiently. "We have to stop it. If the empress declares war, those ships could start firing. Once that happens, it won't matter that it was a misunderstanding. We have to tell them!"

Sigga held up a hand. "Just a moment, Your Highness. We need to think this through."

"I have thought it through!" cried Hazel. "I'm right! You know I'm right!"

"I think you are," said Sigga calmly. "But bursting in on a council meeting is not the best way to address this."

"Why not?"

"Because whoever's behind this wants to discredit your family and start a war between Impyrium and the Lirlanders. Whoever did this might be in that room."

"Is Lord Hyde on the war council?" asked Hob.

Sigga nodded.

"It's got to be him," said Hob. "At the May Ball, all the Hydes paid their respects when Lord Kraavh visited their table. What if they've made some secret alliance with the Lirlanders? What if they're provoking the empress into declaring war so that we're the ones that break the treaty? If the Lirlanders win, they'd be free to rule the seas while the Hydes rule Impyrium."

"It's a possibility," said Sigga. "But you're assuming the Lirlanders would be content with that arrangement. Once the treaty's gone, what's to prevent a demon like Prusias, Tök, or Ahriman from deciding they'd rather rule Impyrium themselves?"

"So, what are you suggesting?" said Hazel.

"A third party could be involved," said Sigga. "Some group that stands to benefit if mehrùn and the Lirlanders go to war."

Hazel gave Hob an apologetic glance. "I hate to say it, but could it be muir? There's been so much unrest."

"I don't think so," replied Sigga. "Even if muir have grievances, I can't believe they'd be foolish enough to think a war with the Lirlanders would benefit them. Within a year, they'd be dead or enslaved."

"Then who could it be?" said Hazel.

"I couldn't say for certain, but it's most likely a mehrùn with an agenda that has nothing to do with politics. But our first priority is to ensure that a war doesn't break out. Your Highness, send a zephyss to Lady Isabel and tell her to meet you in your tower. No questions, no delay."

Hazel conjured a little bulb of golden light and whispered her urgent message. When she'd finished, it zoomed off down the gray beach.

"Why Isabel?" said Hazel.

"We need Violet to open the vault," said Sigga, leading them toward the palace. "Isabel's our best bet for getting her out of that council without drawing undue attention. If one of the culprits is in that room or suspects anything is amiss, they could do something desperate. For example, one of those ships could open fire on the embassy. We must defuse things very carefully."

Thirty minutes later, a breathless Isabel arrived in the triplets' common room. Her black hair was windblown, her cheeks red. Her bodyguard came in behind her and closed the door.

"Tell Agent Rey to step outside," said Sigga.

"What?" said Isabel. "Why?"

"Please," said Hazel. "I need to talk to you."

Isabel caught sight of Hob standing by their breakfast table. "Why is he here?"

"Just do it!" said Hazel impatiently.

"Okay," said Isabel, removing her shawl. "Agent Rey, please wait outside."

Once he left, Sigga shut the door and Hazel explained her vault theory. To Isabel's credit, she didn't interrupt or ask questions. When Hazel finished, Isabel gave a low whistle.

"You're a genius."

"Never mind," said Hazel. "We have to get Violet out of that council to open the vault for us. If we ask the empress or Uncle Basil, they'll stop the proceedings and whoever did this might suspect we're on to them. You have to convince Violet. She'd never come if I ask her. Bring her to the sitting room across from Founders."

"I'll think of something." Isabel ran off. Hazel sighed in relief. If anyone could pull Violet from that meeting it was Isabel.

But Hazel's optimism declined as they waited in the sitting room across from Founders Hall. She paced anxiously, poking her head out now and again. But there were only guardsmen posted in pairs along the corridor.

"Where could they be?" she grumbled.

"Patience," said Sigga.

"War could be declared any minute!"

The Grislander shook her head.

"How can you be so certain?" asked Hazel.

"They keep transcripts of such meetings, Your Highness. If you don't speak up, you're not on the record. The council has fifteen members who will have prepared very eloquent, very *lengthy* remarks to stake their claim on history." She checked her watch. "They'll be in there for hours."

Footsteps echoed in the hallways. Hazel jabbed her head out to see her sisters walking swiftly toward them, bodyguards in tow. The twins stared straight ahead, perfectly in sync down to the swing of their arms. Neither spoke or acknowledged the other.

When Violet reached the sitting room, she nearly poked Hazel in the eye.

"How *dare* you use Isabel to lure me out of that meeting! Have you lost your—?"

"Lower your voice," Hazel pleaded. "Just listen a minute."

Violet stepped closer, so that she towered over Hazel. Her voice was icy calm. "Don't ever interrupt me. Don't ever tell me what to do or summon me from a council. Not now. Not ever. Do you under—?"

"Shut up."

Hazel was trembling with honest rage. For once, Violet was going to listen to her. Her sister looked stunned.

"I'm trying to help," said Hazel. "And if you're too proud or stupid to accept it, we'll end up at war. So you're going to stand there, and shut up, and do *exactly* what I tell you to do!"

Five minutes later, a pale but composed Violet led them into Founders Hall, where a dozen guardsmen stood before the Lirlander

Vault. She marched straight to the man with a black and gold armband. He bowed.

"Good morning, Captain," said Violet. "I need to access the vault." She showed him her nautilus key.

The captain was taken aback. "Yes, but protocols have changed. I wasn't told anyone planned to access the vault, Your Highness."

"That's because no one planned to."

"I'll have to contact—"

Violet showed him her signet ring. "Unless you intend to contact the empress, there is no one whose authority exceeds my own. You will obey my order this instant, or I'll ask the Red Branch to intervene."

The captain's gaze drifted from Violet to the three notorious figures behind her. He cleared his throat. "Of course, Your Highness. Guardsmen, part ranks."

Walking forward, Violet inserted the nautilus and turned it clockwise while whispering words of command. The heavy slab began to move.

Sigga ordered everyone, including Violet, fifty feet back. Even at that distance, Hazel needed her glasses due to the blinding light spilling forth from the vault's interior. Her heart was beating like a bird's as she clutched Merlin. The excitement and anxiety were overwhelming. What if she was wrong?

She glanced at Hob, who stood to the side, shading his eyes with his cap. He watched the door intently, his mouth twisted into a frown. Seconds later, the grating ceased. Sigga was silhouetted against the doorway, a dagger in her hand.

"Omani and Matthias, stand in front of the Faeregines," she called.

"Captain, if anything but me tries to exit this vault your men are to shoot it."

Stepping up to the threshold, Sigga conjured an orb made of swirling shadows and lobbed it forward. The light within the vault dimmed so that it was no longer blinding. Unsheathing her other dagger, Sigga stepped inside and disappeared from view.

Ten seconds passed. Twenty. The guardsmen were perfectly still, their carabines trained on the opening. Everyone stared at the vault in expectant silence. It was too much for Hazel.

"Is it in there?" she cried.

"It is, Your Highness. Captain?"

"Yes, Agent Fenn?"

"Give the boy out there a gun."

"Do you need me to send in my men?"

"No," said Sigga firmly. "Just the boy."

The puzzled captain was not pleased. He thrust his carabine at Hob.

"I'm toward the back," Sigga called. "Watch your step, Mr. Smythe. No sudden movements."

Raising the carabine to his shoulder, Hob walked forward. Like Sigga, he paused on the threshold before disappearing inside.

Isabel whispered in Hazel's ear. "What is in there?"

Hazel could not answer. Her entire being was tense. Why had Sigga told Hob to watch his step? What was on the floor? How big could these things grow?

Crack-crack-crack-crack-crack!

The gunshots made Hazel jump; the ensuing screams nearly caused her to flee. A series of inhuman, ululating cries seemed to be coming from a dozen throats. Isabel gripped Hazel's arm.

The screams trailed away into strangled moans that ended with a final gunshot. Milky liquid dribbled from the rounded archway like rain running off a roof. It pooled on the floor and overflowed into the hall. Sigga appeared in the doorway, wiping her dagger clean.

"The danger has passed," she said, and looked to Violet. "Your Highness, please take the steps we discussed. Follow them to the letter."

Violet lifted her chin. She'd had enough of taking orders. "I'm not doing anything until I see what's in there."

She walked boldly toward the vault until she reached the pooling, pearly liquid. Clamping a hand over her nose, she stood on tiptoe to peer past Sigga. She promptly spun around on her heel.

"It will be just as you ask, Agent Fenn. Captain, no one enters or leaves this room until you receive a direct order from the empress or myself. Is that clear?"

"Yes, Your Highness."

Violet made swiftly for the exit with Omani Kruger. As their footsteps receded, Hazel ventured toward the vault. Like Violet, she soon had to cover her nose. There was a rotten, meaty smell, like a decomposing animal.

Sigga sheathed her knife. "Just a peek."

Hazel was trying very hard not to gag. "Where's Mr. Smythe?"

"Collecting himself."

Hazel heard a series of violent retches within. Peering past Sigga, she spied Hob spitting up whatever remained in his stomach.

The Lirlander Vault was much bigger than she imagined, perhaps eighty feet deep and thirty across. Seals covered the walls and even the high barrel ceiling.

With their radiance veiled, Hazel could see the Seals weren't perfectly round or even white. Rascha had said they were fashioned from dragon scales, but they looked like pure gold with whorls of rose and platinum. No two were alike. Each had a name chased in runes above unique, intricate patterns that encircled the Faeregine sigil.

Hazel almost wept when she beheld them and sensed their magic. Mina I had crafted every Seal herself and no one could match her spellwork for sheer beauty. The Lirlander Seals were poetry in form and function, irreplaceable treasures.

And a monster had been devouring them.

She gazed about the vault at the dwimorleech. It bore little resemblance to the master's specimen. The entire vault looked like it was choked with tree roots. Dozens of twisting, vascular limbs draped the walls and ceiling. Some were fastened upon Lirlander Seals; others hung down to the floor where they coiled like dead pythons.

Most of the limbs protruded from a huge, fleshy mass attached to a far corner where the wall and ceiling joined. But not all. Smaller masses had formed in different areas of the vault, each with their own limbs and feelers. They were connected to one another via bluish cords, but each possessed numerous eyes and perhaps its own brain. From their wounds, it appeared Hob had fired upon the largest mass, while Sigga dispatched the others with her blade.

"It was nearly invisible when I came in," said Sigga. "Excellent camouflage. I didn't even see it until I was ten feet in and brushed an arm." She gazed round at the swollen monstrosity. "I'd say he's grown a bit since they smuggled him in."

But Hazel was still preoccupied with the Seals themselves. She'd always felt a special affinity for Mina I and these Seals were her masterpieces. The scene was an abomination.

"Do you think any of them still work?" she said softly.

Sigga nodded. "If not, there would have been more attacks. We won't know how many have been drained until we dispose of this creature and find a way to test them. But that doesn't matter right now." She stooped to look Hazel in the eye. "You just prevented a war, Your Highness."

Hazel smiled faintly. "Not yet. A lot depends on Violet."

An hour passed. Then another. Old Tom's chiming was faint but audible. Hazel sat on a bench next to Isabel and Pamplemousse, silently marveling how a visit to the master's office had led them here.

"So, is Montague going to give him a job?" Isabel asked, jolting Hazel from her thoughts.

She nodded toward Hob, who was examining a distant portrait of Mina V. He'd spent the last two hours wandering around the room. Hob was not a guardsman, a member of the Red Branch, or a Faeregine. With so many people about, he couldn't talk to Hazel, and no one else would deign to speak with an unemployed page. And so, he perused the paintings.

"I don't know," said Hazel. "At first, the master thought I was crazy for asking. But once they got talking, I think he started to like Mr. Smythe."

"He grows on people," said Isabel. "Not as fast as a dwimorleech, but . . ."

She trailed off. The tromping of many boots sounded from the hallway. The girls rose and bowed low as the Impyrial honor guard marched in bearing the empress on her golden palanquin. The Spider looked very old and small, the hand that clutched her scepter was but a shriveled claw. But those hard black eyes drank in all before her.

The empress did not stay long. Once she'd looked into the vault and understood the grisly scene, she issued a number of commands. The first was that all Impyrial warships were to stand down and return to their bases. The second was that Lord Kraavh should be fetched in the royal coach. Hazel grinned. She really had prevented a war. She had saved lives!

Her smile faded at the empress's third command, delivered in that horrid croak.

"Arrest every person who inspected or inventoried this vault after it was breached. They shall be set adrift in Lirlander waters to suffer the same fate as those they doomed by failing to detect this parasite. Their families are hereby exiled to the Grislands."

The Spider said this so casually she might have been ordering soup. She went on to double the reward for catching the perpetrators and demand the Workshop liaison be brought before her. It was their creature that did this. Once she had finished, she beckoned Hazel to her side and held out her hand. Hazel took it with some reluctance.

"You are responsible for this discovery?"

"Yes, Your Radiance."

An approving nod. "Name your reward, child."

Hazel hesitated. "I . . . I don't want anyone executed. I ask that you spare their lives."

The Spider gave a mirthless laugh. Her fingers closed upon Hazel's hand with surprising force, the nails digging into flesh.

"That is why you will never be empress."

CHAPTER 20
THE ROAD TO TALYSIN

Keep your basilisks and harpies, your trolls and goblins.
There is only one true monster and its name is Dragon.

—Vivek the Younger, playwright and orator
(486–537 A.C.)

T he only summers Hob had known were in Dusk. And while the
Sentries did enjoy a summer of sorts, the season was brief and
hectic. The ground did not fully thaw until July; by September,
blue skies were already turning gray as winter reasserted herself. This
left little time for repairs, tending crops, and laying in stores for the
brutal months to come. Summer meant work.

This was not the case on the Sacred Isle. Its climate was temperate,
its summer a far sweeter season than anything Hob had experienced.

There was a languor in the air, a sense that people were more willing to please and to be pleased. In the weeks since war had been avoided, Rowan's residents seemed almost giddy. Everyone had a bounce to their step, and that included Hob.

He had good reason: Master Montague had offered him a job. The news came three days after they discovered the dwimorleech in the Lirlander Vault. According to the master, Hob's title would be Junior Research Assistant, which was to say he could look forward to long hours and little pay. Hob didn't mind—he was excited to have access to the greatest libraries on earth. In Dusk, books were hard to come by.

Since the job would not start until September, Hob had more leisure time than he'd ever known. The academic year had ended, and Her Highness had passed each class with honors. Their tutoring sessions were on hold until school resumed, leaving Hazel free—if *free* was the word—to spend every minute studying Mystics with Dàme Rascha.

As for Hob, Oliveiro required only that he scrub some pots and pans to earn his temporary keep. Once he started work for Master Montague, Hob would move from the palace to a room on the school grounds. Despite his daily dose of haggish abuse, the arrangement was more than fair and left his afternoons free. Of late, he liked to spend them at the base of a colossal oak in Rowan's Old College.

He was there now, sitting against its trunk as a ladybug meandered across his forearm. He watched its progress and took another bite of his peach. Peaches were a revelation compared to Dusk's native cabbage, which kept you alive but made you wish you were dead. The ladybug flew off and Hob returned to Mr. Burke's latest note.

Do not bring this handbook when you accompany HF on the pilgrimage. You will be searched before you depart and spypaper does not function near the Otherland Gates.

HF may not be the Reaper reborn but she is powerfully magical. Watch her closely, for the dragon may change her. It has happened to Faeregines besides Arianna. With luck, Talysin will exorcise her of the spirit that plagues her. If not, we will address it.

Your new position pleases us. Influencing the royal family and future Rowan graduates will help us achieve the transition I envision. But never forget where your loyalties lie. Do not be taken in by Isaac Montague: mehrün feed and clothe him. He is their pet and chief apologist.

Enjoy your voyage over peaceful seas. War with the Lirlanders would not have served the Fellowship's interests. Thank the gods that crisis was averted. Nothing can stop us now . . .

For truth, equality, and a free Impyrium.

Hob scribbled off a brief reply and finished his peach, wrapping the pit in a handkerchief. He understood Mr. Burke's warnings, but he couldn't pretend he hadn't done some thinking since his talk with Master Montague.

During Hob's Fellowship orientation, Brother Marcos had also shown him a map and discussed how the Cataclysm recast the world.

His account agreed with the master's in almost every way except intent. In the Fellowship version, mehrùn exploited the Cataclysm to rob muir of their history and status. In Master Montague's version, mehrùn were not self-interested or diabolical—at least not in the beginning. Their intent was to protect those who survived the Cataclysm. If that was true, when had things gone bad? Why was Impyrium so different from what its founders had envisioned?

"Mr. Smythe, I almost didn't recognize you. You're brown as bark."

Sigga Fenn stood ten feet away. Hob had no idea how she'd gotten so close without him noticing, but there she was. In the tree shade, her eyes seemed to reflect the sunlight filtering through leaves. The agent could not be human, he decided. Not entirely.

Hob glanced at his tan. "My mother's son, I guess."

"When I left the Grislands, I spent every minute I could in the sun. But I'm not blessed with Hauja blood; I just burn. How is your mother by the way? Did she get the potion?"

"I don't know," said Hob.

"Didn't you follow up?"

"I write every week, but I haven't heard back," said Hob. "I think she's still upset that I left."

"That's probably it," said Sigga. "Of course, there's always the chance she never received anything."

"You think the mails lost that many letters?"

"Unlikely," she replied. "Perhaps someone intercepted them. A lot of that's been happening."

Sigga eased down next to him and stretched out her long legs. It was like having a panther pad up and settle by you, both thrilling and frightening. She looked younger close up, and smelled distinctly feminine. How old was she? Twenty-five? Hob looked at her hands. No hints there—too many scars. He lingered on the Red Branch tattoo on her wrist. *How many people have you killed?*

"We're not strangers anymore," she said. "You can call me Sigga. May I call you Hob?"

He nodded. "What do you mean letters have been intercepted?"

"Last week we caught a man we've been hunting. He works for an organization called the Fellowship. Have you ever heard of them?"

Hob's heart beat faster. He pretended to consider the question. "I think so. Revolutionaries. 'Down with the Faeregines' and all that."

"That's right," said Sigga. "There's lots of similar groups, but the Fellowship's different."

"How's that?"

"They're smarter," she said. "Better funded, better organized. We've been following one of their people, a man they call Brother Jakob for several weeks."

She glanced over at Hob. The mention of Brother Jakob's name stirred something in his subconscious, but it darted for muddier banks. He shrugged.

"What does this have to do with stolen letters?"

"Ah," she said. "When we caught up with this man, he was with a boy about your age, a smile to melt your heart. Brother Jakob was in the process of selling him to an establishment that entertains wealthy and unscrupulous mehrùn. I assume this boy—his name was Badu—was supposed to gather information that could be used for blackmail."

Hob tried not to betray his horror.

"I talked with Badu," said Sigga. "He was cocky at first, all swagger. But beneath it all, he's really just a scared boy from Castelia. We found nineteen letters he'd written to his family stashed in Brother Jakob's apartment. His parents have no idea where their son is."

"What's going to happen to him?"

She sighed. "I don't know. Unfortunately, he can't tell us much. But we'll keep trying. I wish I could work with him, but I've got other responsibilities. Anyway, this Badu got me thinking about you."

The Grislander gazed down at him, her face inches from his own. Hob did not look away.

"Why's that?"

She shrugged. "Badu's bright and capable. Comes from nothing. But he wasn't lucky enough to get a job with House Sylva, much less the royal family. So he fell in with less savory types."

"Life's tough."

"I know. Where I'm from makes Dusk look like this . . ." She gestured at the verdant quad.

"Yeah," said Hob. "Dusk's all rainbows and flowers."

Sigga leaned into him the way an older sister might. "Don't take it the wrong way. I like you, Hob. And I'm not a magistrate. I don't care if you broke some rules to get here and better your life. I'd have done the same. I don't even care if you explored a forbidden dig site. What I do care about is danger. And it didn't go away when we found that dwimorleech in the vault. You remember what I told you about Whitebarrow?"

Hob nodded.

"It turns out we were on to something," said Sigga. "Brother Jakob is a necromancer."

Hob felt like he'd just fallen through the ice at Bear Lake. Fortunately, his shock was a perfectly natural reaction to such news.

"How do you know? Did you give him that potion?"

"We did," she said. "And we learned a valuable piece of information. That particular potion is no longer effective. Its formula is centuries old and apparently necromancers have learned how to offset its effects. It didn't do anything to Brother Jakob. If we hadn't caught him robbing a mausoleum, we might not have tried more exotic means of detection."

She held up another vial containing a silvery liquid.

"I am not drinking that," said Hob pointedly.

She smiled. "No need. A drop on the skin will do—assuming you have no objections."

Hob held out his arm. He didn't care if he burst into flame. He was wholly preoccupied with Sigga's news. If this Brother Jakob really was a necromancer, were there others in the Fellowship? His mind went back to his first encounter with Mr. Burke in Dusk. The man had been loitering in the temple's graveyard when he'd stopped Hob and Angus Dane from fighting. Then there was the cellar where they'd met after his trip to Impyria. That cottage was located right by Rose Chapel's cemetery . . .

Hob blinked as a drop of liquid splashed on his wrist and beaded off onto the grass.

"Congratulations," said Sigga. "You are not a necromancer."

Hob tried to make a quip but couldn't. "So, Whitebarrow wasn't some kind of hoax?"

"No," said Sigga. "That offering to the Shibbolth was very real. Brother Jakob isn't just a necromancer; he's a member of the original Coven . . ."

From her pocket, the Grislander removed a heavy bronze pendant that hung from a silver chain. The chain looked new but the pendant was smooth and pocked with age. Hob stared at it in horror. Mr. Burke had a similar pendant. Hob had seen him tuck it into his robe aboard the Transcontinental.

"What is that?"

"A reliquary," replied Sigga. "It contains the ashes of Brother Jakob's original heart. Necromancers always keep it close." She pointed to a worn infinity symbol within a nine-pointed star. "And that's the Coven's mark. I wish I could say he's the only one."

"You're sure there are more?" said Hob.

"Oh yes," said Sigga. "We've confirmed Brother Jakob was in Impyria when that offering was made at Whitebarrow. He's not alone. There will be others in the Fellowship."

Hob thought he might be sick. "Why would necromancers be involved with a group fighting for muir rights?"

"Many reasons," said Sigga. "Necromancers are parasites. They're very good at hiding their true selves within various hosts—whether it's a corpse, a living person, even organizations where you wouldn't expect to find them. The Fellowship would offer good cover, plentiful resources, and lots of candidates from which to select a potential replacement."

Hob did not like the sound of this. "Replacement . . . as in protégé?"

The agent chuckled. "That's probably what they tell their victim, but it's not innocent. Human bodies don't last forever. Before a necromancer gets too old and frail, he starts identifying candidates to be his next host. They're incredibly selective about choosing that person. They only want the best."

Hob recalled Mr. Burke's description of his father:

Ulrich was a fundamentally superior person—tougher and smarter than the rest. I used to joke he was some kind of Workshop experiment. Best recruit I ever had. You have some big shoes to fill, young man.

The implications were beyond horrifying. Mr. Burke wasn't a muir revolutionary, he was a monster who'd been preying upon people for untold centuries, stealing their bodies and using them as hosts. Hob turned to Sigga, prepared to confess everything.

But something peculiar occurred before he could speak. His mind ran into a soft but irresistible wall. Even as the words formed, they trickled away like smoke. Hob's terror and urgency evaporated. The Grislander's news was disturbing, but there was no need to be squeamish. And he certainly wasn't going to betray Mr. Burke or anyone else in the Fellowship. The very idea was unthinkable.

Instead of confessing, he merely rubbed his temples. "Why are you telling me this, Agent Fenn? And don't tell me it's out of concern for my mother and sister. I know it's your job to protect Her Highness, but these games are wearing me out. I'm here because Dàme Rascha poached me from the Sylvas. I'm not a threat to the princess."

Sigga glanced curiously at him before picking up his handbook and thumbing idly through it. As she did, Hob eyed a slight crease on the page where he received messages from the Fellowship. To his immense relief, she closed the book and laid it down.

"I'm sorry to tread upon your patience, Mr. Smythe. I thought you were interested in these developments. I'm well aware you're not a threat to Her Highness. If you were, we would not be having this conversation."

Hob studied her a moment. And then it hit him.

"That's why you gave me a gun," he muttered softly.

The Grislander said nothing. Hob sat up.

"That's it. You already knew I could shoot. You wanted to see what I'd do if I was armed around the princess."

Sigga's face was impassive; no confirmation or denial. Hob was incredulous.

"What if I *was* an assassin?" he said angrily. "How could you take a risk like that?"

"Her Highness was never in danger."

Something in her tone made Hob a believer. He had never seen Sigga Fenn do anything distinctly superhuman, but one never lost the sense that they were in the presence of something terribly dangerous.

"I will say this once," she continued. "If you are involved with the Fellowship, you are in far over your head. People like Brother Jakob could not care less about muir rights. Their only allegiance is to demons that live beyond this world—beings that make Lord Kraavh look like a kitten. So I'd ask you to consider something."

"What's that?" said Hob, unable to look at her.

"When the Shibbolth tried to invade, it was the Reaper who stood against them," said Sigga. "For all her faults, Mina the Fourth was no coward. She and the dragon Valryka charged through the Otherland Gate—into the Void itself—and drove the Shibbolth back. They were victorious, but Valryka perished in the battle and the Reaper never truly recovered. Two years later, assassins finally got to her."

"So what am I supposed to consider?" asked Hob.

"If the Shibbolth come again, who is going to stop them?"

Hob thought of Mina IV and Hazel, and their uncanny similarities. If Mr. Burke served the Shibbolth, his interest in Hazel took on an entirely different significance. The Coven would view her not as a threat to muir or the Fellowship but as a potential obstacle to their masters.

Again, a silent war raged within Hob. He wanted to tell Sigga everything, to confess, to be rid of secrets, no matter the consequences. But he could not translate impulse into action. It unraveled like string. All he heard were Mr. Burke's words of caution.

Agent Fenn's trying to spook you into switching sides and coming to her for protection. Common tactic.

It was true, Hob thought. He suddenly felt foolish and unworthy. Mr. Burke had been his father's friend, and it was his gold supporting Hob's mother and Anja. The man had a noble vision for Impyrium's future and was making steady progress toward it. Sigga was trying to make it seem like Hob had been told nothing but lies. But this simply wasn't the case. Mr. Burke had shown him photographs; his account of the Cataclysm was almost identical to Master Montague's. The two of them stood upon a buried city! That was a plain and undeniable fact. The only facts he knew about Sigga were that she was a professional killer from the Grislands. Why would he trust her?

He looked at Sigga with suspicion. "If you're convinced I'm taking orders from someone, why don't you have me arrested?"

The Grislander's face hardened into a mask, beautiful but grim. "We all have our orders, Mr. Smythe. We don't have to like them."

The two sat in silence while students and masters walked past. Glancing at Old Tom's clock, Hob saw it was nearly three.

"I need to go pack," he said.

"Are you looking forward to the trip?" Sigga asked.

"Yes and no," Hob admitted. "I'm flattered to be invited, but I don't like crossing ponds, much less an ocean. Have you ever been on a pilgrimage?"

"No. But here's some advice. When we're crossing the Lirlands, stay below deck. People who look overboard often wish they hadn't." She rose to her feet and stretched like a drowsy cat. "The voyage takes a week and Her Highness will be sequestered. If you'd like to continue this little chat, ask a sailor to fetch me." Reaching down, she picked up his handbook again and brushed away bits of grass. "You don't mind if I borrow this, do you?"

A vise closed around Hob's chest. *I'm finished.* "Why would you want that?"

Sigga shrugged. "I'll need something to read, and this can't be as dull as it looks. After all, you can hardly put it down and you're not even a page anymore." She thumped the back cover. "Must be riveting."

Hob watched helplessly as she strode away. There was nothing he could do. How could he protest her borrowing something so trivial? Closing his eyes, he touched each tattoo beneath his shirt and whispered a prayer to Fenmaruq, Vessuk, and Kayüta. He even addressed grim Morrgu, though he knew she'd never listen.

Slowly he got to his feet and crossed the grass to a walkway. Maybe Sigga wouldn't find anything. After all, that mystic had not detected the spypaper when he'd first arrived on the Sacred Isle. Then again, Sigga Fenn was not your average mystic. Hob paused to look about Rowan, at the grand and stately buildings that housed so much of the world's knowledge. And he realized, with a dull pang in his heart, that he would never get to work here. He'd probably never see it again.

Sigga had shaken him deeply. Her news of this Brother Jakob and the Coven was disturbing, as were the implications for himself and Hazel. But as he walked in the warm sun and listened to the twittering birds, he found it impossible to remain frightened or anxious.

As Mr. Burke said, all he had to worry about was doing his job. The Fellowship would take care of everything else. By the time he'd reached the palace, Hob had forgotten Brother Jakob entirely.

Later that afternoon, Hazel sat in a little chair in the triplets' common room. She tried to keep still as a fine sable brush tickled her eyelid. She failed, and burst into giggles. The priestess sighed, set down her brush, and dabbed away the errant line.

"Please, Your Highness. I'm nearly finished."

"I'm sorry," said Hazel. Keeping her eyes closed, she reached for one of the little sandwiches that had been on a tray. What she found was Dàme Rascha's large and hairy hand. She squeezed it. "You're not a sandwich."

"No," said Rascha. "I am not. And you're not taking this seriously."

"Yes, I am," said Hazel. "I can't help if it tickles to have little brushes painting things on my face. And I've been sitting here for hours. I'm famished."

"You've had three sandwiches," said the vye. "Two peaches. And couscous."

"I don't care," said Hazel. "In two hours I start fasting for a week. A *week*! I get to eat as much as I want."

From across the room, Isabel groaned. She was also being subjected to decorative torture. "Shut it, Hazel. You're making me hungry." A pause. "Pamplemousse?"

A preoccupied voice answered from the rafters. "What?"

"Cut up a sandwich and feed me," said Isabel. "I can't move my arms."

"You cannot possibly be serious."

"Deadly serious."

"I'm busy."

"You are not. You're painting your toenails."

An indignant snort. "How did you . . . ?"

Isabel gave a sudden shriek. "I can see! I can see through your eyes, Pamplemousse!"

Hazel felt a rush of air as the homunculus whooshed past. "Oh, my lamb chop," he exclaimed. "This is a happy day!"

While the two cooed and gushed over each other, Hazel felt Merlin turn about in her lap like a puppy disturbed from a dream. His tiny hands gripped her skirt convulsively and then relaxed. Poor Merlin. Pamplemousse already lorded over him something fierce; now he'd be insufferable. Hazel felt a pang of jealousy herself. She'd never been able to see through Merlin's eyes, not even a hazy glimmer.

"What's it like?" she asked.

"It's wild," said Isabel. "I still see normally, but if I concentrate, I see whatever he's looking—"

"Enough!"

It was the first thing Violet had said all day. All afternoon she'd sat with her back to them, perfectly rigid as the priestesses and their acolytes attended to her.

"Can you two sit quietly for five minutes?" she said coldly. "Or are you going to giggle and make jokes all the way to Man?"

"Not all the way," said Isabel. "I'll need a nap."

Violet exhaled slowly. "This is our first pilgrimage. You may not care, but I do. Sit still and let these people finish their work. Or would you rather keep Grandmother waiting?"

No one wanted to keep the Spider waiting. It was going to be bad enough being cooped up with her for a week, much less starting off on the wrong foot. The woman might eat them.

Hazel and Isabel sat in chastened silence while the Ninespire priestesses completed their duties. When the henna had dried, the girls rose and gazed at themselves in a gilded mirror. Each was barefoot and wore a sleeveless gown of plain white cloth. Crowns of twisted rowan sat atop their braided hair. Intricate symbols and runes glistened darkly on their skin.

At first, Hazel thought they looked like witches, for many witch clans were fond of skinscrolling. But she quickly changed her mind. They did not look like witches.

They looked like sacrifices.

The head priestess did little to allay these misgivings. As the girls left the tower, she daubed their foreheads with ashes and lamb's blood and intoned a prayer in Old Impyrian.

"Ayama sundiri un yvas don Ember thùl embrazza."

May Ember's sons and daughters accept you.

They descended the tower in silence, followed by the priestesses, tutors, and bodyguards. Hazel walked behind Isabel, counting the steps as they took a hidden stair that led from the Faeregine wing down through the cliffs and to the beach. The palace had many hidden rooms and passages. Some were still in use, others had been walled off long ago and were popular references in ghost stories. According to legend, no fewer than eighty-seven malicious spirits haunted the palace. Thankfully, Hazel had yet to see one.

Then again, maybe the Spider counted. Their grandmother was waiting for them at the bottom of the stair, her palanquin resting on the grotto's pitted limestone. She also wore henna inscriptions, but her skin shone in the dark, as if moonlight illuminated her. The effect was not magic, Hazel knew, but an ointment made from phosphoroil and powdered lunestones. It looked wonderful in pictures, and there would be hordes of photographers clicking away as they proceeded to the empress's flagship.

The Spider gestured for her granddaughters to take their places. They did so, Violet in the center. Torches were lit, and from up ahead a deep drumming made the rock hum and vibrate. Eight tall priests raised the palanquin and walked forward. Hazel and her sisters fell in step behind them.

They proceeded through a series of dim caves before they exited an archway cut into the cliffs. Thousands cheered as they emerged. Many residents came to see the empress off on her annual pilgrimages, but even more than usual lined the beaches this sunset. Hazel wasn't surprised. The Spider's popularity increased once tension with the Lirlanders had slackened, but the real attraction was Violet.

For the first time since Hazel's mother had died, a future empress was making a pilgrimage to one of the dragons that guarded the Otherland Gates. Many believed the dragons not only protected Impyrium from forces beyond this world but that their presence conferred peace and prosperity within it. It would never do to offend such godlike creatures, and thus it was the empress's duty to pay proper tribute. Now that the triplets were making the journey, people could breathe easier knowing that another crop of Faeregines was in place to continue the hallowed tradition. Other houses craved the Faeregines' wealth and power, but none envied this particular responsibility. Hazel couldn't blame them. For all the excitement, she was terribly anxious. She had witnessed firsthand the Spider's condition after making these journeys. Pilgrimage took a terrible toll on the mind and body.

It took fifteen minutes to make their way to the deepwater pier where *Rowana*, the empress's golden flagship, was moored. A

Lirlander Seal shone brightly on its prow, a reminder that the seas were safe once again. Drums were booming as dancers wearing elaborate dragon costumes snaked through the crowds. Hazel found it impossible not to get swept up in the moment. There was such an electric, festive atmosphere. People were singing, throwing rowan petals, and wishing the Faeregines safe passage across the Prusian Sea. Hazel felt like some kind of hero.

The feeling continued as they marched up the flagship's broad gangplank. Everyone aboard was arrayed in crisp lines to receive them. They stood behind the captain, his officers, and the trio of weather-workers who would conjure winds and calm the seas before them. Hazel spied Hob off to the side, next to his roommate, Viktor. He looked very smart in a new linen suit he'd bought with Sigga's money. Their eyes met and she offered the tiniest of smiles. He returned it before turning his gaze back on the empress.

By now, Hazel attached an almost superstitious faith in Hob's company. The Muirlander was a good luck charm. She would see precious little of him during the actual voyage, but knowing he was aboard gave her confidence that she could handle the upcoming fast and her fear of meeting a dragon. As Hazel was discovering, confidence was half the battle.

The drums ceased as the priests set down the palanquin. Violet helped the empress up from her cushion. Anyone hoping for inspirational remarks from Her Radiance would have been sorely disappointed. Clutching Violet's hand, the Spider hobbled toward a hatchway and promptly disappeared down its steps. Rascha bent close to take Merlin from Hazel.

"Quickly, child. The sun has nearly set."

Hazel turned and saw only a hint of red in the western sky. Purification had to begin at sunset. There wasn't a moment to lose. Hazel hurried into the hatchway after Isabel. Once they were inside, the priests shut the doors and locked them in.

Slowly, Hazel and Isabel crept down into *Rowana*'s belly. All noise from outside had vanished. The air was very still and smelled faintly of tar and incense. As they descended the narrow steps, Hazel sensed the ancient spells about them, spells that had been worked into surrounding timbers like linseed oil. Neither girl spoke. The laughter from earlier that afternoon seemed a distant memory.

How far had they descended? Eighty steps? One hundred? Farther than Hazel would have thought possible, even in a ship of this size. Old Magic was at work here. But the steps were coming to an end. An orange flickering shone below. It spilled from a low doorway to illuminate the strange being on the threshold.

At first glance, the creature looked trollish—gray and gnarled, with glassy green eyes and a bramble beard—but it was no larger than a child of four or five. Although it was short and its goatish legs bowed, its arms were long and corded with muscle. When they came closer, Hazel saw that ram's horns were beginning to grow from its temples. Although its size gave an impression of youth, Hazel felt like she'd never encountered anything older in her entire life. The creature did not speak, but bowed and stood aside so they could enter.

The space they entered felt like a shrine or sanctum, about twenty feet across with a bed of burning coals at its center. The curving walls were made of fragrant sandalwood, darkly stained, and carved into mythological scenes. Gazing round, Hazel saw great wolves chasing the moon and sun, fierce thunderbirds whipping seas into storm, battles between gods and giants, the Hound impaling Astaroth with his spear. . . .

"Sit."

The Spider's voice resonated in the chamber. She and Violet were seated a few feet apart on two of the nine mats spaced round the bed of coals. Isabel sat on the empress's left. Hazel took the mat farthest from her grandmother. She gazed across the burning coals at the frail woman whose limbs were folded about her person. Hazel knew she would always be afraid of her.

The little creature shut the door and brought the empress a mortar, pestle, and several bowls filled with dried flowers, herbs, and berries. The Spider shook some petals into the mortar and began to grind them.

"You bear the Faeregine name, but you are not yet Faeregines," she said quietly. "None of the pampered fools who share your last name are true Faeregines. They think it is an inheritance, a birthright to wealth and power. But they are mistaken. It is a responsibility, a burden too dreadful and heavy for others to bear. So it has been for three thousand years. You are not a Faeregine until you have stood before a dragon and born its scrutiny. . . ."

Sweat beaded on Hazel's forehead and trickled down her back. The room was growing hot as an oven.

"It has been nearly thirteen years since I've had company on pilgrimage," the Spider reflected. "Your mother used to sit there." She nodded at a mat between Hazel and Violet. "Elana made twenty-three journeys with me. The last took her life. She died on Samhain giving birth to you before the Nether Gate." She added rowanberries in the bowl. "Violet arrived first, then Isabel. I took you girls away, for your mother was too weak to hold you and Graazh was restless. That dragon is the least predictable, and I dared not linger."

The Spider's sharp black eyes locked on Hazel.

"I did not know there was a third child until you cried out. When I came, I saw that Elana was dead. She was gone, and you were here. Unexpected and uninvited."

The empress returned her attention to the bowl, grinding the ingredients with grim determination.

"You did not look like something that should live," she muttered. "I thought a curse had befallen our family, that some evil out of time had crept forth from the Nether Gate. You had killed my Elana; I would kill you. If I'd had my way, you would have died that minute."

More rowanberries went into the bowl.

"Fortunately," she continued. "A guardsman restrained me and then Graazh intervened. The dragon licked you clean and nursed you with milk from her body. And then she devoured my Elana."

Hazel was stunned. As girls they were told their mother died in childbirth aboard this very ship. There was no mention of Graazh eating her, much less playing nursemaid to Hazel. And certainly no indication the empress tried to murder her own granddaughter.

"Mother's tomb . . . ," said Isabel. The girls visited it twice yearly: once on Elana Faeregine's birthday and the other on their own.

"Empty," said the empress. "My Elana is with Graazh."

Violet said nothing, but gazed at Hazel with an expression of repulsion and enmity. The Spider had just confirmed all of her doubts and misgivings that Hazel was different, that she didn't truly belong with Isabel or herself. Hazel was an outsider—she was the reason Violet had no mother. . . .

"Why are you telling me this?" said Hazel.

Their grandmother sprinkled herbs into the mixture. "In my bones, I know this is my last Midsummer. There can be no more secrets between us, or between the three of you. You have a right to know the circumstances of your birth and why I have always hated you. But the one who must truly understand this story is Violet."

Violet tore her gaze from Hazel. "Why me, Grandmother?"

"Because you will be empress, and I learned much about ruling that night. The world has its own wisdom and it often lies beneath veils we cannot pierce. Mortals are poor judges of whether our actions will prove good or ill over time. In my rage, I nearly committed an act of unspeakable evil. Not against a child but against Impyrium. We had received a very great gift that night, and in my folly I nearly threw it away. When you are empress, you must not make decisions in haste, happiness, or anger. Do you understand?"

Violet shot a dark look at Hazel. "Yes, Grandmother."

"Soon, the responsibilities of Impyrium and our house shall fall to you. If you are to fulfill your duties as Daughters of Mina, there is lore you must know."

The empress beckoned to the little creature she called Og. He took the mortar's contents and added some sort of spirit to make a brew so vile Hazel gagged when it was her turn to drink. Forcing it down, she felt sharp, hot pains in her belly as she passed the bowl to Isabel. Sweat poured in little rivers down the sisters' faces as they shared the Spider's bitter drink. As the bowl made its rounds, their grandmother talked of dragons.

The Spider spoke of Ember and N'aagha, the Father and Mother of dragons. She told them how Ember hatched from the earth, a wingless stormdrake of gold and fire. She whispered how Astaroth conjured black N'aagha from the ashes of his enemies. The two battled, and pursued each other to the far corners of the world. Their unlikely union produced six children, as varied in appearance as they were in power and temperament.

> Hati the Moon-Snatcher, Midwinter's King,
> Ammech the Sun-Catcher, Master of Spring,
> Talysin Spell-Singer, Weaver of Mists,
> Graazh the Frost-Bringer who kills with a kiss,
> Ran-Tolka the Dreamer who wanders the earth,
> Valryka the Valiant awaits her Rebirth.

The lore was woven into rhymes and songs that tumbled through Hazel's mind and subconscious. Most were new, though some grazed memories buried somewhere deep. She learned the verses for each dragon and the ancient spells binding those that guarded Otherland Gates. She recited words of protection and command, charms to ensure her safety in their presence. She learned where Valryka fell in battle with the daemonic Shibbolth, how all dragons feared Hati, and why Ran-Tolka cloaked herself in human form . . .

The four Faeregines did not eat or sleep. If they grew thirsty, Og mixed more of the bitter concoction. When the coals cooled, he added more and fanned them with a bellows.

When Hazel could sit up no longer, she curled into a ball. Eventually, the Spider's words faded, replaced by the rasp of her breathing, the soft hiss of coals, the creaking of the ship's hull. And when her awareness sank even deeper, and floated on currents of whale song, the Reaper's voice, dry and cruel, sounded in her head.

One cannot hide from a dragon. Not behind thoughts, flesh, or dreams. Talysin will not be deceived. He will perceive you are my vessel, the instrument I set in motion long ago when I knew my doom was at hand. His mind will tear through your little cocoon and lay you bare to me. You will never feel more exquisite pain. And when it is over, we shall be one, whether you wish it or no. And then let my enemies tremble!

Rough hands took hold of Hazel. She moaned as Og raised her to a seated position. Several feet away, Violet and Isabel huddled together, watching her through a curtain of heat shimmer. Their dull eyes were sunk deep within their emaciated faces. Fingers twitched, their mouths hung open, a red-brown crust about their cracked lips. The merciless heat had baked the humanity out of them. Her sisters were strangers, two savages plucked out of time.

"Is she breathing?"

Her grandmother's voice seemed to come from a great distance. Og gave an indifferent grunt.

"Ten minutes," said the Spider.

Hazel had a dim sense of being carried not up, but down a long, dark stairway. Her next sensation was of sea spray speckling her face. Something damp touched her forehead. Her skin absorbed its moisture like a sponge. She opened her eyes to see Dàme Rascha's face, upside down and framed by a sky teeming with stars. Tears glistened in the vye's fierce eyes.

"Am I dead?" croaked Hazel. Her voice sounded utterly alien in her ears.

Rascha hugged her close. "No, my love. You are purifying yourself to stand before Talysin. I know it is hard."

"How long have I . . . ?" Hazel whispered.

"Six days," said Rascha, stroking her limp hand. "Violet and Isabel have been up twice already. We land day after tomorrow."

Hazel nodded dimly. She wanted to feel pride at staying below longest, but she was too exhausted to care. Music carried on the wind, from somewhere—a flute or fife. There were footsteps behind Rascha, and another figure appeared within Hazel's view. Sigga.

The Grislander's concern was plain. "Is this typical?"

Rascha nodded and dabbed Hazel's forehead. "Faeregines bear it. I don't know how, but they do. Something in their blood."

Hazel heard a chorus of cries and shouts, a stampede of footsteps above.

"What . . . ?" she whispered.

Sigga peered over a railing. "We're in Lirlander waters. There's a city below us."

Hazel tried to sit up.

"No," said Rascha. "Lie still."

But Hazel would not. She wished to feel a breeze, and see for herself one of the fabled demon kingdoms. Most of all, she wanted to stand and prove she still could.

"Been sitting too long," she gasped. *"Please."*

Not even Rascha could ignore the desperation in her voice. Propping Hazel up, she and Sigga helped her to stand. Hazel gave a little cry as her cracked and blistered feet made contact with the deck. Her teeth chattered uncontrollably, even after Sigga wrapped a blanket about her. But anything was preferable to that dead, sweltering sanctum.

As she got her bearings, Hazel realized they were on a small deck toward the back of the ship on the starboard side. The main deck was some thirty or forty feet above them. She could see figures lining the rail, their faces lit from below by the sea's shimmering luminance. Among the many soldiers and sailors, she spied Hob's dark face gazing down, transfixed with quiet horror. He might have been watching another phantasia.

It turned out he was.

Pictures of the Lirlands always disappointed. They could not be glimpsed during daylight, and photographs taken at night revealed no more than dim clusters of fuzzy light within a vast black sea. It was like viewing a distant galaxy through an overmatched telescope.

Not so in person.

The waters below were shockingly clear and gave off a phosphorescent glow. Gazing down, Hazel made out distant cities and dwellings like she was spotting coins in a fountain. Some were encased under glassy domes, but many stood in the open ocean, including palaces that looked to be colossal in scale. Every structure and spire had a pearly gleam.

Something huge glided past, trailing streams of shimmering bubbles. It looked like a manta ray, but one with a hundred foot wingspan and luminous markings down its back. It cruised lazily along before veering down and away toward a smoking canyon.

As Hazel followed its majestic dive, she noticed things were floating up toward the surface. It took her a moment to realize they were bodies; hundreds of corpses in various states of decomposition. Most were sailors and merchants, their faces frozen in expressions of frenzied terror. They bobbed up like corks, steam billowing off their rotting flesh. Hazel heard soft thumps as *Rowana* pushed them aside. "Why?" she whispered.

Sigga stared down at the grisly spectacle. "The Lirlander Seals gives us safe passage over their lands, but the demons are not our friends, Your Highness. They're gloating over the ships they've sunk these past months. Whoever hid that dwimorleech in the vault sacrificed thousands of innocent lives."

Hazel's gaze fell upon a young boy. She recognized him at once, for she had been with him during his final moments aboard the *Polestar*.

Danny's skin was gray, but he had not decomposed. His mouth hung open; sightless eyes gazed up at the heavens. He did not look frightened, so much as surprised and even disappointed that his life had ended so soon.

Hazel did not scream or cry out. She was too tired, too disoriented to be certain if what she was seeing was real. But a tear rolled down her cheek, and she watched Danny until he was lost in *Rowana*'s foaming wake.

Her teeth had stopped chattering, but Hazel felt vaguely sick. Looking up, she saw most spectators had disappeared from the railing above. But not Hob. He remained exactly where he'd been, staring down at the nightmare sea.

Sigga sighed and tugged Hazel away from the railing. "I warned him not to look."

When Hazel turned, she saw that Og was waiting in the dark doorway. Rascha lay her hands on Hazel's shoulders.

"I don't want to go," said Hazel softly. "I want to stay with you."

The old vye kneeled beside her and straightened the crown upon her head. "Go to your grandmother and sisters. We'll reach the Isle of Man soon. The worst is over."

Hazel left them. Creeping down through the dark with Og, she could not imagine how she would ever endure another day in that furnace. When they reached the sanctum, the empress was still chanting through black, cracked lips. Violet and Isabel were slumped against each other, their glazed eyes insensate. Hazel tried to go to them, but Og steered her firmly to her mat and poured more of the scalding brew down her throat.

Folding her legs beneath her, Hazel tried to forget what she'd just witnessed in the sea. She resumed her vigil of the white-hot coals and prayed that Rascha's assurances were true. But when the Reaper's whispers returned, she knew the worst was far from over. It was only just beginning. . . .

"Your Highness?"

Hazel found herself staring into the kindly face of a priestess. The woman was dabbing her with a scented cloth while an acolyte added small white flowers to the crown upon her head.

"Yes?" said Hazel.

"It is time," the woman replied. "Are you ready?"

Hazel was so disoriented she had no clue where she was. "Ready for what?" she murmured. She half expected to hear she was late for a test in Old Tom.

The woman smiled. "To stand before Talysin. All is prepared. The Divine Empress is waiting, and it is a beautiful day."

Hazel looked around uncertainly. She was in a cabin of gold and teak, standing in a basin of cool water. She had been bathed and her white skin anointed with oil, which darkened the henna designs. The cabin's curving window showed a dawn sky of pale gold above natural harbor or inlet. Two warships—half their escort—were anchored just behind them. She felt a dull ache in her stomach.

"Can I eat something?"

"Very soon," the priestess promised. "Just a few more hours."

Hazel cursed silently. A few more hours might have been eternity. Taking the acolyte's hand, she stepped from the basin and dried her feet on a soft mat. The skin was pink and badly blistered.

As they left the cabin, Hazel realized the pounding in her head was actual drums. It was not the festive drumming that sent them off from the Sacred Isle. It had different timbre and rhythm. Hazel could not place it but was almost certain she'd heard it before.

Stepping on the main deck, she gazed out at cliffs and hills, green with clover or yellow with gorse. The Isle of Man was one of the few places whose name had not changed with the Cataclysm. A guardian had lived here once, a giant whose magic protected the island and its inhabitants. When the Reaper crafted the Otherland Gates, she chose this land for a portal to the Sidh, a realm ruled by ancient gods who left this world long ago. And when it was finished, the empress set Talysin to guard it and ensure that none could enter but those she approved.

Already, workmen were building bonfires and setting up pavilions to house the small army of people that would be sleeping on the island while the Faeregines made their offerings. Hazel would not get to live in one of them. For three days, she would be sleeping in a dragon's shadow.

Talysin.

A shiver went down Hazel's spine. Today, she would see a dragon. Not some drawing from one of Uncle Basil's storybooks but a true monster from antiquity. The Spider's lessons from the journey surfaced in her mind like champagne bubbles: Talysin's lore and history, the words of greeting and passage, and the rules for dealing with such proud and aged creatures. These were not phrased as guidelines but as dire warnings with potentially devastating consequences: *Never look a dragon in the eye; never let a dragon learn your truename; never assume a dragon is sleeping; never turn your back on a dragon; never speak lies in a dragon's presence; never fail to show courtesy; never fail to bring gifts; never fail to praise a dragon's lineage; never show fear....*

There were dozens. Hazel imagined there must be similar lists for meeting the empress or other members of her own family. She hoped she could remember them all. She also hoped the gate was near, for she feared a longer trek would be the end of her.

Clinging to the priestess's hand, Hazel proceeded down a stone pier to the beach where the Divine Empress was waiting in her palanquin, surrounded by guards and attendants. Violet and Isabel sat astride white horses. Both looked so weak they merely clung to the animals' necks while their bodyguards held the reins. Hazel's horse was pale gray with a white mane. Dàme Rascha and Sigga stood by the animal, but Hob held its reins.

Sigga lifted Hazel into the saddle. Like her sisters, she leaned forward and rested her head against the animal's warm neck. Its mane smelled like seawater and there were small shells threaded onto its coarse hairs. She wondered dimly if it was some breed of stalliana. Maybe there were gentle kinds. Her face was just a foot or two away from Hob's.

"So you're coming to see him too," she whispered.

He nodded gamely, but the hand that held the reins trembled ever so slightly. *How alien this must be for him*, she thought. It was strange for her, and she'd grown up hearing about dragons and Otherland Gates. Hazel always knew she'd make this journey someday. *But a boy from Dusk? He must feel like he's stumbled into a nightmare.*

"Don't be scared," she said. "It's going to be all—"

The dragon horn sounded, a spiraling shell whose hoarse note triggered a primal dread. From somewhere in the hills, the drumming grew louder. When sunlight reached a standing stone, the priests raised the empress's palanquin and they began the slow march inland.

They climbed for hours over hills and streams. They crossed a ravine and still kept climbing toward a windswept ridge where a ring of stones jutted from a grassy pinnacle.

That must be the gate, she thought. *But where is the dragon?*

Talysin was known as the most beautiful and placid of the gate guardians: a golden wyrm like his father, but flightless. Tatters of mist blew across the island, but the landscape was full of color—greens and browns dotted by white and yellow flowers, gray rock formations, and wind-bent saplings. But Hazel saw no glints of gold, much less a dragon. It had been four years since the empress last visited the Isle of *Man. What if Talysin had broken the Reaper's spells of binding? What if he had died? After all, he and his siblings were thousands of years old.*

She caught a flash of movement on a hill. Something was standing upon it, a gangling, man-shaped creature with tall, straight horns. Hazel stared at it. *Was it a kind of goat? Some kindred of Og's?* The creature leaned upon a twisted staff and watched their party. It seemed to regard them as intruders, but intruders that must be suffered.

Others appeared in twos and threes, some beating the drums she had heard since dawn. They were not fauns or satyrs and were not remotely uniform in appearance. Some resembled rams; others had heron beaks or a wide-eyed, staring aspect that was unmistakably fish-like. There was a crippled, ungainly quality to them that contrasted with the nimble faeries that were now buzzing about. Their radiance was subtle in the daytime; at night, the island must have looked like it teemed with fireflies.

Nine standing stones formed the ring of the Sidh Gate, each forty feet tall and thicker than an oak tree. They rose from a flattened hill-top that offered a commanding view of the island's cobalt bays and misty dells. From this vantage, Hazel saw great gouges in the earth below, like jagged wounds with smoke trickling from their depths. Scores of the strange creatures now watched them from hilltops and tumbled cairns. The drumming continued.

Priestesses led forward three white goats, sheep, and bulls to the ring of stones and tied their halters to a maypole in the circle's midst. The priests who'd carried the palanquin placed small chests at the foot of each standing stone. Dàme Rascha lifted Hazel down from the horse. Once again, a priestess daubed an oily mixture on Hazel's forehead.

"Ayama sundiri un yvas don Ember thùl embrazza."

The same rite was being performed with Violet, Isabel, and even the empress. As Hob led Hazel's horse away, his hand brushed hers and gave it a tiny squeeze. And then he was gone, walking with Rascha, Sigga, and the others to another hill some fifty yards away that was crowned with yew trees. Only the four Faeregines remained near the gate.

"Come," croaked the Spider, clutching her scepter.

Holding hands, the three sisters followed their grandmother within the circle of standing stones, the sun shining on their faces. When they crossed the threshold, Hazel felt a subtle energy. It was like standing in the midst of nine tuning forks, each vibrating at a different frequency. She'd experienced similar sensations with the megaliths in Tùr an Ghrian, but this was stronger. The Spider pointed to each stone, and the Ogham runes chiseled upon it.

"Nine stones," she said. "Each gap between them leads to a different kingdom within the Sidh. But only on holy days, and with Talysin's aid." She turned to Violet. "Name the eight kingdoms."

Poor Violet was shivering in the wind. She clutched Isabel's hand, her swollen eyes red as cherries. The words came slowly. "Fionnachaidh, Bodb, Bri Leith, Airceltrai, Eas Aedha Ruiadh, Meadha, Brugh Na Boinne, and Rodrubân."

The empress looked to Isabel. "Which kingdom shall receive our offering?"

She pointed to the gap facing due east. "Rodrubân."

"Why?" pressed the empress.

"That is where the Ard Rí, the High King, lives," said Isabel.

"Aye," said the Spider. "But gods do not stir for trifles we lay at their doorstep. If we are fortunate, the High King will send a shield maiden to offer his blessings."

At last, the empress turned to Hazel.

"Say the words to summon Talysin."

Hazel tried swallowing, but her throat was too dry. No creatures drummed or watched from the glades or hills anymore. They had disappeared, along with the faeries. Clutching Isabel's hand, Hazel spoke softly into the wind.

"Talysin the Golden, Spell-Singer, Dawn-Bringer, Moon-Snatcher's Twin, a Faeregine beseeches thee this Midsummer's Day. Open thy gate so we may honor those beyond."

The island shivered.

CHAPTER 21
BUTCHER, BAKER, AND CANDLESTICK MAKER

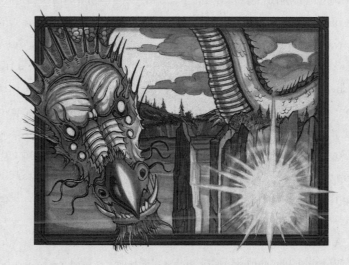

There is no fouler crime than betrayal—
it is the most personal.

—Elias Bram, sorcerer (420 P.C.–1 A.C.)

The first tremor startled Hob. The second nearly knocked him off his feet. Stumbling forward, he caught himself against a yew branch. The entire hillside was rippling as something huge moved beneath the surface. Soil split like seams, bursting in several places all at once. Flashes of gold appeared, only to vanish behind clouds of billowing steam. There was a cacophony of animals bleating, screeching birds, and panicked cries from others in the grove. But they were mere background to the din of the rending earth. Hob's gaze fell upon a line of slim, leafless trees moving along in a body. It was a hypnotizing spectacle, for they were not only sliding easily through the rocky soil, they were moving uphill. It simply wasn't possible.

They're not trees.

What Hob had taken for birch saplings were spines sprouting from the back of a monster whose scale was inconceivable. The grove where he was sheltered remained unaffected by the landslides, as did the ring of standing stones. But almost everything else—topsoil and trees, bushes and boulders—sloughed off like a blanket as Talysin stirred from slumber. Wind blew away the haze of dust and steam, revealing what looked like a river of molten gold with many turnings and oxbows, meandering down the slopes until it disappeared into a dell. It appeared to be flowing uphill, nudged along by pairs of lizard-like legs that sprouted from its sides every hundred yards or so. The dragon was so gargantuan Hob had yet to even see his head.

A shadow fell over him.

Through the canopy of branches, Hob saw a wedge-shaped head and coppery underbelly pass smoothly over the treetops as the wyrm snaked over and around the sacred grove. Hob sank to the ground, unable to do anything but stare at the monster moving toward the standing stones.

Once the dragon reached the circle, he swayed up and peered down at those within it. Framed against the sky, Talysin's great head looked a monument of hammered gold. It was long and lean, with golden barbels that twisted and snaked as they tasted its surroundings. The lower jaw resembled a crocodile's, the upper ended in a hooked beak like a raptor's. Six eyes, round and white as pearls, were fixed upon the circle's occupants.

The Faeregines did not cower. Instead, they stood motionless among the standing stones, the wind whipping their gowns. Hob could see Hazel clearly: head bowed, hands clasped behind her back. Reverent but composed. Hob almost laughed.

And you wonder why Faeregines rule the world?

A black tongue snaked down from Talysin's jaws to curl about one of the bulls. It ripped the animal from the maypole as though picking a violet. The lowing bull vanished down the dragon's throat. No chewing, barely a swallow. The rest of the animals disappeared within the minute, the sheep as a bleating trio.

One by one, each of the Faeregine princesses stepped forward to the maypole where nine torn tethers hung gallows ropes. Talysin lowered his head, peering at each with those huge blank eyes. How they could bear the dragon's attention was beyond Hob's comprehension. He was over fifty yards away, sheltered behind ancient trees, and he was practically paralyzed.

Talysin's attention lingered on Hazel far longer than it had on her sisters. Back and forth he swayed, like the cobras of Ana-Fehdra. A frill of hornlike projections rose along the back and sides of his skull, as though he was readying to attack. Her Highness would not meet his gaze. She kept her head piously down, her eyes averted.

At last, Hazel stepped back with her sisters. The empress's voice now rose above the wind in the trees. The Spider was crying out, pointing her scepter at a gap between the stones. Snaking round, Talysin surged forward and roared.

The sound was deafening. Hob covered his ears and fell to the ground as waves of superheated air tumbled over him. The dragon was breathing a jet of green-gold fire between two stones. Instead of shooting through the gap, the flames fanned out, as though they'd struck a solid barrier. The area began to glow like molten glass. The Faeregines stood well off to the side, but smoke issued from their wooden crowns. At last, there was a flash of light and a thunderclap that rattled Hob's molars.

Hob lay panting in the grass as the thunder subsided. A breeze washed over him, wonderfully cool and smelling of rain. Raising his head, he peered at the space between the standing stones.

He gazed upon a different world.

The megaliths framed a darkening twilight where gray clouds loomed over a landscape of forested hills. White towers rose above the trees, their lights twinkling. A ribbon of road wound through the hills, leading toward the gate itself.

Rolling onto his back, Hob tried to gather his wits. He dearly wished he was back home, drinking cider at Mother Howell's and ignoring Bluestripe's pleas for money. In Dusk, Hob worried about making rent and whether Anja had enough to eat. He kept one eye out for the weather, another for raiders. Life had been hard but straightforward.

Now? There was a dragon fifty yards away—a *dragon!*—and it wasn't even the most remarkable thing Hob was witnessing. The Sidh was beyond that portal. The rain he smelled was falling in a different world. . . .

And yet, to the Faeregines—or at least the empress—this was an annual obligation. It was work. He could hear the Spider barking orders at her granddaughters. Turning, he saw the three girls dragging over one of the chests. It appeared to be quite heavy. Violet lifted the lid and reached inside. At first, Hob thought she brought out a small fox. The animal had reddish-rust fur and a tapered tail, but there were strange glints of sunlight on its back, as though its fur was metallic. Hob squinted, but he was too far and the creature was too small.

Someone tapped his shoulder. Sigga held out a small spyglass. Through its lens, Hob saw that the animal did not resemble a fox so much as an otter with curling claws and silver-tipped quills along its back. Violet was trying to pry the creature's claws from her gown.

"Is that a lymrill?" Hob wondered aloud.

He'd heard of the creatures but never seen one. Every spring and summer, trappers passed through Dusk, searching for them in the high Sentries. Many considered the animals sacred, and it was illegal to hunt them, but this did not dissuade poachers. A lymrill's quills and claws could reputedly be used to craft unbreakable armor and weapons. On the black market, a mature pelt and claws might fetch as much as a Lirlander Seal.

And there was not one lymrill in that chest but six. The empress had one, Violet and Isabel hefted two apiece, and Hazel cradled the sixth, a tawny specimen with coppery claws. The Faeregines stroked their ruffs, calming the creatures. Meanwhile, Talysin loomed over them, his ghostly eyes fixed on the gate.

Rain was blowing through the portal now, gusting in wild billows as the Sidh's showers were turning into thunderstorms. A warning growl sounded deep in Talysin's throat.

Something was coming.

Through the spyglass, Hob watched the figure approach. It was tall and man-shaped, but shone so brightly it was impossible to make out any details other than that it carried a long staff. Against the twilight, the figure blazed like a star.

When the empress caught sight of it, she gave a cry and collapsed.

Violet and Isabel did not move. They stared at the approaching figure as though time had stopped. Wriggling free of their keepers, the lymrills dashed through the gateway like eager kittens. Glancing round, Hob saw that everyone in the grove was transfixed. Something consequential was happening. Something not even the priestesses had expected. Hob turned back to the portal.

Was that a god?

Talysin's body continued to course slowly upon the hillside, looping and coiling like a viper preparing to strike. The dragon bared his teeth. White-hot spittle dripped hissing onto the maypole, which burst into flame. Another growl rose in Talysin's throat. Behind Hob, Sigga was muttering a prayer in the harsh tongue of the Grislands. Dàme Rascha cried out to Hazel.

"Get down, child! Don't look at him!"

But Hazel did not seem to hear her. She glided toward the gate as if sleepwalking. Lifting her crown, she let it fall on the grass. Rain and light streamed through the portal now. Talysin's head swished back and forth behind her. Hazel halted at the barrier's threshold.

The shining figure stood on the other side, just a few feet away from her. Hob had been mistaken. The figure was not carrying a staff but a black spear wreathed in white flames. It towered over the princess, as radiant as the sun. Hazel bowed low and raised her small hand in what might have been a gesture of greeting or denial. The figure in the Sidh reached out its own hand, as though to touch hers. The grass beneath Hazel's feet began to smolder.

When the figure's hand crossed the boundary, dark blood streamed from its side as though a wound had opened suddenly. Snatching back its hand, it withdrew two paces. The instant it did, Talysin gave a roar and the Sidh Gate vanished with a crack of thunder.

Hazel stumbled backward. Turning, she looked straight into the eyes of the dragon.

And when she did, she screamed.

Hob had never heard a sound like that. He never wanted to again. It was hoarse and high-pitched, an exclamation of raw terror mixed with excruciating pain. Hob felt as though Hazel was calling to him, begging him to make it stop.

Hob hardly realized he was running until he was halfway to her. Talysin loomed above him, impossibly huge. The dragon took no notice of the approaching boy. Talysin's eyes were on the youngest Faeregine. He swayed over Hazel, his jaws hanging open like a slavering wolf's. Barbels flicked the air about her upturned face like buggy whips.

Hob pulled her to the ground, covering her with his body. Quick as a cat, the dragon batted him aside so that he landed fifteen feet away. Instantly, a talon pressed down on Hob's chest. It was bigger than he was.

Gasping, Hob gazed up at Talysin. The dragon's head swayed a hundred feet above him. The talon had pierced Hob's shirt and grazed his skin but no more. It was like a tiger pinning a moth without hurting it. But now the dragon's head was descending, his teeth bared and flecked with froth. Six eyes held Hob rapt, as round and cold as a winter moon. His mind opened like a puzzle box . . .

Pale light slanted through a window, wind moaned in the chimney. A red giant looked into his cage and touched two fingers to its lips. Another giant beckoned from the door. It was Mr. Burke, but he was a grinning corpse riddled with coffin worms. The two giants set out. In the corner, a grizzly bear sat in a tub of scalding water. She was in pain. The fox could not stand to hear the sobs. He sprang out of the slatted cage, a silver-white blur that landed lightly and bounded out the door. He dashed through forests and over meadows, feasted on a burrow of squealing mice. Snowmelt coursed through the land. Dormant things were waking. A gliding shadow kept pace with him, its feathered wings ragged shrouds. It was descending, growing big as the world. Clever fox—he darted into an alder wood and doubled back into a stream. But the water was too cold for his warm fox heart, too swift for his padded fox feet. He became a speckled salmon, red and green with an amber eye. He leaped up the stream, gasping and relentless. Something flashed—shiny and tempting. He snapped and felt the bite of a hook. It pulled and jerked; the salmon thrashed and strained. But the line was too strong, the fisherman too skilled. The salmon tired. Cold water lapped over his fine scales. Another tug dragged him up the pebbled bank. He could smell the man's cooking fire. But it was not a salmon this poor fisherman had caught. It was a mountain wolf, as wild as any storm atop the Sentries . . .

"He's waking up," said a distant voice.

Another spoke, its accent gruff and foreign. "Hold this under his nose."

Acrid fumes invaded Hob's mind, burning away the haze. He kicked out his leg, gripped wooden poles on either side. Opening his eyes, he looked into Sigga's inquisitive face.

"Can you hear me?" she said.

He nodded, tried to sit up, and felt a bandage tighten about his chest. Sigga eased him back down onto the travois.

"Lie still a moment," she said. "Get your bearings."

A hand stroked his hair. The palm was coarse as sandpaper. Sharp nails pinched his cheek with rough affection.

"You are a stupid boy," Dàme Rascha growled. "Stupid but brave. I will never forget what you did for my Hazel."

"Where is she?" said Hob.

Sigga hooked a thumb over her shoulder. "Sleeping."

Hob nodded. His eyes wandered around his surroundings. He was in a pavilion some twenty feet across. Yellow light danced on its canvas walls as a crackling fire sent smoke curling out a hole in the roof. A kettle began to sing.

"What happened?" he croaked.

"Talysin had you," replied Sigga. "We couldn't get close for fear he'd crush you both. And then he let you go. I don't know why. He just left and made for the sea. He's gone."

"You saved her life," said Rascha. "Her Highness was in great danger when you broke the connection between them."

"She's okay then?"

The vye sighed heavily. "To meet a dragon's gaze is perilous. No mortal escapes unscathed. It will have changed her. It will have changed you."

Hob allowed these words to sink in. In some ways, he felt like he'd already changed, like a fog was slowly lifting. The dream he'd just woken from was stranger and more vivid than any he'd had before. Propping himself on his elbows, he peered down at the bandage on his chest.

"Just a scratch," Sigga assured him. "A story for your grandchildren."

"Are the other Faeregines all right?" said Hob.

"All unhurt," said Rascha. "They remain at the Sidh Gate. The empress makes a three-day vigil and prays to each stone."

"Will they open the portal again?" asked Hob.

"No," said the vye. "Not after what happened. Besides, Talysin has gone."

Hob recalled the shining figure. "Who was that in the Sidh? That person with the spear?"

Sigga cocked her head. "Is that what you saw? I saw a wolfhound."

"And I saw a youth," said the vye. "The gods appear as they wish to us."

"So that was a god," said Hob.

The vye nodded gravely. "The Hound himself, though he gave up that name long ago. He is the Ard Rí now, High King of all the Sidh."

"Then why was everyone so afraid?" said Hob. "The Hound slew Astaroth. There's a shrine to him in Dusk's temple. I don't understand. Did he become evil?"

"No," said Rascha. "We honor the Ard Rí and all the old gods of the Sidh. But they do not belong in this realm. The Hound's greatest act was not slaying Astaroth but leaving this world before he became its master. If not for his wound, he might have returned. Thank goodness Talysin closed the gate. The High King was much too close to Her Highness."

Her Highness.

Hob climbed slowly to his feet. There was some dizziness, and a few spots swam before his eyes, but he was otherwise all right. His shirt was lying over a footlocker. He slipped it on. Most of the blood had been cleaned away, but a faint stain remained. Buttoning it, he turned to look at Hazel.

The princess lay on a silk sheet draped over a pallet. One arm lay on the sheet, the other clutched Merlin, who was sleeping on her chest. Her Highness's breath came in quick, shallow gasps. Sweat shone on her face and limbs. Hob glanced at Dàme Rascha.

"May I approach her?"

The vye nodded.

He knelt by the pallet. Merlin stirred slightly, but Hazel did not.

Heat issued from her body in pulsing waves. Her eyes were moving swiftly beneath her henna-painted eyelids, darting here and there. She frowned suddenly and gave a whimper. Anja used to do the same when she had bad dreams. Without thinking, Hob folded his hand over Hazel's. It was hot and clammy, but her fingers closed about his like a newborn's. Their pressure was so weak, yet their touch conveyed a desperate need for contact and reassurance.

"She's burning up," he said. "Is that fire really necessary?"

"Yes," said Dàme Rascha. "Fire draws out the dragonspell's fever. It must get hotter before it breaks."

"How long will that be?"

"I do not know," said the vye. "Mina the Fourth slept for eight days after meeting Hati."

"Why aren't her sisters sick?"

"Dragons affect magic like moons govern tides," the vye answered. "Their presence can bring it rushing to the surface, even reservoirs that were hidden. Her Highness's waters run very deep."

At this, Hazel's brow furrowed. The faintest of breaths escaped her lips. It contained a word, but Hob could not catch it.

"She tried to say something," he said.

Dàme Rascha and Sigga came over. The vye mopped Hazel's forehead.

"Can you hear me, Your Highness? It's your Rascha."

A tiny nod. Again, she whispered. This time Hob could make it out.

"Gone."

"What is gone, child?" said Rascha.

A pause. Her eyelids fluttered. Her answer came as a wistful sigh.

"Magic."

"No," said Dàme Rascha gently. "No, no. It has not gone, child. You are under the dragonspell. This will all pass."

The vye spoke earnestly, but Hob could hear notes of fear and doubt. She was speaking out of hope, not surety. Perhaps magic was like a fire that could burn too hot and extinguish itself. Stirring slightly, Hazel squeezed Hob's hand. The pressure was even weaker than before.

"Don't give up on me, Mr. Smythe."

Hob's throat tightened. She was remarkable, the most remarkable person he'd ever met. He'd underestimated her on every dimension. He patted Her Highness's hand.

"Not today," he whispered. "Not tomorrow. Not for all the gold in Impyrium."

A ghost of a smile. Then Hazel's face relaxed, going blank and oblivious. Her lips parted and the fitful breathing returned. Hob placed her hand gently over Merlin.

"I need air," he said quietly. "Can I go outside?"

Sigga nodded. "If you feel well enough."

Slipping out of the tent's entry, Hob saw Cygnet's stars twinkling in the night. They'd set up Her Highness's pavilion a little inland, on a bluff well away from others, but he could hear the surf and see the lights from a dozen campfires. Six guardsmen were stationed outside. Hob nodded to them, recognized the captain from the Lirlander Vault. To his surprise, the man bowed. Viktor sat on a stump just beyond the torchlight, whittling a piece of driftwood. When he saw Hob, he tossed it aside. He looked like he didn't know whether to laugh or cry.

"Is that Hob the Dragonslayer?" he said.

Hob mustered a grin. "More like Hob the Hapless. What are you doing here?"

"I wanted to know you were okay." Viktor gave him a searching look. "*Are* you okay?"

"Of course I am. Talysin's overrated."

His friend's smiled wavered. "Not on your life. I nearly pulled a Dante when I heard that roar. They say you ran right at it."

"I have no idea what I did," said Hob. "It's all a blur."

Viktor peeked at his pocket watch. He swore softly.

"What's the matter?" said Hob.

"Oliveiro sent me to fetch firewood an hour ago. Don't suppose you could lend a hand."

A walk in the cool night air sounded good to Hob. "Lead on."

The two went down to the beach, skirting a virtual village of tents. Most people were sleeping, although a group of soldiers and sailors were making a fair bit of noise by one of the larger fires. A full moon shimmered on the tranquil sea. Viktor pointed to a stand of dark trees jutting from a bluff down the beach.

"There's an old campsite with some fir wood. We can load up the tarp and drag it down that goat path."

Hob grunted. If anyone could figure out the least strenuous way to accomplish a task, it would be Viktor. He was a master of energy conservation.

Leaving the beach, they clambered up the goat path and into the resin-scented shadows. They went deeper into the wood, their path lighted by Viktor's lantern. Ahead, Hob saw a clearing with tree trunks arrayed in a circle. Several figures were seated on them. The moonlight illuminated a familiar face.

"Happy Midsummer," said Mr. Burke.

Hob stopped dead before shooting a disbelieving glance at his roommate.

"You're a part of this?"

Viktor looked almost sheepish. "Please don't be mad. It was better you didn't know."

Overcoming his shock, Hob turned to Mr. Burke. "What are you doing here?"

"Come and sit, Hob. Viktor, keep a lookout."

As Hob walked over, he made out the others sitting by Mr. Burke. The first was Ms. Marlowe. She wore black robes and sat perfectly straight, forever rigid and proper. She might have been making tea in her Fellowship office rather than sitting in a moonlit clearing across the ocean. The third figure was a stranger. He was a big man, middle-aged and solidly built with heavy black brows. Something about him was familiar. Where had Hob seen him?

Mr. Burke rose to embrace him. "Looking more like Ulrich every day. He'd be proud of what you've done. Of what you're about to do."

Hob was still in a state of shock. "And what am I about to do?"

The twinkle left Mr. Burke's eyes. His face became deadly serious. "You're going to rescue mankind from another Reaper."

"But you said she *wasn't* the Reaper," said Hob urgently. "You said we could help her, that she could be useful to the Fellowship."

"I am sorry," said Mr. Burke. "Our scholar was mistaken. Hazel Faeregine has to die, and she has to die tonight."

Hob glanced at the big man sitting behind him. "And this is the assassin?" The man chuckled as though Hob had something unexpectedly funny or even pitiable. Hob suddenly recalled Dante's taunts the night of the May Ball: *The assassin that's going to murder your girlfriend. I hear he's already in position.*

Closing his eyes, Hob merely shook his head. He'd been such a fool. It was the most obvious play in the world. A second later, his fears were confirmed.

"It has to be you," said Mr. Burke softly. "You're the one who's earned their trust. You're the one who can get inside that tent without being searched."

Hob glared at him. "Has this been the plan all along?"

Mr. Burke did not answer. He did not need to.

The big man spoke up. "You said the boy was dependable."

"Patience," said Ms. Marlowe. "Her Highness is his friend. We must respect that. Give him a moment, and Hob will see the necessity. This is our chance to take action while the princess is in a weakened state. If we fail, a second Reaper will be loosed upon the world."

"She's *not* the Reaper," Hob said firmly.

Mr. Burke's jaw tightened. "You saw how Talysin responded to her. When Her Highness stood before the Sidh Gate, the High King himself came to receive the gifts. As we speak, the princess is burning up from the dragonspell. So did Arianna Faeregine. And when she finally woke, the girl was gone and a terror was born. The Hazel you know is already dead."

"Her magic is gone," said Hob stubbornly. "I heard her say so."

"Nonsense," said Mr. Burke. "She's changing. Metamorphosing. Her magic isn't gone; it's growing stronger. We're in the eye of the hurricane. The true storm is coming."

Hob pictured Hazel lying in the tent: feverish and hyperventilating, her eyes swimming beneath their painted lids. Something *was* happening to her. He could not pretend otherwise.

"You know what I'm saying is true," said Mr. Burke more gently. "We will never have this opportunity again. We must strike now."

"Damn right," the big man growled.

Hob glanced at him again. The mustache was gone, which had thrown him off, but now he recognized that face and those mournful, mastiff eyes. Hob had seen the man's photograph many times for it sat on Marcus's nightstand in the healing ward. It was the photo of a hero, the photo of a man who'd died trying to buy Private Finch and Lord Faeregine a few extra seconds.

"You're Beecher," said Hob.

The sergeant cracked a smile, and Hob saw instantly how that big, unassuming face could take in a person like Marcus Finch. The guardsman exuded a comforting solidity. But those eyes and that smile weren't fooling Hob. Beecher was a killer, and not just out of necessity. This man enjoyed it.

"Call me Butcher," he replied. "Burke's our Baker and Ms. Marlowe's our Candlestick Maker. And you're our Jack."

"You're supposed to be dead," said Hob.

Beecher leaned forward. "But I'm here, lad. And so are you. So let's make a night of it."

Hob wheeled on Mr. Burke. "You're the one behind the Lirlander Vault. You planted that creature that sabotaged the Seals."

"Not personally," said Mr. Burke. "I was in the Sentries, if you recall. But, yes, that was one of our initiatives. It just fell short, but this is the bigger prize. We've spent years setting up all the pieces. Now you're going to win the game."

"What game?" cried Hob. "Thousands of people are dead because of those Seals you sabotaged. I saw their bodies." He glared at Beecher. "Have you seen what's left of Finch's face? He still thinks you're a hero."

Mr. Burke sighed. "Every war has innocent casualties. Mehrùn started this, not us. That blood's on their hands. You once told me you wanted to make a difference. Here's your chance."

Hob's hands were trembling. "I'm not shooting my friend."

"Don't be silly," said Ms. Marlowe. "If a bullet could slay Hazel Faeregine, she'd already be dead. She's far too powerful for ordinary measures. This job requires someone who can get very close without being searched. All they need is a weapon equal to the task."

From beneath her shawl, Ms. Marlowe produced a bundle wrapped in cloth. Before she even unwrapped it, Hob knew what it would be.

Bragha Rùn.

He stared at the gladius whose forgery he had wielded during his duel with Dante Hyde. Hob had no doubt this was the real thing. Every detail was already familiar, from its dragon's head pommel to its razor-sharp tip. In the moonlight, its bloodred blade looked black.

"A special blade for a special occasion," said Ms. Marlowe.

Mr. Burke gave his chest a firm tap. "Through the heart, lad. She won't suffer; she won't even know what happened. You're not just saving Impyrium from a tyrant, you're sparing her a terrible fate. Your friend would never want to become the monster she's destined to be."

The word *monster* had a peculiar resonance. It caused a ripple in Hob's mind that stirred a vague memory. He'd had some conversation before leaving on the pilgrimage, something about monsters . . .

Hob blinked and shook his head as though trying to clear his ears. He looked about the group. They were insane. Not only were they rationalizing the murder of a child, their plan appeared to overlook a significant obstacle.

"Have you forgotten about Sigga Fenn?" he said.

"Of course not," said Ms. Marlowe. "When you are back in the tent, there will be an explosion near the standing stones. The Red Branch's first duty is to the Divine Empress. This is not merely protocol—they are chained by magical oaths they cannot violate. The empress's safety takes precedence. Once the explosion occurs, Sigga Fenn will be compelled to ensure the Spider is safe. You will have a window. Not a large one, but sufficient if you are quick and quiet. Once the job is complete, head west along the beach. No one will notice you in the chaos. In a mile you will come upon some caves in the cliffs. We will await you there."

Mr. Burke rested a hand on Hob's shoulder. "By dawn we'll be in Malakos. By next week, Hobson Smythe will no longer exist. You'll have a new identity, a new life. Most important, your fellow muir will have a brighter future. When things settle, we'll begin the next phase of operations."

Hob shook his head. "Dàme Rascha will tear my throat out the instant she sees me draw a blade. And there are guardsmen."

"Sergeant Beecher will deal with them," said Mr. Burke. "You just need to return to the tent, wait for the diversion, and do your job."

"Stop calling it that," Hob snapped. "It's not a 'job.' It's murder."

"Call it what you like, so long as it's done," said Mr. Burke.

Hob looked round at them. "I'm not killing anyone, much less my friend. I'm for muir rights, but not like this. This is sick. You're all sick."

The sergeant grunted. "Sounds like his daddy."

Hob spun on him. "What do you know about him?"

Beecher smirked. "Capable man, Ulrich, but too righteous. Thought he'd get clever and go his own way, not do what he was told. Didn't look so clever tumbling down Hound's Trench."

"You're not helping," said Mr. Burke pointedly.

The sergeant shrugged. "We're wasting time. Speak the trigger and be done with it."

"Not if there's another way," Burke insisted. "Once the trigger's spoken, psychnosis begins to erode and we no longer have Jakob to perform again. The boy would be useless to us later."

"He's useless to us now," Beecher retorted.

Mr. Burke did not agree. "I have bigger plans for him." He looked to Hob in appeal. "Listen, lad. You're going to do this. Don't make me force you."

Hob barely heard him. The name Jakob sent another wave rippling across his subconscious. Memories were rising slowly like those bodies from the deep. Hob had heard of this Jakob, had met the man. An image flashed in his mind—Ms. Marlowe's office. There had been a man in brown robes sitting on the couch. . . .

"What's the matter with him?" said Beecher.

"I don't know," said Mr. Burke. He snapped his fingers. "Hob?"

Hob gazed dazedly at the man. What had the Fellowship done to him? Somehow he knew he couldn't run away or shout for help. The best he could do was resist.

"I won't do it," he murmured.

Mr. Burke snatched a folder from Ms. Marlowe. Lifting a lantern's shutter, he shined its light upon the contents.

Glancing down, Hob saw a photograph of himself standing near the golem's headless body. There were others of him in the dig site, some in Fellowship headquarters, and one where he and Badu were laughing together. There were copies, in his own handwriting, of every report he'd made to the Fellowship. The final piece of blackmail was another photograph. When Hob saw it, he nearly whimpered.

The image showed Hob's mother and Anja fishing a little stream just beyond the palisade wall. Hob knew the spot well. Anja was sitting on their mother's knee, holding Hob's fishing pole and scanning the water expectantly. His mother's expression was distant, preoccupied.

The corners of her mouth curved up slightly, but her eyes were care-worn. Hob never realized how much she resembled her father. She and the shaman each held their heads with a proud, almost defiant attitude. Hob supposed he did too.

It was not this glimpse of his family that distressed him. It was the picture's date. Anja had grown since he'd last seen her, her hair was longer. And the stream they were fishing was swollen with snowmelt. The photograph could not be more than a few weeks old.

"I don't want to have you arrested or have to hurt your family," said Mr. Burke. "But I will. And when you're plunging down Hound's Trench, rest assured you'll be having an easier death than they are. You're not saving anyone by making a useless and misguided stand. You're just ensuring more people suffer."

A twig snapped beyond the clearing. Hob heard Viktor pleading anxiously with someone. "Honestly, Olly. I don't know where he is."

"Lies," said the underbutler. "A cook saw you walking together. Some kind of mischief is going on and I want to . . ."

He fell off as the two entered the clearing. Oliveiro gave a start. His eyes darted from face to face, finally settling on Hob. "What are you doing? Who are these people?"

Beecher turned casually with the rifle.

Pft-pft.

The rounds made almost no sound as they struck the underbutler's chest. Oliveiro staggered back, clutching Viktor's arm, as two stains bloomed like dark flowers on his shirtfront. Sinking slowly to the ground, the underbutler rolled onto his side and lay still.

Viktor gave a disbelieving cry. "What did you do?"

Beecher blew smoke from the rifle's chamber. "My job. If you'd have done yours, he'd still be alive." He looked at Mr. Burke. "We're on the clock."

Mr. Burke gave a disgusted nod of agreement, as though Viktor's incompetence had forced his hand. "This is one sacrifice I didn't want to make."

Sacrifice . . . Whitebarrow . . . Necromancers.

The words triggered a chain reaction that burst a dam somewhere in Hob's mind. Memories came flooding back, vivid and horrifying. He stared at Mr. Burke.

"I know what you are."

"Not for long, my boy. Good luck."

Stepping forward, Mr. Burke spoke in a soft, melodic voice.

"Jack be nimble, Jack be quick, Jack jump over the candlestick."

The rhyme didn't prompt any bells or faerie lights, but Hob felt a subtle humming near the base of his skull, as if an internal switch had been flipped. Shock and fear melted away, replaced by a calm sense of purpose. Hazel was his friend and he cared a great deal about her, but this was bigger than his personal feelings. By taking one life, he'd be saving millions.

Hob looked at Bragha Rùn. "How am I supposed to conceal it?"

Ms. Marlowe smiled and took a log of fir wood from the stack at her feet. When she gave one end a twist, it opened to reveal a hollow compartment.

CHAPTER 22
THE ASSASSIN

The best assassins are never strangers.

—Charon, first disciple of the Atropos

Hazel's body felt weightless, but she had a sensation of movement, of being adrift on a lazy river of mist. The experience would have been pleasantly ethereal if not for the pain. That was all pervading and ever present. Thumbscrews cracked her bones; her heart did not pump blood but boiling ichor that cooked her from within. She'd realized her magic was gone the instant she'd regained a semblance of consciousness. There was a void, an emptiness that felt like her soul had been ripped away. The loss was far worse than the physical pain. Who was Hazel Faeregine without her magic? She did not know.

The only glimmer of it she felt came from Merlin. The homunculus lay atop her. Instead of feeding off her magic, he was sharing what little he possessed. If Hazel could have moved, she would have laughed. Now, she was the parasite.

But not all losses were heartbreaking. Hazel's magic had gone, but so seemingly had the Reaper. When the Ard Rí came striding toward the gate, the Reaper tried to flee deep within Hazel's being. The Reaper had not expected the High King to come himself, and Hazel could sense her terror. But the Ard Rí was not deceived.

The shadow could not hide from him, and he would have drawn it forth—had extended his hand to do so—when his wound opened. It was a famous wound made by an evil knife when the Ard Rí was a mortal hero.

It was in this guise that he appeared to her, and Hazel knew it was no accident. The Hound was tall but surprisingly young, with dark hair and and a thin white scar on his cheek. He carried a black spear and had a warrior's bearing, but his aspect was surprisingly gentle given the deeds attributed to him.

When the wound opened and the blood ran down his side, he drew swiftly back. His expression was not one of pain but surprise, for in his desire to help her, the Ard Rí had nearly forgotten the decision he'd made long ago. But he did speak to Hazel before the gate closed. Five words that resonated even to this moment.

There is always a choice.

When Hazel turned from the gate, she looked straight into the eyes of Talysin and she fell prey to the dragonspell. Paralyzed and helpless, she felt his mind invade her own, shattering all resistance like a battering ram. The pain was unimaginable. Hazel remembered screaming and the Reaper screaming too, their voices intermingling to form a hellish chorus.

And then, all at once, it stopped. When Hazel had regained

something resembling consciousness, she no longer sensed the Reaper's lurking presence. It had vanished entirely, along with Hazel's magic.

The only voices she heard now were ones she wished to hear. At present, they were muffled, but they were growing clearer by the minute. Hob was talking with Sigga. Hazel wanted to see them; she was tired of lying still and quiet. But she could not yet move her body; the very idea was inconceivable.

However, she was beginning to glimpse her surroundings. They came slowly into focus, the images fuzzy at the edges. She made out figures in the pavilion. Hob was stacking wood upon a pile by the fire. Hazel suddenly realized she was seeing through Merlin.

"Where's Dàme Rascha?" said Hob, setting a final log on top.

"She left to get some sleep," said Sigga. The agent looked like she could use some herself.

"And Her Highness? How is she?"

"No change," said Sigga.

Hob peered at Hazel. "Well, Merlin's awake."

He came over, looking anxious and concerned. He stroked Merlin with a fingertip, but his eyes were fixed on Hazel.

"Do you really think Her Highness is going to be okay?"

"Dàme Rascha knows more about these matters than I do."

"Do you care about her?" said Hob absently.

"Come again?"

"Do you care about Her Highness? I mean, are you allowed to get attached to the people you protect? Or does that interfere with the job?"

"I'm not ordinarily a bodyguard."

"I know," said Hob. "But you didn't answer my question."

There were several moments of silence. "I think," said Sigga, "if I were ever to have a daughter, I would be very fortunate if she turned out like Hazel Faeregine."

Hob grinned the grin that Hazel loved—the one where his seriousness vanished and he was just a beautiful boy. "You're not so bad, Agent Fenn. I knew there was a heart in there."

"You're not so bad either, Mr. Smythe. By the way, you don't mind if I hold on to your handbook a little longer, do you?"

"I forgot you had it."

A dry chuckle. "Oh, I doubt that. I'm curious. Did you buy it new or secondhand?"

"They gave it to me at Stock & Trade. Why?"

"Well," said Sigga, "it's just that I found an old parchment embedded in the back cover. It's blank and gives off no aura, but it's very old. I'll need to get it checked by specialists in—"

BOOM!

The explosion shook the ground. The fire's logs shifted, sending sparks swirling up. The tent's roof brightened, as though a vast fireball was rising into the sky. Sigga rushed outside. Hazel could see her silhouette through the flickering canvas. A startled Dàme Rascha rushed in, belting her robe.

"Is Her Highness all right?" she asked Hob.

He nodded and backed away as the vye bent over Hazel. Outside, people were shouting. There were whistles and horns. Hazel heard Sigga barking orders at the guardsmen. The Grislander poked her head into the tent.

"Stay here," she said to Rascha and Hob. "The captain's in charge."

Sigga dashed off. The guard captain stood in the tent's entry, his carabine held at the ready. He looked tense but composed.

"Stay calm," he said. "There was some kind of explosion inland. Don't worry. We're going to get everything under—"

Red mist burst from the man's ear.

He jerked sideways before toppling forward. As Dàme Rascha went to catch him, Hazel saw the silhouettes of guardsmen collapsing outside. She wanted to scream, to warn them to get down, but she couldn't. She could only watch in paralyzed terror as Rascha held the dead captain in the entryway. There she stood, exposed to whoever was firing upon the tent.

The first bullet spun Rascha about. The second sent her stumbling back into the pavilion where she collapsed atop the dead captain. The vye did not move.

Hazel was too horrified to clearly process what was happening. Merlin stared at the scene, trembling like a leaf. Hob knelt calmly by the fire. Why wasn't he lying flat? Why wasn't he scrambling to get the captain's carabine? Whoever was shooting at them, surely they would come into the tent.

Instead Hob retrieved a piece of firewood and opened it like an oversized scroll tube. Reaching inside, he withdrew something. Merlin's tiny claws dug into Hazel's chest.

When she saw Bragha Rùn, Hazel knew she was going to die. She was going to be murdered by one of the few people she trusted. The phantasia flashed in her mind: the scene where the nemones surrounded the Reaper, hiding a blade until one finally plunged it through her heart. Dr. Phoebus really was prescient.

Hazel's indifference surprised her. While she was afraid of dying, she wasn't sure she wanted to live. Rascha was gone. And Hob, a boy she cared about far more than she wanted to admit, was now betraying her in the most painful way imaginable. All of his kindness and encouragement had been a lie. Hob was her enemy.

He stood over her now, his face grim and set. This was not the boy she knew. This Hob was a stranger, a Hauja hunter who'd eaten a Cheshirewulf's heart. He nudged Merlin to the side with Bragha Rùn. The homunculus whimpered and edged away from the blade. Nothing but a thin wall of skin and bone stood between her heart and that razor point.

"I'm sorry," Hob murmured. "It's not personal. It's for Impyrium . . ."

The blade's point quivered as he raised it high. He was breathing with slow deliberation, as though trying to maintain control. What was wrong with him? Hazel suddenly realized he was struggling against something, straining with every ounce of spirit he possessed. Hob did not want to do this—he was being compelled somehow. He was trying to fight.

And he was losing.

Hazel slowly opened her eyes. She didn't know how she found the strength, only that she was gazing at Hob through her own rabbity-red eyes instead of Merlin's. Hob looked away. Tears ran down his dark cheeks. His gaze fell upon her medallion, that silly souvenir from their trip to Impyria.

"Don't look," he whispered. "Please. They'll kill my family. I don't have a choice . . ."

The veins in his neck stood out like mooring ropes. His entire arm was shaking. Bragha Rùn's point hovered a foot above her breastbone. Hazel found that she too was crying. She could not speak, but she tried her hardest to communicate, to let him know that she understood. That she wasn't angry. That she forgave him.

"Do it, lad."

The man's voice came from the entryway. Merlin's vision overlapped with Hazel's. She beheld a big, slope-shouldered man in dark clothes holding a rifle. He stepped over Rascha and the captain.

"Hurry up," he muttered. "We need to move."

When the man came closer, firelight illuminated his face. Hazel recognized him from Private Finch's photograph. It was that guardsman who'd been killed at the Lirlander Vault. Sergeant Beecher. Somehow he was here, in this tent.

"You can do it," he said. "Nice and easy. Let the blade do the work."

Hob brought the sword up, but there it remained. He was sweating profusely, shaking, fighting with everything he was worth.

"I can't."

"You will," the sergeant growled. "We spoke your trigger."

Hob shook his head. "You'll have to do it."

Beecher's expression darkened. He pointed his rifle at Hob. "Now or never, lad."

Hob exhaled and slowly lowered his arm. "Never."

With a flick of his wrist, he flipped Bragha Rùn straight at Sergeant Beecher. The gladius flashed as it tumbled end over end. Instinctively, the sergeant brought up his rifle to bat the lethal blade aside. The instant he did, Hob launched himself at the man. The gun went off as they crashed over a little table and fell onto the floor, where they fought like wild animals.

Hazel focused on Merlin. The little creature obeyed at once, shooting from the tent like a sparrow. But with Merlin gone, Hazel could no longer view what was happening. Though her eyes were open, her body was still paralyzed. She could only stare at the tent's roof and listen to the brutal and desperate struggle.

Hob was no longer worried about the gun. The bullet had grazed his ear and it was bleeding, but a rifle was useless at such close quarters. What concerned him was air. Sergeant Beecher's powerful hand had clamped around his throat, tight as a bear trap. The man would not let go, no matter how furiously Hob punched or scrabbled for his eyes.

Hob had fought for his life on five occasions. Twice against beasts, three times against human beings. The worst was when he'd fled from the Hauja after sitting séyu. His uncles pursued him for three days, hunting him like game. It had been terrifying not merely because his trackers were his relatives but because they combined human cunning with a predator's savagery. You could not outwit them and they would not abandon the chase. By the time they cornered Hob, they'd broken his spirit and desire to keep running. The only reason he survived—albeit half-scalped—was because he'd made it within sight of Dusk's lookout. His uncles cared nothing for warning shots, but they cared greatly about their animals. When the sentry fired at their dogs, the two Hauja left Hob in the snow and returned to their sleds. They'd made their point. Combat was not merely physical. Strength and skill mattered, but so did will. Victory often came down to which combatant could endure more pain. And Hob could endure quite a lot.

He reached for one of the burning logs. When he seized it, there was a searing hiss, but Hob overrode the instinct to let go and thrust it at Beecher's face. The sergeant tried to twist away without easing his grip on Hob's throat. He couldn't do both. Burning wood met flesh. The man grunted, and then bellowed like a branded bull. Releasing Hob, he knocked the log away and struck Hob a powerful blow with his fist.

Lights swarmed before Hob's eyes. An elbow struck him on the crown of his head. Still, he would not let go of the sergeant. But Beecher was considerably bigger and stronger. Seizing Hob's wrist, he bent it sharply forward. Hob rolled with it to prevent the bones from snapping. It forced him onto his back so that Beecher's blistered and bleeding face came into view. The man's eyes were almost inhuman. Howling like an animal, he head butted Hob, cracking his nose. Consciousness hung by a thread.

"What the hell is going on?" hissed a furious voice.

A bleary Hob saw Mr. Burke's upside-down face thrust through the entry. It took Beecher a moment to catch his breath. His voice was thick with blood and rage.

"Your Jack won't do as he's told."

Mr. Burke stepped into the tent and gazed down at Hob from over Beecher's shoulder. "Impossible. He's under psychnosis."

The sergeant ground his forearm into Hob's throat. "That's what I thought, and now my face looks like a chop. I'm gonna gut him."

"Enough," said Burke. "We're wasting time. Where's the blade?"

Hob coughed as the sergeant released him and went to retrieve Bragha Rùn. The sword was lying near the fire, half-hidden by scattered logs. Hob tried to get up, but Mr. Burke pressed his boot on his chest. Hazel lay helpless, her arms folded as though the pallet were a funeral pyre. Beecher lumbered toward her holding the Faeregine House Blade.

A gust of wind screamed into the tent, so swift and strong it nearly blew out the fire. The wind became a shadow. And the shadow became Sigga Fenn.

The Grislander stood in front of Hazel, a long black dagger in each hand. She took in Beecher at a glance.

"Surrender."

Her tone was calm, even courteous. But the sergeant ignored it. Cursing her, he made a lunging slash with Bragha Rùn.

Sigga's counter was a blur. Hob heard only a ringing clash and an abbreviated scream. Sergeant Beecher's body staggered sideways and toppled. Bragha Rùn lay at the agent's feet.

Mr. Burke opened fire with the revolver Hob had used at the dig site. Sigga made no attempt to dodge or move. The bullets slammed into an invisible barrier, leaving an incandescent afterglow as they dropped harmlessly to the floor. She pointed one of her daggers at the fire.

It roared up in response, its flames turning pale green as they snaked round Burke's neck and jerked him off his feet like a noose. He dropped the revolver and clutched at the flames, which held him fast. As Hob watched, Mr. Burke's handsome features began to smoke and bubble. Flesh melted away like candlewax, revealing patches of skull beneath. But instead of screaming, Mr. Burke offered a deathshead grin.

"*Shibboltha nul-savinu, Sigga-fina. Nanska Aionia.*"

With that, the man vanished. The captain's corpse spasmed violently as though it had received an electric shock. And then it, and the tent were still.

Sigga made no effort at pursuit. Instead, she checked on Hazel, looking into her eyes and feeling her pulse. Hob sat up, wiping blood from his ear. The Grislander glanced over.

"Stay there."

But Hob ignored her. He was half-delirious and had a single

objective: catching Mr. Burke and Ms. Marlowe. If they escaped, his mother and sister were as good as dead. He staggered over to Beecher's rifle, which lay a few feet from Dàme Rascha.

As he reached for the stock, a bloody hand seized his wrist. Hob found himself staring into Rascha's eyes. Their icy blue had clouded and the old vye trembled, but her teeth were sharp and bared in a jagged grimace.

"You did this," she whispered. "You're one of them!"

She pulled Hob down to her. He tried to squirm free, but an aged vye—even a wounded vye—was far stronger than a human boy. A savage growl rumbled in her throat. Hob was on the verge of losing his face. Sigga hurried over.

"Stop. He's not one of them."

"Of course he is," the vye snarled.

"No," said Sigga. "Let go of him, Rascha. Her Highness is unharmed. Let me tend to you. You've lost too much blood."

The vye released Hob with a look of savage disdain. As her fury ebbed, so did her energy. Sinking back, she wiped blood from her muzzle. "The empress?" she whispered.

"Secure."

Beecher had nearly crushed Hob's windpipe. Every word he spoke felt like he had swallowed a shard of glass. "They're going to hurt my family."

Sigga was busy examining a bullet wound in Rascha's shoulder. "Take the rifle and go."

"I need your help," Hob croaked.

The Grislander produced a leather case and selected a small scalpel. "I'm not leaving Her Highness."

Snatching the rifle, Hob dashed out of the pavilion. He glanced at the bodies of the guardsmen, and down the path at the beach's bonfires and torches. Witchfire blazed at the prows of *Rowana* and the warships. He couldn't go that way, not covered in blood and carrying a gun. Rounding the pavilion, he saw that it was perched on a bluff some thirty feet above a little inlet. Kicking off his shoes, Hob took two running steps and jumped.

There was a surreal moment of weightlessness, and then the fall. Down, down, with the cool night air whipping about him. He held the rifle high and caught a glimpse of stars before he broke the surface. He plunged in a plume of bubbles as weeds tangled his legs. Shells and rocks cut his feet as he struck bottom. Pushing off, he shot to the surface and gasped for air. Paddling furiously for shore, he clambered out and took off running down the beach.

The night was relatively clear, and there was a fat summer moon hanging over the sea. Hob had plenty of light, but lots of ground to make up. He ran swiftly in the direction of the caves Ms. Marlowe had mentioned. Now and again, he spied a recent footprint the tide had not washed away. When he did, he ran a little faster.

The run became a kind of dream. His own life was finished, but he was desperate to save his mother's and Anja's. He ignored the searing in his lungs, the sting of shells beneath his feet. They did not exist. There was only the next step, the next crunch of pebbled sand. Fenmaruq, Vessuk, and Kayüta were with him. Even Morrgu. They would not fail him. Not when a shaman's daughter was in danger.

He dashed over rocks and sand, little shallows and pools whose edges were crusted with barnacles. A few hundred yards ahead, there was a white monolith that looked like it had been hammered into the sand. Driftwood was piled around it in concentric circles, as though it was a sacred place. Beyond the stone, an inlet fed a series of tidal pools that ran along a limestone cliff pockmarked with caves. Hob saw no people, no fires, no—

There!

His eyes caught a tiny glimmer of blue light upon the ocean—like a lantern whose shutter had been raised for just a moment. There was a sloop moored in the waters off the point ahead. Its dark sails were well disguised among the rocks jutting from the sea. But now that he was looking at it, the details became clearer. The blue light blinked again.

It was a signal.

Hob spied a little rowboat making for it, its oars sending up flecks of white spray. It had nearly reached the ship. Clutching the rifle, Hob raced ahead for a closer shot. He was so focused on the rowboat that he nearly slipped into a tidal pool. Catching himself, he made for some rocks rising from the water. His feet scrambled on the slime coating the lower half, but he wedged the rifle's stock in a crevice above his head, and pulled himself within reach of a proper handhold.

Once on top, Hob shook several drops of water from the rifle's barrel and unscrewed its silencer. He didn't know if such things affected a round's velocity or flight. This was not the time to tinker with something new, and silence didn't matter anyway. Accuracy counted for all.

Tossing the cylinder aside, Hob raised the rifle to his shoulder and peered through its sight. The lens was coated with phosphoroil like his goggles back in Dusk. The night became several shades brighter as he brought the rowboat into focus.

A shrouded figure had maneuvered the rowboat next to the ship, whose crew was lowering a rope ladder over the side. The rowboat's two passengers took hold of it and began to climb. The first was Ms. Marlowe; the second was an ungainly, crippled-looking figure with patches of bare skull that gleamed in the moonlight.

Hob took aim at the thing he'd known as Mr. Burke. He tried to calm his breathing and forget how much depended on this shot. He'd downed caribou from farther distances, but not with his heart beating like this. And the ship was rolling on the swell, causing his target to bob up and down. Then there was the inshore breeze. Elevation. So many factors . . .

Sailors helped Ms. Marlowe over the rail. Mr. Burke was nearly there. Exhaling slowly, Hob whispered a prayer and waited for the next roll.

Crack-crack!

A body splashed into the sea but it was not the one he'd aimed for. An instant before Hob pulled the trigger, Ms. Marlowe had leaned over the railing to extend Mr. Burke a hand. The gesture had proved fatal. As she plunged toward the water, Mr. Burke disappeared safely over the gunwale. Hob's family was still in danger.

He trained his rifle on the ship, but no figures remained visible on deck. Nevertheless, it was getting swiftly under way as though ghosts were at the helm. As for the rowboat, its oarsman had already sculled it to safety behind the rocks.

Leaping down from the boulder, Hob raced up the beach, his feet squelching in the cold sand. Faster and faster, he ran, his eyes fixed on the ship. It was picking up speed, its topgallants unfurling as it steered northwest toward an encroaching fogbank.

"Come on," Hob pleaded. "One shot. One lucky shot."

Scrambling up a little dune, he brought the rifle to his shoulder.

Crack-crack-crack-crack!

But there was no lucky shot.

The rounds struck wood, and perhaps a bit of canvas or rope, but no Mr. Burke. Lowering the gun, Hob watched in silence as both the ship and his hopes faded in the mist.

He spent the next hours on the beach, sitting in a daze with his back against the monolith. Now that the Faeregines were secure, patrols began fanning out over the island. The first to pass Hob took away the rifle but did not arrest him, on Sigga's orders. Apparently, the Grislander intended to come for Hob herself. No one seemed to think that boded well.

The soldiers asked Hob where the attackers had gone, but Hob found that he couldn't tell them anything. Traces of psychnosis remained. The soldiers assumed he was in some kind of shock and continued on. Shortly thereafter, a warship swept north with a mystic at its prow, conjuring a fair wind. It soon vanished into the mist and Hob was alone once more.

A body washed ashore just before dawn. At first, Hob thought it was a seal, for there were many in these waters. But a gull soon landed to investigate, followed shortly by another. Climbing slowly to his feet, he made his way down to the water.

Almost everything hurt. Dried blood caked his ear and neck. His nose was broken, his feet had been cut to ribbons. But the pain in his right hand trumped all. The skin had blistered and peeled away. His palm and fingers were raw, red flesh. Even the wind made it sting, much less holding or touching anything. In the heat of battle, it was an irritant. Now, it was agony.

Hob gazed down at the body on the sand.

Ms. Marlowe's bun had come loose so that her long white hair lay in damp tangles. Hob was glad she lay facedown, for her flesh appeared to be dissolving like sea foam. The reek was sulfuric. Hob backed away, watching in silent horror as her body, maintained perhaps by some dark magic or alchemy, slowly collapsed into sludge.

Gulls cried out behind him. Hob turned to see a lone figure walking toward him down the beach. Mist hung between them, but he knew that silhouette and stride.

Sigga did not hurry. When she reached Hob, she glanced at Ms. Marlowe's remains.

"What's this?"

"The other one," said Hob. "Who's protecting Her Highness?"

"Red Branch," she answered. "The royal family is all together."

Sigga crouched over Ms. Marlowe. Using one of her daggers, she poked about, fishing out whatever might remain among the sludge and wet clothes. There was a belt, a flask, some bracelets, rings, and a bronze pendant. It was the reliquary that interested her. It looked just like the others.

"So they were all necromancers," said Hob.

"Not Beecher," said Sigga, inspecting the reliquary. "He was probably just an acolyte. But that other man was powerful. I'll be going after him. Our business is personal."

"What did he say to you?" said Hob.

"'The Shibbolth do not forget. Neither does Aionia,'" she replied quietly.

"Who's Aionia?"

The Grislander's mouth twitched. "My sister, Mr. Smythe. She died ten years ago." Sigga frowned and pocketed the pendant. "Let me see your hand."

Hob held it out for her to inspect it.

"It'll hurt, but it'll heal," she said. "How's the rest of you?"

Hob shrugged. He felt dead inside. Sigga looked attentively at him.

"They threatened your mother and sister?"

"Yes."

Hob shut his eyes and willed himself not to cry. The last thing he wanted to do was shed tears in front of Sigga Fenn. The agent laid a hand on his shoulder.

"You fought hard for Her Highness. I'll give you five minutes."

She did not have to explain. Hob walked slowly back the way he had come. He stopped after fifty yards or so, and waded into the water. He was tempted to keep walking, but he didn't. He merely stared out at the dark swells as the sun peeked over the horizon and turned the gray mists gold. He didn't think about Mr. Burke or the Fellowship, the Faeregines, or even his family. There would be plenty of time to brood on them. Instead, Hob focused on the cool water lapping about his shins, the sensation of sand between his toes.

"It's time," said Sigga.

He left the water and went to her. The agent bound his wrists, her face as unreadable as the day they'd met.

"Hobson Smythe, you are under arrest for high treason against Her Radiance, the Divine Empress."

CHAPTER 23
HOUND'S TRENCH

Once I became the Reaper, Arianna did not cease to exist.
She had never existed.

—Divine Empress Mina IV (322–401 A.C.)

Hazel did not stir again until *Rowana* returned to the Sacred Isle. When she finally woke, it was in her own room with Dàme Rascha reading at her bedside.

That was four days ago. It had taken Hazel much of that time to process what had happened during her virtual absence. The empress and sisters were unhurt, although they'd suffered quite a shock when the grove by the standing stones had suddenly detonated. Several servants had been injured, but the most grievous loss was that of Oliveiro. Many generations of his family had served the Faeregines.

He received a posthumous medal and his heirs were granted good lands in Southaven. The Spider valued loyalty.

Consciousness had returned, but Hazel's magic had not. She could not even snuff a candle or conjure a glowsphere. Master Montague was kind enough to give her a lunestone that would sustain Merlin until they could find a more permanent solution. At night, the homunculus curled about the glowing shard and absorbed its energies. Hazel remained in Merlin's debt. If he hadn't fetched Sigga, she knew she would be dead.

Hazel and Rascha did not discuss the implications that her loss had for the Mystics examinations, or the vye's potential punishment. If the Spider intended to grant an extension or reprieve, she had not told them. Rascha's conviction that Hazel's magic would return began to dwindle. It was clear she was growing worried. So was Hazel, although she was preoccupied with other matters.

Hob had been arrested. He was being kept in prison until his trial, which was to take place in one week. Sigga explained to Hazel that he was a member of the Fellowship, a revolutionary group whose ranks had been infiltrated by necromancers with a more insidious agenda. There was no real question whether Hob was involved with the Fellowship; Sigga had confiscated a handbook containing an ancient, almost undetectable type of spypaper. While Hob's deceit was painful, Hazel refused to believe it was the entire story. He was caught up in a conspiracy that went far beyond muir rights. And she intended to prove it.

There was a knock and Rascha entered, moving stiffly and leaning heavily on her staff. She looked gravely at Hazel.

"You promised not to look at it again."

The vye was referring to the painting of Arianna Faeregine,

propped against the armoire. They had found it in the fireplace when they returned from pilgrimage, covered in soot, the canvas burned in several places. Hazel could not say precisely when it had been expelled from its interdimensional hiding place, but she imagined it was probably when she had locked eyes with Talysin. That was the last time she had heard the Reaper's voice, the last time she had felt any trace of magic.

The painting was dead now, its image ruined, its depths uninhabited—if it had ever been inhabited at all. Its hold over her was broken. Hazel confessed all to Rascha when she had woken from her slumber—all her whispers at the witching hour with that terrible ancestor. The news upset Rascha deeply. She blamed herself for showing Hazel the painting and wondered aloud if it had been mere chance that led her to find it in the archives. The Reaper had been an unimaginably powerful sorceress—it was not impossible that she would have created some artifact to preserve her spirit and enable her to possess a descendant.

But that was over now. The Reaper was gone. Talysin had burned her away.

Rascha threw a blanket over the ruined painting. "You are ready?"

Hazel smoothed her dress, and checked her appearance in the mirror. "I think so."

"You must be certain," said the vye.

Hazel went to stroke Merlin, who was sitting on the bed. "I am."

Thirty minutes later, Hazel and Merlin arrived in Old College. The campus was in its full summer glory, awash in flowering ivy and sun roses. The July morning was hot and overcast, with storms threatening in the western sky. Hazel made her way to Maggie.

The hallway leading to her uncle's office was unusually crowded for a Sunday. Clerks and secretaries hurried to and fro, making final preparations for the Impyrial Stakes, whose races would take place in the city that evening. It was the sporting event of the year, and Uncle Basil was chairman of the Equestrian Club.

Lord Faeregine opened his office door himself, dressed in a summer suit with a rowan flower stuck through the lapel.

"There she is," he said, pecking Hazel on each cheek. He glanced at the guardsmen who were Hazel's escort. "Where's Agent Fenn?"

"On a well-deserved vacation," said Hazel. "She left two days ago for Afrique."

"I didn't know the Red Branch took vacations," he said with a laugh.

He closed the door once Hazel followed him into his office. Servants had already brought their brunch, which was under silver covers on a little dining table strewn with fresh flowers. The office looked much the same: polished wood and glass cases glinting with curios and artifacts. Harkün occupied an armchair by the window, looking like a mummy made of basalt.

"How is Rascha?" said Uncle Basil.

"Lucky," Hazel replied. "A bullet barely missed her spine. But she's mending."

"She's a tough old girl. And you're a tough young one. It's awful what you've been through."

Hazel nodded in appreciation. "I'm just trying to get things back to the way they were. Like our Sunday brunches. Thank you for doing this. I know today's busy."

"Not at all," he said. "I don't sail until this afternoon. Incidentally, shall I place a bet for you?"

"I don't know the first thing about horse racing," said Hazel.

"Lucky for you I'm an expert. Mistral's at three to two, but Hellfyre's better on a muddy track and rain's not unlikely. He's at four to one, but the odds will shorten once the first drop falls. Of course, you can always take a flier. Tincropper's fifty to one."

Hazel set her bag and Merlin on a nearby windowsill. The homunculus sat on his haunches like a miniature gargoyle. He even had a surly grimace.

"That's okay," she said. "I don't have any money."

Her uncle pulled a chair out for her. "You do, my dear. You come into it on your thirteenth birthday. In a few months, you'll be one of the wealthiest people in Impyrium."

Hazel sat down. "How exciting."

He took the opposite seat. "Never turn your nose up at money. Some fools say it doesn't buy happiness, but that's absurd. Money lets you do what you like when you like. If that isn't happiness, a more philosophical mind will have to tell me what is. Now, let's see . . ."

He lifted the covers off the dishes, and served Hazel eggs, bacon, grapefruit, and a twist of doughy bread. He was a gourmand but believed in simple breakfasts. Hazel poked at her eggs.

"So, how are things with you?" she asked. "After all this unpleasantness."

"Not bad," he allowed. "Trade's recovering, the Lirlanders are behaving, and the riots have ceased. Your grandmother's never been a beloved figure, but no one wants to see an old woman murdered, much less her grandchildren. There are boundaries, and decent people understand them. That business on Man scared even our critics. Who's going to rule Impyrium and tend the gate dragons if not our family? The Hydes?"

Hazel rolled her eyes.

"Exactly," said her uncle. "Speaking of them, Lord Willem's ceased his capers at the bank. He's got enough on his plate without trying to take my job, especially now that the empress is weighing charges of treason. It turns out the Hydes had close dealings with that Mr. Burke who escaped. This necromancy business is rather appalling."

"I actually want to speak to you about these matters," said Hazel.

"Do you indeed?" he asked. "I'd have thought you would want to put all this behind you."

"I would like to, but my friend has been charged with treason."

Uncle Basil darted a look at her. "That page? What about him?"

"Mr. Smythe's trial is next week," said Hazel. "And I happen to think he's innocent."

A laugh. "Come now, my dear. The boy's not innocent. He's a member of the Fellowship. We've arrested a score, including his room-mate in the palace. A whole nest of radicals was in the city. Rascha herself said he was standing over you with Bragha Rùn."

"I think it's more complicated than that," said Hazel.

This brought a frown. "How so?"

"I have some theories," she said. "But I'd like to discuss them privately." She looked over his shoulder at his bodyguard. Uncle Basil took the hint.

"Harkün, please step into the inner office and close the door."

The agent rose, glanced quizzically at Hazel, and walked slowly into the inner office. He closed the door without a sound.

Uncle Basil spread butter on his bread. "So, what's this all about?"

Hazel retrieved *The Little Mermaid* from her bag and laid it on the table between them. Her uncle crowed happily and picked up the beloved volume.

"There she is. My collection thanks you. I was afraid you'd lost it."

"I shouldn't have borrowed it without asking," said Hazel. "It was wrong. And I ended up getting something I shouldn't have."

She placed a square of paper on the table. Her uncle raised an eyebrow. "What's this?"

"A threat," said Hazel. "From people who called themselves Butcher, Baker, and Candlestick Maker. We assumed someone slipped it in my room during the succession announcement. But it was never intended for me. This note was written for you."

Uncle Basil scoffed. "Preposterous."

"I wish it was," said Hazel. "I picked it up the other day and noticed there was glue on the back. Just the tiniest little dab. There's also some on the story's last page. The people who placed it there knew you read that book every holiday. They didn't expect anyone to borrow it."

"And why would anyone leave a threatening note for me?" said Uncle Basil.

"Because they were blackmailing you," said Hazel. "They wanted to remind you they could get to you at any time. But you knew that, which is why you helped them break into the Lirlander Vault."

The blood drained from her uncle's face.

"Are you feeling well?" he asked. "Why are you saying such preposterous things?"

Hazel spoke slowly in an effort to hold back her tears. "Because I want to give you a chance to confess. Because I don't want to lose every shred of love and respect I have for you."

Instead of growing angry, he looked at her sympathetically. "This is about your magic. It's gone for good, isn't it?"

"Maybe it is," said Hazel. "But this isn't about me. It's about crimes you've committed against Impyrium and our family. Were you involved in Dr. Razael's death, Uncle Basil? Look me in the eye and say you weren't involved in the plot against me."

Lord Faeregine sipped his coffee. A vein throbbed at his temple. "I'm going to treat this as a bad joke carried too far. Please tell me you haven't shared your absurd 'theories' with anyone. Your sisters, for example."

"No," said Hazel. "I wanted to give you a chance to explain."

"That's very sporting."

Reaching back, he gestured with two fingers as though calling a dog. A coil of slender gray rope shot from a bookcase display. In a split second, the cord wrapped tightly about Hazel, binding her to the chair. Merlin cowered as Hazel's muscles went slack. She could not move.

"It's a passive fetter," Lord Faeregine explained. "Handy thing. Pre-Cataclysm. I'd apologize, but you should have had your guard up. Everyone always underestimates the Faeregine men. We can do magic too."

Hazel was heartbroken. "You betrayed us, Uncle. Why?"

"I didn't want to," he said. "But people don't mind their own business. First Razael poked her nose in my affairs. Then that smudger, Gus Bailey. And now, you."

"Please tell me you didn't kill Dr. Razael," said Hazel. "She was your tutor."

"I had no choice," said Lord Faeregine. "I have debts, girl. Serious debts to serious people. I had to skim the bank's coffers, but Razael spotted discrepancies in the ledgers. She was furious—always expected too much of me. I stopped embezzling, but that only played into

Burke's hands. Instead of money, he demanded access to the Lirlander Vault."

"And so you pretended to stumble upon a crime," said Hazel.

"The whole thing was a disaster," he admitted. "Razael got suspicious when I left the festivities and followed me. Once word got out about the vault, she'd have known I was involved. I had to silence her. Regrettable, as were the injuries to that young soldier. Poor lad, but we needed a witness to corroborate my story. Someone wide-eyed and credible—someone who'd never seen the vault and wouldn't realize I'd left it unlocked earlier that day. The imposters never had the key."

"So who were they?" said Hazel. "These imposters."

"That Ms. Marlowe who washed up on the beach. And her prize student." He gestured toward his inner office.

"*Harkün?*" Hazel hissed. "But he's in the Red Branch."

"Necromancy's his first love. He started dabbling years ago and crossed paths with Marlowe. She practically became his mother. She convinced Harkün he was the empress's slave, a prisoner of the vows he'd taken when he joined the Red Branch. But the Coven found a way to break those bonds and Marlowe pried him away from us. I won't describe what Harkün would like to do to your friend for shooting her. But he intends to revive his teacher."

"How is he going to do that?" said Hazel. "Ms. Marlowe's dead."

Uncle Basil shook his head. "Death isn't the end for a necromancer, Hazel. Harkün can resurrect her using blood magic. Very dark stuff. All he needs is her reliquary."

"There's just one problem," Hazel observed. "Sigga Fenn has it."

Lord Faeregine sopped his bread in some yolk. "He'll take it from her soon enough. Harkün's not fond of your Grislander. She's tried to keep tabs on him. Dangerous mistake."

"Sigga's dangerous too."

"Not like him," said her uncle. "Gus Bailey almost died of sheer terror before Harkün cut his throat. Between the two of us, I think Harkün was behind the *Typhon* explosion."

"But why would he do that?"

Lord Faeregine smiled bitterly. "To put me further in Burke's debt. Harkün isn't my servant, Hazel. He is my keeper. Once *Typhon* ruined me, Burke and his partners demanded Bragha Rùn as collateral."

Hazel was puzzled. How could Uncle Basil have stolen it? Every Faeregine had to swear before the empress's shedu they hadn't taken the blade. The creatures were born lie detectors. "We all took oaths," she said. "How did you lie to the shedu?"

He chuckled. "I didn't. The thief was your young cousin Amelia. You met her the night *Typhon* exploded—that little brat visiting from Southaven. Toddlers can be most cooperative and no one thinks to question them. She took the blade from Prime while I gave her a tour of the throne room. It cost me two squares of chocolate. Of course, no one would have known it was missing if you hadn't tried to give our ancestral blade to a page. Very disappointing, Hazel."

"You're one to talk. You gave Bragha Rùn to our enemies."

This did not appear to trouble him. "Look, my dear. If you hadn't revealed what was in the Lirlander Vault, we wouldn't be sitting here right now. We'd be at war. I could have made a fortune on supply contracts, settled my debts, and ended this sordid business with Burke. When you ruined those plans, he demanded that I smuggle his people aboard one of the warships escorting *Rowana*. Not an easy task, I can assure you."

Hazel was appalled. "All so they could murder me? You're my uncle!"

He sighed. "I wasn't happy about it, but they have these absurd theories. Think you're the Reaper reborn. That's why they want you dead, Hazel. I couldn't talk them out of it."

"Why didn't they have Harkün use Bragha Rùn?" said Hazel. "Why involve Hob at all?"

"They needed to wait until you were under the dragonfever," he answered. "I don't make pilgrimage so we couldn't send Harkün without arousing suspicion. Besides, they had faith the boy would come through. Who knows what went wrong? Perhaps the boy's psychnosis was weakened when he fell under Talysin's spell."

"So you admit Mr. Smythe is innocent, that he was under Mr. Burke's control."

"What does it matter?" he said. "The boy's going to be executed."

"It matters to me," said Hazel. "And he won't be executed if I have anything to say about it. There's still a week until his trial."

Uncle Basil gave her a pitying look. "Don't be naïve, Hazel. You cannot help the boy. The person you should be worrying about is yourself."

"Why?" she said. "Are you going to murder me, Uncle Basil? Twenty people saw me enter this room. My guards are right outside that door."

He shook his head. "These offices are soundproofed. Sound comes in, but it doesn't leave. Even without the passive fetter, you could scream yourself hoarse and no one would hear you. But I have no interest in seeing you die, Hazel. You're my favorite niece. Besides, it would raise questions and Harkün has more subtle tools at his disposal. You're going to have a seizure, my dear, a fit that leaves you brain-dead. Here we were having a delightful brunch and you just pitched over, frothing and choking. There was nothing I could do. Your recent sickness must have caused the seizure. After all, you've always been frail and dragonfever is notoriously unpredictable."

"Please don't," said Hazel. "I'm warning you."

"Sorry. It's pushing noon and I've got a busy day."

Wiping his mouth, Lord Faeregine pushed back from the table and went to knock on the door to his inner office. "Come out, Harkün. I need you."

The door opened, but it was not Harkün that emerged.

It was Sigga Fenn.

The Grislander had hidden herself in that office for the last two days, lying in wait to ambush Harkün once Hazel asked her uncle if they could speak alone. Hazel doubted there had even been a struggle. Sigga's daggers were both red to the hilt.

Lord Faeregine staggered backward. Toppling over an ottoman, he retreated from the Grislander like a frantic crab.

"Guards!" he cried. "Help! Murder!"

Hazel watched him with real sadness in her heart. "No one's coming, Uncle. You said it yourself: no one can hear you."

Lord Faeregine bolted for the door, only to find Merlin hovering before him. He tried to swat the homunculus aside, but the familiar transformed into a seven-foot vye.

"Rascha!" he gasped.

She lifted him by his neck, her voice thick with rage. "*Dàme* Rascha. Witch, mystic, and cousin to Dr. Razael—the vye you murdered. The vye that raised you!"

Uncle Basil kicked weakly as his face turned purple. Sigga looked up from untying Hazel. "We want him alive."

With a snarl, Rascha slammed Lord Faeregine onto his massive desk. He lay sprawled, his face squashed against the mahogany.

"This is a mistake," he sputtered. "You're making a mistake!"

Hazel eased up from her seat. Her weakness and nausea had nothing to do with the passive fetter. The plan she'd devised with Sigga and Rascha had played out to perfection, but it did not change the fact that her uncle—a man she'd loved and trusted—had betrayed them. Isabel would be devastated. So would Violet. The Spider? Who knew what she thought of her son. Hazel turned to Sigga.

"What about Harkün? Is he still alive?"

The Grislander shook her head. "Harkün's too dangerous to subdue. I had to eliminate him."

Hazel removed Mei-Mei Chen's recording device from her bag and pressed the stop button. "We have plenty of evidence. It's certainly enough to reduce the charges against Mr. Smythe."

Sigga looked less sanguine. "Hob's not a murderer, but he's not innocent, Your Highness. Spying is a capital offense."

"My grandmother can pardon him," said Hazel. "I'm sure she'll listen to me."

Hazel heard smothered laughter. It came from Uncle Basil.

"What's so amusing?" she demanded.

"That page you're going to pardon?" he said innocently. "He's being executed."

"Nonsense," said Hazel. "Mr. Smythe's trial is next Saturday. The empress promised I could give testimony."

Lord Faeregine grinned. "And you believed her. There are no trials, girl. Just executions today at Hound's Trench. At noon, each traitor takes a plunge."

Hazel's insides turned to icy sludge. She stared at her uncle. "You're lying."

Outside, Old Tom began to chime twelve o'clock. Uncle Basil tutted. "Better hurry!"

Hazel ran to the door, yanked it open, and rushed past the startled guardsmen. Rascha shouted her name and Sigga was on her heels, but Hazel did not stop. There wasn't a moment to waste on debate or hand-wringing. Her footsteps rang in the hallway. Rounding a corner, she burst out Maggie's front doors. As she dashed down the steps, Hazel felt a tug at her elbow.

"Your Highness," said Sigga. "Hound's Trench is miles away. Even a zephyss couldn't get there in time."

Hazel pulled free and flew down the pathway, scattering a group of masters opening umbrellas in the drizzle. She couldn't feel the rain on her skin, only the heart beating in her chest, pounding so furiously she feared it might rupture. She'd never run so fast, had never done anything with such reckless desperation. Her magic was gone, but she nevertheless focused her mind and all her desire on transformation. She needed to become a deer, a bird, an arrow—*anything* swifter than herself—something fast enough to reach Hound's Trench before . . .

Another bell. Was that the six or seventh? Hazel ran even faster. One shoe flew off, then the other. Sigga was calling her. The Grislander sounded anxious, even frightened, but Hazel did not stop. And yet, she had not even reached the Old College gates. She was sobbing now, weeping. Fear and frustration boiled over, became blind, incandescent rage. It was burning her, engulfing her from within. The pain was unbearable.

AT LAST!

The Reaper's cry nearly broke Hazel's mind. She had not gone anywhere. Like Sigga, she had been lying in ambush, gathering herself, awaiting the moment when Hazel's magic would rekindle.

It returned in a wild rush of energy, like the fires of a dormant forge roaring suddenly to life. But these flames burned fiercer than ever before. Their heat was all consuming, as was the Reaper's desire to seize control and devour whatever remained of her descendant, her chosen vessel.

But Hazel fought. She fought as she never had before—with a frantic, desperate need to exist, to persist, to live and love, to save her friend. But the Reaper was desperate too. Within her mind, Hazel encountered a tidal wave of hate and hunger that had waited too long. There was no shame in surrendering to such an indomitable will. Hazel was not her own person; this life was never intended to be her own. She was a sacrifice—a sacrifice the Reaper had made to herself over two thousand years ago.

It was time to die.

But Hazel refused to surrender. She would not fade. She would fight until the end, until the Reaper, the Spider, and everyone else in this flawed and beautiful world understood exactly who she was.

She was Hazel Faeregine.

The strain became unbearable When Hazel screamed, her body burst asunder.

Rain fell steadily on Hob as he studied his killer's face. The guardsman stood ten feet away. He was young—little older than Marcus Finch—and there was something vaguely ridiculous about his professionalism, his rigid refusal to make eye contact with the prisoner he was about to execute. Instead, he looked over Hob's shoulder, carabine clapped across his chest, rigid as a toy soldier waiting for his key to be wound.

There was a toy soldier for each of the twenty-two prisoners arrayed along this stretch of Hound's Trench. Each prisoner was a member of the Fellowship, but Hob only knew a few. Viktor was four spots down on his left, Badu eight spots on his right.

Early that morning, a warden had roused Hob and marched him to a holding cell where other prisoners were dressed in gray robes. Some were sobbing; others protested they hadn't had their trial. Hob said nothing until the priest offered him a thimble of sinwine to atone. He declined. Morrgu didn't care about sins or sacraments. She cared only that Hob had been so stupid and weak as to find himself in this predicament. No afterlife awaited him. Only nothingness.

At least the magistrate had finally shut up. Hob did not want to spend his final moments listening to a flabby judge sputter outraged invective on the subjects of moral rot, the ingratitude of the masses, and the empire's duty to mete punishment.

The speeches had ceased when Old Tom began to chime. Hob tried not to count the tolls. Instead he listened to the soft rain, the murmuring surf, even the wind moaning in the dead black gorge behind him. There were many tales of hauntings and evil deeds at Hound's Trench. Right now, Hob believed them all. Would he become a ghost? Or would his body simply shatter on the rocks and be swept into the harbor? At least he would be with his father.

He tried to focus on this as Old Tom neared the stroke of twelve. He spied the Divine Empress among the spectators. The Spider was in her palanquin, a frail and wizened figure watching with grim intensity. Hob stared at her, hating her. Lady Sylva was in the crowd too. Her pretty face looked more haggard than when he'd last seen it. She must have had many sleepless nights, wondering if her contact with the Fellowship would come to light. Inquisitors visited Hob three times during his brief captivity, but he had not been able to give any information. Psychnosis faded slowly.

The next toll made ten.

Lightning flashed in the southern sky. Above the palace and Old College, storm clouds were swirling with unnatural speed, their depths turning greenish-black. Spectators turned as a curtain of heavy rain swept toward them. Some took shelter beneath the nearest trees.

Eleven.

Bowing his head, Hob gave thanks for his life and said farewell to three people. He would miss them.

Twelve.

He straightened as the guardsmen hefted their carabines and took two brisk steps forward. Hob wondered if the soldier would finally look him in the eye.

He never did.

The gun's stock struck Hob squarely in the chest and sent him over the precipice. He fell like a stone. Wind screamed in his face, muffling several cries around him. There was a jolt of pain as his foot struck an outcropping. The impact flipped him over. Below, black water swirled amid jagged, foam-crusted rocks. It was rushing up to meet him. There was a searing flash of light, an earsplitting thunderclap. And then . . .

He stopped.

Hob stared at the sloshing brine below. Crabs were scuttling among the rocks, clambering over bits of clothing and splintered bone. Glancing over, Hob saw that the other prisoners were suspended. Their faces exhibited the same shock and disbelief that he was feeling.

An invisible force enveloped him, a tension like the field between two opposing magnets. Hob began to rise. All the prisoners were floating upward, their gray robes dripping rain. Hob gazed dully ahead at a wall of charred rock. He heard some prisoners crying and giving thanks to whatever gods they worshipped. Not him. He'd heard too many tales of false or prolonged executions. It was a form of torture.

But when he reached the top, Hob realized he was wrong.

A god *had* answered their prayers.

It stood before them, so blindingly radiant Hob could barely look upon it. At first, he thought it must be the High King, but then he realized the figure was much too small. Several seconds passed before he understood he was gazing upon Hazel Faeregine.

The princess stood with her back to the hovering prisoners. She was breathing heavily, her fingers twitching as crackling white fire writhed about her body. The ground beneath her smoked and hissed as though a meteor had struck. No guardsman or spectator remained within fifty yards of Her Highness. They sprawled at a distance in the muddy grass. Even the empress's palanquin had been blasted back and tumbled onto its side. The Spider crawled out slowly. She, like everyone else, stared in stunned silence at the terrifying presence before them.

Hazel's voice rose above the dwindling thunder.

"There will be no executions."

All eyes turned to the Divine Empress, whose sharp black eyes were fixed on her granddaughter. At length, the Spider nodded her acquiescence. And then she smiled. A cold little smirk that smacked of pride.

And triumph.

CHAPTER 24
A MUIRLANDER IN JULY

The cell was built for two, but Hob was the only occupant. He sat in a corner, squinting at the sunlight that poked from a slat near the ceiling. It appeared each morning for a few minutes before it was gone—his only glimpse of the outside world. Closing his eyes, welcomed its warmth, and hummed the tune he'd heard so many times at Mother Howell's.

> *A likely young lad sought his fortune.*
> *He set out one day in July,*
> *with shoes newly soled and a rucksack too old,*
> *he strode past fields of barley and rye.*

> *His ma had not wished him to leave.*
> *She offered two bits of advice:*

If you're looking for gold,
best be lucky I'm told.
And if not,
learn to reef, knot, and splice.

He rode the rails east to the ocean.
He rolled his pants up to the knee
and bathed his feet fine
in sea foam and cold brine
'til they sparkled like fey from the Sidh . . .

Footsteps came down the hall. Hob recognized one heavy tread, but also heard lighter steps and softer soles. The jailer had company.

When a key rattled in his lock, Hob opened his eyes. The door was over six inches thick and steel plated, but it had no magical runes or wards. This cell was built for muir prisoners, and they could not change into spiders or mist or summon homunculi to their aid. Muir could only sit and hum and molder in the dark.

The door groaned open; the jailer's bulk nearly filled the opening. "On your feet."

Hob twisted up, using the wall for support as his ankle chains stretched taut. They no longer hurt. The skin had been chafed to leather. Hob was ordered to go stand by the restraints bolted to the wall.

"No need for those," said a female voice.

The jailer was well suited for the monotony of his job. He was dim-witted and clung to routine as if it were a holy object. And so, these instructions—a deviation from said routine—caused him to frown before shuffling aside.

Sigga Fenn walked into the cell, followed by Dàme Rascha and Hazel Faeregine. Her Highness no longer resembled the godly being Hob beheld at Hound's Trench. She wore different robes, but she was the same, unassuming girl he'd tutored on the Muirlands. Hob had not seen any of them since Her Highness's astonishing manifestation at his execution. He could not even say how many weeks ago that was. After a few days in prison, he'd stopped keeping track of time. Too depressing.

He assessed the faces around him. Sigga's expression was inscrutable; Dàme Rascha's predictably hostile. Hazel seemed uncertain of what she was feeling. Her eyes met his for only a moment before they gazed about his cell. They lingered longest on his privy, a round hole cut into the floor, which lent the room its ammoniac reek. Hob hardly noticed it anymore.

"I want his ankle chains removed," she said to the jailer.

Her tone was strangely wounding. Her Highness spoke like Hob wasn't a person, but a dog whose kennel was unsatisfactory. Aside from that initial glance, she did not look at him.

Dàme Rascha scowled. "He should remain chained, Your Highness. The boy is a spy. A spy who tried to murder you."

Hazel pursed her lips. "We've been over this, Rascha."

The vye glared down at Hob. "You are a spy, no?"

He was capable of answering, for his psychnosis had almost faded completely. But he had not spoken aloud for days. His voice sounded like a stranger's. "I was," he croaked.

The vye grunted as though this settled all. "Spies are executed."

Hazel stroked Merlin, who was clinging to her wrist. "So are traitors, Rascha. But my uncle's still alive." The princess's expression was inward, distant. She did not look at Hob but at his sleeping pallet, a lumpy canvas filled with sawdust. "I'm sorry to say my uncle was involved in the crimes involving the Lirlander Seals, the theft of Bragha Rùn . . . everything. Apparently your Mr. Burke blackmailed him. Did you know anything about that, Mr. Smythe?"

Hob shook his head. He'd known Lord Faeregine had debts, but he was stunned by the man's crimes against his own family. Hazel had been deeply attached to her uncle. The betrayal must have been unspeakably painful.

Betrayal.

Hob had betrayed her too. Not her life, perhaps, but her trust and friendship. He'd mused on it many times since his arrest, but not with her standing a few feet away. Now, the ugly truth struck home.

"I'm sorry," he said. "Mr. Burke promised they wouldn't hurt you."

Her Highness merely nodded. Dàme Rascha took her hand and turned to Sigga.

"This was a mistake. She has been through enough."

"No," said Hazel. "I want to hear what Mr. Smythe has to say about this Mr. Burke." She turned impatiently to the jailer. "I said I wanted those chains removed."

The jailer reluctantly obliged. Once freed, Hob tried to stamp the life back into his prickling feet. He nearly lost his balance, but Sigga caught him.

The Grislander eased him to a sitting position against the wall. With a flick of her fingers, she summoned a glowsphere that brightened the dim cell. Crouching beside him she removed a photograph from a dossier. It showed Mr. Burke standing on the Bank of Rowan steps.

"You recognize this man," she said.

"Of course," said Hob. "That's Mr. Burke."

Sigga held up another photograph of an elderly black woman in a foreign bazaar. "What about this person?"

"Never seen her."

The Grislander showed him more. Most were census photographs of men and women, young and old, even children of various races and ethnicities. All were strangers.

"Who are they?" he asked.

Sigga smiled grimly. "They're all the same person. Your employer has used many aliases and identities over the centuries. He's been Edmund Burke for the last thirty-one years."

Hob sat up. "So, who is he really?"

The Grislander showed him another photograph, pointing to a young man with a high forehead and long dark hair sitting with a dozen other people in a stony hall. They wore no robes or mage chains, but there were strange inscriptions on the floor and a pair of domanocti in the rafters. His gaze returned to the man sitting nearest the fireplace.

"That's Mr. Burke?"

"I believe so," said Sigga. "His real name is Pietr Lanskova, a founding member of the Coven who were devoted to the Shibbolth. When the Red Branch stamped the cult out, I think Pietr and his sister, Yvanna, escaped. The two have been swapping out bodies for centuries. Mr. Burke and Ms. Marlowe were just their latest creations."

"How do you know this?" said Hob.

The agent removed a bound stack of papers that looked to be copies of legal documents.

"Look at the signatures," she said.

The names and dates varied greatly, but each signature was written in the same spidery hand.

"They're all made by the same person," he said.

"Correct," said Sigga, packing up the documents. "For generations Pietr has passed down his wealth and possessions to various people he's groomed as his replacement. Through necromancy, he transfers his mind and soul into the host's body. They die; Pietr lives."

"So he's like a vampire," said Hob. There were many Hauja tales of vampires in the Northwest, disembodied heads that feasted on the unwary and streaked across the winter skies like shooting stars. On certain nights, the tribe painted lamb's blood on their doors in the hope it would appease them.

"Pietr's not undead," said Sigga. "Neither was Yvanna, which is why your bullet killed her. They're mortals—but mortals who have been accumulating wealth and knowledge over many lifetimes. Pietr's profoundly dangerous and must be caught. I think you can help me. In doing so, you'll be avenging someone I think you care about."

Sigga's next photograph left Hob numb. It seemed to be an official photograph of the ill-fated expedition to the Sentries in pursuit of ormeisen. The Grislander tapped one of the soldiers. "I think you know who that man is," said Sigga.

Hob's jaw tightened. "That's my father." He glanced at Hazel. "Mr. Burke told me my father was there when you were born."

Hazel did not look at him. "So I understand. My grandmother told me the story."

He tried to keep the anger out of his voice. "Did she tell you she had him executed? Did she tell you she had him killed for saving your life?"

"No," said Sigga. "The empress promoted Anders Smythe to captain and named him to the Order of Orion. She had nothing to do with his execution. That came later, and was for desertion. Another member of his Sentries expedition had survived after all. The man accused your father of abandoning the regiment when they fell under attack. Here is the affidavit."

There was no mistaking the document's spidery script. It had been Mr. Burke who betrayed Hob's father. As Hob read, he saw that another soldier—a Sergeant Beecher of the Impyrial Guard—had confirmed the accuser's story. Beecher testified that he had heard an identical account from another member of the expedition who later died of his injuries.

Hob laid the paper down. "Why?"

"I think your father refused a direct order," said Sigga. "Probably one involving the newborn princesses. With Lady Elana's passing, the triplets represented the last of the dynastic Faeregines. And the Fellowship had a newly promoted captain in place, one trusted by the royal family . . ."

"But my father refused to hurt them," said Hob. "And so Burke had him killed."

"Reluctantly, I would think," said Sigga. "As I told you, necromancers are very selective about their next body. The fact that Burke personally recruited you after knowing your father, leaves no doubt in my mind. Pietr had chosen your father to be his next host. When that was no longer a possibility, he turned his attention to you."

Hob trembled with horror and rage. "I'm going to kill him."

"Unlikely. But you can assist me by answering some questions."

Hob leaned forward. "But I want to help you hunt him down."

"I work best alone," said Sigga. "There's also the pesky fact that you are in prison. And, by direct order of the Divine Empress, you are to remain here."

"But my mother and sister," Hob pleaded. "Mr. Burke threatened them, they could be dead already—!"

Sigga held up a hand. "They're safe, Mr. Smythe. I had them moved to Cey-Atül."

Hob leaned back slowly. It was the best news he could have possibly hoped for. He took a deep breath. "What do you need from me?"

"Every snake has its bolt-hole," said Sigga. "I would be willing to bet that Pietr has fled to his. If we're lucky, he's given hints where it might be."

The Grislander questioned Hob about the time he'd spent with Mr. Burke. She listened closely to his account of Mr. Burke's appearance in Dusk, their descent into the dig site, and their train trip to Impyria. Time and again, she pressed him to go into small, seemingly irrelevant details. Hob had nearly exhausted his memory when something occurred to him.

"The wine," he said slowly. "Aboard the Transcontinental, Mr. Burke asked for a Lansalian red. The concierge recommended something else, but Mr. Burke joked he wasn't ordering bad wine; he was ordering good memories. The Lansalian coast was his favorite place on earth. He said he missed the taste of its soil."

Sigga raised an eyebrow and sorted through her files. Holding up a document, she studied it closely by the glowsphere. "He's lived there twice. Once in the nineteenth century and again in the twenty-fifth. An estate outside Taraval . . ."

Extinguishing the sphere, Sigga rose and tucked her files under her arm. Hob caught a predatory gleam in the Grislander's eyes. "If this helps me find him, I'll put a word in with the empress."

Dàme Rascha chuffed. "Put in a word for what? Better quarters? The boy should be turned into a boatman!"

With a parting glare, the vye followed Sigga out of the cell. "Come along, Your Highness."

Hazel remained where she was. "In a minute."

A wolfish head instantly poked back into the cell. "Now."

The princess turned to her tutor. "Rascha, I love you, but please get out."

The vye's brow furrowed but she withdrew. Her grumbling could be heard from the hallway. "To think I used to bathe her . . ."

Hazel turned back to Hob. While she was no longer the radiant goddess from Hound's Trench, it was nevertheless remarkable how much she'd changed. Her Highness was still petite and wore a barrette in her white hair. But she had seen something of the world, and that awareness—for both good and bad—had robbed those rabbit-red eyes of their innocence. Hob found it difficult to believe she was the same girl he'd first seen at Lady Sylva's.

He gestured at her robes, black silk with amber trim. "I knew you'd do it. Third Rank?"

"Fourth."

"The empress must be pleased."

"Mainly with herself. My grandmother placed Sigga under orders to leave you in place and not to interfere in our friendship. She wanted me to care about you before she took you away. I . . . I wasn't supposed to find out about the executions until they'd already happened."

"Why?" said Hob. "What was the point?"

"Mina the Fourth lost her brother when she was young. I guess some scholars believe that her grief—and the hatred that came after—made her more powerful. My grandmother wanted to turn me into a weapon, to make people fear our family again. She wanted me to be another Reaper."

Hob hesitated before speaking. "Did she succeed?"

Her Highness did not reply right away. Her expression turned inward. "The Reaper would have let you die," she said quietly. "Then she would have burned the empress to ashes. No, Mr. Smythe. I am not the Reaper. I chose to be Hazel Faeregine."

A flicker of pain passed over the princess's face, subtle but unmistakable. He realized she had been through some sort of trial—something far beyond anything to do with the Lirlander Vault, the Fellowship, or the Coven. And Hazel had won.

"So what now, Your Highness?" said Hob.

"Back to work. I'm going to make Fifth Rank. Not even the Reaper made Fifth Rank before she turned fourteen."

"No rest for the weary."

"I'm a Faeregine," she said drily. "We don't get to rest. If it's not a Great House or revolutionaries that want us dead, it's body-snatching necromancers."

Her Highness smiled but it was fleeting. Its departure left a surprising ache. Hob hadn't realized how much he missed spending time with her. She gazed at him contemplatively.

"Were you ever my friend?"

There was no hurt or judgment in her tone. She simply sounded like a girl who was tired of guessing at a riddle. Hob did not answer right away.

"Not at first," he confessed. "At the beginning I thought you were stupid and spoiled. I couldn't believe how little you knew or cared about the empire your family rules. It made me angry."

He fell off. A volatile mix of emotions was rising dangerously near the surface.

"But I changed my mind," he continued. "Not about equality or muir rights, but about you. I believe you're going to do great things. *Good* things. And that makes me proud." Hob looked at the stone floor and fought to keep his voice steady. "I know it sounds ridiculous, but I think you're the best friend I've ever had."

A pause. "Even better than Mole?"

Hob laughed and thumbed away a tear. "Yeah, I guess so. Poor Mole. He'll be crushed."

Hazel cradled Merlin and stroked the homunculus's wings. "Well"— she sighed—"thank you for answering my question. Unfortunately, I have to go. Impyria's playing Tropique and I don't want to be late for kickoff."

She turned in a soft swish of silk. Hob cleared his throat. "Don't give up on me, Your Highness."

Hazel Faeregine paused in the doorway, an elfin silhouette against the torchlight.

"Not today. Not tomorrow. Not for all the gold in Impyrium."

ACKNOWLEDGMENTS

When I completed the Tapestry, I came to realize that I was not quite finished with the world I had created. The story of Max McDaniels felt complete, but I remained intrigued by what might unfold after the demons had been conquered and Rowan emerged as a global power. Would all that energy and optimism result in a better society, or might the passing centuries twist good intentions into something that bore little resemblance to David Menlo's "Pax Rowana"? A curious writer and amateur historian wanted to know. With the signing of the Red Winter Treaty, *Impyrium*'s seeds had been planted.

While I nurtured these seeds in their infancy, others played crucial roles in bringing them to harvest. Special thanks to my agent, Josh Adams, who placed *Impyrium* with the peerless Antonia Markiet and her team at HarperCollins. A writer could not ask for better partners. I am deeply indebted to Toni and Abbe Goldberg for believing in my vision, and for lending their wit, warmth, and insight to the story's characters and narrative. They are true professionals, as is Amy Ryan, who designed a beautiful book and made an inspired choice in Antonio Caparo, whose artwork graces its cover. Copy editor Martha Schwartz not only imposed order upon *Impyrium*'s complexity, she taught me that magnolia do not bloom in July. An invaluable lesson. As Dàme Rascha might say, little things make big differences.

Of course, none of this would be possible without my dear friends and family. Without their support, Hob might still be arranging chairs in Mother Howell's. And when it comes to Danielle, Charlie, and James—no words are adequate. Your love and patience have made all the difference. Thank you.